S0-CJM-776

MISSING HEAVEN

Caroline Wagner

ATHENA PRESS
LONDON

MISSING HEAVEN
Copyright © Caroline Wagner 2003

All Rights Reserved

No part of this book may be reproduced in any form
by photocopying or by any electronic or mechanical means,
including information storage or retrieval systems,
without permission in writing from both the copyright
owner and the publisher of this book.

ISBN 1 931456 39 9

First Published 2003 by
ATHENA PRESS
Queen's House, 2 Holly Road
Twickenham TW1 4EG

Printed for Athena Press

MISSING HEAVEN

Prologue

Present Day

Hannah Kirkland had no choice but to get there before the plane crashed. If she waited and pretended to be drawn to the disaster like any other passer-by, she might not be able to get into the wreckage and reach the boy before he was dead too long. So it was with grim resignation that she allowed herself to be guided on the two-hour drive west from home that beautiful spring morning. By the time she turned her Jeep north off Route 30 onto Route 34 out of Gettysburg, she had no more mind of her own than the needle of a compass. Eventually, a few miles down a narrow dirt road that she thought probably did not exist on any map, she saw the twin blue silos in the distance across the newly-cultivated field and knew that she had arrived.

She drove further along the road to the woods that bordered the west end of the field and backed her Army-tan Jeep into the shadow of the trees until the rear bumper and license plate were buried in the thick branches of a blue spruce. As she turned off the ignition, she noticed the shiny Massachusetts 2000 quarter she had found last month on her twenty-seventh birthday, lying in the space under the parking brake. She picked up the coin and rubbed it between thumb and forefinger, liking its solid silkiness, and zipped it into the breast pocket of her black jumpsuit where it rested against her small cell phone. Found money is good luck, she thought, and I need all the luck I can get.

She checked her efforts at disguise in the Jeep's rearview mirror. The short, shag-cut blond wig she'd bought on a lark several years ago concealed her unruly auburn hair, and the disposable brown contacts she'd picked up at the pharmacy covered the blue-green of her eyes. She wondered if even Rose would recognize her at first glance.

Stepping out of the Jeep, she locked the door and wedged the key behind the front tire. Then she squared her shoulders and set off into the field, occasionally glancing at the sky to the west as she angled toward the silos, her Reeboks sinking slightly into the soft earth. Eventually she stopped walking and looked into the cloudless blue of the April noon, the sun warm on her face as she breathed in the cool, earthy fragrance of the air.

"Here," she whispered, and sank cross-legged onto the ground.

Resting a hand palm up on either knee and closing her eyes, Hannah attempted to clear her mind and calm herself. Today it was impossible. The violent images that brought her here were too vivid. The best she could do was to focus on her breathing: in through her nose, long and deep, hold it, count slowly to four, out through her mouth, emptying her lungs, count slowly to four again and repeat.

After a time, Hannah felt a change in the busyness of life around her. The birds came to roost, the insects in the soil paused in their scurrying, and the breeze suspended itself like a held breath. The earth beneath her lost its resilience, and all of life seemed to stretch itself toward the west in silent, awed anticipation.

Withdrawing her cell phone, she stood and tapped the emergency button.

"Nine-one-one," said the operator.

"I'm reporting a plane crash."

"Location?"

Hannah gave it, breaking the connection when the operator asked for her name. She replaced the phone in her jacket pocket as she watched the plane, sleek and silver on the horizon, coming fast and low over the tops of the trees, the shrieking of the jet's engines pressing on her eardrums.

Within Hannah, the familiar change began. A deep and soothing hum blanketed all other sounds in her ears and thoughts in her mind. Her vision shifted, the infinite shadings of blue, green and red transforming into degrees of light. Most familiar of all, the pulsing heat began to radiate from her solar plexus upward, throughout her chest, into her neck, shoulders, and arms, finally concentrating in her hands.

Hannah crouched and hunched in on herself, pressing her hands over her ears and narrowing her eyes against the wind as the world around her became an enemy, assaulting her body. Still, she forced herself to watch as the airliner, devoid of its landing gear, its engines roaring with stress, plowed into the soft ground with a force that created massive fountains of earth as it began its nightmare slide across the field. Halfway between the woods and Hannah, the left wing engines sheared off into dual infernos, while the plane's tail section broke away and exploded, sending fiery and unrecognizable bits of seats and luggage and human beings flying hundreds of feet into the air. The front carcass of the plane continued on its shrieking path across the field until it shuddered to a groaning stop, its nose half buried in the earth a hundred yards east of Hannah.

After the cacophony of sound, the moment's silence was eerie. Then the screams began.

Hannah was up and running toward the wreckage when she nearly fell over a small body. It was a child, a boy—about two years old, she thought—the odd position of his head revealing a critical neck injury. She picked up his limp body, stunned by the clean, baby-powder smell of him, and pressed him into the heat of her chest as she continued to run. Soon she felt his heart flutter and begin beating rapidly. He was whimpering softly as she neared a teenage girl kneeling on the ground a few yards from the wreckage, wailing and gesturing wildly at everything and nothing.

Hannah put a heat-pulsing hand on the back of the girl's neck and looked into her eyes. "You're all right," she said over the girl's cries.

Immediately the teenager quieted and gaped at Hannah.

Hannah handed her the little boy, leaned forward and said into her ear, "Take him over there. Help will come." She pointed toward the silos.

The girl stood and did as she was told, walking stiffly but steadily and holding the whimpering child firmly against her body.

Hannah faced the remains of the jetliner then, suddenly unable to go any further. The whole world seemed shrouded in smoke. Small fires of something indefinable had sprung up everywhere, and Hannah's throat gagged with the revoltingly sweet smell of burning flesh.

I can't do this, she thought. It's too much. There are too many between the child and me. I'll never make it in time.

For a moment she was lured by a powerful impulse to turn and run, but suddenly her courage lifted like a mainsail in a stiff breeze, and she moved forward through the jagged opening at the back of the wreckage.

What awaited Hannah inside was a scene from hell. Her senses were assaulted by the dense, acrid smoke and the smell of blood and fear, vomit, urine and feces.

Directly to her left, a blood-soaked woman shrieked over the corpse of the man next to her as she wildly tried to prop his head back onto his neck. Other screams and cries for help pierced the murky air from every side. One man's voice wailed the rosary, and another's repeatedly shouted, "Ohmygod! Ohmygod!" Somewhere in the horror a baby screamed, and that sound above all the others knifed into Hannah's ears and heart.

Survivors struggled with each other, fighting to get into the narrow aisle and out of the plane, apparently oblivious that they might kill or be killed in the effort. A stocky young man rushed at Hannah, his face a mask of terror. He reached to shove Hannah out of the way, but she grabbed his wrist with her hot right hand and brought him easily to his knees. He gaped at her then as she wordlessly conveyed to him what he must do. Quickly he got to his feet and moved back the way he had come. She could hear him raising his voice, telling those who would listen to calm down, help was here.

Hannah turned her attention then to the woman on her left whose screams had turned to whimpers as she continued to struggle with righting the head of the man beside her.

"Sweet Jesus," Hannah murmured, lightly touching the woman's arm and unfastening her seat belt.

The woman released the man's head and it lolled grotesquely as she turned to look at Hannah, her eyes wild with pain, words rushing out with tears. "He tried... he wouldn't... then this thing came flying... what it was... and I told him but he never... and now it's not… I can't… see here… but he shouldn't have—"

Hannah stopped her with one hand on the back of her neck and the other on her quivering cheek. "He's with God now. You'll be okay. Will you help me?" She gestured to two elderly people, a man and a woman, on the right side of the aisle who stared at her with blank expressions of shock.

With a mechanical stiffness, the woman stood and moved across the aisle as Hannah stepped forward to the next row of seats.

The din was subsiding. The emergency doors were open, flight crew and volunteers helping survivors out of the wreckage.

Hannah persevered toward the front of the plane, touching, calming, and healing wherever possible. Four rows behind the first class, in seats to the left of the aisle, she came across a hysterical young girl pulling on the right arm of a man who slumped in the seat beside her. He appeared to be unconscious, and blood seeped from a wound on the side of his forehead.

"Uncle Ethan!" wailed the child. "Please, Uncle Ethan! It's me, it's Jenny. Wake up, Uncle Ethan. Wake up!"

Hannah calmed Jenny with a light touch to the back of her neck, and the girl swiveled, looking up at her. She grasped Jenny's arms and pulled her into the aisle, turning her forward and speaking into her ear, "Everything's all right now, Jenny. There's an exit right up there. Follow that man in the plaid shirt. Okay?"

"Okay," the girl said softly, moving out into the aisle and forward.

Hannah sat next to Jenny's unconscious uncle. "Ethan?" she said, laying one hand on his wrist and the other on his forehead. "Ethan? Can you hear me?"

He blinked a few times, then opened his eyes.

Hannah watched him focus, feeling a strange connection with him as his eyes locked on hers. Suddenly flustered, she looked away as she said, "If you can get up now, your niece is waiting for you."

Quickly she stepped back into the aisle, but when Ethan stood behind her and touched her shoulder, she felt an electric shock arc through her chest. My God, what's happening? she thought, steeling herself from looking at him again.

"I know you, don't I?" he said, his voice reminding her of her father's in its depth and warmth.

She turned her head only slightly as she said, "You have to move on out now. Hurry!"

"I need to…" He touched her arm, and she pulled away from him.

"Go! Please!" she begged him, moving to help a woman on the right of the aisle. She sensed Ethan hesitating behind her, but when he finally stepped away to the exit she willed him out of her mind.

Halfway into the first class section, Hannah found the child she was seeking. The captain and first officer were urging the boy's mother to give him to them so they could carry him out the forward-most exit. The mother, a slim black woman in a dark suit, seemed frozen in place, her arms locked around her son's lifeless body.

"We'll have to carry them both out," the captain said. "Can you get to her other side, Bill?"

Hannah glanced at the first officer's face and her heart skipped a beat. God, no! she thought. It's Bill Tyler.

Ducking her head slightly, Hannah put a hand on each man's shoulder. They both straightened and looked at her, then at each other. Nodding in silent agreement, they stepped aside and Hannah slipped into the seat beside the mother. She put her right hand on the woman's neck for a few moments until she relaxed her hold on her son. Sighing deeply, the woman shifted her child and cradled him gently, as if she were showing her newborn baby to Hannah.

"Lily? That's your name, isn't it?" Hannah began, her voice little more than a whisper. "I love the name Lily. That's what I called the doll my mother gave me. Do you know, I still have that doll."

As she spoke, she pressed her burning left hand against the boy's chest.

"And this is your son, Micah, isn't it? What a handsome boy. Is he about five years old?"

"He's dead," Lily breathed.

"No. No, he's not dead, Lily. I promise. Look at his eyes. See there? See his eyelids flutter? He's going to be just fine."

The mother looked at her son, the expression on her face a mixture of confusion and hope.

"We need to take Micah outside the plane now, Lily. There's an ambulance coming."

With those words, Hannah heard the first siren sounds in the distance and knew she had little time left.

"Here," she said, slipping out of her seat into the aisle. "Let the captain carry Micah out for you."

"Oh, God! Oh, God!" cried the boy's mother. "Be careful! Please be careful with him."

"I will. I promise," the captain said, lifting Micah easily and stepping back into the aisle.

Lily's eyes never left her son while she struggled blindly with her seatbelt.

Bill Tyler was studying Hannah's face intently. He seemed on the verge of speaking to her when the captain said, "Bill, give this lady a hand with the belt."

When the captain started forward with Micah, and Bill leaned down to help Lily, Hannah saw her chance. She turned and moved quickly back down the aisle and out through the jagged opening at the rear, racing into the field toward the woods and covering the distance between the plane and her Jeep in a fraction of the time it had taken to walk there.

Gasping for air like an asthmatic, Hannah retrieved the key, unlocked the door and stepped in, turning on the ignition. She whipped off her wig and shook out her wild auburn hair. Her hands, cold now and bloodstained, trembled on the steering wheel, and the pain behind her eyes throbbed mercilessly as she maneuvered the Jeep onto the road, heading east.

The color was returning to her vision as she pulled out her cell phone and pressed a speed-dial number. The call was answered on the first ring. "It's over, Rose," she said, still struggling with her breathing.

"Hannah! Praise the Lord! Are you all right?"

"Yes. Pretty shaken, though."

"I don't wonder! How about the boy, did you get to him in time?"

"Yes. He'll be okay."

A couple of beats, then Rose said, "But something went wrong, didn't it."

"There was a little glitch."

"What happened?"

"I'll tell you as soon as I'm home and get cleaned up. I'll call you."

"All right. Hurry. But drive carefully."

Pocketing her cell phone, Hannah glanced to her left and thought she saw Ethan with his niece, and Bill Tyler, the two men looking in her direction. She cursed under her breath and pressed the gas pedal to the floor, racing wildly down the narrow road until the field was out of sight. Slowing then merely to fast, and swerving a good bit, she scrubbed at her hands with some Wash 'n Drys from the glove compartment, disposed of her contacts, tapped on a CD of Yo-Yo Ma, opened a Wild Cherry Pepsi, and popped a mini 3 Musketeers in her mouth, all before she turned south onto Route 34.

With her first bite of the candy—the sweet rush of milk chocolate—the steel band around her chest began to loosen. By the time she had driven south a half-mile with Yo-Yo Ma's cello soothing her soul, her tears were pouring. She wiped them away with the backs of her hands, thinking she should pull over until she could get control of herself, when a bright yellow fire truck sped past her heading north, its sirens blaring. She decided she'd better keep going.

Don't want to be caught at the scene of the crime, she thought, giving a rueful little laugh.

She was certain that Bill Tyler recognized her, and it seemed like a cruel cosmic joke that he was on that flight. Hannah had known "Billy" since childhood and they had shared some of the same classes in high school. A party after graduation was the last time she had seen him. Until today.

He'll come looking for me now, she thought. And when he finds me, what then?

Her mouth went dry at the thought of being discovered. What would people make of her inexplicable gifts?

"I'll be torn apart," she murmured, her eyes welling up again.

She started just then as Grampa appeared beside her on the passenger seat, his winter white hair bright in the afternoon sun.

"Everything's going to be okay, honey," he said through his beautiful, crookedy-toothed smile. "God loves you and so do I."

Hannah reached to touch him, but he was gone. "Oh, Grampa, I can't do this anymore. Help me. Please help me."

By the time she reached Route 30 and turned east toward home, a resigned calm had settled over her. She programmed the Jeep's mapping system and allowed her mind to wander back into the summer of 1982—the summer when she decided she was a witch.

Book One

21 Years Earlier

Chapter One

It was an unusually sultry morning for early June in southeastern Pennsylvania. Six-year-old Hannah sat on the front porch steps of the old, stone farmhouse she shared with her Papa and her grandmother, Vivie. She chewed on one of her auburn braids as she fanned away gnats, and she worried. Vivie called her a terrible worrywart, and sometimes Hannah worried about that too. Did Vivie mean she looked like a wart when she worried? Or, even worse, did she mean that Hannah might actually grow warts from worrying too much? Either way, Hannah didn't like the sound of it.

But this particular morning, Hannah couldn't stop herself from worrying about the fate of the princess she and Grampa had invented by the crackly-warm fire just before bedtime last Christmas Eve. Remembering, Hannah was filled again with the fragrance of cinnamon and evergreen, and with the sense of perfect safety she felt only with Grampa.

Leaning into Grampa across the arm of his wheelchair, Hannah had been the one to start the story that night, imagining the beautiful princess who was kidnapped and locked in a tower by an evil wizard.

Grampa added the princess's long blond hair. "It's so long, she trips over it sometimes," he'd said, making Hannah giggle. "Her name is Isabella, but everyone calls her 'Izzy'."

"Izzy?"

"You see, she's a very down-to-earth sort of princess, and she wants people to call her Izzy because she thinks it sounds like a regular person's name." Grampa was gently stroking Hannah's hands. "Anyway, Izzy is very unhappy about being kidnapped and imprisoned, and she's crying as she looks out of the tower window."

"She's lonely," said Hannah.

"Indeed she is."

"And she's hungry, too."

"Positively starving."

"And it's Christmas, so she wants to go home and open her presents with her mommy and daddy."

"Right, the King and Queen of Happyland, who have sent out vast hordes of soldiers to find their beloved daughter. But it's snowing."

"And there's a tornado, too."

"Really, honey? A tornado. Those soldiers have their work cut out for them."

"And even an earthquake. That's why Izzy's crying so much, Grampa. She thinks she'll never ever get rescued, see?"

"I certainly do. Things aren't looking very good for Izzy."

"And the evil wizard was just there and ate a bunch of 3 Musketeers bars in front of Izzy but didn't let her have any."

"My, oh my! That is a very evil wizard."

"Yes! And he wants a million million dollars for Izzy."

"My goodness! Is it possible that even the King and Queen of Happyland have a million, million dollars?"

"Oh, yes! They have a zillion million dollars, but, see, they already paid it and the wizard still won't give her back."

Hannah had suddenly run out of ideas. Her eyes stung with tears.

Grampa lifted her chin and kissed each eyelid. "It's okay, honey. Everything will be all right."

"But I can't think of anything to help her."

"You're just tired. You'll see, by tomorrow morning you'll feel right as rain again, and you'll know exactly what to do to rescue Izzy."

But the next morning had been Christmas, and Hannah hadn't even remembered Izzy again until weeks later. She and Grampa never did finish the story—story-telling didn't work well over the telephone—and that morning, in the summer before first grade, she was thinking again about Izzy, worrying that the poor lonely princess would have to spend her whole life in that evil wizard's tower. She worried and chewed on one braid and the other, idly watching the dancing patterns of bright sunlight that filtered through the ancient walnut trees.

Intent on the snowflake design of one of those patterns, she suddenly noticed a little bird lying on the ground directly in its center. She jumped down and knelt beside the still creature, her throat closing up and her eyes stinging because it was so tiny, so sweet and so lifeless.

She decided to bury it. She knew about dead things and burials. Two years ago, when her mother's car had been crushed by a truck, Hannah had seen this doll that only looked like her mother lying in a big, shiny, satin-lined coffin. Later she had seen the same coffin at the cemetery and had put a beautiful red rose on top of it when Papa told her to. After they left the cemetery, Vivie had explained that the coffin would be lowered into the ground and covered with dirt. Hannah thought it was a strange way to get to heaven, and wondered why they didn't take the coffin up in an airplane and place it carefully above the clouds. Still, there was much about the world that was very strange to Hannah; she hoped Papa was right every time he told her, "When you're grown up, baby, that's when you'll understand."

So she knew about burying dead things, and although she didn't have a big shiny coffin and a beautiful red rose for the little bird, she could at least bury it in a very special place: she would take it out past the barn and down to the creek. Going to the creek wasn't a problem—Hannah was allowed free rein on the property—but touching a dead animal, that was something serious.

The two-hundred-year-old, serpentine stone farmhouse where Hannah lived was surrounded by acres of woods and uncultivated fields, and was approached only by a long, winding driveway. Hannah knew that Papa had left for his construction work early that morning and that there was no one to see her pick up the dead bird—except, of course, Vivie, who saw everything. Hannah was sure that Vivie had eyes under her hair on the back of her head and could see through walls and around corners. Some of Hannah's scariest dreams were about being followed everywhere by a giant, invisible eye that saw everything she did—especially the bad things—and reported back to Vivie. And what Hannah was planning now was very bad; Vivie had repeatedly told her to steer clear of wild animals because of their dirty germs that could cause terrible diseases. Hannah worried that touching a dead one might make her dead, too.

Still, she couldn't stop herself. The poor little bird needed to get to heaven, so it needed to be buried. She perked up her ears and heard a hymn playing loudly on the kitchen radio. "Vivie's making a pie," she whispered to the little dead bird. "She won't catch me this time."

Taking in a deep breath and holding it, Hannah slipped her hands under the bird from each side and lifted it, light and lifeless as a dry leaf.

Immediately, with that contact, the ground fell away, the trees started to spin, and the world around her lost its color as the familiar heat started in her stomach. Quickly, the heat spread throughout her body until her hands and fingertips felt as if they were on fire. Then, within moments, the tiny bird's heart began to beat and the bird quivered in her hands. It stood and shook itself, blinking its eyelids and then staring at Hannah, moving its head sharply back and forth to view her with one eye and then the other. Finally its neck puffed up and it trilled its melodious song and flew off.

Hannah clapped her hands over her mouth to keep herself from screaming as she stood and raced to her special place in the center of the huge lilac bush at the far corner of the barn. She huddled there, shivering in spite of the morning's heat, and thought about what she had done. That's when it came to her that she must be a witch. Who else but Jesus, angels and witches could make dead birds be alive again? She knew for sure that she was not Jesus or an angel. What was going to happen when Vivie discovered she was a witch? Hannah was more worried than she'd ever been in her whole life.

For as long as she could remember, she had known that she was different, that not everybody could hear thoughts or see how big someone's heart was or, sometimes, even know what was going to happen next. Mama and Grampa were different, too. But then Mama had gone away to heaven and Hannah hadn't seen Grampa since last Christmas, wheelchair-bound as he was, all the way out in Cincinnati. Grampa was the right one to help her figure out how to stop being a witch, and even *he* might be upset if he found out.

But nobody was going to be more upset than Vivie. Like last summer when Hannah had discovered five fluffy gray kittens in the barn one morning and rushed to tell Vivie about them. Later, Hannah was very angry at herself for bothering Vivie; she should have just put the kittens in a basket and left them at the back of the neighboring witches' house, knowing that witches liked cats. But she hadn't thought of that at the time, so she'd told Vivie and then forgotten how to breathe when Vivie got upset and said she was going to have to drown the kittens.

"I'm afraid they carry dreadful diseases that could kill us all," Vivie had said. Hannah had watched in screaming silence as Vivie put each of the tiny, helpless kittens into an old potato sack with a rock and tied the top with twine.

"I'm so sorry you have to see this, Johannah," Vivie had said. Then she'd suggested that Hannah accompany her to the pond. "That way, we can make this like a little funeral."

She had trailed along behind her grandmother and watched her throw the sack with its wiggling, mewling cargo out into the pond. Hannah's whole body had been suffused with the familiar burning that day as she watched the sack of kittens sink quickly into the brownish-green water.

But at least she hadn't done anything witchy then. Not like this morning with the dead bird.

"What am I gonna do?" she whispered to herself in the lilac bush, putting the end of one of her braids into her mouth and chewing it. Then she let out a small cry as the tiny bird landed on a branch, not a foot from her face, and trilled at her merrily.

"Oh, no, little birdie! You gotta go away!"

But he didn't. Instead he flew to her right knee and sang. Oh, how he could sing! Hannah was so taken by the sound of his song and by the delicate beauty of him that she didn't shoo him away again. Instead, she tentatively put out a forefinger and lightly brushed the tip of his head. She thought he looked like he was smiling at her.

"Okay, birdie, I guess you can stay," she whispered. "But we have to be really careful. Vivie will have to put you in a bag and drown you if she finds out."

The bird trilled at her again.

"Oh, no! You have to stop that, okay? It's really pretty, but you just have to stop 'cause she might hear you, okay? I wish you could whisper like this. Can you do this, little birdie?"

Hannah didn't expect him to answer her, but at least he didn't sing anymore. He seemed perfectly happy to sit on her knee and let her pet his silky feathers.

"You're my friend now, aren't you, birdie? My very first real bird friend. I'm gonna give you a name, okay? Let's see... how 'bout Gabriel. D'you like that?"

The tiny bird responded with a single peep. Hannah laughed. "You do! You like it!" She wanted to hug him, but instead kissed her fingertip and touched it to the top of his head.

"There. Now we are friends forever and ever, amen. And nobody is gonna find out what I did, right? 'Specially not Vivie, okay? I'm not gonna tell anybody, and you won't 'cause you're my friend, right?"

Hannah's breathing came to a sudden halt. "Oh, Gabriel! But what about the lordgodamighty? He knows what I did. He always knows everything, doesn't he? He'll have to punish me, won't he?"

Gabriel was looking at Hannah as if he understood every word. He hopped to her left knee, turned around and hopped back again. Then he hopped up and down in place as he chirped a single peep, three times. She laughed with delight.

"Johannah?" Hannah nearly let out a screech at the sound of Vivie's voice just outside the bush. "Who are you talking to? You know how filthy you get when you play in there. Now come on out here."

"Run away, Gabriel," Hannah whispered. He flew off and she scrambled out of the bush, confronted immediately by her grandmother's kewpie-doll face, wearing the look that always made Hannah feel like somebody was stomping on her toes.

Vivie straightened and frowned at Hannah. "Look at you, child. You've gone and gotten yourself filthy again, haven't you. I swear, I'll have to get your father to burn down this old bush one of these days if you can't learn not to play in there." She threaded her fingers in Hannah's thick hair and gave it a little tug. "And look at this mess. Here it is out of its braids already and back into a rat's nest. For goodness sake, Johannah, do you think I have nothing better to do than clean up after you all day long?"

Hannah had discovered long ago that Vivie was bothered by the sight of her weird turquoise eyes, so she kept her gaze trained on the ground as she replied, "Yes, ma'am."

Vivie began swatting the dirt off of Hannah's clothes. "Now, I'm sure you don't mean to answer 'yes' to that question, Johannah."

Uncertain of her mistake, but knowing she had made one, Hannah inadvertently looked up at her grandmother. "Oh, no, Vivie. I'm sorry. I guess... I mean... I don't..."

"It's all right, child. I know you don't mean to be rude. You know full well how the Lord God Almighty feels about children who don't respect their elders. Now stand up straight and let me fix this hair."

Vivie took her fine-toothed metal comb from the pocket of her apron and began to pull it through Hannah's thick auburn hair, stretching it up and back into two long, tightly plaited braids, all the while humming tunelessly to herself.

Vivie's routine with Hannah's hair had always been painful, not only because of the pulling and tugging of the metal teeth that made her eyes water, but also because of the tuneless humming that made Hannah's back itch like it was covered with marching centipedes. Long ago, Hannah had taught herself to fly away in her thoughts to keep from crying. Crying in front of Vivie only made things worse. This time Hannah thought about Gabriel, wondering if he was nearby, glad Vivie apparently hadn't seen him.

Wherever you are, don't say anything, Gabriel, okay? Hannah said to him in her mind. *Be really quiet. And don't worry about me, okay?*

Hannah silently sang the first line of her favorite hymn. She thought about Gabriel singing along with her, imagining them flying together over the barn and the house and the trees, out over the creek and the pond, Hannah singing and Gabriel trilling in tune with her. "Jesus loves me, this I know, for the Bible tells me so. Jesus loves me, this I know, for the Bible tells me so..."

Finally the braiding was finished and Hannah had made it

through without letting go of a single tear. Vivie stepped back, put the comb in her apron pocket and pulled out a 3 Musketeers bar. Hannah tensed as soon as she caught sight of her favorite candy. As Vivie tore off its wrapper, Hannah stopped breathing when a faint growl in her stomach betrayed her hunger.

"I heard that, dear. I suppose you'd like to have some of this."

"No, ma'am," she said as her stomach growled again.

Vivie took a bite of the candy and leaned close, her breath so chocolatey, Hannah had to fight an impulse to bite the air. "You're saying no, Johannah, but your tummy is saying yes. Now, I want you always to tell me the truth. You *would* like some of Vivie's candy, wouldn't you."

Hannah desperately wanted to chew her braid. "Yes, ma'am."

Vivie straightened as she said, "Thank you for being honest, dear. But you understand why you can't have any, don't you."

"Yes, ma'am."

"And why is that?"

"Because it's too close to dinner—"

"Lunch, this time. So start again."

"Because it's too close to lunch and I'll spoil my appetite…"

"And what else?"

"And because I'll get fat and get big pimples."

"That's right. Very good." Vivie folded the wrapper over the last of the candy and put it back in her pocket. "But one of these days, Johannah dear, I do hope you'll learn to not even ask for candy." Vivie patted the top of Hannah's head. "You may play outside until I ring the bell, but please do stay out of that filthy bush, all right?" She turned then and walked toward the house.

Hannah watched Vivie go, holding her breath.

Suddenly a white splotch appeared on the back of Vivie's navy blue skirt, just below the bow of her apron. Hannah looked upward for its source and found Gabriel, sitting on the branch of the huge red oak under which Vivie had just passed.

Oh, no! Hannah wanted to scream; instead she nearly giggled as her grandmother went on, oblivious of Gabriel's revenge.

Chapter Two

As soon as Vivie disappeared into the house, Hannah turned and ran. She loved to run. If she could, she'd never walk anywhere, only run. Sometimes she was sure her feet weren't touching the ground, she was going so fast. She ran past the barn, into the woods, skirting the trees, then out into the field. There she picked up speed, despite the tall grass, and nearly flew as she headed for her special place by the creek.

Hannah laughed when she saw the brown blur that was Gabriel flying on ahead of her. He knows where I'm going! she thought.

And, indeed, when she arrived at the creek, Gabriel was already there, sitting on the top of Hannah's rock in the sunshine, clearly waiting for her. She settled herself into the concave curve of the rock that seemed to have been shaped for her back. From there she could watch the shallow water as it danced over the stones of the creek bed on its way to the pond.

There was always something interesting to see at the creek—bugs of every variety, squirrels, rabbits, frogs, raccoons and all sorts of birds. Once there'd been a doe and her fawn. Hannah always held herself very still so that she wouldn't scare the animals, and with the deer she'd been so still for so long that it hurt a little to move once the fawn and its mother loped away.

Hannah used to love the pond, too, until Vivie drowned the cats there. Now she couldn't look at the pond without thinking of those fluffy kittens, imagining them still trapped and crying in that bag, somewhere in the water's murky depths. She thought if she ever learned to swim, she'd go down there and rescue them. Then she'd give them a proper funeral so that they could get to heaven.

As she sat in her spot by the rock that morning—in spite of the nearness of her new friend, Gabriel, in spite of the warmth of the sun on her skin and the breeze rustling the willow leaves—

she began to cry. Gabriel flew to the ground in front of her and trilled his song repeatedly, but she didn't hear him. She felt as if someone with long fingernails was scraping the inside of her chest and throat as she worried about being different and bad and a witch, as well as whatever punishment the lordgodamighty would have in store for her.

While she wept, an image formed in her mind's eye. It was Grampa, and she found herself looking over his shoulder as he sat in his wheelchair gazing at something he held in his hands. The image became clearer: it was a photograph of Hannah herself, taken with Grampa and Mama in Cincinnati three Christmases ago. Their faces were full of smiles.

She watched Grampa turn his head and look at her, his dark-lashed turquoise eyes mirroring her own through his rimless glasses. He smiled at her then, his big, crookedy-toothed smile that always felt like an angel's kiss.

"It's okay, honey," he said. "Jesus loves you and so do I."

"I love you too, Grampa," she said, smiling and kissing the air toward him before the image vanished.

Hannah noticed Gabriel then, hopping up and down in front of her, and she let out a laugh as merry as his song. She threw herself onto her stomach beside the tiny bird so that her nose was just a few inches from his beak.

"You know what, Gabriel? You know what? The lordgodamighty isn't gonna punish me! Know how I know? 'Cause of Grampa. Did you see my Grampa? He told me everything'll be okay. And he always knows, too!"

Hannah crooked her right elbow and lay her head on her arm. She made dancing legs of the first two fingers of her left hand and danced them in the dirt around Gabriel, thinking about her pictures. She had been getting them for as long as she could remember, since long before Mama went to heaven.

It was about a month after her funeral that Mama began to come to Hannah regularly in her mind's-eye pictures, wearing a long white gown covered with tiny diamonds, and carrying a large, fragrant bouquet of wildflowers. Hannah would first be surprised by the fragrance of the flowers and then know that Mama was coming. She never stayed long, and she never said a word, but afterwards Hannah always felt as if she had been held and rocked for a while.

Once, last January, Mama had come to Hannah in the hospital. Hannah had fractured a small bone in her wrist when she tripped over Vivie's foot and fell off the front porch. The wonderful part was Mama arriving with her flowers right there in front of Emergency's waiting room bench, where Hannah sat next to Vivie. When Hannah smelled the wildflowers and knew her mother was coming, she looked up at Vivie nervously. But the whole time Mama was there, Vivie never glanced away from her magazine. That's when Hannah knew that those pictures were just for her, one more thing that made her different from everybody else.

She sat up suddenly. "I gotta go now, Gabriel. Vivie's gonna ring the bell for lunch soon, and I have to be there, okay?" Hannah didn't know that she had an uncanny sense of time; all she knew was that she could be where she was supposed to be exactly when she was supposed to be there.

She stood but then paused, looking down at her little friend. Gabriel was watching her as if awaiting instructions.

She sat on her haunches. "Now here's the thing. You can come up to the house with me, but you can't come inside 'cause Vivie'd have a conniption. And you have to promise me something, okay? You must never, never, *ever* let Vivie know you and me are friends, okay? Just don't even let her see you. You have to do this stuff just like I say, Gabriel. You promise? Shake?"

Hannah put out the thumb and forefinger of her right hand and very gently touched Gabriel's right foot. "Shake," she repeated. Then she jumped to her feet and began to run back through the pasture and the woods toward the house. Passing the barn, she heard the first clang of the old bell by the back door. She ran around the side of the porch and arrived at the foot of the back door steps before the bell's fourth and final clang. Vivie scowled at her from the back stoop as if she were late.

She was slipping off her sneakers as Vivie said, "All right, Johannah, come on up here and wash your hands and face and use the facilities. Mind you keep your feet on the runners and off my clean kitchen floor."

As Hannah tried to brush past her grandmother, Vivie put her fingers in Hannah's hair and stopped her.

"Lord God Almighty, child! Would you look at this rat's nest. Worse than an hour ago." Vivie was reaching for the comb when a car horn sounded from the driveway. "Well, I wonder who that could be," she said.

Hannah knew exactly who it was, and crossed her fingers behind her back in the hope that now she could eat her lunch outside with Gabriel.

Vivie turned and headed out of the kitchen, fluffing her permed helmet of blonded hair, and Hannah couldn't suppress a small gasp when she saw that the white blob on the back of her grandmother's skirt appeared to have grown bigger.

Vivie glanced back. "Clean yourself up, Johannah, and then wait right here in the kitchen for me and our guest."

Hannah did as she was told, in the bathroom off the kitchen, and then took a moment to gaze at the large glass jars of cookies and candy bars that Vivie kept in the pantry closet, on a shelf too high for Hannah to reach. Was there time to pull over the stepstool and climb up? No, Vivie was coming back. Hannah scampered to a chair.

Vivie entered the kitchen trailed by one of the women Hannah saw every Sunday at church and regularly here at the house, usually at lunchtime.

"Look who's here, Johannah. Stand up and say hello to Mrs. Thornbekker." Hannah got off the chair and effected the little curtsy Vivie had taught her, pulling the sides of her baggy bluejeans out as if she were wearing a skirt. "Hello, Mrs. Thornbekker."

Mrs. Thornbekker clasped her plump hands under her double chin and exclaimed, "Vivian, this child's manners just get better and better! How fortunate your stepson is to have you to teach her."

"Thank you, Louise. I do my best."

"Goodness," said Mrs. Thornbekker, "I seem to have arrived at your lunchtime once again. I do apologize."

"Nonsense. We can have a nice visit over lunch. Johannah was just going to take her meal outside anyway, weren't you, child?"

"Yes, ma'am."

"Well, go ahead, then. There's your milk and your sandwich and your grapes. You run along, and be sure you put your paper in the trash can when you're done. I'll ring the bell when I want you to come in for your nap."

"Yes, ma'am."

Hannah picked up the paper plate and paper cup and went to the screen door, where she tried to balance the cup of milk on the flimsy plate so that she could open the door with her other hand. The cup fell and splattered the floor with the milk, and Hannah stopped breathing.

"Oh, my, will you look at that," Vivie said sweetly.

Hannah breathed again, remembering that she wouldn't be in real trouble with Mrs. Thornbekker here.

"That's all right, Johannah. Accidents will happen." Vivie offered a bright kewpie-doll smile as she handed a dishcloth to Hannah. "Now, dear, you blot that up and I'll get the mop."

"I must say, Vivian, you're a saint. I see red when my grandchildren make a mess in my house."

"Oh, well, there's no reason to cry over spilt milk, eh, Louise?" Vivie said with a chuckle. She ran hot water into the head of the mop and squeezed out the excess with her hands. "Johannah, dear, bring me that cup and I'll pour some more milk for you."

Hannah took the soggy paper cup to her grandmother. Vivie filled it from the ten quart dispenser in the refrigerator and handed it back to her.

"Now, dear, I'll open the door for you while you carry these out, all right?"

Mrs. Thornbekker said, "Children these days simply aren't as agile as we were in our day, are they, Viv? I remember when I was younger than Johannah here. I had to carry trays full of food to the dining table for my mother, and I never dropped a one."

Hannah was starting down the back steps by the time Vivie was saying, "Isn't that the truth, Louise. Why, I can't begin to tell you about all the accidents that child has had. Seems like several a day, always tripping over her own feet. And mine. Just last week she fell nearly halfway down the stairs and almost gave me a heart attack."

"You poor dear."

Hannah was almost out of earshot and began to run, milk sloshing from the paper cup, as she heard Mrs. Thornbekker saying, "Vivian dear, I'm sorry to mention this, but there is a large, white spot on the back of your skirt, and I think it can only have come from…"

While Gabriel watched her from a nearby root, Hannah sat on the wooden swing that hung from the old walnut tree by the driveway and ate her peanut butter and jelly sandwich and grapes. She pushed the swing back and forth with her feet while she ate, watching Gabriel and making up a story about him going on a dangerous mission to find a magical golden worm.

She was still hungry after she finished eating. It's 'cause I'm a witch, she told herself. Witches need lots of food—'specially candy and cookies—so they can do spells and stuff all day.

When Vivie came out on the back stoop to ring the bell for naptime, Hannah was already standing at the foot of the stairs.

Vivie nodded and stood aside, gesturing for Hannah to come into the house, so she brushed the loose dirt from her jeans and shirt and hastily removed her sneakers. Then she lowered her eyes, ducked her head, held her breath and raced past her grandmother through the kitchen and into the front hall. As she rounded the corner and headed up the stairs, she had a fleeting glimpse of Mrs. Thornbekker sitting in the small parlor where Hannah knew Vivie and her friend would spend the next couple of hours watching soap operas on TV.

Hannah fairly flew up the switchback stairs and into her bedroom. There she breathed again, happy to be in another of her special places. Not that Vivie couldn't come into Hannah's bedroom whenever she wanted. She could and did frequently, especially since last summer when she had insisted that Papa remove the bedroom door.

"You know she's always having accidents, Paul. I have a horror of what would happen if I couldn't get into her room quickly enough to help her."

Except for Mama to be alive again, and except for going to visit

Grampa, there was nothing Hannah wanted more in the whole world than to have her bedroom door back. She tried to remember to ask Jesus for it every night before she went to sleep.

Still, it was her own bedroom with her own furniture and, best of all, her own closet. Hannah's closet was wide and deep, with wooden accordion doors giving easy access to all but a few inches on each side. Papa had built two racks for hangers on the right side of the closet, one at normal height and another at Hannah's level. On the left side of the closet Papa had built wooden cubicles, floor to ceiling. The upper ones were mostly empty because Hannah couldn't yet reach them, even on tiptoes, but the lower cubicles held almost all of her most precious possessions.

Along with her handmade toys—carved, sanded and finished by Papa in his workshop in the barn—the accessible cubicles on the left side of Hannah's closet held books, most of which had been given to her by Grampa. She loved her books. Early on, Mama had taught her the basics of reading and writing. And since Mama had gone to heaven, Papa read to Hannah nearly every night before bed, running his fingers under the words as he read them so that she, at a little over six, could read a whole new book practically on her own, especially if it had pictures to give her clues for the bigger words.

It was Mama who had given Hannah her very favorite thing, a soft baby doll with pretty auburn hair and big blue eyes, dressed in a lacy pink nightgown with satin ribbons. Nearly four-years-old now, "Lily" sat on Hannah's pillow during the day, slept wrapped in her arms at night, and knew all of her secrets.

For Hannah, being in her room made her feel closer to Papa and Mama and Grampa, all of whom she missed for different reasons: Mama was in heaven, Papa was here but often seemed like he wasn't, even when Hannah was right beside him, and she had been able to visit Grampa only a few times since Mama's funeral.

Hannah had been praying very hard that Papa would take her to see Grampa this summer, "all the way out here in Cincinnati," as Grampa would say. She was afraid he wouldn't. She'd overheard Vivie saying to Mrs. Thornbekker once, "Paul hasn't been himself since Elizabeth's death. So thoughtless and forgetful." As much as Hannah hated it, she knew Vivie was right. She worried that Mama might have accidentally taken Papa's happiness with her to heaven.

Hannah kept a photograph on her bureau of Grampa in his wheelchair, wearing his clerical collar, his beautiful white hair longer than she'd ever seen it, with Mama and Papa standing on either side and Grampa's church in the background. She knew it had been taken the day Grampa had married Mama and Papa, and one of her favorite things to do was to gaze at the faces of the people she loved most in the world and wonder what it had been like then for herself, still in heaven when the photo was taken. She wished she could remember more about heaven and more about Jesus, whom she was certain she had met there.

Grampa had often told Hannah that he had loved her from "way before you were born, honey." Hannah couldn't remember a time when she didn't love Grampa too; she knew she must have loved him since way before she left heaven. Every week she looked forward to their Sunday evening telephone conversation. The trouble was, neither Hannah nor Grampa much liked talking on the phone, it was such a poor substitute for being together.

That afternoon, Hannah was too worried about being a witch to read any scary books like *Alice in Wonderland*, so she selected a favorite happy one from Grampa, *Bible Stories About Jesus*. Feeling a little sleepy, she lay down on top of her bedspread, snuggling Lily into the crook of one arm and pressing the book against her with the other. As always, she faced the doorless doorway so that, if she stayed awake, she would have some warning of Vivie's approach.

She lay there on her right side for some time, gazing unseeingly at the sunshine framed by the window at the far end of the hall.

This is bad, she said in her mind to Lily. This is really bad, being a witch. They burn witches and drown them, and nobody cares 'cause everybody hates witches.

But Papa won't let anybody do that to you, Lily argued. *Besides, nobody's going to ever find out, and Grampa already said it's okay.*

"I know he did," Hannah whispered. "But Grampa's all the

way out in Cincinnati, and Vivie always finds out everything, and what if she puts me in a bag and drowns me when Papa's not here?"

She won't, silly. You're too big. And, anyway, Jesus and Mama will protect you.

"You really think so?"

I'm positive. So stop worrying, and think about some happy stuff, like Gabriel and going to visit Grampa soon, and stuff like that.

Eventually Hannah fell asleep and dreamed about dead birds and dead kittens and a blond witch with a kewpie-doll face who stirred the poor animals in a huge, black pot. Then, just before she slipped into a time of deep, dreamless sleep, she saw Grampa—without a wheelchair and standing taller than Hannah's house—putting Vivie in a burlap bag and drowning her in a pond full of bird poop.

Chapter Three

Hannah was startled awake from her nap that afternoon by Vivie shaking her shoulder.

"Time to get up now, Johannah. We've a lot of work to do before your Papa gets home."

Hannah stood beside her bed, holding Lily tight against her chest as Vivie went to work with the metal comb.

"Aren't you getting a bit too old to be so clingy with that doll of yours, Johannah? You're not hoping to take it to school with you in September, are you?"

"No, ma'am," Hannah said softly.

"Let's show how grown up we can be now, and let me have it," Vivie said, taking Lily out of Hannah's arms and tossing her toward the closet.

Watching Lily land face down on the floor, Hannah's head started to buzz, and for the next several minutes she was in Cincinnati with Gabriel and Grampa.

When Vivie finished with the braids, she said, "All right. Let's get busy," and gave Hannah a push in the small of her back that nearly sent her sprawling.

"Oh. I'm sorry, child. Sometimes I don't know my own strength."

Downstairs, Hannah silently helped Vivie prepare supper. She set the table meticulously, as Vivie had taught her, the everyday linen napkins placed just so under the everyday forks, and the matching knives and spoons in order, a plate-and-a-half's distance away. She carried crystal water glasses from the kitchen cabinet, one at a time, and carefully placed them on the table just above the knives and spoons. It was also her job to stir various foods in saucepans on the stove burners to keep them from sticking; for this she proudly stood on the footstool that Papa had made just for her.

At the right time, Hannah left the kitchen by the back door, pausing at the bottom of the steps to brush off her feet and slip into her sneakers. Then she raced around the side of the house and down the long driveway, laughing when she noticed Gabriel flying ahead of her.

She arrived at her spot by the mailbox and shooed her tiny friend away. "No, no, Gabriel! You wait up there in that tree, okay? Maybe I'll tell Papa about you later, okay?"

As Hannah retrieved the day's mail from the box, Gabriel obediently settled himself on a branch of the designated dogwood and began to trill resoundingly.

Hannah laughed with delight. "How do you do that, Gabriel? You're so little but you sing so big."

At just the right moment, she peered down the road and there was Papa's blue pickup truck rounding the bend.

Hannah jumped up and down, waving her free arm and hollering, "Papa! Hi, Papa!"

He turned his truck into the driveway and stopped, reaching over to open the door for her.

"Hello, baby," he said in his low, warm voice.

He tossed the last of his cigarette through his open window and gave Hannah a half smile as she scrambled up onto the seat with a little help from his strong right hand. She dropped the mail on the floor and moved over as close to him as she could, resting her head on his arm as he shifted gears and started up toward the house.

For a few moments, Hannah was in heaven, sitting there next to the very center of her everyday world. But soon a familiar heaviness settled on her shoulders. She chewed on a braid, trying to think of something to say to cheer up Papa, and was tongue-tied by the time he parked his truck by the barn, next to Vivie's black sedan.

As usual, Vivie was waiting for Papa inside the front door with a wide smile and a, "Welcome home!" She put her arms around his broad shoulders and aimed a kiss at his lips, planting it instead on the cheek he quickly turned to her.

With a tight little smile barely touching his mouth, he said, "Hi," and hastily separated himself from her. He went to the kitchen for a beer and then headed straight upstairs for his shower.

Hannah followed Vivie to the kitchen to help with last minute chores.

Papa was back downstairs within fifteen minutes, freshly shaved, his sun-streaked dark blond hair still damp. He grabbed another bottle of beer from the refrigerator and took it with him to the dining room as Hannah helped Vivie carry in the bowls and platters of steaming food.

Once they were all seated, they bowed their heads while Vivie said grace, talking to the lordgodamighty about something, Hannah didn't know what. She didn't want to know, and always shut her ears to Vivie's grace.

During the meal, Vivie chattered at Papa while Hannah went away into the story about Gabriel and the magical golden worm.

She had just begun to think that Gabriel might find a way to rescue poor imprisoned Izzy, when Papa brought her back to the table by asking, "What did you do today, Jo?"

Hannah remembered her day as a witch and immediately reddened with guilt, stammering, "Oh... well... um... oh, I just played and stuff." To get the spotlight off herself, she asked, "What did you do today, Papa? Did you build a house or something?"

He chuckled as he said, "I sure did."

Hannah smiled and blushed over the light in his sea green eyes.

"Do you have any plans for this evening, Jo, or would you like to go for a walk with me?"

Flustered, Hannah glanced out of the corner of her eye at Vivie. "I, um, well, I guess not. I mean, I guess so, but I have to help do the dishes."

"Yes you do, Johannah," said Vivie. "Now, Paul, don't go getting the child over-excited just before bedtime."

"She's hardly over-excited, Vivian. We're simply going to take a walk."

Hannah looked down at her hands clasped tightly in her lap.

"You're going out again tonight? That's three times this week already, Paul. Drinking with your buddies, I suppose. And don't give me that look."

Papa stood noisily and went to the kitchen for another beer.

"Liquor killed your father," Vivie called after him, "and if you keep on like this, it'll do the same to you."

"I'm going on a job estimate tonight with Carl," he said as he returned to the dining room, twisting off the bottle cap. "Not that it's any of your business."

"Of *course* it's my business. I'm left here taking care of your daughter."

"You've got something better to do?" he said, leaning against the door jamb. "Is it card night? Get a sitter. Bertha's always available." He took a long drink of his beer. "Anyway, it's not as if you have to do anything for Jo before I leave." Crossing his arms, he regarded his stepmother. "You know I'll tuck her in and she'll be sound asleep before I'm out the front door."

"You just have no idea, Paul, how much work there is in taking care of you and your daughter and this big old house. All day long, laundry, cleaning, ironing, shopping and cooking. And then I have the responsibility of listening for Johannah all night while you and your buddies guzzle beer at Vincent's."

Light flashed in Papa's eyes as he said, "If we're too much of a burden, I'll be happy to help you find a place of your own in town." Papa had said this many times before, but tonight he added something extra that thrilled Hannah. "Or maybe it's finally time to sell this place. Hannah and I could move to Cincinnati and live near Elizabeth's father. Ethan's been after me for years to do that, you know. He's always telling me that there are plenty of opportunities for a good builder out there."

Vivian pushed herself up from the table and began to clear the dishes. "Johannah!" she said.

"Yes, ma'am." Hannah stood and began to help.

After the dishes were rinsed and put in the dishwasher, and after the pots and pans were cleaned and dried and put away, Hannah hurried out of the kitchen toward the front of the house.

Vivian called after her, "Johannah! Do not run in this house, you hear me?"

"Yes, ma'am," Hannah said, running down the hall to find Papa sitting in his favorite chair in the big parlor.

Putting aside his beer and the *Philadelphia Inquirer* Sports'

Section, Papa stood up and smiled. "Ready?"

"Ready!"

Together, they walked out to the front porch. "Where'll it be tonight, kiddo?" Papa said as he lit a cigarette.

Hannah had been thinking about this all day. "I was wondering, can we go to the witches', Papa?"

"Why not."

Walking on their well-trodden path through the woods toward the road, Hannah hiccupped with nervousness when she noticed Gabriel keeping slightly ahead of them from one tree to another.

She was wildly trying to think of something to distract Papa when he said, "Your mama loved wrens."

"Huh?"

"See there, that little bird?"

Hannah carefully looked at everything except Gabriel. "A bird? Where's a bird? I don't see anything."

"There," Papa said, pointing at Gabriel staring at them from the low branch of the walnut tree just ahead. "That tiny bird, that's a wren. The smallest bird in the garden with the biggest song. Mama used to say wrens mean good luck."

"Really?" said Hannah, looking at her little friend with delight. "Mama says Gabriel's good luck?"

"Hm? Gabriel?"

Hannah put a braid in her mouth and chewed frantically.

Papa looked at her then and gently pulled the end of the braid out of her mouth. "Did you call the wren 'Gabriel'?"

Hannah looked down at her sneakers. "Um... well, I guess maybe I did, but just by accident maybe, I guess."

Papa patted Hannah's shoulder. "It's a good name for the little fellow."

Hannah put her hand in his. "I love you, Papa. "

"Mm. Me too, you."

They continued their walk in silence, and when they reached the blacktop, Papa pointed toward a small dogwood beside the grassy verge. "Look at that," he said. "The wren's still with us."

"Is that okay, Papa? I mean, to kind of be friends with a bird?"

"Sure. Why not? Better not touch it, though."

Hannah gritted her teeth and said nothing.

A few minutes down the road their destination came into view. In spite of the warm evening and the early hour, the huge old structure that Hannah had dubbed "the witches' house" did look quite sinister, the soft evening sunlight merely lengthening the shadows that crept over its gray stone walls, dark windows and ancient slate roof.

Normally, by the time they reached the witches' house, Hannah would be bursting with a dozen questions she had asked countless times before, such as, "How come nobody ever sees the witches?" and, "Do they have a black cat?" But tonight, fully aware of being a witch herself, Hannah was silent.

"Looks different tonight, doesn't it, Jo?"

Hannah could barely bring herself to focus on the horrible structure. "I don't see anything."

"Look at the grounds. Somebody's been clearing them. See there?"

"I want to go home now."

He looked at her in surprise. "What's the matter? Don't you feel well?"

Hannah managed a smile. "Uh-huh. I just want to go home, okay?"

"Okay," he said, glancing at his watch. "It's getting late anyway."

Papa pointed out Gabriel again on the way back but Hannah said nothing.

When they stopped for Papa to light a cigarette, Hannah asked, "Do witches *have to* live in houses like that, Papa?"

"I don't know," he said, inhaling deeply. "Can't they conjure up any sort of house they want to live in?"

Hannah liked that idea. "Oo, like Glinda in *The Wizard of Oz*! She probably had a really pretty house, I bet."

"Right."

"But so why do our witches live in a house like *that*?"

There was no laughter in his eyes as he said, "We're just teasing about them being witches, Jo. Remember, I told you they're just elderly sisters who don't have the money to fix the place up. And now, with the grounds being cleared like that, maybe a whole new family has moved in."

Hannah brightened. "You mean maybe like the Munsters live there now?"

He shook his head and smiled. "Whatever you say, Punkin."

Hannah giggled and suddenly wasn't afraid.

Someday when I get big, she thought, I'm going to go right up and knock on the door and find out.

Back at home after her bath, Hannah found Papa waiting for her in the overstuffed chair in the corner of her room.

"What'll it be tonight, kiddo?" he said, gently freeing her hair from its braids and combing it with his fingers.

Hannah retrieved her book of Jesus stories from the bed. "This one, okay?"

"Sure," he said, helping her nestle beside him on the chair.

He put his left arm around her and opened the book. "Where do you want me to start?"

"With the baby and then the kings, Papa."

He began reading, Hannah resting her head against the front of his soft shirt as she followed along. She loved the clean, woodsy smell of him and the low, rumbly sound of his voice in his chest.

When he finished he said, "We can do one more. Then you have to get to bed."

"So can we read the one about the little girl who died and Jesus fixes her? You know the one?"

Hannah helped Papa look for the picture she knew so well, of Jesus sitting at the foot of the bed with his arms out and the little dead girl not dead anymore, starting to sit up.

When he finished reading the story, Hannah said, "How did Jesus do that?"

He gave her a half smile. "*You're* the expert on Jesus, kiddo, you and your Mama and your Grampa. I'm the wrong person to ask. Never have been much of a churchgoer."

"Oh! I wish I could be not much of a churchgoer too, Papa. Could I stay home with you on Sundays?"

"I thought you liked going to church, Sunday school and all, learning about Jesus."

"I like the Jesus part, but…" She stopped herself from mentioning her fear of the lordgodamighty. "Anyway, I already learned about Jesus from this book," she said, tapping *Bible Stories about Jesus*. "And from Grampa and Mama, but mostly from heaven, way before I was born."

Papa looked into Hannah's eyes and caressed her cheek with his hand. "Sometimes you say the most amazing things."

Thrilled by the expression on Papa's face, Hannah wanted to freeze the moment forever. But all too soon she saw his big heart closing up again.

Softly she asked, "So could I stay home with you on Sundays, Papa? Please?"

He shook his head. "Sorry, Jo. Vivie thinks church is important for you, and I guess she's right."

"I wish I could go to Grampa's church, then."

He stood and lifted her in his arms. "Enough, now. Time for you to get to bed."

After he tucked her in and put Lily in her arms, he sat on the bed, smoothing her unruly hair back from her face.

"Papa, can I ask you just one more thing?"

"Not about church, I hope."

"No. I just wanna know, could I get my hair cut off?"

"Oh, baby, why? I love your hair. It's just like your mama's."

"It's a rat's nest, Papa. It's always a rat's nest. And it hurts, too. I mean, um, well sometimes it hurts when, um… Well, I just wanna get it cut off, is all. Can I, Papa?"

"I don't know. Let me think about it. Maybe we could get it cut a little shorter so that Vivie wouldn't have to work so hard to take care of it."

"That's a good idea, Papa. Vivie would like that a lot."

"Well, we'll see."

"And Papa? Just one more?"

"Just one."

"Are we really gonna live with Grampa like you said?"

"Oh." He was silent for a moment as he closed his eyes and rubbed the center of his forehead. "I'm sorry. I shouldn't have said that. Vivie's worked hard to take good care of us since Mama died. And, with my work, I don't see how we could move away from here. At least not anytime soon."

Hannah wasn't really disappointed. She knew it had been too good to be true. "Well, but so could we just go *visit* Grampa again soon?"

"Yes, soon."

"Very soon?"

"*Pretty* soon."

"Is pretty soon like very soon?"

He chuckled. "As soon as possible. I promise."

Hannah smiled and wrapped her arms around his neck. "I love you, Papa. Forever and ever, amen."

He hugged her and said, "Yes, Jo. Forever and ever, amen."

Standing, he leaned over and kissed her cheeks, forehead and nose, then turned on the bureau lamp, draped with a pale blue kerchief to soften its light, and left the room.

Hannah turned on her side and watched the doorway for a while, listening for his footsteps. She heard him go into his room, into the bathroom, then down the stairs and out the front door, with a quick "g'night" to Vivie in the little parlor.

The moment Hannah heard the front door close, something inside her tightened as it always did when she was alone in the house at night with Vivie. Sometimes she would awaken in the middle of the night to find Vivie standing by the head of her bed—just standing there, staring at her. The first two times it had happened, Hannah had screamed and Vivie had covered her mouth with a hand, telling her to, "Hush! You'll wake your father." Then she'd told her she was "just checking on you, child—just making sure you're all right." So Hannah had learned not to scream. She was ashamed of being what Vivie called "afraid of your own shadow". She thought that if she could just get her bedroom door back, she could find a way to lock it at night so that she wouldn't have to be afraid of her shadow anymore.

That night, in spite of how terrible it felt to be a witch, in spite of wanting to try to guard her doorway with her eyes, and as much as she wanted to stay awake and think about Grampa and Mama and Papa, and continue Gabriel's adventure with Izzy and the golden worm, Hannah fell sound asleep soon after she said in her mind, "Dear Jesus, could I please visit Grampa soon, and could I please, please have my door back? Amen. Thank you a lot."

A while later, Hannah was awakened by a sharp pain above the elbow of her right arm. Tears sprang to her eyes, and she sat up quickly and began to rub the sore spot with her left hand.

Was it a spider? she wondered fearfully, her sleep-clouded eyes peering warily above her and around at the corners of the room.

From down the hall, she heard the faint sound of a door being closed, its catch slipping into place.

Maybe it was Vivie, she thought. It wouldn't be the first time Hannah's arm had hurt after Vivie checked on her at night.

Hannah stared out the doorway and into the hall for a few moments, then slipped off the bed with her pillow, Lily and her lightweight blanket. She carried everything into her closet, curling up on the floor and pushing the doors together behind her.

After awhile, she felt safe and she slept again.

Chapter Four

The following Sunday, seeing that Vivie's small heart was thornier than ever, Hannah was silent and working hard at being invisible on the car ride to church. They arrived a little earlier than usual that morning, finding nearly half of the auditorium's seats empty and Reverend Stiles not yet behind his pulpit in the center of the stage.

Hannah and Vivie made their way toward their usual row, near the front of the room, where they sat in the third and second seats from the right aisle. As always, Vivie saved the first seat in for her friend Helen MacGill, and the aisle space itself for Helen's daughter, Maybelle, in her wheelchair.

Maybelle was a year older than Hannah, deaf and mute, her body severely twisted and crippled.

"Born that way," Vivie had said to Papa, within Hannah's hearing. "Poor old Helen and Ike, married twenty-three years, praying for a baby all that time. Finally blessed with one, and look what happens. Now Ike's gone off and Helen's killing herself, working all day long, all night too, looking after Maybelle. And for what? That child's nothing more than a vegetable."

Later, alone with Hannah, Vivie had added, "You must always stay away from Maybelle, you hear me? I don't want you giving Mrs. MacGill any more trouble than she has already. And you should count your lucky stars, Johannah, that the Lord God Almighty didn't see fit to make you just like that child."

Maybelle was one of the reasons why Hannah dreaded church. Not that she didn't like Maybelle; the trouble was, she loved her. As soon as she saw her each Sunday, the burning would start. Hannah would look into Maybelle's dull brown eyes and be suffused with longing to climb onto the wheelchair and wrap herself around her silent sister.

Waiting in their seats for the service to begin, Hannah was pleased that her mind wasn't picking up the crowd of noisy thoughts she usually heard in church. But as soon as she became aware that Maybelle's chair was being wheeled down the aisle, the heat began in her stomach and she remembered that she was a witch. Suddenly her head was filled with a bright neon voice saying, "*Help me, Hannah. Please help me.*" Knowing full well that the voice was Maybelle's, and that she might do something very, very bad if she obeyed it, Hannah clenched her teeth, sat on her hands, and flew away with Gabriel for a brief visit with Grampa.

Later Hannah imagined herself back in the auditorium with Maybelle, taking her hand, lifting her out of her wheelchair, Maybelle's body becoming straight and strong, Maybelle laughing and the two of them flying right out of the building, high into the air, up and out and away, laughing and singing and laughing some more, Gabriel flying with them, Maybelle turning and looking at Hannah, saying...

"Johannah! Wake up!" Vivie whispered, surreptitiously pinching Hannah's arm just above the right elbow. "Go on, now."

Hannah followed the other children to the Sunday School rooms, where she spent most of the next forty-five minutes listening to the teacher read from the Bible for Children and watching Billy Tyler hawking spitballs at the younger girls. Even though Hannah wished Sunday School had some playtime, she liked it because all the children had great big hearts—even Billy Tyler. Hannah knew that Billy was having his heart squeezed day after day by troubles in his family, so she liked to sit near him and think happy thoughts his way.

After church, Hannah found Vivie in the meeting room and followed her, keeping her eyes lowered as Vivie spoke to this person and that. As they approached the door where Reverend Stiles stood greeting his parishioners, Hannah was surprised by the minister's voice separating itself from the others in her head, saying, "Christ! Here comes that bitch, Vivian Kirkland." Hannah glanced up and discovered the minister apparently intent on shaking hands with the man in front of Vivie. Then Reverend Stiles nodded and smiled briefly at Vivie, shook her hand and said, "Good morning."

"Good morning, Reverend. That was a very interesting point you made in your sermon about the importance..."

But Reverend Stiles had already smiled at Hannah and turned his attention to the elderly woman who was moving forward behind her. Vivie scowled at Hannah, took her hand and pulled her out the door, toward the parking lot. Hannah twisted backwards and found Reverend Stiles looking at them. He gave her a little wave, and Hannah decided that her mind must be playing tricks on her. After all, everybody loved Vivie.

On the drive home from church, Hannah left the car and flew away again with Maybelle, this time soaring over the barn and the pond, telling Maybelle about the kittens.

Maybelle turned, her dark brown eyes now brilliant with light, and astonished Hannah by saying, "It's okay about Gabriel. It was a very good thing you did for him. It's what I want you to do for me."

They floated quietly on the breeze for a while, then Maybelle stopped in mid-air, put her hands on Hannah's shoulders, looked straight into her eyes and said, "You have to go to the witches' house by yourself."

Hannah returned to the sedan's passenger seat with a thud and remained there for the rest of the ride home, dazed with worry about what it all meant.

That evening, after the supper dishes were cleared away, Papa and Hannah went to the phone in the front hall. Papa dialed Grampa's number and left Hannah to talk with him in private.

"Hello, honey," said the beloved, scratchy voice from "way out here in Cincinnati".

Hannah giggled. "You *always* know it's me. I never get to surprise you."

Hannah heard his warm chuckle, could imagine the merry light in his eyes.

"I miss you so much, Grampa."

"And I miss you. More every second."

"How are you? Are you okay?"

"I'm right as rain. Right as rain. How about you?"

Giggling, Hannah said, "I'm right as sun."

Grampa laughed. "That you are, honey. Right as sunshine itself."

They lapsed into silence. This was the part Hannah hated about talking on the phone. You couldn't just talk when you felt like it, you had to sort of plan what to say and get it said in a hurry. And tonight there was so much to say that she didn't know how to say any of it.

Maybelle's words hung over Hannah like a small storm cloud. Her plan to do as Maybelle had told her to was a secret she could share with no one—not even Grampa, and she never kept secrets from Grampa. Well, until recently that is. Now, with being a witch and what happened with Gabriel and her plan about going to the witches' house by herself, Hannah felt like there was more to keep secret from Grampa than there was to tell him. And Grampa always seemed to know everything about Hannah. Whenever she asked him how he did that, he would smile and say, "Why, the Spirit tells me, honey."

So tonight, Hannah wasn't surprised when Grampa asked, "What's the matter?" The cheerfulness was gone from his voice.

"Nothing," she lied. "Really." Flushed with shame, she made the lie worse by adding, "Honest!"

Grampa was silent for a moment. "You do know you can tell me anything, don't you?"

"Um… yes."

There was silence again from Cincinnati. Then, "Okay. I won't press you. Just remember I'm only a phone call away."

"Okay. I always remember that," Hannah said, trying to sound happy. But her tone dropped a few notes as she said, "I just miss you so much and I want to see you, is all."

"I know, honey. I know." Grampa paused. "Is your Papa nearby? I'd like to have a word with him tonight, if he is."

Relieved that she had kept her secrets, Hannah brightened. "Uh-huh. He's right in there," she said, pointing toward the big parlor.

"Could I speak to him for a moment?"

Hannah hollered, "Papa!" into the receiver, realizing too late that the sound was going directly into Grampa's ear. "Ooo, I'm sorry Grampa," she was saying, as Papa came out of the big parlor, a question on his face.

"Here," Hannah said, standing so that Papa could sit in the

phone chair. "Grampa's here for you."

Putting the receiver to his ear, Papa said, "Hi, Ethan. How are you?"

Hannah waited nervously beside Papa, shifting from one foot to the other, wishing she could hear more than Papa's end of the conversation, which consisted mostly of words like "Okay," "Yes," and "Sure." She could see in Papa's eyes that they were talking about her.

Finally, Papa handed the phone back to her but stayed seated. "Say goodbye, Jo."

Filled with worry, her eyes fixed on Papa, Hannah said, "Goodbye, Grampa. I love you."

"Goodbye, honey. Remember, you can call me anytime, not just Sunday evenings. Okay?"

"Okay. I love you."

"And I love you."

Hannah replaced the receiver in its cradle, still staring at Papa. "Are you mad at me?" she asked.

"Not a bit," Papa said, smiling as he put his hands on her shoulders. "Grampa is just worried about you, that's all."

"But why?"

"I guess it's because he hasn't seen you for such a long time."

Hannah felt like someone had lifted ten pounds of rocks from her shoulders.

"Oh! Me too, Papa. I didn't see him either!"

Papa gave a sad little smile. "I know, Punkin. And I'm sorry. It's just... well, it's that I have so much work to do."

"But can I see him really really soon, Papa, like you said?"

Hannah's stomach churned at the look in his eyes.

"I wish I could say yes, but I just can't. To be honest, I don't know how I'll be able to get away before winter, and even then..."

Papa stopped speaking and pulled Hannah into a warm hug. "I'm sorry, Jo. I know I let you down. But Grampa gave me a good idea. Want to hear about it?"

"Okay," she murmured against his chest, not really caring.

"Here," he said, shifting her position so they could both look at the phone dial. "Grampa thinks you should be able to call him all by yourself, whenever you need to, and I agree."

By the time Hannah went to bed that night, she was feeling a little bit better. For the first time Grampa really was as he always said, "only a phone call away," and it was a phone call she could make without help from anyone.

Mama visited Hannah in her sleep that night. She talked to Hannah about Grampa, Maybelle and Gabriel, and about Hannah's "wonderful" differences. The trouble was, the next morning Hannah couldn't remember a thing that Mama had said.

It's 'cause I was asleep, Hannah told herself. Mama never says anything when I'm awake. It was just a dumb old dream.

It was raining heavily, so Hannah spent the morning in her bedroom, working on a letter to Grampa, trying to find a way to talk to him about Maybelle and Gabriel. She kept having to scrunch the letter up into a ball, put it in the wastebasket and begin again with a new sheet of lined paper. She was very worried that the Spirit would tell Grampa that his only granddaughter was a witch.

Eventually, the letter that survived scrunching read,

Dear Grampa,
Hello. How are you? I am fine. It's raning today. I met a litle burd. Papa told me it is a renn. I named him Gabereel. Do you think thats OK? Do you know Mabell? She is 7 and she has a weel chare like yores and she cant talk and heer. I miss you! I love you!!!!! Hugs and kisses!!!!! Hannah. P.S. Papa shoed me how to dile the fone!!!

She folded the paper neatly, put it in an envelope from her bottom bureau drawer and retrieved a stamp from the booklet that Papa had supplied.

Her letter ready, Hannah idly leafed through some of her books, frequently gazing out the window and repeating the nursery rhyme, "Rain, rain, go away…" She couldn't wait to see Gabriel and get started on her secret adventure.

The rain finally did go away, shortly before noon. After taking Grampa's letter to the mailbox and eating lunch in the kitchen with Vivie, accompanied by Vivie's favorite weekday radio church service, Hannah was given permission to play outside, "as long as you wear your galoshes and don't come in all muddy at naptime."

Hannah had an idea. Could she possibly… "Vivie?"

"Yes?"

"I wondered, um, could I maybe not have to take a nap today? I mean I sort of rested this morning."

Leaning back against the kitchen sink, finishing her cup of coffee, Vivie regarded Hannah through narrowed eyes. Finally she nodded and said, "But you be back by four to help with supper, you hear me?"

"Yes, ma'am."

Hannah found her galoshes in the front hall closet, pulled them on over her sneakered feet, and raced out the back door, hollering behind her as she flew down the stairs, "Thank you!"

She rounded the corner of the house and was delighted to see Gabriel sitting on the swing, under the chestnut tree. He flew straight onto her shoulder when she ran to him, but she quickly whisked him off, whispering, "Not now, Gabriel. Wait till we get away from the house more, okay?"

Her little friend flying near her, all the way to the woods, Hannah headed not down to the road but cross-country toward the back of the witches' property. Before long she was staring at the big old house across a field of tall grass.

Suddenly Hannah wasn't so sure about what she intended to do. She had never before done anything on purpose that she knew Papa wouldn't like.

She sat cross-legged on the damp ground, put a braid in her mouth and began to chew thoughtfully. Gabriel perched on her shoulder, and she gently stroked his back with the tip of her forefinger.

"What should I do, Gabriel?" she said through her braid. "I really want to go there, but what if Vivie finds out? Or Papa?"

She thought about it a while longer and then said, "Maybe we could just go a little bit closer."

She got on her hands and knees and began crawling across the open, overgrown field toward the back of the huge old house. Uncertain about what was going on, Gabriel fluttered nervously around her, finally perching himself on her head.

Hannah thought that was the perfect place for him. "You're a lookout, Gabriel," she whispered. "Tell me if you see the witches, okay?"

When she'd approached within fifteen feet of the edge of the field, she realized with a start that she was becoming very wet and very muddy. Water was even getting inside her galoshes from the tall grass.

She stood up suddenly, frightening Gabriel off her head and also frightening the white-haired woman, not twenty feet away, who was carrying an aluminum lawn chair in her direction.

"Oh, my!" said the woman, dropping the chair and putting a hand to her throat.

"Oh!" yelped Hannah, putting her wet, muddy hands to her cheeks. She turned and started to run, her water-logged clothes and boots weighing her down.

"Wait!" called the woman. "Don't go. Please wait."

Hannah stopped, but didn't turn around.

"I'm sorry I scared you," the woman said in a pleasant voice. "I didn't know anyone was there."

Hannah still didn't budge, and the woman said, "My name is Jeli. Won't you tell me yours?"

Forgetting that she was talking to a grown-up witch, Hannah turned and said, "Jelly? Your name's really Jelly?"

Walking slowly through the grass toward Hannah, the woman said, "Well, as a matter of fact, that's my nickname, short for Anjelica. Do you know what a nickname is?"

"Uh-huh. Grampa and me call it a nickel-name, and mine's Hannah."

"Ah! Well, Hannah is one of my most favorite names. Did you know it means 'grace' or 'gift from God'?"

Suddenly shy, Hannah looked down at the muddy knees of her pants. "Well, but my real name is Johannah."

"Johannah. That's lovely."

"That was my Mama's mommy's name."

"And that makes it even more lovely, doesn't it."

Jeli was standing in front of Hannah now, holding out her right hand. "How do you do, Hannah-Johannah. It's a pleasure to meet you."

Hannah put her right hand in Jeli's. "How do you do, Jeli."

Jeli smiled and Hannah decided she was the most beautiful old lady in the whole world. How could somebody so beautiful be a witch?

"Would you like to come to the house with me, Hannah? You could dry off a bit."

Go into *that* house with one of *them*? She might get turned into gingerbread. "I guess not," she said, looking at the ground, prepared to run again.

"Mm. Of course. I'm being thoughtless. Your mother undoubtedly wants you to come home and dry off there."

"Mama's in heaven," Hannah said, glancing up at Jeli briefly. "She went there when I was four 'cause a truck hit her car."

Jeli immediately went down on her knees in front of Hannah, reaching out and lightly touching her arm. "Oh, my dear child!" she exclaimed. "How terrible!"

Hannah felt funny inside as she looked into Jeli's clear blue eyes; then she burst into tears. Jeli took hold of her shoulders, and Hannah moved forward into Jeli's arms. She stayed there for some time, weeping into Jeli's neck and absorbing the woman's warm, sunny fragrance.

Eventually the tears stopped, but Hannah didn't want to move. She hadn't felt like that in anybody's arms since Mama's.

It was Gabriel's landing on Hannah's shoulder that finally broke the spell.

"My goodness!" said Jeli. "It's a *wren*."

"He's my friend. His name is Gabriel."

Jeli sat back on the wet grass and watched with interest as Hannah softly stroked Gabriel's head and chest.

"I've never seen anything like that," Jeli said. "Wrens are notorious for keeping their distance from people. How in the world did you and Gabriel become friends?"

"He was…" Hannah began, remembering just in time that she couldn't tell anybody the truth about how she met Gabriel. She put a braid in her mouth as she said, "Um. Well, see, he was just kind of sitting there on the ground and he let me pet him, is what happened."

"That's amazing! I'm very impressed, Hannah. I wonder if he

would let *me* touch him."

Hannah stopped petting Gabriel and looked earnestly at Jeli. "Do you think it's okay to touch him? I mean I, um, heard someplace that you're not supposed to touch wild animals 'cause of germs and stuff."

"Yes, I suppose that's true as a general rule. But he doesn't look a bit wild or germy to me. Does he to you?"

Hannah felt so relieved that she decided Gabriel should be Jeli's friend, too. She moved Gabriel's perch in Jeli's direction. "You can go ahead and pet him if you want."

Jeli slowly extended an index finger, and when it was an inch away from Gabriel, he darted off Hannah's shoulder and flew out of sight.

"I'm sorry. I guess he got scared or something," said Hannah, embarrassed.

"It's all right, dear," Jeli said as she stood and brushed at the knees of her olive green khakis. "Clearly you and Gabriel have a very special friendship."

"Yes," said Hannah, wondering how a witch could have such a big heart.

"I have a special bird friend, too. His name is Oliver. Would you like to meet him?"

"Oh, yes, please!"

"Good. Oliver loves to meet new people—especially children." Jeli turned and started toward the house, stopping when she noticed that Hannah wasn't coming with her. "What's the matter, dear? Don't you want to meet Oliver?"

"Well, but, um, I thought he was outside, like Gabriel."

"Oh. I see. But Oliver is a canary, and he lives in a cage. Have you ever seen a canary? No? Well, they're very pretty, usually combinations of yellow and green and black and white. Oliver is a beautiful butter-yellow with just the prettiest little band of white along each wing and at the tip of his tail. And he sings a beautiful song when he's happy, just like Gabriel does. Wouldn't you like to meet him?"

Hannah squished the toe of one boot into the mud as she said, "I guess not."

Jeli looked at her for a few moments and then glanced back at the house. "I think I understand. It's this big old monster of a house, isn't it? It's pretty scary looking."

Hannah felt her face get hot with embarrassment.

"That's quite all right, dear. I understand perfectly." She glanced up at the sky. "It's become a lovely afternoon, hasn't it. I think I'll bring Oliver out here into the shade of that big old maple tree for a while. It will be a very special treat for him, and that way you can meet him without going inside. Would you like that?"

"Oh, yes, please. I really would."

Jeli headed again toward the house, saying, "I'll bring you a chair like the one I was just going to set up for myself."

Hannah found the collapsed chair that Jeli had dropped and dragged it with her to the maple tree where she pushed and pulled at it in an effort to get it to unfold.

"Here we are," said Jeli in no time at all.

In one hand she carried a large, white cage with a bright yellow bird perched inside on a swing, and under the other arm she held a chair identical to the one Hannah had been struggling with.

"Here," she said, extending the cage toward Hannah. "Would you hold Oliver's house while I set up our chairs?"

Hannah took the cage in both arms, glad that it didn't weigh much of anything, and stared admiringly at the beautiful bird inside who was staring back at her.

"Good," said Jeli. "He likes you."

"How do you know?"

"If he didn't, he'd be flapping around his cage making a terrible ruckus."

"What's that, that 'rucks' thing you said?" asked Hannah, as Jeli relieved her of the cage and placed it on the ground between them.

Just then Gabriel landed on the white metal loop at the top of the cage. Oliver saw him and immediately began to flap his wings, ricocheting off the cage bars and screeching. Gabriel watched him for a few moments and then calmly flew to Hannah's shoulder. Oliver immediately settled back on his swing.

Jeli laughed. "That, my dear Hannah, was definitely a ruckus!"

"You mean he doesn't like Gabriel?"

"I think it's safe to say that he wouldn't like any other bird on or even near his house. Oliver is fiercely territorial."

"He's so pretty, too."

The canary seemed to know that he was being admired. He began grooming himself.

"Will he sing for us?" asked Hannah.

"I expect he will in a little while, when he thinks we aren't paying attention to him."

Hannah giggled. "He's funny."

Jeli smiled and nodded. "You're absolutely right, Hannah. One of the things I love best about Oliver is the way he makes me laugh."

Hannah absent-mindedly stroked Gabriel with one forefinger as she studied Oliver.

Jeli said, "How about some cookies and lemonade? Would you like that?"

"Oh, yes, please, thank you."

Jeli returned shortly from another trip into the house carrying a pitcher of lemonade, some paper cups, plates and napkins, and a dish of cookies, all on a lightweight plastic table, which she set beside Oliver's cage.

As Hannah bit into a soft chocolate chip cookie, she wondered for a moment if she might be asleep and dreaming. She looked up at the house, gloomy and menacing as ever, and then at her new friend, this witch named Jeli who smiled and winked at her when she caught her eye.

"Tell me about yourself, dear," said Jeli, as Hannah finished her cookie. "Is your father still living? Yes? Thank heaven!"

Over the course of three cookies and a big glass of lemonade, Hannah told Jeli almost everything about herself except, of course, that she too was a witch. She told Jeli how old she was, where she lived, about Papa, and especially about Grampa and how much she missed him.

"Your grampa sounds wonderful, Hannah," Jeli said, pouring more lemonade into her own glass. "I'd like to meet him sometime."

"He'd like to meet you too, I know he would," said Hannah

proudly.

"Where does he live?"

"Way out there in Cincinnati. Do you know where that is?"

Jeli smiled. "Sure do. In fact, I have some good friends who live in Cincinnati."

"Really?" Hannah asked excitedly. "Do they live near Grampa? Could you go see them and take me with you and then you could maybe—" Hannah stopped abruptly and felt her cheeks burn with embarrassment.

Jeli smiled brightly. "That's a lovely idea, Hannah. Maybe I *can* do that sometime. Now tell me, who takes care of you all day when your papa's at work?"

As they continued to talk, Oliver began to ask for attention by singing loudly. When Gabriel chimed in with his own tunes, Hannah and Jeli were forced to raise their voices in order to be heard.

"SO YOUR GRANDMOTHER ALLOWS YOU TO GO WHEREVER YOU WANT ON THE FARM ANY TIME AND—" Both birds stopped singing abruptly, catching Jeli in mid-holler. She and Hannah laughed.

"And you mean to tell me, Hannah, that she doesn't worry about you?"

"I guess so," Hannah replied, wondering if that was the wrong answer.

"And what about your Papa? Doesn't he worry about your safety?"

"I don't know," said Hannah, feeling ashamed and looking down at her muddy galoshes.

"Oh, dear! I'm sorry. Forgive me, Hannah. It's just that I would be so worried if you were my little girl, and that's silly of me. I mean, look at you. Obviously you can take very good care of yourself, and you even have your brave little Gabriel to keep you company."

Feeling better, Hannah asked, "Do you have a little girl too?"

"In a way, I do. But my little girl, Celeste, is all grown-up now. She's a nurse in Philadelphia."

"Ooo!" exclaimed Hannah. "My Mama and Papa took me to the zoo in Phildeelphia one time when I was little. I don't remember it much, but Papa says we took rides on a camel. Did you ever see a camel?"

Just then a black cloud covered the sun, a gust of wind lifted the paper plates and napkins, and the hair on Hannah's neck rose straight in the air.

As Jeli ran after the paper goods, Hannah jumped from her seat and looked around warily, certain that someone was watching her. She thought of the giant invisible eye of her nightmares, but saw only the darkening sky, the overgrown field and the woods beyond.

"Looks like it's going to rain again," called Jeli, scrambling after the last flying plate. "Sure you won't come on inside with me?"

Without giving it another thought, Hannah picked up Oliver in his cage and went into the witches' house with Jeli. A short time later, Hannah opened the back door, spotted Gabriel and called him into the house with her.

Chapter Five

At three-fifty-seven that afternoon, as Hannah pulled off her galoshes and damp sneakers on the stairs at the back of her house, a terrible thought stole her breath: Vivie knows!

She stood, ran up the steps and opened the screen door, jumping and giving a little yelp when she found Vivie standing there, arms crossed, jaggedy red thoughts flying out of her head. Wordlessly, Vivie took hold of Hannah's arm and propelled her toward the basement door, beneath the front hall staircase.

"Oh, no! Please, Vivie. I'm sorry, really, honest I am. Please don't!"

It was useless. Vivie locked Hannah in the basement.

Next to being put in a bag and drowned in the pond, being locked in the basement was the worst thing Hannah could think of. There was a light on the landing, but the switch was outside the door. The light downstairs had a string hanging from it for turning it on, but it didn't hang low enough for Hannah to reach —and, anyway, she didn't want to go downstairs into the basement itself. Too dark, too creepy, and filled with little rustling noises that she could hear all the way at the top of the steps. Best to just huddle up here in the corner by the door, chew on her braids and be very still until Vivie let her out.

She tried to make up stories and sing songs and fly away to visit Grampa, but when she was in the basement even her imagination abandoned her.

Hannah's time in that dark little space at the top of the basement steps lasted forever that afternoon. She believed that Vivie would let her out to go meet Papa, but when that time came and went, Hannah felt as if she had a big rubber ball in her throat. She couldn't swallow. She could barely breathe. Would Papa be so mad that he'd make her stay in here too?

When the door was finally unlatched and opened, it was Vivie who stood there. "Go wash your hands and face and then sit on the kitchen stool," was all she said.

Hannah did as she was told. Soon after she was seated in the kitchen, she heard Papa at the front door. "Where's my girl?" he hollered cheerily, as the screen door flapped shut behind him.

"We're back here," said Vivie.

Before Papa reached the kitchen, Vivie was saying, "Your daughter snuck off to the old Whitney sisters' property this afternoon. I waited awhile after I saw where she was heading, and when she didn't come back, I went after her and found her going right inside that house, with one of those women."

"Is this true?" said Papa, staring down at Hannah, the look on his face making her stomach hurt.

"I'm sorry, Papa."

"Why on earth did you do that, Jo? You know you're not allowed off this property when you're alone. You know you're never to go into a stranger's house. How could you have done that?"

"I'm really sorry, Papa. I didn't mean…"

"No," said Vivie. "You never *mean to*, do you?"

"Let me handle this, Vivian."

"She must learn a lesson, Paul. Spare the rod and spoil the child," she said as she moved closer to Hannah.

"I said I'd handle this, Vivian." He put himself in front of Hannah.

Vivian turned her glare on her stepson. "You're not the one who's been worrying all afternoon."

"Will you get out of here!"

"No, I won't! You leave her with me every day and expect me "

Papa turned abruptly. "Go to you room, Hannah!" he barked.

Hannah did so in a flash, grabbing her pillow and Lily from the bed and heading straight for her closet. She crawled into her spot under the hanging clothes and pulled the doors closed behind her. Curling up on the floor, she put the pillow around her ears, squeezed her eyes shut, and distanced herself as much as she could from the angry voices.

There was little that frightened Hannah more than Papa and Vivie fighting. As she huddled there on the floor, tunelessly repeating, "La-la-la-la-la-la," to further muffle the noise from the kitchen, she was wishing she could *really* fly away now, sprout wings and fly out of the window. She would find Gabriel and they would go say goodbye to Jeli, then they would fly all the way out there to Cincinnati, where they would land and spend the rest of their lives with Grampa. And Papa would come out there too, as soon as he discovered where she was, and then they would all live there together, happily ever after.

But that afternoon, Hannah could not even fly away in her mind. Instead she felt chained to the floor by thoughts of how bad she was. Even Lily was silent.

She told herself it was because she was a witch. Witches are bad, she thought, so bad things happen to them. Except for Jeli. But maybe Jeli's not really a witch after all. Or maybe she's one of those really good witches, angel witches, like Glinda.

Her mind drifted into *The Wizard of Oz*. She remembered the beautiful field of red poppies where everybody became so sleepy. The poppies transformed themselves into the fragrant wildflowers that made up Mama's bouquets, and after awhile Hannah herself drifted off to sleep.

When she awoke sometime later, she found herself lying on top of her bedcovers, her hair freed from its braids, and still wearing the clothes she'd put on that morning. The house was quiet and the nightlight on the bureau illuminated the dried mud on her jeans, reminding her of the bad thing she'd done that day. She sat up and was swinging her legs over the side of her bed, planning to change into her pajamas, when the room was suddenly filled with lightning and a long roll of thunder. Hannah shrieked, grabbed Lily and ran down the hall to Papa's bedroom. Not even knocking as she normally would, she pushed the door open and raced to his big bed, clambering up and yelling "Papa!" just as his room was briefly and brightly illuminated by a crackling flash of lightning.

Papa's bed was empty. Still, it felt safer than her own, so Hannah pulled the covers over her head and sang to herself, every bit of every song that she could remember. Later, as the storm subsided, she thought about what had happened that afternoon, what a bad thing she had done, and worried that maybe she should go back to her own room before Papa got home.

But then she heard him coming up the stairs. Listening to his cautious footsteps, Hannah's heart sank with the knowledge that he was "bleery"—her own made-up word for what happened to him when he drank a lot of beer.

He came into the room and flipped the switch beside the door that turned on the bureau lamp. Then he nodded at Hannah as if he had expected to find her there. "Was 't the thunder?" he asked, moving unsteadily to the side of the bed.

"Uh-huh," she said in a very small voice, flinching from the smell of his breath. "Are you mad at me, Papa?"

"Not mad." He sat heavily on the side of the bed with his back to Hannah. "But you shouldn't'a done it, y'know."

"Oh, I *do* know, Papa," she said, sitting up, talking to the back of his head. "I'm really, really sorry. I know it was very bad. But see, Maybelle… um, well, see I had this idea I was supposed to go to the witches', and so I… well, I was just going to get close, but there was Jeli and I scared her, and she's so nice, Papa. And that's her real name, Jeli, it's a nickel-name for Angelica like Hannah is mine, and—"

"Whoa," he said into his hands as he rubbed his face. "Maybe better wait till t'morrow…"

"But could I tell you now, Papa? I'm not sleepy at all. Honest! And anyway you always go to work way before I even wake up, so could I tell you now?"

He turned and looked at her, smiling slightly. "I guess, but skootch over and let me lie down."

She did, and he kicked off his shoes and lay on top of the sheet beside her, resting a forearm over his eyes. "So tell me."

"Well, see, what happened was I went to the witches' house the back way and when I got to the big field there was this beautiful old lady—you wouldn't even know she's a witch, she's so pretty—and she has a little yellow bird named Oliver, and she gave me cookies and lemonade, and then it was going to rain again so I went inside with her, and…" Hannah paused to catch her breath. "And inside, well, it was just so big and kinda nice—Jeli's been cleaning it up. She says her aunts lived there and they died and left it to her, and her husband died too, but before the aunts, so she moved here 'cause she has a little girl who's a nurse in Phildeelphia. And, guess what! She's looking for somebody just like you to fix up her house for her."

Papa lifted his arm and looked at her then.

"And I told her about how you do building stuff and now she wants you to go see her and I just know you're gonna like her and she's gonna want you to fix everything, so it's really a good thing I went there, isn't it?"

He gave her a small, weary smile. "Maybe it is, kiddo."

"So, well, then, can I visit her tomorrow?"

He was silent for a moment and Hannah worried he'd fallen asleep. Then he said, "I should meet her first, I guess."

"Will you tomorrow, Papa? Meet her, I mean."

"Can't promise, but I'll try."

"Oh, thank you! You're the best Papa in the whole wide world."

"Love you too, kiddo." He yawned. "Sleepy now. Better get back to your own room."

"Okay, sure," she said, sliding off the bed with Lily. She stood beside him then and, even though he looked as if he'd already fallen asleep, she said earnestly, "And I cross my heart and hope to die, I'll never go to somebody's house again without asking first. 'Kay?" When he snored lightly, she whispered, "'Kay," kissed his cheek, and made her way on tiptoe back to her room.

Hannah was dancing with Gabriel in the air three hundred feet above the farm. She wore a pale green chiffon tutu sprinkled with silvery stars. She was the most graceful ballerina in the whole universe, and Gabriel dipped and swooped around her, as big and colorful as a flamingo. Then they were above the pond and Hannah glanced down, thinking of the poor drowned kittens. The pond looked strange somehow, eerie, making Hannah stop her pirouettes and Gabriel transform into his small, gray-brown self. Together they watched the waters of the pond churn and darken in the center, while its elongated shape rounded itself somewhat, and the green pond grasses receded to both sides, turning brown as if they had suddenly died. The dark green water became slate gray and the entire pond, now perfectly resembling a human eye, separated from the ground and began to rise into the air toward Hannah and Gabriel. Hannah watched the eye in fascination until it was about ten feet below her, when she recognized it: the giant eye, no longer invisible. And it was Vivie's.

She awoke with a shriek and the certainty that Vivie knew about Gabriel.

"No!" she cried.

Within two minutes she was dressed and practically tumbling down the stairs in her rush to protect her little friend.

The kitchen was empty. "No!" she cried again as she raced out the back door and ran around the house, looking in every direction for Gabriel or any sign of Vivie. She found nothing. Vivie's car was there and Papa's truck was gone.

She knew, she just knew, that Vivie was at that very minute trying to kill Gabriel.

Wait. That noise. Is that in the barn?

Hannah raced to the barn, pulled open one of the doors and slipped inside, finding Vivie swatting at the air with a straw broom.

"Wait!" Hannah screamed. "What are you doing?"

Vivie barely glanced at Hannah. "Get on out of here now, Johannah. This is none of your business."

"What is it?" Hannah persisted. "Is it a bat?"

"Not a bat. It's that filthy wren that's been following you around."

"But, wait! Please, Vivie! Mama says wrens are good luck."

"Well, Mama's not here and I am, and I say they're filthy pests."

Hannah saw Gabriel dart from under the threshing floor and fly toward the highest rafters.

"Oh, look!" Hannah cried. "Now you'll never be able to catch him." Under Vivie's glare, she stuffed some braid-less hair in her mouth.

"Stop chewing your hair, and close that door again."

Hannah obeyed, pulling the large, left-hand door inward until it met its right-hand twin. She remained by the doors, ready to push them open again for Gabriel's escape, when she realized that

Vivie was going into Papa's office, to his gun cabinet, sorting through a ring of keys.

Her heart beating as fast as a hummingbird's, Hannah lowered the bar that locked the barn doors from the inside and scuffed her sneaker into a large opening under the doors as she thought with all her might: HERE, GABRIEL! GO! RIGHT HERE! RIGHT NOW!

Just as Vivie came out of Papa's office, raising a shotgun to her shoulder and sighting up its barrel toward the tiny bird in the rafters, Gabriel flew straight down and out the opening by Hannah's foot.

Vivie hurried to the doors, apparently intending to open them and have a shot at the fleeing bird, but stopped in her tracks by the bar Hannah had put in place. She was forced to put the gun on the ground as she lifted the bar out of the way, grumbling under her breath. When she finally opened the door, there was no sign of the little wren.

Vivie stiffened and turned toward Hannah. "You did that on purpose, barring the door like that so I couldn't get out."

"I couldn't let you hurt him, Vivie. I'm sorry, honest I am, but I just couldn't let you—"

Vivie silenced Hannah with an open-handed smack to her face, knocking her down.

Hannah's head hit hard on the rocky dirt and light spun behind her eyes for a moment. Then she found herself being half-carried up the steps into the kitchen and plunked onto a chair at the table.

"You had that slap coming, Johannah, disobeying me that way," Vivie said as she set a glass of orange juice in front of Hannah and poured some Cheerios into a bowl. "I don't know what's gotten into you lately, but I don't like it one bit." Vivie added some milk to the Cheerios, gave Hannah a spoon, and then stood behind her, going to work on her hair. "Now, eat. Then I expect to you to get up to your room and stay there for the rest of the day. You may come down only for lunch. Do you understand?"

When Hannah said nothing, Vivie yanked on a half-done braid. "I asked if you understand. Or would you rather spend the day in the basement?"

"Oh, no, please, Vivie. I'll go to my room, I promise."

Hannah silently ate her meal, her Cheerios mixing with the flavor of the salty tears she could not stop. She knew exactly what had gotten into her lately, but there was no way that she could explain to Vivie about being a witch. Her head hurt where it had hit the ground, her hair hurt from Vivie's braiding, and her cheek was stinging as if it had been poked with a thousand tiny needles.

When she rose from her chair to go to her room, she heard Vivie say from the pantry, "I want you to know, Johannah, I am not giving up. I will not have any sort of filthy, wild creature hanging about this house."

Hannah was miserable all day. She couldn't occupy her mind with a single happy imagining, so certain was she that Gabriel had flown away forever. Her only comfort was Lily, who sat with her quietly and listened to her worries.

When it was time to go to the road to greet Papa, Vivie called from the foot of the stairs, "You stay in your room, Johannah. I'm going out to speak with your father."

After a time, Papa came up the stairs and into her room.

Hannah's throat closed up when she saw the look in his eyes. "I'm sorry, Papa," she squeaked.

"I know, baby." He sat next to her on the bed and put his arm around her. "But this is two days in a row now that I've come home to find trouble between you and Vivie. It has to stop."

"I make her crazy," she said. "I try to be good, but I just can't help being bad."

"You're not bad, Jo." He raked his free hand through his hair. "I know Vivie can be a little tough sometimes, but she works very hard to take good care of us, and we just have to try a little harder to cooperate. Do you know what I mean?"

"Uh-huh."

He put a finger under her chin and tilted her face up toward him. "Look at you." He kissed her forehead. "I know you miss your mama, baby. So do I. But Vivie's all we have now, and I don't know what we'd do without her.

"Anyway, it's over. She's upset, but I told her it's okay about your little wren friend. Gabriel, that's his name, isn't it? I told her that I knew about him and that it was okay for you to play with him."

Hannah sat up straight. "Really, Papa? You really did?"

"I really did. And you'll have to be extra nice to Vivie tonight, okay?"

"But what if Gabriel's already gone away?"

"I'll bet you anything he's outside waiting for you."

"Oh! I'll go see." Hannah jumped off the bed and ran out of the room, down the stairs and straight out the front screen door, practically dancing a jig when she saw Gabriel on the porch railing.

"You are!" she said aloud, kneeling beside him, wishing she could hug him. "You are waiting for me."

He sang to her, and she knew he too had been lonely and sad all day.

Hannah nearly flew to her lilac bush, Gabriel flying with her, and they spent time there together until the bell rang her in for supper.

Hannah was lying in her bed that night, determinedly wide awake with the bedside lamp still on, when Papa returned from visiting Jeli.

He came into her bedroom with a happy smile on his lips.

And not one little bit bleery. "You like her!" Hannah exclaimed, sitting up.

"Yes I do," he said as he sat on the bed beside her. "Very much."

Hannah listened in delight then as Papa recounted some of what he'd learned about Jeli—whose whole name was Mrs. Anjelica Whitney Thayer. Jeli was a professional writer who had lived most of her life outside Seattle, Washington, and had spent the past year caring for her ailing husband. Papa said that Jeli had loved her maiden aunts' big, old house every time she visited there as a child, and had decided to move here permanently when her daughter Celeste took a job with a Philadelphia hospital.

Hannah was relieved to hear that Jeli laughed at the notion that witches lived in her house, saying she'd had the same thought from time to time. Apparently Jeli's aunts grew quite crone-like in their advancing years, furthering the idea that they were witches, except with anyone who knew their sweet nature.

"Are you going to fix the house for her, Papa?" Hannah asked.

There was a lively spark in his eyes as he said, "I think so, sweetheart. There's a lot of potential there, and it's a very big job, so she naturally wants to put it in the hands of someone she trusts."

"And she trusts *you*!"

Just then Vivie hollered up the stairs, "Paul, it's past nine-thirty. Johannah needs her sleep."

Hannah lowered her voice to a whisper. "So it's okay if I go see Jeli tomorrow?"

"As a matter of fact, Jeli and I think it would be best for her to come over and introduce herself to Vivie before you go visit her again."

"Oh, but—"

"Don't worry, Punkin. Jeli promised she'll be here tomorrow morning."

"But, well, what if Vivie doesn't like Jeli or something?"

Papa stood and turned off the bedside lamp. "I can't imagine anyone not liking Jeli. Can you?"

"I guess so. Do you think maybe Jeli is an angel?"

"Maybe. Just not the kind who flies back to heaven every night."

Hannah giggled.

"Now, you get to sleep. You've had a long day."

As Papa headed out the doorway, Hannah asked, "Are you going out again?"

He returned to the side of her bed and leaned over her, regarding her thoughtfully. "Does that worry you, being here without me?"

Her heart leapt into her throat. Should she tell him the truth?

But he didn't wait for her answer. "But I'm not going out tonight. Just to the barn office to call Carl about meeting me at Jeli's early tomorrow morning, then I'll come right back upstairs and go to bed."

He kissed her cheek. "That'll be okay, won't it, Jo?" he said, straightening and blowing her another kiss as he left the room.

Hannah caught the kiss and held it tightly in her hand as she listened to Papa go down the stairs and out the front door.

That'll be okay, Papa, she thought. Maybe now that there's Jeli, and I can be friends with Gabriel, maybe I won't be scared of my shadow anymore.

Chapter Six

"Wait in your room until I call you, Johannah," said Vivie the next morning as she put water on to boil for tea.

Hannah looked down at her faded green shorts and yellow T-shirt. "Should I put on a dress like you?"

"No. You're fine in shorts. Mrs. Thayer is coming to see me, not you. So just get on upstairs."

Hannah was slowly climbing the stairs—backwards, so she could see if Jeli arrived—when she heard Vivie call from the kitchen, "And don't let me hear you calling Mrs. Thayer by that silly nickname. You must always address your elders with respect, Johannah. Do you hear me?"

Hannah scuffed her way along the hall and into her bedroom, plunking herself down on the bed. She sat there for a while, chewing on a braid, cuddling Lily and keeping watch on the part of the driveway she could see from her front windows. Eventually she retrieved her Crayolas and drawing paper from the closet, settled herself on the floor with Lily propped against a leg of the bed, and began drawing a picture of Maybelle.

When she heard Jeli arrive, Hannah hurried to the top of the stairs and listened as Vivie greeted her.

"Welcome, Mrs. Thayer. I'm so pleased that you could take time out of your busy schedule to visit with me this morning."

Hannah couldn't hear Jeli's reply, but Vivie's words clanged up the stairs as if they were meant for Hannah's ears.

"Well, it's nice of you to say so, but I'm sure you haven't fifteen minutes a day to call your own, much less to spend with a demanding six-year-old like Johannah."

Hannah didn't want to hear anymore. She went back to her drawing of Maybelle.

She'd been thinking about Maybelle a lot, about the things that Maybelle had said to her. She wished she knew what Maybelle meant. She wished she could talk to Grampa about it, but didn't know how to without admitting that she was a witch.

She began to draw Grampa next to Maybelle, thinking that she really wasn't much of a witch if she couldn't make things happen the way she wanted them to.

She was looking for the right Crayola for Grampa's eyes when she heard Vivie call, "Johannah! Come on down now and say hello to Mrs. Thayer."

She raced down the stairs but stopped short when she saw the strange woman sitting next to Vivie on the big parlor's sofa. Hannah almost wouldn't have recognized Jeli. Gone were the well-worn khakis and shirt, replaced by a longish summery dress, white with tiny flowers. She was even wearing lipstick, her soft white hair was smoothed back from her face, and she didn't seem all rosy and sunshiny like two days ago. In fact, the way she looked today, Jeli could almost have been any one of Vivie's regular church friends.

Almost. Except that when she smiled, it was with Jeli's beautiful smile, and Hannah breathed again.

"Hello," Jeli said, her voice putting a happy tickle in Hannah's ears. "It's so good to see you again, Hannah. I guess you know I had a nice visit with your father last night. I like him very much, and he certainly is proud of you."

Hannah felt her cheeks redden. "He really likes you too, Je— … um, Mrs., um…"

Jeli's smile widened. "Please call me 'Jeli', dear. And won't you come give me a hug?"

Hannah started across the room, but was stopped by Vivie's saying, "Now, Johannah. I don't think you should hug Mrs. Thayer in those dirty old clothes. You go on upstairs and change into a nice dress."

"But—" began Hannah.

"No buts, child. Upstairs with you."

Hannah was heading out of the room as Jeli said, "It's all right with me, Mrs. Kirkland. I think shorts are just the ticket for a hot day like this."

Vivie's response—"Well, I'm just surprised she would greet you in such filthy clothes"—sent Hannah scurrying up the stairs.

It took her less than five minutes to wash her face and hands, put on one of her best dresses, her socks, her white Mary Janes, and unsuccessfully try to tame her hair a bit.

When she returned to the parlor, both women spoke to her at the same time.

"That dress looks very pretty on you, Hannah," said Jeli, as Vivie was saying, "I hadn't realized those shoes were so dirty."

Then no one said anything for thirty seconds, Vivie pouring herself some more tea, Jeli stirring the spoon in her cup, and Hannah wishing she could disappear into the floor.

Finally Vivie spoke. "I hear you like to write, Mrs. Thayer. I like to dabble in writing myself."

"Actually," said Jeli, "writing is my profession."

"Yes, of course," said Vivie, nodding. "Your profession. And what sort of pieces do you write?"

"All sorts," said Jeli, warming to the subject. "But I've been published primarily with my murder mysteries under a pseudonym."

"Mm. I'm sorry to say I've never been much interested in murder mysteries. Give me a good romance any day of the week, though. Have you ever tried your hand at romance?"

Jeli shook her head. "No, I'm afraid not."

"Mm. Too bad. I hear tell there's a great deal of money to be made in romance novels."

"Yes. Well. Just not my forté, I guess."

"Perhaps you should give it a try sometime. A dear friend of mine, Bertha Samuels—maybe you've heard of her? No? Well, she writes romances as good as any I've ever read. She's even had one of them published in *Modern Romance*. I know it won't be long before she gets a book published, and then, well, the sky's the limit."

Jeli looked slightly dazed as she said, "Isn't that nice."

"Indeed. You'll want to remember her name—Bertha Samuels. You'll be hearing a lot about her."

"Marvelous."

Silence fell, and just when Hannah thought she'd have to say something—anything—Jeli spoke. "And what do you write, Mrs. Kirkland?"

Vivie made a sweeping gesture with her hand as she said,

"Well, of course, what with taking care of Hannah and my stepson and this house, I don't have much time for my writing. But what I do have, I devote to Biblical meditations."

"Ah."

"Yes. I've been a deacon of our Christian Endeavor Bible Study group for more than eight years now, and I've written nearly one hundred meditations based on scripture."

Jeli blinked a couple of times.

"I must confess, I'm quite proud of them. If you'd like, I'll let you read some of them one day. I think you'll get a lot out of them."

Vivie turned in her seat to face Jeli more directly.

"Have you ever studied the Bible in depth, Mrs. Thayer?"

"Why, no, not since childhood."

"An understanding of the Bible would benefit your own writing. Don't you agree?"

"I believe that an understanding of virtually anything benefits one's writing."

"Surely you're not classifying the sacred word of the Lord God Almighty as just *anything*, I hope."

When Jeli didn't reply immediately, Vivie said, "You *are* a Christian, aren't you, Mrs. Thayer? You have been saved, haven't you?"

Jeli regarded Vivie steadily as she said, "Are my religious beliefs so important to you, Mrs. Kirkland?"

"Why of course they are! I'm quite certain that Paul wouldn't want Johannah in the company of a person who is not a true believer."

"Your stepson hardly strikes me as a religious fanatic, Mrs. Kirkland."

Vivie drew herself up straighter. "Are you saying, Mrs. Thayer, that a person who acknowledges our one true Savior is a religious fanatic?"

Seeing the expression on Jeli's face as she regarded Vivie, Hannah wanted to race over and clap a hand on her mouth.

Whatever it is, please don't say it, Jeli! Hannah shouted in her mind.

As if she had heard her, Jeli looked at Hannah and the

expression in her eyes softened.

"Of course not, Mrs. Kirkland," Jeli said, lowering her gaze and smoothing her skirt where it rested on her crossed knees. "I apologize if I gave that impression. In fact, I am a Christian."

Vivie turned away and brushed heavy-handedly at her own dress, as if trying to push herself back into control. "Yes," she said. "Yes. Well. Good."

In spite of another stretch of silence, Hannah knew the worst had passed.

"More tea?" Vivie said eventually, reaching toward the pot.

"No more for me, thank you, Mrs. Kirkland."

"Please, you must call me Vivian. And I shall call you Anjelica."

"'Jeli' will be fine."

Vivie shot a glance at Hannah, who managed to keep from giggling.

"But Anjelica is such a graceful name. I positively enjoy saying it." Vivie nodded at no one in particular, apparently settling the matter. Then she added, "I'm thinking, Anjelica, that perhaps you would be interested in participating with our Bible study group when we start up again in September. We meet every Wednesday evening from seven-thirty to nine-thirty."

"Well," said Jeli, setting her empty teacup on the coffee table. "Well. I will give that some thought, Mrs.... Vivian."

"Everyone should be fully versed in the word of the Lord God Almighty, don't you agree, Anjelica?"

"I'm sure that's so," said Jeli, glancing at her watch. "Now, if it's all right with you, I wonder if Hannah might show me her room before I leave?" Jeli stood and smiled at Hannah.

Vivie fussed with the tea service for a few moments. Then she looked at Hannah and said, "All right. You may show Mrs. Thayer your room, Johannah, but for heaven's sake don't go on and on about all your little *things*."

This was a first for Hannah, and she was thrilled by the expression on Jeli's face as she ushered her into her bedroom.

"Oh, my, Hannah! What a beautiful room."

Hannah felt her cheeks redden and toed the rug with a Mary

Jane.

"So bright and cheerful. And I love these little flowers," said Jeli, lightly brushing her fingertips over the wallpaper. "Like spring bouquets. I can almost smell their freshness."

Hannah sniffed the air and thought that maybe she could, too.

"Did your mother decorate this room for you?"

"I guess so," said Hannah, looking around the room with new eyes.

"I can see that she loved you very much."

Jeli bent over Lily where she still sat by Hannah's drawings, and lightly touched the doll's reddish-brown hair. "This must be a friend of yours."

"Lily's her name," said Hannah, picking her up and holding her out toward Jeli. "Mama gave her to me when I was a little girl."

"Mm," said Jeli, a smile brushing her lips. "That long ago." She took Lily carefully in her hands and cradled her like a baby. "She is beautiful. She looks just like you."

Hannah nearly giggled with embarrassment.

Jeli noticed Hannah's drawing of two figures in wheelchairs, and bent over it with interest, holding Lily against her shoulder like a baby needing burping.

"My goodness. You have a fine talent for drawing! I would guess that this is your grandfather, but who is the little girl? Surely not you."

"It's Maybelle," said Hannah, sinking cross-legged on the floor. "She's, um... I know her at Vivie's church."

"She looks very sweet. Such lively brown eyes. Is she confined to a wheelchair like your grandfather?"

"Yes. But not like Grampa, though. I mean, she had to have a wheelchair even when she was born. And she can't talk or hear, and her bones are all bent up, too."

Jeli continued to study the drawing. "I like your friend Maybelle very much. And that's just from your drawing. I'd like to meet her some day. And your Grampa—does he know Maybelle? The way you've drawn them together, they look like good friends."

As with her room, Hannah was looking at her drawing with

new eyes. "They never met yet, but…"

When Hannah said nothing more, Jeli asked, "But, what? That is, if you want to tell me."

Hannah searched Jeli's eyes for a moment before she said, "You know how you think something and you're sort of sure it's going to happen even if it's not going to happen for a long time? You know?"

"Yes," Jeli said, through a gentle smile.

"Well, so I think Grampa and Maybelle are going to be friends, too, but, well, I just don't know how 'cause Grampa is all the way in Cincinnati and Maybelle's here."

Encouraged by the look in Jeli's eyes, Hannah rushed on. "And you know what, Maybelle can't talk, but sometimes I hear her say things to me, and she told me I should go to the… um, to your house by myself, and I think I'm supposed to talk to Grampa about her, but I don't know how 'cause he never even met her yet."

Jeli had knelt at Hannah's eye level. "Hm. Could you tell your Grampa what you've just told me?"

"Well, maybe…" Looking into Jeli's caring eyes, Hannah felt tears come to her own. She lowered her gaze to the floor. "But I guess it's really weird, isn't it."

"What's weird, sweetie?"

"I mean, that I hear Maybelle say stuff and she can't even talk."

Jeli sat on the floor and took Hannah's hands in her own. "I don't think it's the least bit weird, Hannah. I think it's a gift you have."

"A gift?"

"Yes. Like a talent. You know what a talent is, don't you. Well, that's what I mean by a gift. Perhaps you can hear things that most people can't."

"I think Mama told me stuff like that sometimes," Hannah murmured, looking at her hands resting in Jeli's. "So you don't think I'm crazy or, um, well… bad or something?"

"Sweetie!" said Jeli, lightly squeezing Hannah's hands. "You're one of the most un-crazy, un-bad people I've ever met."

Hannah was concentrating very hard on believing what Jeli

was saying when she heard Papa's voice from downstairs. "Where's my girl?" he called, to the accompaniment of the screen door slapping into place.

"Oh," said Hannah, jumping up. "Here I am, Papa! Up here with Jeli."

Jeli stood and was straightening her dress when Papa bounded into the room like a big happy puppy.

He lifted Hannah into his arms as he said to Jeli, "It looks very, very good. Structurally, everything is in excellent condition. A real testimony to the way houses used to be built. Of course, you'll want the restoration architect—"

"Well, hello to you too, Paul," Jeli interrupted with a little laugh.

"Oh. Hi. Sorry," he said, grinning sheepishly. "Guess I got a little carried away. It's just that your house... this is going to be an exciting project. Well, I mean, if I get the job. And then your daughter—"

"Celeste?"

"I was just going to tell you that she showed up."

"She's at the house?"

"She's downstairs. She rode over with me."

Jeli was already halfway out of the room. "Cellie?"

"Mom!" a woman's voice called from the first floor as Jeli hurried down the stairs.

Still in his arms, Hannah was staring at Papa in surprise. Something was different about him.

"You okay, Papa?" she asked.

He seemed surprised himself when he looked at her, as if he'd forgotten he was holding her. "Sure I am, kiddo," he said, setting her on her feet. "And don't you look pretty."

"You really think so?" she asked, smoothing her dress and looking up at him, discovering he had already turned his attention to the voices from downstairs.

"C'mon, Jo," he said, taking her hand. "I want you to meet Celeste."

Hannah felt something like mice playing tag in her stomach the moment she saw the slender woman with honey blond hair who stood with Jeli near the foot of the stairs.

"Celeste," said Papa, "This is my daughter, Hannah."

"Hello, Hannah," said Celeste through a warm smile.

"Hello," Hannah replied softly, mesmerized by the light in Celeste's clear blue eyes and the sprinkling of freckles across her nose. "You're pretty," she blurted out, and then felt her cheeks burn.

But Celeste didn't laugh. She knelt to Hannah's eye level and said, "Thank you, Hannah. You're pretty too."

"Did you know me before?"

"You mean, before now?"

"Uh-huh."

Celeste looked thoughtful. "I don't think we've met before, but it does seem like it, doesn't it."

"Uh-huh… like maybe from when we were in heaven."

"Of course. In heaven."

"Hey, gorgeous," interrupted a tall black man coming through the screen door. "You got a hello for me?"

"Carl!" exclaimed Hannah, rushing to hug him.

He lifted Hannah easily with one arm, and she readily planted four loud kisses on his cheek.

Grinning, Carl Kingsley explained to Jeli and Celeste, "That's one for me, one for my wife, Claire, and one each for my twin boys. They're fourteen and madly in love with this little princess."

"I don't think so, really," said Hannah, so seriously that everyone laughed.

"No, *really*," she added.

"No, really, what?" asked Vivie as she came into the hallway from the kitchen, drying her hands on a tea towel.

Her expression darkened when she saw Carl, who quickly set Hannah on her own feet.

"This is Celeste Thayer, Vivian. Jeli's daughter," said Papa.

"How do you do," Vivie said, giving Celeste a nod and a brief smile.

"How do you do," said Celeste. "I apologize for intruding like this, but I drove out to see my mother this morning, and…"

"Oh, that's quite all right, I'm sure. You're very welcome," said Vivie, turning her attention to her stepson. "Now, Paul, I think you know how I feel about your boys tramping dirt in the house," she said.

"Sorry, Miz Kirkland," said Carl, turning toward the door.

"Wait a minute, Carl," Paul said, taking hold of Vivie's arm and steering her toward the kitchen. "I want to have a word with Vivian, if you all would wait in the parlor."

A half hour later, everyone except Vivie was seated around lunch at Burger King. Papa had told them that Vivie sent her apologies, that she had a headache and needed to rest. Secretly, Hannah was glad that Vivie always got a headache when Carl Kingsley was around.

Coming to Burger King for a meal was one of Hannah's favorite treats, and today she thought she might burst out into bright balloons of laughter, she was so happy.

She was looking back and forth between Papa and Celeste when she saw that their hearts were having a conversation that no one could hear. Her mind got busy trying to figure out what to do, and then Mama suddenly appeared between them in her diamond-covered gown. Hannah couldn't contain a happy little "Ooo!" when Mama blew her a kiss.

"What is it, princess?" asked Carl.

"Oh, um, well... nothing," Hannah stammered as she watched Mama vanish. "I mean, you didn't see anything, did you?" She put a braid in her mouth.

"Nope. Just a bunch of happy people chowing down. And one beautiful little girl eating her hair. So what'd *you* see?"

Aware that everyone was looking at her, Hannah took her braid out of her mouth and said, "Nothing. Honest. Can I have some of your french fries?"

The subject changed and the moment passed. Soon Hannah was thinking about how nice it would be to get Grampa and Maybelle and Gabriel and put all of them—Burger King too—in one of those glass globes you shake and sparkly bits of something fly all around, and the scene inside never changes.

Chapter Seven

By Saturday of the Fourth-of-July weekend Hannah was miserable. Jeli was away while Papa, Carl Kingsley and their crew did the major deconstruction work on her house. Celeste was at work in Philadelphia, and Papa drove the thirty-five miles to see her once or twice a week. Vivie's small heart had been at its thorniest since the day she met Jeli and Celeste, and Hannah was more on guard than ever for Vivie's giant invisible eye.

But worst of all, Uncle Bruce was coming.

Hannah sat in her lilac bush in the mid-afternoon heat, idly brushing Gabriel's feathers with a forefinger. "I wish you could help me, Gabriel. I wish you could fly to Cincinnati and... wherever, and ask Grampa and Jeli what to do, and then come back and tell me." Gabriel looked at Hannah as if he were earnestly waiting for her to send him off on this mission. She kissed her finger and gently touched his beak.

"And I *really* wish you could make Uncle Bruce go away forever," Hannah whispered plaintively.

Three or four times a year, Uncle Bruce would bring his family to visit his mother. Although he towered over her, Vivie called Uncle Bruce her "baby boy," and liked to say that the household was "one big happy family" when Bruce and his wife and daughters were there. Hannah thought that was the biggest lie Vivie ever told.

Uncle Bruce scared Hannah, even more than Vivie did. With Vivie, Hannah knew what to expect; with Uncle Bruce, she never knew what scary thing would happen next. She thought he was like that funhouse at Birmingham Amusement Park last year, where she had been so frightened by things popping out and screeching and laughing maniacally that Papa had to carry her out the way they'd come in, and fast! Papa was "*so sorry*, baby!" that he'd taken her inside that place, and Hannah hadn't been able to fall asleep that night until he had held her and read Jesus stories to her for an hour.

Hannah had told Papa that the funhouse reminded her of Uncle Bruce because of the way he would jump out from any shadowy place and scare Hannah or his own children, laughing uproariously at their reactions. He said it was good to keep children on their toes.

Papa had told Bruce what he did with his own kids was his business, but he was scaring Hannah and to knock it off. Bruce had told Papa to lighten up, he was just having a little fun. But he did leave Hannah alone for the rest of that visit. When he resumed with the next one, he was careful not to taunt her around Papa.

Hannah particularly hated Uncle Bruce's big hands. He was always touching her with them, whatever part of her he could reach, especially pinching or patting her bottom. Twice, he had put his hand under her, palm up, when she sat near him. As a result, Hannah went far out of her way not to sit close to Uncle Bruce, and was a little nervous about sitting anywhere without first checking the seat.

Hannah saw that Uncle Bruce's daughters were afraid of him too. Marcie, age ten, and Lynnie, eight, were petite versions of pale-blond Aunt Marcia, who looked too young to be their mother. Shy and reserved, the girls rarely played with Hannah, instead spending most of their time together in the room they shared, or watching television. Hannah understood. She could see how their hearts were being squeezed by their papa.

And Hannah didn't know why, but it made the centipedes march on her back to see the way Aunt Marcia was with Uncle Bruce. Once, when Papa was tucking her in bed, Hannah said, "Aunt Marcia's like his little girl, too, isn't she."

Looking startled, Papa had hesitated. "Don't let it worry you, Jo. You can't tell much of anything about a marriage from the outside." Hannah didn't think about it anymore after that, knowing she didn't want to see anything on the inside of that marriage.

Hannah dreaded those times when Uncle Bruce and his family would visit, dreaded not just Uncle Bruce, but the weird feeling in the whole house when he was there. Still, when she heard Uncle Bruce's station wagon coming up the driveway that July afternoon, she was excited about seeing Marcie and Lynnie. She ordered Gabriel to stay out of sight, hurriedly scrambled out of the lilac bush, brushed at her shorts, and tried to smooth her unruly hair as she raced to the driveway around the back of the barn so that Vivie wouldn't know for sure where she'd been. She arrived alongside Vivie's sedan to find Uncle Bruce already out of his car and being fussed over by his mother.

"There's my big, handsome baby boy. Give your mother a nice big hug."

"Hello, Mother. You're looking young and beautiful as always."

Marcie stepped out of the back door nearest Hannah and gave her a little wave, then trained her eyes on her father and Vivie. Lynnie also got out of the car on that side, closest to Hannah and furthest from the grownups who continued to hug and praise each other.

Hannah peered into the car, then said, "Where's your mama?"

Both girls looked wide-eyed at Hannah, and Lynnie responded in a quavering voice, "Mommy's sick. Daddy put her in a nuthouse 'cause she's crazy."

Marcie squeezed Lynnie's arm and whispered urgently, "Shut up, Lynz! We're not supposed to talk about it."

Lynnie retorted, "I don't care, Marce! I don't!"

"Don't what?" said their father, startling all three girls as he appeared behind Hannah and quickly lifted her into his arms.

"Well, look what we have here," he said, turning her around and holding her tightly. "This can't be our Hannah, can it? A beautiful swan princess practically overnight."

Hannah tried to squirm away from him and his sour breath. He laughed as he kissed her cheek and patted her bottom. "A wiggly swan princess, too."

"Put her down, son," called Vivie from the porch steps. "She'll get your shirt dirty."

"I don't mind a little dirt from a princess," he said, nevertheless setting Hannah on her feet and seeming to notice his daughters for the first time.

"Come on," he said as he watched Hannah disappear around

the corner of the barn. "Help me with the bags." He clapped his hands twice. "Hop to, girls."

Hannah trembled as she raced along the back of the barn, scrubbing at the cheek he'd kissed, as if he'd brushed it with a spider.

I hate him! she thought. I wish he was dead! I wish the lordgodamighty would make him dead!

Once safe again in her lilac bush, she hugged her knees and burst into tears. Gabriel flew in and perched on a branch near her head, chirping nervously. After a time, as her weeping subsided, he moved to her head and began rustling around in her hair as if trying to make things more homey.

Not only did his little feet tickle Hannah's scalp, but also the thought of her friend making a nest in her rat's-nest hair seemed so silly that she went from her last small sob straight into a happy giggle.

"Hey!" she said. "You can't live there." She carefully lifted him off of her head and brought him to her eye level, just a few inches away from her nose.

"You're my best friend in the whole, wide world," she said, kissing his tiny beak. She thought he was smiling at her.

"How come I'm not the kind of witch who can make Uncle Bruce disappear?" Gabriel seemed to consider Hannah's question earnestly. "I wish Jeli really was a witch too, so she could help me with this stuff."

She was thoughtfully petting Gabriel's tiny feet when she suddenly straightened up and exclaimed, "I know! You could poop on Uncle Bruce like you did on Vivie that time." She giggled as he hopped up in the air a few times. "Right on his greasy old head, okay?"

A while later, Hannah reconnoitered the front yard. Spotting Vivie and Uncle Bruce absorbed in conversation on two of the porch's Adirondack chairs, she snuck around to the back door, in through the kitchen and up the stairs, as quiet as a kitten.

At Marcie's and Lynnie's bedroom door, she knocked softly and whispered, "It's me, Hannah."

Marcie opened the door, reached out and grabbed Hannah's arm, pulling her quickly into the room. "You're not supposed to be here," she said. "We're supposed to be resting before dinner. You're gonna get us in trouble."

"I'm sorry, Marcie. I just wanna know what happened to your mama."

From her perch on the room's double bed, Lynnie said, "Let her stay, Marce. We can talk real quiet."

"But we're not supposed to talk about it, Lynz," Marcie cried in frustration. "He's gonna *kill* us."

"Oh, Marce, it's just Hannah. You won't tell anybody, will you Hannah?"

"No, really, I won't. Honest."

"Promise? Cross your heart and hope to die?" asked Marcie.

"Promise! Cross my heart."

"So, okay, Marce, what do you say? Let's tell her."

Marcie looked uncertain for a moment, but finally nodded and said, "Okay. But you have to keep it a secret. Okay?"

Hannah nodded, then she and Marcie climbed onto the bed with Lynnie, the three settling themselves cross-legged in a small circle. Hannah put a braid in her mouth and chewed.

Lynnie began, her voice so soft that Hannah had to lean closer to hear her. "Well, the thing is, you know Mommy cries a lot—at least at home she does. And he, well, see, Daddy gets mad 'cause she's always crying, and he calls her awful names, so she just cries more. And then, sometimes she doesn't even get out of bed all day long and he gets even madder and yells at her, like he says she never takes care of the house or cooks the meals or anything. And then, all of a sudden last week, he took her away."

Marcie interrupted. "And when he got home he told us she was crazy and he put her in a *nuthouse*." She burst into tears, covering her face with her hands and leaning against her younger sister.

Lynnie put her arm around Marcie and patted her back. "It's okay, Marce. It's gonna be okay."

Marcie shook her head and wailed into her hands. "No, it's not. It's never gonna be okay. Mommy's gone and she's never coming back."

"Sure she is, silly," said Lynnie, smoothing Marcie's silky hair. "Don't be such a scaredy-cat."

"You're as scared of him as I am," Marcie cried. "I know you are. 'Specially at night!"

Lynnie looked down at the bedspread and said nothing, but Hannah saw a tear start down her cheek.

"It's true, Lynz, isn't it," Marcie whispered. "I feel so bad. I'm the oldest and I'm supposed to take care of you, but I don't know how."

Lynnie put her arms around her sister and said quietly, "It's okay, Marce. It's not your fault."

Unaware of the burning in her hands, Hannah leaned forward and put her arms around the sisters, resting her teary cheek on Marcie's shoulder. The three of them hugged that way for a while, their tears drying, their heartbeats slowing, their breathing becoming calm.

It was Marcie who finally broke the silence, murmuring, "Your hands are so hot, Hannah."

Mortified, Hannah pulled away and clasped her hands behind her back.

"Don't stop!" said Marcie and Lynnie simultaneously.

"It feels really good," said Lynnie, Marcie nodding in agreement.

"But I wasn't doing anything," said Hannah, crimson with shame and fixing her gaze on the bedspread.

When the sisters said nothing, Hannah glanced up and found them looking at each other as if they were acknowledging a shared secret.

"We need a grownup to help us," Marcie said calmly.

"What about Papa?" exclaimed Hannah. "He'd help. I know he would."

"No," said Marcie. "He's Daddy's brother and brothers can't help against brothers."

"But they're not *real* brothers," said Hannah.

"Aunt Millie!" said Lynnie. "She's the one."

"Yes!" said Marcie, becoming animated. "Aunt Millie. Good idea, Lynz! You're right, she's the one. And Uncle George, too. You remember when they came to see us and we went on that trip and Uncle George tried to race us up the Washington Monument?"

84

Both sisters giggled. "That was so funny, Lynz, remember? He was only halfway up when we got to the top."

Feeling disoriented by the abrupt change in the sisters, Hannah shyly asked, "Who's Aunt Millie?"

"She's Mommy's sister," said Marcie, with only a brief glance at Hannah. "I don't know why we forgot about her, Lynz, except they hardly ever come to see us."

"That just 'cause they live so far away, I bet. We just have to find out her phone number, and I know she'll help us get Mommy back."

"Maybe we could even go live with her and Uncle George."

"I bet we could. Just Mommy and you and me."

Marcie and Lynnie laughed out loud, and this time Hannah joined in. The sisters looked at her then and smiled as if they were happily surprised to find her there.

"It's good you came in, Hannah," said Lynnie.

"Yeah, it is," echoed Marcie.

"So could we maybe play together?" Hannah asked excitedly. "I mean, I could show you some of my best places around the farm, and you can meet Gabriel—but you have to be really careful with him 'cause he's so small."

Hannah was telling the sisters about Gabriel when the bell by the back door clanged.

Quickly Hannah slid off the bed, saying, "I have to go help Vivie get supper ready."

She stopped at the door and looked back, saying, "You wanna go with me?"

They did.

With Marcie and Lynnie in the kitchen that evening, for the first time Hannah enjoyed helping Vivie with supper. Eventually, Vivie shooed all three of them from the kitchen and they went in search of Gabriel.

As soon as they came out onto the front porch, a brown blur flew to Hannah's shoulder.

"Here he is!" she said, feeling all filled up with happiness.

"Ooo, look!" exclaimed Lynnie. "Can I hold him?"

"You can't hold a bird, silly," said Marcie. "You'd break him."

Gabriel patiently permitted the sisters to do a little one-fingered feather stroking until, at the right time, he and Hannah flew down the driveway to meet Papa.

When she was settled on the seat beside her father, Hannah tripped over her words with excitement about Marcie and Lynnie, then silenced herself when he asked about Aunt Marcia.

"It's a secret," was all she would say.

Marcie and Lynnie looked worried as they greeted Papa, each offering him a tentative smile. Hannah wanted to tell them that it was okay, that her Papa would never hurt them, but she couldn't untie her tongue.

"Would you two wait out here for a minute with Hannah?" Papa said. "I'd like to have a word with Vivie and your father. All right?"

They nodded, but both looked questioningly at Hannah as Papa headed up the porch steps.

"I didn't tell," Hannah whispered. "I promise. Only about us being friends, is all."

The three of them waited quietly, the sisters taking turns pushing each other on the swing. Hannah sat at the base of the tree, Gabriel on her shoulder, and thought about Grampa as a real wizard king casting a spell on Uncle Bruce, turning him into one of those slimy bugs that live under rocks.

Finally Papa, fresh from his shower, opened the screen door and smiled at them. "Vivie says to come on in now and wash your hands, supper's ready."

As Hannah followed the sisters into the house, Papa put his hand on her shoulder and said, "Come with me for a second, Jo."

They went into the big parlor, where Papa sat and lifted Hannah on his lap.

"I don't want you to worry about Aunt Marcia, sweetheart. Uncle Bruce told me all about it. She just needs to rest for a while, that's all. Then she'll come home again and everything will be fine."

"But Lynnie and Marcie said he—" Hannah stopped herself.

"He, what?" Papa said, brushing her cheek with the backs of his fingertips. When she didn't respond, Papa said, "Well, I wouldn't worry about whatever they said. Bruce tells me that they don't understand and that they... well, that they tend to exaggerate."

"What's that mean?"

"It means, making something sound much worse than it really is."

"You mean, like *lying*?"

"No, not really lying. Just blowing something out of proportion."

Hannah stared at him in confusion, and he gave a little shrug. "I'm sorry, Jo. I don't seem to be able to explain this to you very well. The point is, there's nothing to worry about. Aunt Marcia will be home before long, good as new."

Hannah looked down at her hands and murmured, "Uncle Bruce is who zaggerates."

"Hm? What'd you say?"

"Nothing, Papa."

"So, will you promise not to worry about Aunt Marcia?"

Hannah quickly put her right hand behind her back and crossed her middle finger over her index finger as she said, "Promise."

It wasn't until a whispered conversation as they helped Vivie with the dishes after supper that Hannah was able to reassure the sisters about her talk with Papa.

Marcie wasn't easily reassured. "He believes *Daddy*," she whispered plaintively. "What if Aunt Milly does too?"

"She won't, Marce," Lynnie said softly, touching her sister's shoulder. "It's just that they're brothers, like you said, and Uncle Paul, he thinks Daddy's telling the truth 'cause Uncle Paul's just so nice."

"Who's so nice?" asked Vivie.

Hannah came to the rescue with the truth. "Lynnie just said Papa is so nice, that's who."

"Indeed he is," said Vivie, looking speculatively at Lynnie. "You might also say how nice your own father is, child."

When Lynnie concentrated on the dish she was drying and didn't reply, Vivie clucked her tongue and put her hands back into the dishwater.

Even though it wasn't yet six-thirty and still quite warm, Marcie and Lynnie didn't feel like playing that evening after all, preferring to stay in their room so that they could talk about their plan. Hannah understood. She knew she'd be the same way if her Mama was in the nuthouse instead of heaven.

Papa had office work to do, and Vivie and Uncle Bruce had settled in front of TV, so Hannah and Gabriel flew to the creek by themselves. There, with Gabriel on her shoulder and her bare feet in the shallow water, she sat on the mossy bank, thinking about Mama. She missed Mama's arms around her, Mama's kisses and her soft hands as she wiped away tears. She missed smelling the soft, clean warmth of Mama's hair and skin, and hearing Mama's voice, soothing her to sleep. Tears from her heart began to course down her cheeks.

She cried for a long while, and when the tears finally slowed and she was drying her face with her T-shirt, Hannah inhaled the fragrance of wildflowers and felt something pressing on her ears.

"Mama?" she whispered, wiping her vision clear and standing, searching the glade but seeing no one.

An unfamiliar voice in Hannah's mind told her to sit and to close her eyes. Unhesitatingly, she did so, lying back on the rough ground, feeling as comfortable as if she were cocooned in a feather bed. She inhaled the wildflower-scented air, heady as pure oxygen, and drifted away into timelessness.

When Hannah opened her eyes, she was lying on her left side, curled comfortably. She lay still for a time, feeling as if something very special had just happened. Idly she wondered what it might have been, if perhaps Mama really had been there, holding her and rocking her for a while.

Gabriel landed a few inches from her nose, and she reached out a finger to smooth the feathers on his chest. In a whisper, she said to him, "Everything's gonna be okay, Gabriel. Everything's gonna be okay."

Hannah lay there, perfectly peaceful, and gently stroked her little friend until it was time to return to the house.

"Are you all right, Punkin?" Papa asked, as he tucked her in bed later. "You're so quiet tonight."

"I'm right as rain, Papa. Right as rain and sunshine too."

The corners of his mouth turned up in a smile and he shook his head. "You're a wonder, Jo. I don't know how I got so lucky to have you for my daughter. I sure do love you."

"Me too, you."

Sometime well after midnight, Hannah awoke as if from a nightmare, knowing that Uncle Bruce had just left her room.

Horrified, she jumped quickly off the bed and looked at the sheets, certain she would discover the bugs that had just been crawling all over her body. There was nothing to be seen.

She took her pillow and Lily and went into the closet, closing the doors behind her and curling up on the floor. Wide awake, she thought about the day before, about Uncle Bruce and Aunt Marcia and everything Marcie and Lynnie had said. She thought about being a witch, and about what had happened at the creek after supper. Eventually, she drifted off to sleep again, knowing exactly what she needed to do.

Early the next morning, as soon as she awoke, Hannah hurried on tiptoe to Papa's room. Finding the door slightly ajar, she pushed it open and saw Papa, clad in his pajama bottoms, asleep on top of his covers. She climbed on the bed, sitting cross-legged facing him, and gently tapped his shoulder.

"Mmph," he grunted sleepily.

"Papa."

"Hmm?" He opened his eyes slightly.

"G'morning, Papa."

"Jo?" He sat up, looking worried. "What's the matter?"

"Nothing. Except I need to have my door back. Can I, Papa?"

"Your door? What're you talking about?"

"My bedroom door. Will you put it back for me, please?"

"Oh. Your door. But what if Vivie needs to get to you in a hurry?"

"I promise she won't," Hannah said calmly. "And I won't lock it unless there's a mergency."

He gave her a sleepy smile. "What kind of 'mergency' are you expecting?"

"Well, you know. Like robbers and bad people. Like that."

"Ah, yes. I see."

"So can I have my door back, Papa?"

He looked at her for a few moments and then shook his head, saying, "I can't remember why it seemed like a good idea to remove it in the first place." He cupped her chin. "How about if I put it back up while you're at church?"

"Okay! Oh, thank you, thank you," she said, hugging him, his morning whiskers prickly against her cheek. "Everything's gonna be okay, isn't it."

"You bet, baby. It sure is."

Chapter Eight

When Maybelle was wheeled into church later that morning, Hannah suddenly knew that she was going to do as Maybelle had so long been asking her to do: she was going to touch Maybelle with her burning hands.

Except that her hands weren't burning. She studied them curiously.

Oh, well, she thought. I guess not today. But someday soon.

In Sunday School, she sat next to Billy Tyler and even touched him lightly on the arm. But her hands weren't hot and nothing happened, except that Billy turned and stuck out his tongue at her. Still, she wasn't discouraged. She decided that the very next time the burning started, she would touch something and see what happened.

As long as I don't hurt anything, it must be okay, she told herself. Maybe I really am like a Glinda kind of witch.

Uncle Bruce was sitting on the porch steps waiting for them when they returned home after church. Marcie and Lynnie watched wide-eyed from the swing as their father ignored Hannah and said to Vivie, "Our little princess here has gone and persuaded her daddy to put her bedroom door back in place."

"What!" cried Vivie, her voice shrill. "Without discussing it with me?"

"It's already done, Mother," Bruce said, through a dark little grin.

Hannah winced as Vivie grabbed her wrist and pulled her up the front porch steps. "You come with me, Johannah. I warrant it can still be *un*-done."

Hannah scurried to keep up with Vivie until they reached the second floor, where they both stood and stared at Hannah's bedroom door.

"Paul!" called Vivie. "Paul, where are you?"

"He's in his workshop, Mother," said Uncle Bruce from downstairs.

Vivie faced Hannah. "Now you get in your room and stay there while I have a word with your father." She turned on her heel and descended the stairs, stopping at the switch-back and calling up to Hannah, "And don't even *think* about closing that door! Do you hear me?"

"Yes, ma'am," Hannah responded meekly, her fingers crossed behind her back. As soon as she was sure that Vivie and Uncle Bruce were on their way to the barn, she raced into her room and closed her door firmly in place. Then she opened her arms wide and leaned against it, hugging it as well as she could and whispering, "Oh, thank you, thank you, Papa. Thank you forever."

Wishing she could see the barn from her room, she quickly changed into shorts, T-shirt and sneakers, and only then did she open her door again. By the time Vivie stormed into the room, Hannah was sitting in the chair by the windows, looking at a book with Lily.

Vivie leaned over Hannah, took her by the shoulders and said in a low voice, "You think you're so smart, don't you. Well, you'll be sorry, I promise you that. You'll wish you never went sneaking to your Papa behind my back. You just better keep a good watch on your own back from now on, Miss Priss." With that she left the room, pausing only for a moment to push Hannah's door flat open against the wall.

"Bruce, dear," Vivie called as she went down the stairs. "Take me out to lunch, will you? And maybe we'll see a movie. Paul and the girls can fend for themselves."

Hannah and Lily stared at the doorway awhile after Vivie had gone downstairs.

Don't be scared, said Lily finally, in a scared little voice.

"You too," whispered Hannah.

Okay. But what does that mean, what she said about watching our back? How can we watch our own back?

"I don't know. Maybe she just made a mistake, is what. Maybe we're supposed to watch *her* back, or something."

Well, that would make more sense.

"Yeah," Hannah whispered, hugging Lily to her chest. "That's what we'll do. We'll watch out for Vivie's back."

And her giant eye, too, remember.

"Yes, and her eye. And we'll tell Gabriel to watch out too."

When she heard Uncle Bruce's car going down the driveway, Hannah put Lily down for a nap on their bed and went to find Papa, Marcie and Lynnie.

After a cheerful lunch of sandwiches and potato chips, Hannah asked Papa if she could show Jeli's house to Marcie and Lynnie.

Papa looked thoughtful. "Well, not inside, of course. We have it pretty torn up. But, if you're very careful, around the outside would be all right."

"Thank you!" Hannah said, giving him a quick hug.

"Thanks, Uncle Paul," chimed in the sisters.

"You're welcome, girls. Just go by the back way, not down on the road, and don't touch any of our equipment around there, all right? And be home by four."

"I see why you thought witches live there," Lynnie said, once Jeli's house was in view across the field of long grass.

"Me too," said Marcie. "I would've been too scared to come here. How'd you ever meet this Jeli lady?"

"I was just out here in the field, and she was right over there, and we started talking."

"Is it scary on the inside?" asked Lynnie.

"Not really," said Hannah, proud that they thought she was brave. "Jeli was fixing it up, and now Papa and Carl are *really* fixing it up."

Hannah gazed at the big old structure with a sense of wonder that she could have ever been frightened of it. "I think it's gonna really be pretty. Somebody's even gonna clean off all the walls on the outside with some big washing machine thing. Papa says I can watch when they do that."

"How do they get the walls in a washing ma—" Marcie was interrupted by the sound of screeching tires and two loud thuds from the road on the far side of the house. The girls raced toward the front yard, stopping abruptly when they saw a heavyset man

93

in jeans, T-shirt and Phillies cap standing over the large animal that lay in front of his pickup truck.

He was aiming curses and vicious kicks at the helpless creature.

"Oh, no!" whispered Hannah. "It's a deer."

The girls backed away and flattened themselves along the side of the house, watching apprehensively as the man grabbed the deer by its front legs and dragged it off the road and onto the edge of Jeli's yard. There he kicked it one last time, then climbed back into his truck and gunned the engine before tearing away down the road.

When they were sure he'd gone, Marcie and Lynnie raced toward the deer. Hannah, with Gabriel on her shoulder, held back. Her hands were on fire.

Lynnie looked over at Hannah. "It's okay, Hannah. It's dead."

"Yeah," added Marcie, beckoning. "C'mon. Don't be scared."

Slowly, her hands clasped behind her back, Hannah walked over to them.

Lynnie was petting the still creature. "It's a girl. A doe."

"How can you tell?" asked Marcie.

"'Cause it doesn't have horns, silly. That's how."

Marcie tentatively reached out and touched the doe's back. "She's so warm and soft." She looked up at Hannah. "C'mon, Hannah. You gotta feel how soft she is."

Hannah knelt beside the deer's head, marveling at the beauty of the animal, even with its eyes glazed by death.

Seeing Hannah's tears, Lynnie said, "Yeah, it's really sad, isn't it. I feel like crying too."

I'm gonna do it, Hannah said to herself, looking at her hands. Marcie and Lynnie are gonna see that I'm a witch, but I don't care. I said I was gonna touch the next thing, and here it is and I just gotta do it.

Tense with anticipation, Hannah reached out, laying her right hand on the deer's neck and her left on its chest. She began to stroke the animal tenderly, alert for the tremor of life that would flow through it at any moment.

Nothing happened. Not the movement of an eyelid, the quiver of a nerve, the tensing of a muscle.

And Hannah's hands were becoming cold.

"No!" she cried plaintively, wrapping herself around the deer's side, pressing her face into its neck.

"Hey, c'mon, Hannah," said Marcie.

"Don't do that," Lynnie said, kneeling and tugging on Hannah's shirt.

"You're gonna get really dirty, Hannah. Pull her off, Lynz."

"You can't fix it, Hannah," said Lynnie, prying Hannah's clammy hand loose from the deer's neck.

Hannah was sobbing loudly.

"C'mon, Hannah. Stop it now," said Marcie, standing and backing away.

"Yeah. It's dead," said Lynnie, still trying to separate Hannah from the doe. "Get away from it now."

"You don't understand!" cried Hannah.

"Maybe we should go get Uncle Paul," said Marcie.

"No! Don't!" pleaded Hannah, turning to look at the sisters.

"Well, stop it then!" cried Marcie. "You're scaring us!"

Hannah blinked a few times, then sat back on her haunches and gazed at the deer, wiping the tears from her eyes and face.

"I don't know what happened," she said, her voice small and fearful.

Lynnie sat beside her and patted her shoulder. "It's okay, Hannah. You just wanted to make the deer all better again. So did I."

"Yeah, me too," said Marcie, squatting at Hannah's other side.

"Animals die all the time," said Lynnie. "That's just the way things happen."

"But, see, I... um... Gabriel... well..." Hannah trailed off into silence.

"Yeah, it's okay," Marcie said. "Gabriel's right there, see?"

Hannah looked to where Marcie was pointing, seeing Gabriel watching them from the grass a few feet away. He flew to her shoulder and trilled his prettiest song, making Hannah smile and the sisters laugh with relief.

Suddenly Hannah got gooseflesh and an image flashed in her mind. She stood and looked at the tall grass and trees across the road.

"What is it?" said Lynnie, standing beside her.

"There's a fawn."

Marcie stood at Hannah's other side. "What? You see a fawn over there?"

Hannah was walking to the edge of the road. "It's there."

"Where?" said Lynnie.

Hannah pointed to a huge blue spruce whose lowest branches swept the ground. "Under there."

"I can't see anything," Marcie said.

"Well, I'm going over," announced Lynnie.

"No, you can't!" said Hannah. "Papa told me never to cross the road by myself. He says maniacs drive here all the time."

"Yeah," added Marcie. "Like the maniac who killed the poor mommy deer."

The three girls looked anxiously in one direction and the other along the curving road.

"There's nobody coming," said Lynnie. "We could hear them if there was."

They listened carefully… and heard an engine. Moments later a car appeared from nowhere and drove by so fast that the girls couldn't see it clearly. They all moved back further from the road.

Marcie and Lynnie looked at Hannah, waiting for a solution. She stroked Gabriel's feathers and continued to gaze across the road.

Finally, decidedly, she said, "I'm the littlest, so I'm the fastest."

Marcie and Lynnie nodded solemnly.

"So you two listen real careful and keep watch, and I'll go at just the right second."

Moments later, Hannah was peering under the low limbs of the blue spruce as Gabriel flitted about excitedly. Two big brown eyes peered back at her from a trembling golden-beige softness.

"It's here," she cried. "Ooo, it's so beautiful!"

Maniacs forgotten, Marcie and Lynnie were quickly at Hannah's side.

"Ooo!" they said simultaneously.

The sisters reached in and gently, carefully, slid the tiny fawn out from under the branches.

"It's cold," said Marcie, stroking one of its downy-soft ears.

"Yeah. Look how it's shaking," Lynnie said, lightly patting its back. "I bet it's scared, too."

Hannah said nothing. Her hands were on fire.

"Let's take it back to the house," said Lynnie.

"Can we, Hannah?" asked Marcie.

Hannah leaned forward and rested her hands on the fawn's neck. A moment later, it blinked its eyelids several times and the trembling stopped.

"Look!" said Lynnie.

"Yeah. It's okay now," Marcie said. "And it likes us, I think."

Gabriel chose that moment to land squarely on the fawn's head between its overlarge ears. Hannah thought her wren friend looked like he was smiling.

Thirty minutes later, the girls triumphantly carried their beautiful, living treasure into Papa's barn workshop.

"Can I keep it, please? Please can I, Papa?"

"Whoa, baby! We don't know anything about taking care of a fawn."

"I do," said Lynnie. "I saw *Born Free* four times."

"That was a lion, silly," scoffed Marcie.

"But it's the same thing, isn't it, Uncle Paul? I mean, you just have to give it baby milk or something and keep it warm till it can be on its own. Right, Uncle Paul?"

He was watching Hannah as she sat on the floor, holding the fawn across her lap as if it were a contented, overgrown puppy.

She looked up at him. "Can I, Papa? Just for a little time, till he's stronger?"

He squatted beside her and stroked the fawn's velvety coat. "Vivie will have a fit."

"But I'll take care of it, I promise. She won't have to do a single thing. And I'll keep it out of her way all the time. I could even sleep out here with it if she wants me to."

"I'm pretty sure that's one thing she *won't* want you to do."

He petted the fawn in silence for a time.

"Such pretty markings. It really is a beautiful creature, isn't it," he said eventually. "You're sure the mother was dead?"

"Yes! I know it," said Marcie.

"It really was, Uncle Paul," said Lynnie.

"I'm sure," said Hannah.

Papa stood and brushed off his jeans. "Okay. Here's what we'll do. I'll fix up a place for this fella in the old stall. You'll have to make sure to keep the gate closed so he won't wander around. And do you remember your Mama's friend, Jean Liotta? I guess you don't, you were too young, but she's a vet, an animal doctor. I'm sure she can tell us what to feed a fawn like this, so I'll give her a call. Okay with you?"

Hannah was looking at him, her face suffused with delight.

"But this has to be only for a little while, Jo. When he's big enough and strong enough, no matter when that is, we'll have to set him loose. You can't keep him as a pet. Do you understand?"

"Yes."

"And you promise you won't argue with me when it's time to set him free?"

"I promise, Papa. Really, I promise."

Solemnly, a loving smile on both their faces, they shook hands over their agreement while Marcie and Lynnie beamed at them like proud parents.

By the time Vivie and Uncle Bruce returned from the movie theater, the fawn—a male, Papa had determined—had been named Joey and was quietly settled in his new home, well protected by the girls and Papa.

Vivie was furious. First Hannah's door, and now a wild creature as a pet. For a full half hour she was vocal with her complaints about everything from the diseases the fawn surely carried to the expense of feeding it. Finally, she lapsed into silence on the matter, a silence so dark and cold that Hannah was afraid to even look at her.

Hannah was busy feeding Joey that evening when Grampa phoned. She was using a Playtex nursing bottle filled with the baby formula Dr. Liotta had recommended and that Papa had bought at the drugstore.

Even though Grampa was waiting to talk to her, it was with reluctance that Hannah turned the nursing over to Marcie and

Lynnie and went to the extension in Papa's workshop.

It was Hannah's and Grampa's shortest phone conversation ever. He was happy to hear about Joey, and told her he understood completely that she wanted to get back to the little fawn. Just as they were about to hang up, Hannah said, "Oh, and guess what else, Grampa. I got my bedroom door back!"

"Your bedroom door stays open tonight and every night," Vivie said to Hannah at the foot of the stairs that evening. "That's that. Don't even *think* of disobeying me!"

After Papa tucked her in and left the room, Hannah took her pillow and Lily into her closet, closing the bifold doors and curling up on the floor under her hanging blouses and dresses.

They lay there for a while, looking at the soft stripes of the nightlight glowing through the louvers.

"I'm not sleepy," Hannah whispered.

Me neither, said Lily.

"I been thinking. How come I couldn't help the mommy deer?"

I don't know, said Lily. *I wish we could've made her not dead anymore.*

"Me too. But then maybe I wouldn't have seen Joey."

Yeah. But, still, if we could've helped the mommy, she could've helped Joey.

They were quiet for a time.

Then Lily said, *Maybe the mommy was just too big. Maybe we can't fix a big animal like her.*

"Maybe it's good only Jesus and angels can do that, huh?" Hannah said.

And maybe I'm not really a witch after all, she thought. And felt a little sad about that.

During the night Hannah was awakened by angry voices.

"Get the hell out of here! Now!" raged Papa.

Hannah rushed to her doorway and peered anxiously around the jamb, discovering a bleery Papa shoving Uncle Bruce backwards up the hall in her direction.

"Hey! Lighten up, little brother!" said Bruce.

"I'm not your little brother, you son'fabitch. Getoutta my house. Now! And you better damn well never show your ugly face around here again."

"Jesus, man. What's the matter with you? I was just tucking her in."

"Hell, you were!" He shoved Bruce again in the center of his chest.

"Whoa, watch it!" Bruce backpedaled further. "She's *my* kid. Why don't you ask her what I was doing?"

"Right. Like you don't have her scared shitless."

"Paul! What on earth?" Vivie said, coming out of her room, wrapping herself in a bathrobe.

"Get back in your room. Your precious baby boy here is a goddam child molester—his own daughter, for crissake—and he's getting the hell out of my house, *now!*"

"Paul, stop it! You're drunk!"

"Out!" Paul gave Bruce another hard push toward the stairs.

Bruce turned just in time to catch the banister and stop himself from falling. "You self-righteous bastard!" He lurched and threw a sloppy punch that missed Paul by a couple of feet.

Paul caught Bruce's wrist and twisted it behind his back, using his free arm to pin him in a solid half-nelson.

"No!" shouted Vivie, tugging on Papa's arm. "Stop it, Paul! Let go of him. You're hurting him."

Bruce grunted as he tried to free himself.

"Keep out of this," growled Papa at Vivie, tightening his grip on Bruce.

"I live here, too, Paul."

"Don't make me regret that." He pushed Bruce's arm further up his back.

Bruce moaned.

"Stop it!" screamed Vivie, her face purpling. "You're crazy drunk!"

"Stay the hell out of this, or get out of my house with this bag of shit."

Her hand pressed to her throat, Vivie backed off. "You're wrong, Paul. They're lying to you. Bruce would *never* hurt his daughters."

"I saw it myself." He pushed Bruce forward toward the stairs.

"I don't know what you thought you saw, but you're wrong. It's dark, you're drunk, you made a mistake. And you're making a terrible spectacle of yourself in front of the children."

Papa glanced toward Marcie and Lynnie, who retreated quickly into their room. Then he looked for Hannah and found her trembling in her doorway. Instantly he released Bruce and moved toward Hannah, saying, "Sorry, kiddo."

Bruce landed a weak punch to the side of Paul's head. Vivie screamed as Paul rounded on Bruce and slammed his fist into the taller man's gut. Bruce doubled over, groaning, and Vivie tried to push by Paul to get to her son.

Paul gripped her shoulder. "Get away."

He turned to Bruce and yanked at his arm. "That's it, shithead. Get up and get out."

"My clothes, my car keys," Bruce groaned, struggling to his feet, his fleshy chest flushed above his pajama bottoms.

"Where are the keys?"

"My bureau."

Paul went to Bruce's room, and Vivie moved quickly to her son, putting her arms around his middle and whispering urgently in his ear. She stepped away when Paul returned and threw Bruce's keys at him along with khakis, shoes and a shirt. "Vivian will send you the rest of your clothes."

"But my daughters…"

"I swear to God, if I have anything to do with it, you'll never spend another minute with either of those girls. Now, GET OUT!"

Bruce hurried down the stairs with Papa behind him. Hannah could hear their angry voices moving out to Bruce's car.

Vivie turned on Hannah with a vengeance, stalking into her room and poking her hard in the chest. "What have you done! Always sneaking around, causing trouble for people, pretending you're so sweet, butter wouldn't melt in your mouth. What have you done now?" She stopped abruptly when she heard Papa coming back into the house. "Don't think you're going to get away with this," she hissed, before she scurried away to her bedroom.

A moment later, Papa was in Hannah's room, lifting her in his arms. "God, Jo, I'm sorry you had to see that." He held her on his lap as he sat on the bed. "You okay?" he asked, rocking gently.

She saw that he wasn't as bleary anymore, and the tension began to run out of her. "I'm okay," she murmured into his chest. "Did he hurt you?"

"No."

"Why'd you get so mad at him?"

"He… hurt Marcie."

"Oh! Is she okay?"

"I think so. I'll go see her in a minute."

"Did he hit her?"

"No, but he hurt her just the same."

A shiver ran through Hannah's body. "I was so scared, Papa."

He tucked her head under his chin and rocked again. "I know, baby. I know."

"Will he really go away forever?"

"Away from here, yes he will. I'll see to it."

"What about Vivie? Will she go away too?"

"I don't know. That'll be up to her."

Hannah made a quick wish in her mind.

Apparently misreading Hannah's silence, Papa said, "Don't worry about Vivie leaving, kiddo. I'm sure things will work out."

"But what about Marcie and Lynnie? Are they going to live here with us?"

"I don't think so, but I need to talk to them, and I need to get in touch with Aunt Marcia." He gave her a squeeze. "This is going to take a while to sort out."

Hannah heard the strain in his voice. "It's gonna be okay," she said. "Really it is. It's good you did that. They were always scared of him and I… well, I was too."

He stopped rocking. "Did he ever hurt *you*?"

"No. He just pinched me and stuff."

"What sort of *stuff*?"

"Just like always hugging and kissing me with his big, smelly lips, is all."

"Oh, baby. I'm so sorry. I wish I'd known. I should have known."

After a time he said, "Are you okay to go back to bed now? I want to check on Marcie and Lynnie."

"Can I come, too?"

"Sorry, kiddo. I need to talk to them alone. Do you understand?"

"I guess so."

"You're all right?"

"Yes."

"Sleepy?"

"A little."

He glanced at the head of her bed. "Were you sleeping in the closet?"

"Uh-huh."

"Why? Did something scare you?"

"Uncle Bruce and… um, well, Uncle Bruce scares me."

He retrieved her pillow and Lily, and soon Hannah was settled comfortably, her eyes already at half mast.

"Would you like to have your bedroom door closed tonight, Jo?"

She opened her eyes fully and began to sit up. "Oh, Papa! Could I?"

He gently pushed her back down. "Of course. I don't want you to be scared ever again."

"Maybe not even of my own shadow," Hannah said softly. Or maybe even the giant invisible eye? No, that was too much to hope for.

Chapter Nine

The following Friday morning, Hannah stood at the foot of the driveway with Gabriel on her shoulder and watched her father's truck disappear around the bend. She caught one last glimpse of Marcie and Lynnie waving back at her through the cab window, and Papa tooted the pickup's horn three times, his signal for "I love you."

Gabriel flying ahead of her, she raced back up the driveway to the barn, where she found Joey standing with his nose pressed between the rails of the stall gate.

"It's okay, Joey," she said, opening the gate slightly and maneuvering herself into the stall. "See, I didn't go away. I won't go away, not ever." She scratched him lightly between his ears.

Joey licked her, his rough tongue feeling scratchy on her cheek, and then once again pressed his nose between the gate rails.

Hannah knelt beside the fawn, stroking his soft back. "You want to leave, don't you, Joey. You want to find your mama. But she's gone away to heaven and you're still too little. I wish you could understand."

Gabriel trilled a few notes from his perch on the top railing.

"You like him too, Gabriel, don't you. So we just have to make him happy and take good care of him." She thought she saw Gabriel nod in agreement. "'Specially till Sunday when Papa comes home, right?"

Suddenly Gabriel flew into the barn rafters, Joey skittered back from the gate, and the hairs on Hannah's neck stood on end. There was a slight rustling sound outside the stall.

"Who's there? Vivie?"

"Why, of course it's me, Johannah," Vivie said, stepping out from the shadows. "Who did you expect? The boogey man?" Vivie smiled. "I came out to see how you and your little friends are doing."

Although Vivie's tone and manner were friendly, Hannah trusted her less than ever. For the past four days, since Papa had kicked Uncle Bruce out of the house, Vivie had been very sweet to everyone, Hannah included. Hannah could see that Papa was glad; after all, he had his hands full with work on Jeli's house and arranging to return Marcie and Lynnie to Aunt Marcia. As for the sisters, Hannah watched them move around all week in a fog without their feet on the ground, and watched Vivie treat them like little princesses.

Still, Hannah believed that Vivie was up to something, something so awful that her heart had become invisible, surrounded in the blackest of darkness. Now, with Vivie watching her over the stall gate, Hannah felt like the ground had fallen out from under her.

Three days alone with Vivie. No Papa. No Jeli. Hannah's stomach rose and choked off the back of her throat.

"We're okay," Hannah said, her voice shrill in her own ears. "You don't have to come out. I'll take care of Joey all by myself. Good care, I really will."

"Of course you will," Vivie said with a nod. "But that's quite a job for a small child, don't you think? Taking care of a dirty wild animal is no easy chore."

"Joey's not dirty! You should see how good he smells."

"Oh, my," Vivie laughed. "I'm afraid the only kind of deer I like to smell is the cooked kind." She gave Hannah a bright smile, then turned and left the barn.

Hannah stared at the spot where Vivie had stood, her heart thudding in her ears. This is bad, she thought. This is really bad.

There was a soft blow of air from Joey, and Hannah hurried to him where he stood trembling in the far corner.

She wrapped her arms around his middle and rubbed her cheek on the irregular white markings of his soft golden coat. "Everything's gonna be okay," she said, wishing she believed that. If only Jeli were home. If only Celeste would come out for a visit. If only there were somewhere safe that she could take Joey and hide him until Sunday. But there was nothing she could do. Nothing at all.

She spent the rest of the morning tending to Joey. She cleaned his stall, removing the soiled straw and replacing it with fresh, as Papa had taught her to do. She fed him his formula and some granola that Dr. Liotta had suggested, and gave him fresh water. And for a long while, with a braid in her mouth and Gabriel on her shoulder, she brushed Joey with an old soft hairbrush that Papa had found for her, and hummed "Jesus Loves Me" into the still, hot air of the barn.

Except for lunch and supper with Vivie at the kitchen table, Hannah spent all that late afternoon and evening in the barn with Joey and Gabriel. She could tell that even Gabriel wanted to be outside in the open air, and she decided to ask Papa, when he phoned that night, if there was something she could use to make a leash for Joey so she could take him on walks.

But she never did talk to Papa that night. After her bath, when she was lying on her bed, tense and wide awake, hoping to hear the phone ring, she heard instead Vivie calling from the foot of the stairs.

"Oh, by the way, Johannah. Your father phoned while you were in the tub. I told him you were fine. He sends you his love."

Hannah's heart sank. She *needed* to talk to Papa.

"Okay," she whispered to Lily. "It's okay. It's gonna be hard, but it's only two more days, and we won't let anything bad happen to Joey or Gabriel. Right?

Lily didn't say anything.

Then and there, Hannah made up her mind to go out to the barn and sleep beside Joey after Vivie went to bed. And although she did everything she could to stay awake until Vivie came upstairs to bed, eventually she lost the battle and fell asleep.

When she awoke the next morning, the play of sunlight and shadows on her ceiling was so pretty that it took a minute before she remembered Joey and Gabriel. As soon as they came to her mind she leaped out of bed in her shorty pajamas, raced out of her room, down the stairs, along the hall, through the kitchen… and was stopped in her rush to the barn by the locked kitchen door. The inside key had been removed from the lock. She raced to the front door, discovering it also locked and its key removed.

All she could think of was Joey and Gabriel. She had to get out of the house, she had to get to them in the barn. She ran into the big parlor and tried to open the windows onto the porch. Both were locked. She dragged a cherrywood captain's chair to the nearest window, climbed on it and wrestled with the lock. It was too tight; she wasn't strong enough to budge it. She pushed the chair to the other window and found its lock equally stiff.

Help me, please! she hollered in her mind, kicking at the glass in frustration. It cracked. She kicked it again and felt a small, sharp pain in her big toe. She drew her foot back to give the window another kick when a loud, "Johannah!" from behind her froze her in place.

Vivie was standing in the doorway, her face cratered with anger. "What in the world do you think you're doing?" She rushed forward and grabbed Hannah off the chair, carrying her quickly out of the room and down the hall. "Have you completely lost your senses?"

Hannah saw where Vivie was taking her. "Oh, no! Please, no! I'm sorry, really I am. I'll be good."

"You should have thought of that before you broke the window." Vivie opened the basement door

"But I just wanted to see Joey," Hannah cried, as Vivie dropped her on the dark landing at the top of the basement stairs.

Without another word, Vivie stepped back into the hall and closed and locked the basement door.

Hannah pounded on the door and wailed, "Please, Vivie! Please let me out. I'm sorry! Honest I am! I think my toe's bleeding, and I have to go to the bathroom too. Papa's gonna—"

Vivie's voice immediately outside the door nearly made Hannah wet herself. "Don't you dare try to threaten me with what your Papa is going to do. You're the one who kicked a hole in the window."

Hannah sat and curled herself into a tight ball as she listened to Vivie marching up the stairs. "Please don't leave me here, Vivie," she whispered into the musty darkness. Misery welled up in her and she began to cry.

Please, Jesus. Please help me now, she sobbed in her mind. *I'm sorry I broke the window, honest I am. I just wanted to get to the barn.*

Please, Jesus. I have to go potty so bad! And what if she leaves me here forever and all my blood leaks out of my toe and then I'm dead and nobody even finds out till Papa comes home. Please, Jesus! I don't wanna die. I'll do anything. Just please get me out of here. She shivered from the damp cold.

Sometime later, Hannah was controlling her bladder and ignoring the pain in her foot and the noises in her head by thinking about her own funeral, wondering who else might be there besides Papa and Vivie. Her teeth chattered as she thought maybe it might not be so bad to die, so she could be with Mama again. She wouldn't have to be a witch anymore, would she? Maybe she'd even get to play with those little kittens Vivie drowned. And she'd see Jesus again.

Yes, maybe it would be good to be dead, she was thinking, when Vivie unlocked the door and flung it open.

"Go use the toilet before you wet the floor."

Hannah did so, in the bathroom off the kitchen, and was pulling up her pajama panties when Vivie walked in. Grimly silent, Vivie put hydrogen peroxide on the cut in Hannah's toe, wrapped it with a Band-Aid and then hauled her back to the basement.

Hannah lay there for a long time, shivering and coughing until her throat was sore. Occasionally she could hear Vivie, walking along the hall, using the phone, climbing the stairs. Once in a while she thought Vivie was standing just outside the basement door, listening. Probably smiling. Maybe even laughing, only without making any noise. Yes, she could picture Vivie out there laughing and laughing, keeping the sound of it inside herself with all the other scary noises.

Hannah must have fallen asleep because she was startled awake by the chiming of the doorbell. She coughed as she sat up and pressed her ear to the door. She heard Vivie greet someone, then a man's voice she didn't recognize. Before long she heard hammering.

Just somebody fixing the window, she thought, and lay down again.

When Vivie next opened the basement door, Hannah felt too tired to sit up. She blinked in the light and peered up at her grandmother.

"All right, Johannah. You can come out now and have your lunch."

Hannah closed her eyes again, thinking she'd rather go to sleep. But Vivie put her hands under Hannah's arms and lifted her to her feet.

Hannah felt like a rag doll as Vivie carried her to the kitchen table and deposited her in a chair.

Hannah lay her head on the table, facing away from her plate, but Vivie grasped her shoulders and pulled her upright. "Eat now," she said.

"Can't I please go to bed?" Hannah said, punctuating her sentence with a sharp cough.

"Cover your mouth when you cough, for heaven's sake. And, no, you may not go to bed. I told you, I want you to eat now."

Hannah picked up her sandwich, bit into it, chewed it slowly a few times, and then spat it out onto the plastic tablecloth.

Vivie shrieked, "Are you out of your mind! Pick that up and put it back in your mouth."

Tears welled up in Hannah's eyes. She picked up the pinkish-white lump of food and put it on the edge of her plate. "It's tongue. I hate tongue. It makes me throw up."

"Don't be ridiculous. Tongue is a delicacy and you *will* eat it."

Hannah picked at a small piece of bread and mumbled something.

"What? What was that?"

"Could I just eat the bread? Then you could keep the delicate thing for yourself."

Roughly, Vivie swiveled Hannah's chair around to face her. "I can't believe this," she growled. "You are actually back-talking me, aren't you!"

Speechless with fear, Hannah watched a shadow shift in Vivie's eyes. Abruptly, Vivie turned the chair back toward the table, picked up the plate and went to the sink.

Hannah sat still, her head lowered and her shoulders hunched forward stiffly as if to protect herself from the next blow.

A short time later, Vivie plunked a different plate in front of Hannah.

"There, Miss Priss. Peanut butter and jelly. You satisfied?"

With the smell of the peanut butter, Hannah's spirits lifted. She ate quickly and in silence, aware that Vivie was leaning against the kitchen sink watching her all the while.

Swallowing the last bite of her sandwich, Hannah said, "May I please be excused?"

"Eat the apple first."

Hannah did, wishing it was something easy like a pear, something that didn't take so much time to chew. Finally she was done, and asked again to be excused.

"Not yet. I want to have a few words with you first." She sat in the chair adjacent to Hannah's, opened a bag of M&Ms and began popping them in her mouth, a few at a time.

"It's quite clear to me, Johannah, that you have become a very bad child," Vivie said, chewing the sweet morsels. "It's important for you to understand that. Somehow, Satan has taken a foothold in your spirit."

Hearing these things, Hannah felt the room begin to spin. She lowered her head and closed her eyes.

"You are a millstone around your poor father's neck, and a constant thorn in my side. Now I've been talking with the Lord God Almighty and he has again reminded me of his words in the Bible, 'Spare the rod and spoil the child.' Do you know what that means, Johannah?"

When Hannah said nothing, Vivie popped a few more M&Ms and continued, "It means that you are bad because you have not been properly taught. Your papa doesn't have the strength of will to discipline you the way he should. He spoils you, and it shows. So the Lord has been disciplining you, as he did by taking your mama to heaven, and by what happened this morning. Your cutting your foot like that, well that was the Lord God Almighty's way of showing you just how bad you are. Bad things happen only to bad people like you."

Vivie shook Hannah's arm. "Are you listening to me? Are you hearing what I'm saying?"

Hannah didn't raise her head. "Yes, ma'am." Her eyes burned with unshed tears.

"All right. Now, the Lord God Almighty told me that I'm the

one who has to straighten you out. That's why I didn't go with your Uncle Bruce. I would have gone in a second, but the Lord told me to stay here and see to you. So that's what I'm doing. Do you understand? Do you hear me?"

Hannah nodded.

Vivie ate the last of her M&Ms and began making accordion folds in the brown bag. "Even when your papa finds you a new mama, I'll stay because the Lord has told me to. This is my calling, you see, to shake that spoiled badness out of your hide. Do you understand?"

Hannah could barely breathe, but managed to squeak out a "yes."

"And one other thing. The Lord God Almighty told me loud and clear that this calling of mine is just between you and me and him. If you tell anyone else about anything that goes on between me and you, the Lord God Almighty will take your papa to heaven, just like he did your mama. You wouldn't want that, now, would you, Johannah."

Hannah shook her head.

"All right. So we have a new understanding now, don't we. You stop being so bad and you won't have to spend another minute in that basement. Just remember, there's no point in sneaking around and trying to get away with things. The Lord God Almighty and I, we see everything you do."

With a shudder, Hannah thought of the giant invisible eye and knew that what Vivie had said was true.

Vivie stood and carried Hannah's plate to the sink. Over her shoulder she said, "Well, you might at least thank me."

In a very small voice Hannah said, "Thank you." She remained hunched and perfectly still, fearfully wondering if it would be okay to again ask to be excused.

Vivie settled the matter. "All right. Go on. Get dressed. I'll do your braids and then you can see to that filthy animal of yours."

Hannah spent the afternoon with Joey and Gabriel, worrying about what Vivie had told her. She fed Joey and brushed him, thinking it was her own fault that she was a witch. She cleaned out Joey's stall and put in fresh straw, thinking that these terrible things were happening—like with Joey's mommy and Uncle Bruce—because she was a witch. Maybe it was even her fault that Gabriel had died in the first place. Or maybe the lordgodamighty did that to Gabriel so that she'd find out that she was a witch. Yes, that made sense. If the lordgodamighty would take Mama away to punish Hannah, then he wouldn't have any problem killing a little bird for the same reason. But would he really take Papa away, too, just because she was a spoiled bad witch? Every time she worried about that, she forgot how to breathe for a little while.

After supper, Hannah again went to the barn. She found Gabriel perched on the stall railing, and the thought that he and Joey had become real friends made her smile for the first time that day.

When it was time to go inside for a shampoo and her bath, Hannah sat with Joey's head in her lap and luxuriated in the warm beauty of him. Suddenly she was overcome with the feeling that once she went into the house, she would never see this sweet creature again. A sob burst out of her throat. She pressed her cheek into Joey's neck and wept. She felt like she might cry for the rest of her life.

But it was getting dark, Gabriel had gone to his nest, and Vivie had called her twice already. So eventually she sniffed back the last of her tears and kissed Joey once more, watching as he closed his moist, dark eyes. Then she latched the stall's gate firmly and walked slowly to the house.

Hannah lay awake that night waiting for Vivie to come up to bed. Although she had no plan for dealing with the locked doors and windows, she was determined to find a way out to the barn so that she could be with Joey. When Vivie finally came upstairs, Hannah shut her eyes tightly and pretended to be asleep. She felt Vivie stand over her for several long moments, and tensed herself for a pinch. But nothing happened, and Vivie finally left the room.

Hannah relaxed a bit then and waited to hear Vivie's bedtime sounds stop. Just when she thought it might be safe to go, she heard Vivie coming back down the hall. She closed her eyes and held her breath.

This time Vivie wasn't just standing by Hannah's bed, she was busy doing something. Hannah heard the sound of metal on metal, then an unfamiliar movement of air followed by the clicking of a lock into place.

Hannah opened her eyes, sat up and gaped at her doorway, where her newly-restored door was firmly closed. Knowing, but not caring, that Vivie was waiting just outside in the hall, Hannah jumped off her bed and rushed to the door. She turned the knob and pulled, finding the door solidly locked. Vivie had removed the key from the inside and locked the door from the outside.

"No!" she cried. "No! Please!"

"Johannah?" Vivie asked. "Why, I thought you were sound asleep. Now you get back to bed. I want you to have a nice, uninterrupted sleep."

"Please don't lock me in! Please!"

"Just tonight, dear. Just this last night while your Papa's away. Don't worry. I'll let you out first thing in the morning."

Hannah sank to the floor. "Please, Vivie," she cried softly. But she could hear her grandmother's footsteps retreating down the hall.

Exhausted, Hannah dragged herself to her bed. She lay flat on her back, placed Lily on her chest, straightened her legs and pressed her arms against her sides, thinking about how it might be to lie dead in a coffin like Mama's. There would be a satin pillow under her head and the casket would be open so that people could see her and say how nice she looked and how much they would miss her.

After awhile she drifted into a light, restless sleep, interrupted by spells of coughing.

Chapter Ten

The next morning, Hannah was wide awake and dressed in shorts and T-shirt, standing by the door when Vivie unlocked it.

"Hi, 'scuse me," she said, racing past Vivie, down the stairs and to the kitchen, where she was again stopped by the keyless lock. She ran back to the stairs and intercepted Vivie on her way down.

Breathlessly she asked, "Please can I go out to the barn now?"

"It's 'may I,' not 'can I.' And you might first say good morning to me, Johannah."

"Uh, uh… um."

"Say good morning to me, Johannah."

"Oh! Good morning."

"There, that's better."

"So can I go to the barn now, please?"

"'May' I, Johannah. Say 'may I' go to the barn."

"May I go the barn now, please?"

"Only for a little while, after I braid your hair. Just remember, you have to have your breakfast and change clothes before we leave for church. Go use the bathroom and get your braid holders."

Hannah did so and then shifted from foot to foot as Vivie pulled her hair into place.

Finally, the job done, Vivie unlocked the back door and Hannah flew down the steps toward the barn. She was so focused on Joey, she didn't notice that Gabriel had not been waiting at the house for her, until she saw him chirping and flitting nervously just inside the barn doors.

Even as she said, "What's the matter, Gabriel?" she knew what the matter was. Joey was gone. The stall gate was wide open, and there was nothing inside but straw and Joey's water bucket.

"No-o-o!" Hannah wailed. "Joey!"

Her heart racing, she inspected every accessible area of the barn and found no sign of the fawn. Hurrying outside and looking everywhere her vision could reach, she thought of Joey's mama, dead at Jeli's house.

Joey went back home! she thought, and set off in that direction.

Gabriel darted about her head, chirping the harsh single note he used to frighten away predators.

"Where is he, Gabriel? Do you know?"

He persisted with his angry call, and it seemed to Hannah that he was trying to tell her something. She picked up speed, racing along the back of the house.

Vivie's voice from the back door stopped her. "Where do you think you're going? Get back here immediately."

"I gotta find Joey! I gotta go look at Jeli's for him."

"Johannah, you get yourself back here this instant or I promise you'll regret it."

"Oh, please, Vivie. Just let me go look for him."

Vivie had come down the steps and was charging in Hannah's direction. "Come here now, right now, or you're going to the basement."

Hannah could easily have outrun Vivie, but fear glued her where she stood.

Vivie reached her, turned her by her shoulders and propelled her back toward the house. "Forget about that animal, Johannah. This is the Lord's day. It's time to get ready for church."

"But he's still so little. He needs me."

"I doubt that. He ran away, didn't he?"

"I don't know. Maybe he didn't. Maybe—"

"Maybe nothing." Vivie prodded her harder. "Now, I've told you to forget about this, so that's what you must do if you know what's good for you."

Hannah fell silent. She put a braid in her mouth and climbed the steps, moving on ahead through the kitchen, up the front stairs and to her bedroom. She closed her door and flopped face down on her bed, pulling Lily to her side.

"What am I gonna do, Lily?" she whispered, choking back a cough.

An answer came into her mind. She slipped off the bed and knelt at its side. Closing her eyes, she bowed her head over her clasped hands.

Softly, she said, "Please, dear Jesus. Please help me. I know I'm a witch and I'm spoiled very bad, but Joey's good and he needs me. Please let me get to him. I'll do anything you say if you'll just please help me find him now."

She didn't know what she expected, but it wasn't what she received. Vivie burst into her room.

"You are never, ever to close your door without my permission. Is that clear? Now get up and get dressed. You just have time for some cereal and then we're leaving for church."

Thirty minutes later, as Vivie drove down the driveway and onto the main road, Hannah looked everywhere for some sign of Joey. There was nothing. The way to the church was in the opposite direction from Jeli's house, and Hannah felt tears welling up again at the thought of Joey there at Jeli's, maybe curled up against the dead cold body of his mother, lost and terrified.

These thoughts remained with Hannah when she followed Vivie into church. So concentrated was she on Joey, she didn't notice that her hands were on fire.

Apparently she and Vivie were late; Maybelle and her mother were already in their places. As Hannah started to walk in front of Maybelle's wheelchair to get to her seat, she stopped suddenly, turning to look the crippled child directly in her darkly-clouded eyes.

In her mind she heard Maybelle say, *Yes, Hannah. Yes!*

Without a thought, she reached out her burning right hand and placed it on Maybelle's twisted shoulder.

Maybelle elevated out of her chair as if she'd been hit by lightning. Her mother shrieked and the congregation surged into an uproar as Maybelle's spasming body collapsed on the floor at Hannah's feet. There, Maybelle gagged and twitched as foamy mucus bubbled from her mouth and nostrils.

Ice cold now, Hannah gaped in horror. Before she could move to help, Vivie had jerked her off her feet and was carrying— dragging—her up the aisle, out through the door and into the parking lot. Vivie didn't stop until they were beside her black sedan. There, she pinned Hannah against the car by her shoulders and glared into her face. "What in the name of the Lord God Almighty has possessed you?"

An image flashed in Hannah's mind of Vivie in the early morning hours, carrying Joey into the woods and then holding a large, smooth rock and bringing it down repeatedly on his gentle head until she had crushed the life out of him.

Hannah thought the sun had opened up and shot an arrow into her heart. "You killed him," she said softly but clearly, staring straight into Vivie's eyes.

"What?" Vivie shrieked.

"You killed Joey."

"What on earth are you ranting about?"

"This morning. You killed Joey. I saw it."

"Don't be ridiculous," Vivie said, her round eyes narrowing as she looked at Hannah. She opened the back door of the sedan and pushed Hannah inside. "Get in there and keep your mouth shut."

Hannah did as she was told, lying down and curling in on herself. But within moments of Vivie's climbing into the front seat and starting the car, Hannah's mind and heart had flown out of the window in search of Joey.

She looked first at Jeli's, finding only an empty spot on the grass where the fawn's mother had been. Then she flew home to the woods below the barn, and there she found him—her gentle, golden friend—with his tender head mangled into bloody bits of bone. She lay down in the ferns behind him, wrapping herself around his lifeless body and shutting her eyes against the sight of his empty eye socket. She willed her hands to burn so that she could bring life back into Joey. But there was no heat. Not in Joey, not in Hannah. The whole world had gone cold that humid July morning. Hannah felt the deadness of Joey's body creeping into her own and began to give herself up to the thought of following Joey wherever he had gone.

Then the fragrance of Mama's wildflowers filled Hannah's senses, and Gabriel flew to her cheek, tucking in his tiny feet and nestling just in front of her ear, his warmth and the rapid beating of his heart bringing her back to the woods.

She stood then and went to the barn, retrieving Papa's smallest shovel and returning to the woods, digging a hole for Joey. After a while, she stepped back and looked at what she had accomplished. She knew it wasn't much of a grave, barely deep enough to hold Joey below ground level. And she worried that the dirt and leaves she'd put over his golden body weren't packed in well enough to really protect him. That he no longer needed protection made no difference; she had not kept him safe in life and was determined to keep him safe in death.

She lay face down on the rough mound, doing her best to embrace it. With her face to the side and her cheek pressed into the leaves and loose dirt, she whispered, "I'm sorry, Joey. It's all my fault. It's 'cause I'm a witch, a spoiled bad witch, and it's me who shoulduv got punished, not you."

She was quiet then, imagining Jesus watching Joey and his mama prancing about in heaven. It was a happy scene that nearly made her smile, but then the image began to change. Dark clouds gathered in heaven's sky and Joey and his mama vanished. In the growing gloom, Jesus turned and calmly regarded Hannah. He seemed to be waiting for her to speak.

And she wanted to speak to him, to ask him why he hadn't saved Joey and Mama, why he didn't help Maybelle, and why Vivie and Uncle Bruce could hurt people so much, and he didn't do anything to stop them. Most of all, she wanted to ask him to please, *please* make her not be a witch anymore.

But she said nothing to him. She was afraid. What if Jesus didn't really love her after all? What if she made him mad and he did as Vivie warned and took Papa to heaven too? No, she'd better not ask Jesus for anything. She wasn't sure about him anymore. She wasn't really sure about anything, anymore.

She began to float above the mound of Joey's grave, higher and higher, until she was hovering over the woods themselves. She thought she heard Gabriel's heartbeat again, and suddenly was drawn back into her body, finding herself closed in the basement with her own heart beating rapidly in her ears.

"Noooo!" she wailed, pounding on the door. "Vivie, please! Let me out!" She broke off in a spasm of coughing.

When she could breathe again, she pressed her ear to the door, but heard only the silence of an empty house. Vivie's gone out to bury him, she thought. Or maybe just to put him somewhere so I can't find him.

She wrapped her arms around her bare legs, trying to get warm. There were ice cubes all over her body and a squeezing pain in her chest, and she thought that even if she had a hundred blankets, she would still be shivering.

Some time later, just when she was wondering if a person could actually turn into an ice cube and break into small pieces, she heard the front door open and close, and Vivie's footsteps going up the stairs.

Standing, she screamed, "Vivie! Let me out!" Needles of pain shot through her chest and throat, but she pounded on the door and continued to scream, "Please! Let me out! Let me out!"

When she heard Vivie coming down the steps, she silenced herself and stood there, ready to push through Vivie and anything else in her way as she went in search of Joey. She'd find him, she promised herself, even if it took her forever.

There was a click outside the door and the light over Hannah's head came on, surprising her with its brightness. She shut her eyes for a moment, and when she opened them, Vivie was standing there in front of her on the landing, arms crossed over her chest.

"No need to be screaming at me like a crazy person, Johannah."

Hannah tried to push by her, but there wasn't room. "Let me out, Vivie. Please. I need to—"

"Yes, please tell me what it is you need to do," interrupted Vivie. "What's so important that you've been acting like a maniac all morning, pinching poor little Maybelle, and saying horrible things to me."

"I didn't pinch her, I just… I touched her, is all. I didn't mean to hurt her."

"Ah. There we are again with Johannah's favorite words, 'I didn't mean to.'"

"Well, but I didn't. And now I just have to go find Joey. Please let me go, Vivie."

"Yes. What about Joey? You said some dreadful lies about me, you know."

Hannah had moved back from the door, as far as she could go

from Vivie in that small space. Now, without a conscious thought, she stepped forward, looked straight up into Vivie's eyes, and said, "I know you killed Joey this morning. I saw it. Now I have to go bury him so he can get to heaven."

Vivie's face turned bright red. She aimed a roundhouse whack at Hannah, but Hannah ducked it. Off balance, Vivie fell down the cellar stairs, taking the full force of her momentum on her right elbow against the basement's cement floor. Hannah heard the sharp, clear sound of breaking bone.

Vivie rolled onto her back and stared up the steps at Hannah, then followed Hannah's gaze to the jagged bone protruding from her upper arm. Vivie looked at it curiously, as if it belonged to someone else. Then her eyes rolled up in her head and she fainted.

Hannah left the basement landing and raced to the front door, throwing it open, pushing through the screen onto the porch and jumping across the stairs to the ground. She started to race toward the barn and the woods when she felt pressure against her shoulders, as if a giant were standing in front of her, holding her back, telling her to stop.

She noticed then that her hands were on fire. She studied them, wondering at their betrayal. Then, looking up at the bitter yellow sky through the canopy of trees, she soundlessly cried, *Please, Jesus! Please don't make me do this.*

When Vivie regained consciousness, Hannah was sitting on the basement floor beside her.

"You're making a mess of yourself, Johannah, sitting there in your nice dress." Apparently surprised by her weak voice, Vivie clutched at her throat.

"What…" Vivie said, struggling to a sitting position. She examined the arm that had been broken, looked at the floor where she'd fallen, looked at Hannah, and examined her arm again.

"What happened?" she said, suddenly out of breath, her voice small and uncertain.

"You just fell down, is all. Your arm didn't get broken."

Vivie's voice went up in pitch. "How did you know I thought

my arm was broken?"

Realizing what she had said, Hannah sucked in her breath. "I just saw you staring at your arm, is how." She ached to chew on a braid.

Vivie studied Hannah for a long moment, then pushed herself to her feet and brushed at her housedress. "Whatever happened here doesn't change anything, you know."

Hannah stood up too, wondering if now she could finally go look for Joey.

"Pinching Maybelle like that, screaming at me, knocking me down... it all just proves that I was right. You are a very bad, spoiled child."

Hannah started up the stairs, but Vivie pushed her aside and went up ahead of her.

"By rights, you should spend the rest of the day in the basement, Johannah, but just to show you I harbor no resentment, you may stay in your room instead."

Hannah was already out the front door and racing toward the barn when Vivie hollered, "Johannah Kirkland, you get back here this instant!"

By early afternoon, having searched for Joey everywhere on the property and even at Jeli's house, Hannah was ready to give up. She was hungry and tired, and she'd coughed so much, she felt as if her throat was bleeding.

As she made her way back toward the house from the creek, she was thinking maybe she could get some food and take a little nap, and then start looking for Joey all over again.

Rounding the corner of the barn with Gabriel on her shoulder, she stopped abruptly at the sight of Maybelle's mother standing with Vivie at the foot of the front porch steps.

Mrs. MacGill saw her and waved. "Hannah! Come here, dear. Hurry!" she called, a big, friendly smile baring her nice even teeth.

If it weren't for that smile, Hannah would have been terrified. If she hadn't been so exhausted, she would have turned and run. Where was Maybelle? What *had* she done to Maybelle?

Mrs. MacGill was walking quickly toward Hannah. "The

Lord blessed us with a miracle in church this morning, dear. Maybelle can hear and she is talking and moving her arms! Praise God, isn't that wonderful!"

"Maybelle's all right?" Hannah whispered. And coughed, remembering to cover her mouth.

"Oh, she's much more than all right, dear. You and your grandmother left so suddenly, you didn't see what happened after my baby had her little spell. But now she's at the hospital, praise God, and she's asking for *you*."

"For me?"

"For you, dear child. I was just asking your grandmother if you could come with me now to see her at the hospital."

Vivie put a heavy hand on Hannah's shoulder. "And I was just about to say that Johannah here can't go anywhere until she gets thoroughly cleaned up. Did you ever see such a filthy mess on a child's church clothes, Helen?"

Mrs. MacGill knelt before Hannah. "To tell you the truth, Vivian, all I see is a little girl who is very important to my Belle." She opened her arms to Hannah.

I never saw her smile before today, Hannah thought, easily moving into Mrs. MacGill's hug.

Mrs. MacGill made some calls on the hall phone while Hannah had a bath, changed into clean clothes, and nibbled on a sandwich at the kitchen table. She'd somehow lost her appetite and her head was buzzing as if it were filled with bumble bees.

Vivie stood behind her, brushing out her hair and rebraiding it. "I hope you realize how the Lord God Almighty saved your skin today. It seems that the Lord and I are the only ones who saw you pinch that child, and then just look at what he did, stepping in and performing a miracle with her. I can't imagine why she's asking for you, but whatever the reason, just you remember that the Lord God Almighty saw your sinful behavior and made something good of it. And don't think for one minute that anything has changed, Johannah. No one sees you like I do, and I will always keep my eye on you. Do you hear me?"

Hannah couldn't swallow, and icicles were sliding down her backbone.

Vivie poked Hannah's shoulder. "I said, do you hear me?"

"Yes, ma'am," she breathed.

It wasn't until they were just a few minutes from the hospital that Hannah was able to stop worrying about Vivie's giant invisible eye and listen to Mrs. MacGill's happy chattering.

"My lands, Hannah, I had no idea my Belle was so attached to you. Imagine, your name was the first word she has ever said in her life. Did you know that she cared about you so much, dear? I don't suppose you did, if I didn't. And your grandmother didn't, I'm sure, or she would have said something. But there we were, all hovering around my baby there on the floor, in front of her chair, and suddenly she stops, and her hands uncurl, and the clouds lift off her eyes and she says, 'Hannah! Hannah!' just as clear as a bell. Well, I suppose her words weren't quite as clear as a bell for everyone, but I knew she was saying 'Hannah.' She was even gesturing at the chair where you usually sit. You could've knocked me over with a feather!" Mrs. MacGill patted Hannah's knee. "Oh, I wish you had stayed, dear, you and your grandmother. Weren't you feeling well, was that the problem? I notice you've got quite a cough. Was that it? Well, it doesn't matter really, you don't have to tell me. It's just that it seemed so wrong, my Maybelle Rose saying your name and your not being there like that. It seems quite clear to me that you were a big part of that miracle this morning." She sighed happily. "Not a soul in that church who didn't know we'd witnessed a genuine miracle. Praise God!

"And here we are," she announced, steering her station wagon up the long drive and parking in the small lot directly in front of the hospital. "In a minute you'll see our miracle for yourself."

She looked at Hannah then and seemed surprised by what she saw. "Good heavens, child, you really aren't feeling well, are you." Mrs. MacGill put a cool hand to Hannah's forehead. "And I think you might have a fever. Oh, my dear! I'm so sorry! Plenty of time to see Maybelle when you're well. I'll take you right back home."

Hannah wanted to say no, please, that she never wanted to go home again, but her voice wouldn't work and all she could manage was to put her head down on the seat between herself and Mrs. MacGill and close her eyes.

Chapter Eleven

Mrs. MacGill silently stroked Hannah's hair as she drove her home, nearly lulling Hannah to sleep.

Hannah knew she should be thinking about where to look for Joey next, but there were too many fearful images tumbling over each other in her mind. Before she could make sense of any of them, Mrs. MacGill was bringing the station wagon to a stop in front of the house.

"Well, here's a piece of good luck, dear," said Mrs. MacGill, turning off the car's engine. "Your grandmother must have run an errand, and now she's back."

Hannah heard a car go by and head for the barn, and a hazy picture began to take shape in her mind. She sat up quickly, immediately clapping her hands to either side of her head to keep it from splitting in two.

Mrs. MacGill was out of the car and crossing the yard to Vivie when Hannah's head stopped hurting and the picture returned, slowly becoming clearer. Something about Vivie's car...

"Come on, now, Johannah," Vivie said, opening the passenger door. "Come on out of there and let's get you and your germs up to your room where they belong."

Hannah obediently slid out of the car, half hearing Mrs. MacGill say, "I promise, dear, as soon as you're well, you and my Belle can spend lots and lots of time together. I'm just so sorry it couldn't work out today."

"Nonsense, Helen," said Vivie. "Johannah is the one who should be apologizing, putting you to all this trouble. Thank goodness you caught on to how poorly she was feeling before she could get up there to your daughter's hospital room and give her who-knows-what sort of disease."

Mrs. MacGill bent down and put a hand under Hannah's chin, lifting her head, looking into her eyes. "You get well now, dear, all right?" She gave Hannah's forehead a light kiss.

"Maybelle and I will be praying for you."

The warmth in Mrs. MacGill's face and words suddenly made Hannah feel like crying, and she lost sight of the picture in her mind while she watched Mrs. MacGill return to her car and wave out of the window as she headed down the driveway.

When the station wagon was out of sight, Vivie took hold of Hannah's arm and pulled her toward the porch steps.

And the picture returned to Hannah's mind, bright and clear and fully-formed. "You put Joey's dead body in your car," she said.

Vivie dropped Hannah's arm as if it had burned her hand. "What did you say to me?" she shrieked.

"You put Joey in your car, I know it. I saw it."

Vivie grabbed Hannah by the shoulders and shook her, screaming down at her, "You horrible, horrible child! If you don't stop these lies, I'll give you a spanking you'll never forget!"

Hannah pulled away from Vivie and raced to the black sedan parked by the barn, hoping Vivie had left her keys on the seat as she sometimes did.

Vivie trundled along behind her, screaming, "STOP THIS INSTANT! STOP RIGHT NOW!"

But Hannah had already retrieved the keys and was trying to figure out which one would open the car's trunk. *I'm coming, Joey,* she called to him in her mind. *I'm almost there.*

Vivie grabbed Hannah's arm and yanked her back, away from the car. "Give me those keys!" she screeched.

"Let me go!" Hannah cried, keeping a tight hold on the keys as she pulled out of Vivie's grasp. "You killed Joey! I'm telling Papa that you killed Joey."

"I said give me those keys!"

"No! I gotta get Joey out of the trunk."

"JOHANNAH! Give me those keys right now or you're going to the basement."

"NO I'M NOT! I HAVE TO GET JOEY!"

Vivie put a choke hold around Hannah's neck from behind. "I SAID GIVE ME THOSE KEYS, YOU HORRIBLE BRAT!" She lifted Hannah off her feet and began to shake her as she tightened the hold on her neck.

"VIVIAN!" roared Papa.

Vivie dropped Hannah and lurched around.

"Paul! What are you—"

He grabbed her wrists and shook her roughly. "What in hell do you think you're doing?" He gave her no chance to respond, dropping her wrists in disgust and quickly lifting Hannah into his arms. "My God! I can't believe this."

Hannah was hit with a coughing spasm as Papa hugged her close, kissed her, smoothing her hair and murmuring, "Aw, baby, I'm so sorry."

Vivie watched, apparently speechless. When Papa finally looked at her again, she jerked back as if she had been hit.

"I saw and heard it all, Vivian. I want you out of here, now."

"But this is my home," she wailed.

"Not anymore. And never again." He gently set Hannah on her feet. "Go on up on the porch, Jo."

Vivie was shaking. "Whatever you thought happened here, I assure you—"

"I should have thrown you out of here with that sick, sonofabitch son of yours."

"You can't just throw me out of my own house. It's against the law."

"Sue me." He advanced toward her, and she scurried backwards, tripping over a root and going down hard on her tailbone. Her mouth twisted grotesquely as she wailed with pain.

Papa stepped behind her, put his hands under her arms and lifted her to her feet. "A taste of your own medicine," he said. "Now get going."

She spun around to face him again. "I'm not leaving! You can't make me!"

"Want to bet?" He grabbed her upper arm and propelled her to the car, opening the door and forcing her into the driver's seat.

"My handbag! I need my bag."

"Where is it?"

Vivie pointed toward the porch steps where Hannah stood with Gabriel on her shoulder, wondering if she was dreaming. Excitement had bubbled up and washed away the pain in her chest and throat.

"Jo," said Papa. "You see her handbag there? Can you bring it to me?"

"Uh-huh," she said, picking it up and running to his side. "But can I look for Joey in the trunk before she goes, Papa?"

Vivie pulled herself back out of the car. "Of course you can, Johannah," she said, her voice as shaky as her hands. "If only you had asked me nicely." She hurried to the rear of the sedan, fumbled a bit with the keys and then unlocked the trunk and threw it open. "There! See? Nothing but some old rags."

"But he was there, Papa. I know it!"

"Can we end this nonsense now, Paul?" Vivie said, closing the trunk. "I didn't do a thing to that filthy animal of hers. Why don't we just go inside and I'll make you a nice—"

"Nothing's changed, Vivian. I want you off this property. Permanently."

"But I didn't—"

"I saw you choking my daughter, Vivian. Now get your sorry ass out of here before I choke *you*."

Hannah put a hand in Papa's, trembling at the sight of the fiery red spears flying from Vivie's mind.

"You have not heard the last of this!" Vivie growled at both of them.

"Vivian, if you ever try to hurt my daughter again, I swear I will kill you!" He slammed the car door shut and stepped back, firmly putting his arm around Hannah's shoulder and pulling her close to his side.

Vivie gave them one last, long glare before she turned the key in the ignition.

Papa lifted Hannah into his arms and they watched in silence as Vivie's black sedan disappeared down the driveway. Then he carried her to the porch steps, set her down and sat beside her. "Are you okay, Jo? Let me see."

She lifted her chin and he ran his fingers and his eyes along her neck. "Does it hurt, baby?"

"A little inside, 'cause of coughing a lot."

"You've been coughing?" He put his warm hand on her forehead, then her cheek.

"Mrs. MacGill said maybe I had a fever."

"Feels okay to me."

"It's okay, now you're home. When'd you get here?"

"With her screaming at you like that, it's no wonder you didn't notice me pull up." He hugged her close and rested his cheek on her head. "I should have known, baby. All this time, I should have known."

She felt his tears wetting her hair, and wrapped her arms more tightly around him. "Don't cry, Papa! Please don't cry." She patted his broad back.

"Can you ever forgive me, Jo?"

Hours later Hannah was lying in bed, on her side and under her coverlet, with Lily in her arms.

Papa sat on the bed beside her, lightly brushing his fingers through her hair. "Are you feeling all right now, baby?"

"Mm-hmm. I didn't cough since a long time, did I?"

"Right. You're doing great."

She closed her eyes for a few moments, absorbing the warmth of his touch. Then she opened them wide as Vivie entered her thoughts. "Is she really gone?"

"She really is."

"But what if she comes back tonight when I'm sleeping?"

"She won't be able to get in. As soon as you go to sleep, I'm going down to put deadbolts on both doors."

"But she's gotta get her stuff."

"No, she doesn't. I'll send it all to her."

"But what about stuff like her bed and chairs—that kind of stuff?"

"I'll hire a moving company for her furniture."

"But she's gonna be so mad at me!"

He lifted her chin and looked into her eyes.

"You never have to be afraid of her again. Never. I will not let her near you. I promise."

Hannah wished she could believe him, but Papa didn't know as much about Vivie as she did.

"Do you believe me, Jo?"

"I guess so," she said softly, sliding her eyes away from his.

"I will protect you, Jo. I swear I will."

Hannah put a hand on his arm. "Is everything really gonna be okay, Papa?"

"Yes, baby. Everything's going to be okay."

She just wished she could believe him.

Hannah was startled awake and sat up in her bed, fully alert. The nightlight on her bureau was out and she was blind in the darkness.

She felt someone enter the room and stand by her bed. An icy coldness prickled her skin.

Pushing back against the headboard and pulling her coverlet up under her neck, she searched for her voice and managed to whisper, "Who's there?"

"Why, it's me of course, Johannah," said Vivie, her face suddenly illuminated in garish yellow, as if a flashlight were shining on it from beneath her chin. "Who did you expect? The boogey man?"

Hannah wanted to scream, but the sound was stuck in her throat.

"You're wondering how I managed to get in, since your dear Papa changed the locks on me, aren't you? Of course you are. Have you forgotten that I've never needed doors? Or windows, for that matter. No, indeedy." Vivie cackled, just like the wicked witch of the west.

Something moved on the opposite side of the bed from Vivie. A deathly cold, boney hand touched the top of Hannah's head and rested there. She gagged with the stink that filled her nostrils.

"You're wondering who is here with me, aren't you? Of course you are. Have you forgotten that everywhere I go, the lordgodamighty is with me? Yes, indeedy." Again, the cackling.

"We've just dropped in for a moment to make sure you remember that the lordgodamighty and I know exactly what you are. And we want to promise you something, Johannah. Do you want to know what it is? Of course you do. The lordgodamighty and I want to promise you that for the rest of your life we are always, always, always going to *keep our eye on you*."

Hannah woke screaming and didn't stop until Papa came into the room and put his arms around her.

"S'okay, baby," he slurred. "Thing's'okay. Jus' a nigh'mare, s'all."

She wanted to believe him, but his bleeryness felt like ice in her heart.

By the time she was willing to lie down again and try to get some sleep, a recognition had settled in her mind, as if it were written there in stone: she would never be free of the fearful coldness of Vivie and the lordgodamighty.

Book Two
Present Day

Chapter Twelve

Nearing West Chester from Gettysburg late that afternoon, Hannah cast a clinical eye on the vibrant red-orange of the sunset sky and its pale gold mare's tail clouds. She judged it beautiful, along with the evening's freshening coolness, but she felt nothing; her heart was still trapped in the chaos and horror of the plane crash. She wondered if she would ever be free of it.

Then, as she maneuvered her Jeep off Birmingham Road and down the long, back driveway leading to her house, the thought of home soothed her into a smile. Pulling into the driveway circle, she spotted Clancy exactly as she had left him that morning, standing by the front door, his tail wagging his sleek, golden body. In a flash she was out of the car and on her knees with him, his slobbery greeting turning her smile into a belly laugh. He leaned his full fifty-five pounds into her and she rested her head on his, enjoying the sunny warm smell of his fur.

Nearly three years old, Clancy was the third golden retriever Hannah had owned and cherished since Grampa had given her a Clancy puppy on Christmas day in 1982. Grampa, home and Clancy. "Thank God I still have you and home," Hannah said, her nose an inch away from his. She gave his brisket a hearty scruff, then stood, opened the front door with her electronic key and turned off the house alarm system. After she unloaded the car, she fed Clancy and poured herself a Wild Cherry Pepsi over ice. Sipping it, appreciating its sweet bite, she watched Clancy wolf his kibble and smiled again. "You might enjoy it more, pal, if you took the time to chew. You remember chewing, that up-and-down thing with your teeth?"

She let him out for a run and took her Pepsi into the greatroom, turning on the CD player and sinking into the deeply-cushioned sofa. The exquisite dissonance of Barber's *Adagio for Strings* filled her senses as she gazed out through the wall of windows at the patio and trees, softly illuminated in the waning light. Her eyes were drawn to the large, gray-green rock by the creek, the rock with its indentation that had been a perfect fit for her six-year-old back.

Only the rock hasn't changed in all these years, she thought.

Clancy appeared at the French doors; letting him in, she thought as she had countless times before that she loved this house far more than she should love any *thing*. Built for Grampa in 1992, here by the creek at Hannah's request, it had become his home when he decided to retire from the pulpit and bring the mountain to Mohammed.

Papa and Carl Kingsley had worked with an architect and created a classic, with wide-open spaces, hardwood floors, and outside exits from nearly every room. The west wing beyond the greatroom and kitchen held Hannah's bedroom, bath and study. The east wing was comprised of one spacious suite for Grampa and a second for Sophie Muller, the genial woman who had been his nurse, housekeeper and cook "forever," as Grampa would say. Most of all, Sophie was Grampa's devoted friend; her sudden, untimely death a few weeks after his was a sad blow, but not a surprise. Hannah herself sometimes wished she could follow Grampa into what he had called the "next dimension of life."

Settling back into the sofa, Hannah tapped in numbers on her cordless phone and listened to her home and office voice mail. Her chiropractic assistant, Kyla Morgan, would deal with the office messages on Monday, but her unlisted home number held two calls that Hannah was glad she hadn't been here to receive. She was in no state to lie to people she loved about how she had spent her day.

The first message was from Papa and Celeste in Jackson Hole, Wyoming. Hannah could hear her brothers, Michael and Matthew, in the background, Celeste shushing them, and Papa raising his voice over theirs, asking if she could still meet their plane at seven the next evening. "Let us know if you can't, baby. We can always grab the shuttle." Hannah's heart lifted briefly at the sound of her father's clear, unboozey voice, until she realized he'd been calling in the early afternoon, well before five o'clock. Well before cracking open the evening's fifth of vodka, she thought. Or scotch. Or both.

Hannah used to talk to Grampa about Papa's drinking. He would listen with understanding, but his advice would be unvarying: "Just keep lifting him up in prayer, honey," he would say. "Keep trusting that God is at work in this." Hannah finally decided that if God really was at work in this—or in any of the other troubling issues in her life—his pace was far too slow to be meaningful. She stopped praying for her father—in truth, she pretty much stopped praying, period—once Grampa died.

The second message was from Craig in Japan. Hannah's throat closed as she listened to him say he was sorry she wasn't home, that he missed her, he loved her, and he couldn't wait to get back to her. "Only ten more days, doll," were his last words before the electronic female voice announced that there were no more messages in her mailbox.

She stroked Clancy's head where it rested on her thigh as she thought about Craig Stafford. She had been dating him for nearly two years, and lately had begun to see he was thinking marriage just when she was thinking it was time to move on. She did care for him. Though he could be overbearing, he had a solid career as a computer systems consultant, and he had done his best to encourage her during Grampa's illness and after his death. She appreciated that. Still, she knew she couldn't trust Craig with the truth about herself and her healing gifts. After his initial surprise, he would be pushing for Hannah to turn her extraordinary abilities into gold. It was Craig's materialism—his lack of faith in any greater reality—that was at the core of Hannah's dissatisfaction with him. Religiosity she could not tolerate, but neither could she be in sync with anyone whose thinking was entirely in terms of what he could know with his five senses.

He'd be after me to turn a profit off what I did today, Hannah thought. And the "doll" thing, as if I were entirely controllable—how I hate that.

"No question, Clancy my friend," Hannah said aloud. "It's time to end this. Way past time, really. As soon as he gets home, I'll tell him it's over." She thought about Craig's probable reaction to the news, and added, "Unless you'd like to tell him for me."

She closed her eyes and pressed on them lightly with her fingertips, wishing she could fly away in her mind like she used to. Everything was so much easier then. Grampa was alive then. Sometimes she thought her imagination had died with Grampa.

She pressed a speed-dial number on her cordless phone.

"Hello?"

"It's me, Rose. I'm home."

"Thank God! How are you feeling?"

"Tired."

"I don't wonder. But okay otherwise?"

"I guess so."

"Well, it's all over the news. Not *you*, but the crash and the, quote, beautiful blond, unquote, who appeared out of nowhere, saved lives and then vanished like a flaxen Wonder Woman."

"Is that all they have? Nothing about my Jeep?"

"Not that I've heard, but I've been jumping around the channels. They're showing interviews with some of the survivors, and everyone's talking about angels and miracles. You should see it, Jo! I feel like I won the lottery, sitting here knowing you're the angel they're all talking about."

Exhaustion swept through Hannah. "Please don't glorify it, Rose."

"I'm sorry, Jo, but it *is* glorious! How many people get to see God at work like this in their lifetime?"

Hannah said nothing, sipped her Pepsi, and wished she could go to bed.

"Well, at least you should be glad to hear that nobody remembers your face clearly."

"Maybe, just nobody they've interviewed yet."

"They're also making you very tall."

"I'm no midget, Rose." Hannah blanched, realizing what she'd said.

There was a weighty silence before Rose replied, "Not like little old four-foot-eleven me, right?"

"You know I didn't mean that, Rose. I meant five-eight *is* tall for a woman."

"I know, I know. I'm just saying you should be glad you probably won't be traced."

"Maybe."

Rose was quiet a moment before she said, "There is one weird thing that's happening, and I guess I should tell you."

"What?"

"Well, you know those fanatical second-advent groups, always screaming at each other that *they* are the ones who've got the handle on the *genuine* second coming of Christ?"

"Like that baby at Jerusalem's Golden Gate?"

"Exactly. Well, have you heard of the Disciples of the Shepherdess?"

Hannah's mind instantly made the connection, and she felt as if she'd been punched in the stomach. "Don't tell me—"

"Yup. You're her, the one their prophet has been predicting."

"Goddamit!" Hannah said, jumping up and beginning to stride angrily around the room.

"I'm sorry, Jo. I just thought you should hear it from me."

"How bad is it?" When Rose hesitated, Hannah said, "*Tell* me!"

"You don't have to yell at me. I was going to answer you. It's just... well, it's not really bad, it's just very weird."

"How do you mean?"

"Their predictions are so close to the truth. They have you... I mean, the Shepherdess, she's supposed to be your age, appearing out of thin *air*—read airplane crash—and saving lives, and it was supposed to happen around this time, around Easter, within the next few years."

"Is that it? That's not so bad."

"That's what I said. Not bad. But the really weird part, I think, is that they predicted you'd, she'd, appear near a famous sight where there had been a lot of suffering. Most people thought a concentration camp, but—"

"Gettysburg."

"Uh-huh. It *is* pretty strange, isn't it. I mean, there *are* a lot of coincidences."

"You're not buying into this, are you, Rose?"

"No... well, not really, although I've always thought their ideas were pretty interesting. I mean, why shouldn't God come as a woman this time?"

"Fine. Just not *me*, all right? It's me, good old Jo, we're talking about here."

"Well, you know I've always taken your gifts more seriously than you have."

Hannah felt like screaming; instead, she raked her hand repeatedly through her hair as she said, "Dammit, Rose! The very last thing I want in my life is to get in the middle of one of these religious whacko battles. If you don't drop all this crap about me and this Shepherdess, I'll…" Hannah ran out of steam. I'll what? she wondered. There was nothing she could do that wouldn't send Rose into an emotional tailspin.

"Jo! Wait… I… don't hang up!"

Hannah continued to pace, the phone to her ear, but said nothing.

"I'm sorry! Really I am. I'll let it go completely, I promise. Forget I ever brought it up. It's just that they've come forward in a big way with all this, and when they said—"

"I don't want to hear any more about it, Rose."

"Okay, okay. Of course, if you change your mind, you can always turn on the TV yourself."

"Obviously."

"So…"

Hannah could hear Rose's mind struggling for a new foothold in the conversation.

"So… tell me about the glitch you mentioned."

"I'll tell you, but not now. I reek and I've got to get a shower."

"Okay. While you do that, I'll come over and start dinner."

"I was thinking I'd just go to bed."

"For heaven's sake! After such a day, you have to eat."

"I'm really not hungry."

"I see. So, let me guess… peanut butter M&Ms?"

"Mini 3 Musketeers."

Rose gave a dramatic sigh. "One of the first things I plan to ask God when I see him is how you stayed so thin."

"Maybe it's a trade off," Hannah said. "I clean up some of his mistakes and he lets me eat what I want."

"Absolutely nothing happens in God's world by mistake, you know."

Hannah was too tired to argue. "Come over if you want, and I'll see you after my shower."

"Good. I've got my key. And I'm bringing dinner and I expect you to eat it."

"Yes, mother."

Hannah replaced the phone in its base and went to the kitchen. She poured the rest of her Pepsi down the sink, staring into the drain, feeling claustrophobic over the thought of spending this particular evening with Rose. These days, nearly any time spent with Rose felt confining.

An icy resolve gripped her as she stood there by the sink, and she entered a mode where rational thought was not permitted. She went to the liquor cabinet, pulled out a bottle of Jack Daniels, and poured and drank three shots straight up. Moments later, the bottle back in place and the whisky burning its way to her stomach, she took a handful of salted jumbo cashews from the jar on the counter and popped a few into her mouth as she headed for her bathroom.

While the shower water was heating, Hannah took off her clothes and dropped them in the hamper, then stood in front of the wide mirror over the double sinks to pull her hair up off her shoulders and neck with a rubber band.

Observing her full breasts, flat stomach, and slender waist and hips, she felt only shame. "You don't deserve to look so fit," she told her reflection.

When the water temperature was just right she stepped into the shower stall, smiling to herself over the pleasure she took in the simple ritual of bathing. Dependably, the feel of water on Hannah's bare skin would quickly relieve her of tension and unclutter her mind. She wished she could feel so free and fully alive without being naked in water.

She breathed deeply, filling her lungs with the heavy air. Then she let go and gave herself up to the sensual pressure and play of the water on her skin.

Later that evening at the kitchen table, dressed in black jeans and a soft old, red flannel shirt, Hannah pushed spaghetti marinara around on her plate, wanting nothing more than to go to bed and sleep for a week.

Across the table, Rose watched her, dark brown eyes glittering wide in her small, pale face. "Are you all right, Jo? Can't you eat?"

"I'm all right. Just numb."

"You want some Parmesan cheese on that?"

"Doesn't matter."

Rose went to the refrigerator, her limp revealing her agitation. "It makes perfect sense that you're numb," she said, pushing up the sleeves of her too-large, pale peach sweater. Everything Rose wore was too big, furthering the illusion that she was still a child. "God is protecting your mind and body from overload."

"Mm."

Shaking Parmesan cheese on Hannah's spaghetti, Rose said, "The thing I can't get over is Billy Tyler as an airline pilot. I haven't thought of him since we graduated from high school."

"Me neither," Hannah said, turning her attention to Clancy where he sat next to her, regal and still as a statue. Clancy's way of begging, low gear.

"I remember what a jerk he was," Rose said.

Hannah thought, do you remember what jerks *we* were, Rose? Me, afraid of my own shadow, and you, preaching Christianity at anybody who would listen?

Rose continued, "He was so ornery, a lot like the Hooper twins in my afternoon kindergarten. If I'd been you, I would've tried my magic on him."

An image flashed in Hannah's mind. "Huh. I'd forgotten, but I did once, when you were still called Maybelle and Vivian was dragging me to your church every week. I touched Billy's arm in Sunday school one morning because I felt sorry for him. I wanted to see if I could help him."

"What happened?"

"He stuck out his tongue at me." Hannah gave a rueful smile. "One of my early failures."

Clancy chose that moment to shift his begging into high gear, pressing himself against Hannah's leg and resting his head on her lap, looking up at her with his liquid amber eyes.

"And twenty-something years later, Billy Tyler turns up as the First Officer on that flight." Rose shook her head. "It can't be a coincidence."

Hannah grimaced inwardly, sensing what was coming.

"Coincidences happen all the time, Rose."

"But don't you think that God just might be trying to tell you something here? Don't you think the Lord just might be urging you to finally come out into the open? Isn't it possible that the plane crash today was part of God's plan being revealed right before our eyes?"

"Makes sense to me, God revealing his plans for the extraordinary Johannah Kirkland by killing off dozens of ordinary people." Hannah gave her garlic bread to Clancy, who swallowed it whole. She idly wondered if she'd ever have to do a Heimlich maneuver on him.

"You don't have to get sarcastic, Jo. And I bet Grampa would agree with me in a heartbeat."

"Don't be trying to tell me what Grampa would do. One thing he never did was lecture me."

"Oh, well, I'm sorry. I don't mean to lecture, and I know you hate it when I speak for Grampa. Still, don't you think he might have said that Bill Tyler's being on that plane was an essential part of God's plan and that eventually we'd see how everything worked together for the—"

"You're doing it again."

Hannah took a sip from her glass of spring water as Rose regarded her thoughtfully.

"You seem awfully bitter, Jo."

"What, *me*, bitter?" Hannah hated the self-pity in her own voice.

"Don't you realize how blessed you are? I'd give anything to trade places with you. You simply have to get over your paranoia about being discovered."

Hannah put her head in her hands and said nothing, her mind toying with the idea of trading places with someone.

"God saved lives through you today, Jo—all those people, knowing God's love now *because of you*. Clearly, it's time for you to stop hiding your light under a bushel basket."

Hannah was thinking that she definitely wouldn't trade her life for Rose's—one sort of imprisonment for another—but she wondered if that pretty, young pharmacist at CVS might be up for a swap.

Rose continued, "I know you still dwell on what happened to Grampa, but even his dying in such pain was for the glory of the Lord, as he prayed it would be."

Hannah's pulse beat hard behind her eyes. "Drop it, Rose. Please."

"But it's true. Grampa's unwavering faith through his suffering was an inspiration to everyone."

Hannah closed her eyes and gritted her teeth against the bile of anger that rose up in her. *Blind* faith, she thought.

"Are you listening to me, Jo?"

Hannah raised her head and glared at Rose for a moment before her eyes focused. "Not really," she lied. "Sorry."

"It's okay. I know how you hate it when I preach at you."

Do you really? Hannah thought bitterly. After twenty-some years of it, then, do you think you might stop anytime soon?

Rose put her small hands palm down on the table and gazed at them. "And I know you have a hard time understanding why God didn't let you use your gifts for Grampa."

Hannah looked down at her own hands. "I think I loved him too much, and I got in my own way somehow."

"But it does make sense, Jo, if you look at the big picture."

Hannah's thoughts had taken a different turn. "Maybe I'm just a fluke of nature, and my gifts have nothing to do with any sort of God. Maybe we all have these gifts, and mine are just bigger, like some people's noses are bigger than others."

"You can't take God out of the picture." Rose leaned across the table and rested her hand on Hannah's. "I wish I had the words to open your eyes and your mind."

Deliberately, Hannah looked into Rose's eyes as she said, "The sooner you stop trying to fix me, the better off we'll both be."

Rose slid her gaze away and stacked Hannah's plate on her own. "I'm not trying to *fix* you. That's an awful thing to say."

Hannah murmured, "Sorry," not meaning it.

"I believe God is using me to get through to you, and I just haven't succeeded yet."

Hannah worked hard to stay silent as she scratched Clancy's head.

"But I'm not giving up," Rose said, standing and carrying dishes to the sink. "Who knows, maybe you'll get your faith back through the sheer force of mine."

Hannah slid to the floor beside Clancy and held his head close to her own. "What do you think, pal? Think that might work?"

Clancy gave a small, noncommittal woof.

Pleading genuine exhaustion, Hannah persuaded Rose to leave soon after dinner, and by nine-thirty was alone with Clancy in the greatroom. She settled comfortably in the sofa, propped her legs on the massive coffee table, and sipped a Bourbon-on-the-rocks as she watched the reflection from the gas fire in the hearth dance merrily among the subdued lights and shadows visible through the wall of windows. This is, she thought, one of the most peaceful views in all of Chester County. At least it is tonight. At least it is until they find me. "*Then* what are we going to do, Clance? How are we supposed to get privacy with a wall of windows and a cathedral ceiling? Do we paint the windows black or do we move to Tibet?"

Clancy lifted his head from its resting place on Hannah's thigh, and looked at her as if he were mulling over the best way to respond to her questions.

"Well, pal, they may drive me out of my home, but wherever I go, you go with me. Right? Right." An old song came to mind and she thought Clancy looked as if he were smiling as she sang, "Wherever we go, whatever we do, we're gonna go through it together. Through thick or through thin, all out or all in, who cares if it's win—"

The phone rang. Hannah checked the Caller-ID screen and quickly picked up the receiver. "Jeli! I'm so glad you called!"

"Hello, sweetie. How's my favorite granddaughter-in-law?" Jeli's normal lilt was in her words, but not in her voice.

"Is something wrong?"

"I was watching the news about the plane crash near Gettysburg, and when I heard about the mysterious miracle-worker, I knew I had to call you."

"Oh."

"It was you, wasn't it."

Hannah didn't hesitate. "'Fraid so," she said, sorry for the way these things affected Jeli.

"Oh, Hannah. I wish you would have called me."

"I only knew about it this morning, when I woke up. What could you have done from San Francisco?"

"Prayed for you, at least, and sent a lot of positive thoughts your way."

"Wouldn't you have tried to stop me first? And then wouldn't you have worried about me all day long?"

Jeli was quiet a moment before she admitted, "I suppose so. But are you all right? It must have been terrible."

"It was, but I am all right. Only tired. And angry. And a little scared."

"Angry?"

"Mm. At God, as usual, for letting these damn things happen in the first place, and I'm scared because there was someone on the plane who may have recognized me."

"No! Who was it?"

"Someone I knew growing up and in high school. Bill Tyler. I don't think you ever met him."

"No. Unless... his mother's name isn't Ramona, by any chance?"

"I don't know. Why?"

"There's a Ramona Tyler who volunteers at the Brandywine Conservancy. I've known her for years, and she often speaks of her son. He's an airline pilot."

"Oh, God, Jeli. This just gets worse and worse. Bill Tyler was the First Officer on that flight."

Jeli's voice became brisk. "Listen, it's good that I know Ramona because I can tell you she's a very kind soul, and surely some of that will have carried over to her son."

"I hope so."

"Have you thought of contacting him yourself? That way he wouldn't stir anything up, looking for you."

"But all he has to do is check the phone book and he'll find me. Even in the white pages, my practice is listed in bold print. And I don't know for sure that he did recognize me."

"Of course. That's something to pray for."

Hannah was stung by her own utter lack of prayerfulness and said nothing.

"You really are okay, Jo?"

"Yes. Really. And speaking of prayers, I did tell Rose this morning because I wanted hers. She's been a rock, as usual."

"And about as open-minded, I'm guessing."

Hannah smiled. "You got that right. I should never have told her. I had an awful time with her tonight, telling me that what happened today—Bill Tyler and this Shepherdess nonsense—that it's all proof I'm supposed to come out in the open. As she says, stop hiding my light—"

"Under a bushel basket. Ah, sweetie, that's been poor Rose's theme song for ages."

"I just wish Grampa…"

"I do too. I do too."

"He was with me for about two seconds on the way home."

"Was that an encouragement?"

"Not really. Left me wanting more," Hannah said, then lapsed into silence under the pressure of loneliness.

"Hannah?"

"Mm."

"Do you want to talk about what happened?"

Hannah felt a rush of gratitude for Jeli and Clancy, her two confidantes. "Have I thanked you for always being there for me?"

"Repeatedly."

"Doesn't matter, I'll keep on thanking you, and I'll probably talk your ear off when you're home. But for now, I need to think about something else. So, tell me how the tour's going."

"I understand." The music came back into Jeli's voice. "The tour couldn't be better. I just got back from a book signing at Borders that went on for a full hour longer than it was supposed to, there were so many people in line."

Hannah chuckled. "I told you so. But then, so did everybody else."

Jeli's smile came through the line. "Thank you, sweetie. You've always been one of my best encouragers."

"My pleasure."

For a few beats there was silence across the miles. Then

Hannah said, "You're coming home on Good Friday?"

"I was just thinking about that. I have one more signing at Barnes & Noble in L.A. tomorrow afternoon that I really need to make, but I think I'll push my return flight ahead to Monday morning."

"Don't, Jeli. Not for me. I'm okay, really."

"It's for me too, Jo. I have a strong sense of where I need to be just now."

Hannah felt the relief of waking from a nightmare. She expelled a deep breath before she said, "Thank you. I had no idea how much I wanted you home till you said that."

She heard Jeli's loving smile. "I'm glad to do it. Maybe I can intervene a bit with the pressure you're getting from Rose."

"If any living person can, it's you. Let me meet your plane."

"No, that won't be necessary. I'll take the shuttle or ask Celeste to come for me."

"Speaking of Celeste—I've been wondering, does she know about me?"

"If you mean have I told her, the answer's no, of course not. But as for what she knows intuitively, I suspect it's quite a lot."

"Mm. I guess I do too."

"Are you wondering if you can trust her, Jo?"

"Not really. I guess it's simply the idea of one more person knowing about me."

"With Celeste, you could think of it as one more person supporting you."

"But then I'd probably have to deal with Pop and Michael and Matthew finding out, and I see the whole thing snowballing out of control. When that happens, all I want to do is run for the hills. And this Shepherdess business, on top of everything else! I wish I had run for the hills years ago." Hannah could hear Jeli's quiet compassion. "Anyway, I can't wait to see you. You always help me feel like I've got my feet on the ground, the way Grampa did."

"You, my dear Hannah, are one of the most solidly-grounded people I know."

After they said goodbye, Hannah replaced the receiver, finished her drink, turned off the lights and the gas fire and headed for her bedroom.

Hannah read the latest mystery novel by Elizabeth George until after eleven o'clock, then finally turned off the bedside lamp and settled back, cocooning her head in her goosedown pillows.

She lay there for a while with her eyes open, staring into the darkness, thoughts and images swirling in her mind. She wondered about the boy, Micah. Why had she been sent specifically for him? What made his life any more important than the lives of all the others on that jetliner? She felt the fear again, the pain, the chaos, heard again the screams.

She remembered again the man named Ethan. Were his eyes blue? She guessed they were, a deep sapphire blue. And his hair, she thought it was golden brown like her father's. He was tall; she liked that. And she liked his face, its openness, its strength. *Ethan*. She had always loved that name, Grampa's name. "Ethan," she said aloud, liking the feel of it.

Clancy padded to her from his favorite spot beside the bedroom's easy chair. Hannah heard his collar tags jingling and rested her right hand on top of the blanket, knowing what was coming. Soon her hand was lifted by his cold, moist nose nuzzling its way underneath.

"Just for a few minutes, pal," she said, moving over to make room for him.

Seconds later he was lying beside her on top of the covers, his head inches from hers, his breath moist warmth against her face.

For the first time since the ride home, Hannah began to weep. She rested her cheek on Clancy's head, her tears flowing into his thick, silky coat.

"Oh, Clance," she murmured, "I'm so lost."

Later, when her tears stopped, Hannah knew she was still a long way from sleep. She nudged Clancy off the bed and turned on the lamp. After throwing on an old sweatshirt over her pajamas and slipping into socks and Birkenstocks, she went to the kitchen, poured herself a few fingers of Jack Daniels, grabbed some dog biscuits for Clancy and the jar of cashews, and headed to her studio. There she sat cross-legged on the chair in front of her Macintosh, put a disk of Russian choral music in her CD ROM, and played different variations of solitaire for over an hour.

Finally, when the whisky was gone and her eyelids were drooping, she and Clancy returned to the bedroom. She pulled off her sweatshirt and socks, kissed Clancy soundly on the top of his warm head, and crawled under her covers.

She lay in bed for a while, sleep still eluding her, her mind drifting back to the last real conversation she had had with Grampa, a few days before his death.

Having refused continual morphine infusion, he had been in what he called a grace period, a brief time of unexplained remission from pain. Hannah sat on a straight chair beside his bed, pressing his skeletal palm to her cheek.

"I can't let you leave me, Grampa."

"It's only my body that's leaving, honey."

She had been unable to stifle a sob, and he had stroked her hair as she wept into the soft blue cotton blanket.

"There, there, my love. Everything will be all right."

"You always say that," she said, sniffing, pulling a tissue from the box on the bedside stand. "And it's not true. Not this time. The only way for this to be all right is for my hands to start burning so I can heal you."

"God has his reasons," Grampa said, putting a forefinger under Hannah's chin and lifting it so that he could see her eyes. Whatever he saw there made him wince.

Hannah wrapped her hands around his and took it from under her chin. "I'm sorry," she said, kissing his blue-white skin. "I'm so sorry my lack of faith hurts you. That's the last thing in the world I want."

"All these years, my dearest Johannah," said Grampa, his voice quavering. "All these years we've had together, all this joy—remember that. I know you can see God in that. Don't let your mind dwell on what's happening to me now."

Hannah said nothing, gazing into his faded turquoise eyes that had once been the mirror image of her own.

"Remember the love and the joy. Someday you'll see God in the pain as well, but for now, just think on the love."

"If only I could understand *why*, Grampa. I have all this love for you, and if God is in that, why doesn't he let me use these gifts of mine now, when it really matters to me?"

Grampa took in and expelled a few shallow breaths. "You know I've never been one to presume to understand these mysteries, honey. Let other people give you the answers—as I'm sure they will, although none will satisfy you. But someday, I pray before long, you'll find the answers you need within yourself." Stringing so many words together appeared to exhaust him, and he lay his head back against the pillows, closing his eyes.

Hannah thought he was asleep when he softly added, "Bloom where you're planted, honey. Acceptance, that's the key."

The key, Hannah thought now, lying in her own bed, feeling rage stirring in her heart. It's the key to having no control over my life, that's all.

Gradually her mind was pulled down into the whirlpool of sleep, and the last conscious thought she had was a childlike wondering if she might still be afraid of her own shadow.

Chapter Thirteen

Hannah woke the next morning flushed, her pulse racing and her breath coming in short gasps. She had been dreaming about Ethan—passionate, erotic dreams in which she experienced more sexual pleasure than she had ever known in her waking life.

She groaned and turned onto her stomach, pulling a pillow over her head.

Having such a dream was nothing new; only Ethan was new. In fact, this was the first such dream in which Hannah's partner was someone she had actually met. Previously they had been actors, politicians or famous sports figures. One time the lovemaking had been with a living, breathing version of a raven-haired man she had seen in a nineteenth-century painting at the Philadelphia Museum of Art.

These vivid dreams had begun when Hannah was only fifteen, years before the night she finally relinquished her virginity. The actual experience was pitiful, next to what she had known in her dreams, as were all her moments of lovemaking with other men over the following years. Up to and including Craig.

As deeply as she could care about a man, she was unwilling to release her self-control long enough to achieve sexual fulfillment. Except in her dreams.

Silenced by shame, she spoke to no one about the problem. Instead, she did some research, and with the help of a little book she found at the Chester County Library, she became proficient at controlling specific muscles in order to feign the deepest sexual pleasures. Over time, she grew confident of her ability to "fake it", and felt certain that Craig believed her fulfilled by their lovemaking.

This morning all she felt was disgust with herself. She wished she could go back to sleep and undo the dream, but knew there would be no more sleep now. Without checking the clock, she pegged the hour at six. Time to get started on the day.

Hannah had woken at six almost every morning in the past several years, no matter what she had done the night before or how late she had stayed awake. She felt lucky that she needed little sleep, and lumped this personal quirk together with her ability to eat unwisely without apparent consequence, and to keep her drinking secret and under control.

She sensed movement and lifted the pillow to find Clancy standing beside the bed, smiling and wagging his tail. "Good morning to you, too," she murmured as she tenderly stroked his head. "I sure would be lonely without you, my friend."

A few minutes later, Hannah and Clancy were at odds in the mudroom. He had watched her pick up his leash and her umbrella and flip the switch that turned off the invisible fencing. In response, he glared at her, sat firmly on his rear end, and somehow bulked himself to twice his weight.

"Clancy! It's raining," Hannah said, unnecessarily. "I refuse to let you out for your run and then have to spend forty-five minutes washing you and drying you and brushing you out. You're coming out with me on a leash, like it or not. You hear me?"

Clancy said nothing, just continued to glare.

Looking at him, Hannah unbent a little. She squatted in front of him and began to stroke his silky ears. "Look, I'm sorry. I know you're disappointed. You want to go for our run, and so do I. And I know you love to run in the rain. But we're going to have to compromise, that's all there is to it." She cupped his jaw in her hand and stroked the top of his head. "How about, we'll run an extra mile the next clear morning if you'll just do it my way today. Okay?" She could see that he was softening, his eyelids were drooping in pleasure. "I'll even let you use the treadmill."

The treadmill offer did the trick. Within minutes Hannah had taken Clancy out near the creek, waited patiently while he did his business, and taken him back in again, removing his leash and drying his feet. Then they headed for the home gym that Hannah had created in what had been Sophie Muller's bedroom. There, to the accompaniment of U2, Aaron Copland and Bruce Springsteen, Hannah worked out on the Nautilus while Clancy ran on the treadmill. Then she spent twenty minutes on the treadmill and another twenty on the exercycle before she headed to her bathroom for a shower.

With the music and the physical exertion, Hannah's mind had gone into autopilot. Now, drying her hair after her shower, her thoughts were again spinning with yesterday's plane crash and Bill Tyler, underscored by her erotic dream experience with the man named Ethan.

It's going to be mighty tough to stay present in this day, she thought, as she dressed in washed-out jeans and a buttery-soft, blue silk shirt. Slipping on a U. of Penn sweatshirt and old sneakers, she set the house alarm, clucked her tongue at Clancy and went with him to the Jeep. He proudly assumed his place of honor, riding shotgun in the front passenger seat.

Hannah decided to collect yesterday's mail on her way to buy the Sunday papers, so took the route past Papa's house to the mailboxes at the end of his long, winding driveway. She tossed into the back seat the letters and catalogs from both boxes. There was nothing of interest, and she would sort it out later.

When she entered the Wawa, a few miles east on Birmingham Road, and smiled a hello to Sally, the forty-something employee manning the cash register, Hannah suddenly wanted to turn and run. Sally was staring at her with an aggressive "Aha!" scrawled on her face.

"I knew it!" Sally said. "I told Andy this morning, that picture is the spittin' image of Dr. Kirkland, I said, and I was right!"

"What picture is that, Sally?" Hannah heard the tremor in her own voice.

"Front page of the *Inquirer*, Doc. Look here." Sally held it up triumphantly. "That dame they're talkin' about from the plane crash yesterday. If that isn't you, I'm a monkey's uncle!" Sally barked a laugh that reverberated in Hannah's ears.

Andy came out from behind the deli counter and stood at Hannah's side. "I told her, Miz Kirkland. I said it looks like that actress—"

"Julia Roberts," interrupted Sally. "But, kid, you got such a crush on Julia Roberts, you think everybody looks like her."

Curious onlookers had gathered around to judge for themselves, and Hannah felt everyone's eyes on her as she looked at the astonishing likeness of herself on the front page of the *Philadelphia Inquirer*. Her heart rose into her throat and her eyes lost focus.

"'Course, I know you're not her," Sally said. "You got those green eyes and that red hair. But still, you gotta admit she's your double, 'cept for that."

Hannah forced a smile. "Oh, I don't know, Sally," she said, trying to put some lightness into her voice. "I think Andy might be onto something here. Maybe it *was* Julia Roberts."

Andy beamed and blushed.

Sally scowled. "Well, like I said, she's not you, but I wondered, you got a sister 'round Gettysburg, Doc?"

"Afraid not. Only my brothers right down the road from here."

The onlookers were losing interest and returning to their shopping. Andy went back to the deli counter.

"Too bad, 'cause you could've collected that fifty grand."

Hannah stopped breathing again and glued her unseeing eyes to the newspaper. "Fifty grand," she croaked. "A lot of money."

"You're telling me!" Sally said. "It was that rich black mother, you know? The one who swears her kid was dead till this blond comes along? She's the one put up the fifty grand."

"Why on earth?" Hannah said to herself, but out loud.

"I bet she's one of them Shepherdess people, 'cause where else does a black broad like her get that kind of money? Of course, she's sayin' she just wants to thank this blond, but I don't believe it. Who puts a reward on somebody's head to say thank you?"

Unnerved to find herself in agreement with any thoughts that came out of this woman's mouth, Hannah murmured a weak, "Mm," and moved off toward the coffee machine, the folded *Inquirer* tucked under her arm. On legs that felt as supportive as overcooked spaghetti, she filled her twenty-ounce travel mug with black coffee and picked up a box of Entenmann's chocolate-covered donuts, along with a copy of the *Daily Local News*.

Back at the checkout counter, Hannah was grateful to find Sally busy in conversation with another customer. She left more than enough money on the counter for her purchases, and somehow made it back to her Jeep without collapsing.

As soon as they were home and she had dried Clancy's feet, Hannah set the house's perimeter alarm. Then she took her newspapers, donuts and coffee into the greatroom, planning to finally watch the news on the large-screen TV. She opened the TV cabinet doors and was reaching for the remote control when, from the corner of her eye, she saw a quick, furtive movement outside among the trees. Her heart jumped into her throat and she found herself unable to do anything but gather her newspapers and food and hurry from the room, remembering to breathe only when she reached the hall behind the kitchen. There, she stood frozen, straining to catch any sounds beyond the pounding of her heart.

Clancy was in the kitchen doorway looking at her, his head cocked in curiosity. Then he padded happily into the hall and stood beside her, wagging his tail and gazing up at her expectantly as if to say, "Okay. Whatever's going on, count me in."

Thankful as she was for Clancy's presence, Hannah could not even summon a smile for him. Instead, she put the donuts, newspapers and coffee mug on the floor and sat with her back pressed to the wall, drawing her knees up against her chest and wrapping her arms around them. Clancy lay down beside her.

This is insanity, she thought. Total paranoia, hiding out here in the hall of my own home. I'm being ridiculous. It was probably just a squirrel out there in the trees. There's no way Bill Tyler could have found me yet. And he'd call me first, he wouldn't just show up here and prowl around. Would he? Anyway, he doesn't know where I live. Or does he?

"God, I need to talk to somebody," she whispered.

She thought about the time and knew it was around eight-thirty; Rose would already be on her way to the Tel Hai Nursing Home to visit her mother and Jeli was probably still asleep in California time.

What I need is a therapist, she thought. A woman I can trust, who knows all about me and is consistently there for me, always ready and able to help me sort everything out. She should be in her mid-fifties, but youthful, athletic, and with no husband or kids to consume her time. In fact, Hannah thought wryly, why doesn't she just move into Grampa's empty room and have no life beyond helping me with mine? That's not asking too much, is it?

Hannah noticed Clancy then, inching his muzzle ever closer to the box of donuts, his nostrils quivering with anticipation, even as he kept his eyes angled on his master. The sight of him in his stealthy pursuit of chocolate restored her to herself, and a ripple of laughter escaped from her throat.

"Oh, Clance," she said, putting her arms around him and resting her head on his. "You're my touchstone, did you know that?"

Hannah checked the back of the house through the greatroom's wall of windows and found nothing alarming. She was disgusted with herself for being so nervous. Nevertheless, she decided to watch the news in her bedroom where she could close the blinds and give herself all the privacy she wanted.

"All the privacy any self-respecting fugitive could need, eh, Clancy?" she said as she sat cross-legged in her bedroom's easy chair and reached for the TV's remote control.

Clancy rested his head on Hannah's crossed ankles and gazed up at her prayerfully.

"Okay, pal. You can bag the melodrama." Hannah scratched the top of his head and handed him a donut. "You may have one, but only one. Don't even think about asking for more."

She skimmed through the TV channels, finding nothing about the plane crash and eventually settling on CNN. They were giving a stock market report, so she muted the TV sound, took a donut for herself and began to peruse the newspapers.

Hannah read that the cause of the accident had not yet been made public, but that there was no indication of terrorist involvement. NTSB investigators hoped to release a thorough report by the end of the week, with the complete cooperation of the flight's captain, co-pilot and navigator, all of whom had survived the crash.

She drew in an anxious breath when she read the number of people who had died in the plane crash: seventy-nine, with all but seven of them in the rear section that had broken off on impact. Hannah vividly recalled the seven crash victims in the front section of the plane who had been beyond help. They were etched permanently in her mind with all the others not healed through her over the years.

Glancing at the TV screen, she saw a young male reporter standing in the foreground of the plane's wreckage. She unmuted the sound and heard him commenting on the fact that, of the more than one hundred survivors, not one had suffered an injury requiring hospitalization or any sort of significant medical treatment. "The remarkably stable condition of virtually all of the crash survivors has been attributed to the blond woman who is being called the 'angel of Angler's field.' It was in this newly-plowed field of Boyd and Myra Angler yesterday that seventy-nine men, women and children lost their lives, and where the mysterious blond saved the lives of countless others. Correspondent Marianna Rodriguez reports from the Church of St. John the Baptist a few miles south of here."

An attractive Hispanic reporter appeared on camera, standing in front of a gray stone building. "Thank you, Jeff. Hundreds of people are gathering this morning in this impressive, century-old church, for a special service to honor the victims of yesterday's plane crash. Among the congregants today are family and friends of those who died, along with many of the crash survivors and their loved ones."

The camera focus broadened to include a middle-aged man and woman whose faces appeared ravaged with grief. "With me now are Joel and Linda Walston, whose son Joel, Jr., was one of those who died in yesterday's tragic accident." The reporter turned to the couple. "Let me say first that we are all terribly sorry for your loss."

The husband nodded somberly; the wife stared at the camera like a rabbit caught in car headlights.

The reporter continued, "Mrs. Walston, you were telling me that you and your husband are distressed by the attention being given to the survivors rather than to those like your son who were not so fortunate."

"It's just too…" said the woman, her voice so low and broken that the rest of her words were lost.

The reporter held the microphone closer to Mrs. Walston and gently asked if she could speak up a bit.

"I said it's just too hard to take. Our boy is dead. Only seventeen, and he's dead and gone forever. But all anybody's thinking about is the ones who lived." She turned and looked into the camera as her voice rose in anguish. "Why is that? What about our child, our only son? Doesn't he matter as much as the ones who lived?" She closed her eyes and leaned into her husband.

"Mr. Walston?" said the reporter. "Did you want to add anything?"

"Just that I don't believe that woman was any angel, because if she was, why didn't she save our boy and all the others?" He looked directly at the camera then, as if he were challenging someone to respond to him. "Wasn't my son just as good as the rest? If God really had a hand in this, wouldn't they *all* still be alive?"

The reporter turned to face the camera as she said, "Mr. Walston has voiced questions heard from many of those who lost loved ones in Angler's field yesterday. Early this morning, in her home on Philadelphia's affluent Main Line, a very different perspective was offered by Mrs. Lily Severill, mother of five-year-old Micah Severill and the source of the fifty-thousand-dollar reward for the identity of the so-called Angler's angel."

The reporter went on to explain that Mrs. Severill owned and operated a successful real estate firm in Philadelphia, and had been widowed six months before, when her husband and partner in the firm had died suddenly of a pulmonary embolism.

And there was Lily, with Micah on her lap, in a tight camera shot that artfully revealed nothing of her home. In Lily's eyes, Hannah saw both exhaustion and a luminous serenity. The serenity unnerved Hannah; she realized that Lily was not going to be easily deterred from her resolve.

"Mrs. Severill," said Marianna Rodriguez' voice, off camera, "you've heard the claims that the Angler's angel was no angel at all because seventy-nine people did lose their lives in yesterday's crash. I understand you have more than one reason for offering this extraordinary reward for the identity of someone who may simply have been a helpful passerby."

"No, she was certainly not just a passerby. I don't know why she didn't heal everyone, but then, of course, I don't expect to know why things happen in God's world as they do."

Hannah whispered, "Amen to that, Lily."

Lily continued, "And I won't waste time pondering questions for which there are no answers. You see, I know that my son Micah *was* dead. I gave him CPR and so did a flight attendant, and there were virtually no signs of life in my son."

Micah had his head against his mother's chest and was staring at something or someone beyond the camera. Lily stroked his cheek as she spoke.

"But isn't it possible, Mrs. Severill, that you were in shock and unable to adequately determine your son's condition?"

"I admit I probably was in shock, but not until *after* I was certain that Micah was dead. And then the young woman appeared. She knew our names, so I thought she was part of the flight crew. Then she placed her hand very deliberately on Micah's still chest, and I could sense his life returning to him, through her."

"That's a compelling story, Mrs. Severill, but the question remains. Why offer money to find this woman who clearly does not want to be found?"

"For two reasons. I believe she was a divine being sent by God—possibly even the reincarnation of Christ, so long predicted and anticipated with this new millennium."

Pain stabbed into the back of Hannah's neck.

The reporter asked, "Does this mean you are a member of the Disciples of the Shepherdess?"

Lily shook her head. "No, I didn't even know much about their beliefs until yesterday. I do think the coincidences are remarkable, and I obviously believe Christ may be reincarnated as a woman, but my hope with the reward is to encourage this woman to step forward so that the world can see for themselves that God exists and is deeply involved in our lives."

"And you say there is another reason for offering the reward?"

Here the camera focus tightened even further on Lily's face.

"Yes. For me, the more important reason. I have another son, Isaiah, eighteen months old, who was born with a defective heart."

The TV screen filled with a photograph of a child apparently asleep in a hospital crib. The skin of his bloated body was more gray than brown, and his arms were strapped to boards, preventing him from bending his elbows and pulling out any of the tubes to which he was attached. Words at the bottom of the screen identified the child as Isaiah Severill.

Hannah felt as if the floor had opened up beneath her.

Lily was saying, "This is a photo of Isaiah that was taken late last night at the Mayo Clinic Transplant Center in downtown Rochester, Minnesota. Isaiah has been hospitalized at the Center for over a month, awaiting a donor heart."

Lily's face appeared again, with a toll-free phone number displayed at the bottom of the TV screen. "So you see, my hope and my prayer is that this woman can be found and persuaded to save my other son, as she has saved Micah."

Hannah used the remote to turn off the TV and then stared at the blank screen, feeling as trapped and helpless as Lily's youngest son.

She leaned back in the chair and closed her eyes, imagining Rose exulting, exclaiming: *Here's more proof, Jo! Here's perfect proof that God wants you to come out into the open with your gifts!*

"Shit!" Hannah said aloud. Then, at the top of her voice, she hurled every filthy epithet she could think of at the blank white ceiling, stopping only when she felt Clancy's weight pressing against her legs. He was trembling, so she sat up and hugged him.

"Sorry, Clance. Sorry, pal."

Apparently reassured, Clancy lay down, turned onto his back and pawed at Hannah's hand. She obediently leaned forward and moved her ministrations to his favorite scratch spot at the indentation just below his ribcage.

"I envy you, Clancy. I wish all I needed was a belly scratch."

Hannah stayed there awhile, scratching Clancy and wondering what she was supposed to do, where she could turn.

Grampa's voice in her mind said, "Go to church, honey."

She silently answered him. *That's not always the solution to everything, Grampa. I need something more practical right now.*

"Just go to church, honey," she heard again.

It made perfect sense that Grampa was saying this to her. He had been adamant about getting to church every Sunday. Even during his year of cancer, he rarely missed a service. In fact, he died on a Sunday morning in early March of 2002, just after asking Sophie and Hannah to help him prepare for church.

"Anything for you, Grampa," she said aloud, and imagined she heard him chuckling.

Twenty minutes later she left the house, having changed into a fawn-colored shirt and slacks, and slipped into Mephistos and her black Burberry. Steering her Jeep along the drive to Birmingham Road, she was surprised that, in the midst of her despondency, she felt a feathering of pleasure over going to the church where she and Grampa had worshipped for ten years. Since Grampa's funeral, she had felt obliged to attend Church of the Loving Shepherd only once, this past Christmas Eve, but not until this morning had she looked forward to being there.

Hannah was grateful that the greeting she received at Loving Shepherd was friendly, but not overbearing. Settling into a seat at the back and to the right of a young family she didn't recognize, she felt her neck and shoulders begin to release their tightness.

You may have been right, Grampa, she thought. And felt his smile.

Then, not ten minutes into the service, the hairs rose on the back of her neck and she knew that someone was staring at her. Unthinkingly, she glanced across the room and locked eyes with a man. Ethan! She gasped audibly and sank so low in her seat that she nearly slipped off the edge. Wildly she wondered how she could get out of the church immediately without calling attention to herself. She felt ridiculous, and her lower back protested her awkward position on the chair, but she couldn't see Ethan and was hoping he couldn't see her.

Anger coursed through her like fire in dry wood. Grampa had betrayed her in bringing her here today. She railed at him in her mind. *What are you doing to me? You and the lordgodamighty, you're working together now, are you, sending me out to do your bidding, like crawling out on the limb of a tree to rescue a kitten, and now you're sawing off the branch. And I'm supposed to humbly say,* thy will be done? *Like hell!*

I've got to get out of here *now*!

Some shaky minutes later, when the congregation stood up to sing a hymn, Hannah ducked her head, slipped out through a doorway, grabbed her raincoat in the foyer and left the building without glancing back. To her horror, she heard footsteps hurrying behind her.

She was nearing her Jeep when Ethan called out to her, "Please don't run away from me."

His voice, with its strangely familiar timbre, took Hannah's breath away, and she turned to face him on knees gone to Jell-O. "I'm not…" She couldn't complete the lie.

"I saw you here Christmas Eve," he went on. His eyes *were* a deep sapphire-blue and just as compelling as she had remembered, and his hair was the same golden-brown of her father's. "And I saw you yesterday, didn't I? It *was* you."

Hannah couldn't seem to put a sentence together. "What… ?"

"After you'd gone yesterday, I remembered where I'd first seen you. I wanted to meet you at Christmas, but you left in a hurry then too, didn't you. God, I hoped you'd be here today." He moved closer as he spoke.

Hannah stepped back and untangled her tongue. "Why are you doing this?"

He looked abashed and held his palms out to her. "But I couldn't let you go without—"

"So what do you want?"

"Only to talk with you, I swear. At least tell me your name, tell me how I can contact you."

She meant to ask, *Why should I trust you?* but before she could, Ethan said, "I can't convince you to trust me, and I don't want to ask anyone who you are. But I can't let you go… without…" His words trailed off as he seemed to lose his own ability to speak.

Hannah was looking into his eyes, searching his heart, and the knowledge washed over her in that moment that she could trust him completely.

"My name is Hannah. But, please, let's leave it at that for now. This is much too…"

"I understand."

"Do you?"

"I think so. I think privacy is as essential to you as breathing."

She suddenly felt lightheaded and slid her gaze away from his. "Yes."

He said, simply, "Hannah," and for the first time in her life she thought her own name held beauty.

"Will you get in touch with me?" he asked, holding out a blue-gray card to her.

She took it and tucked it into her coat pocket.

"That has my home and office phone numbers. Please say you'll call me."

She looked at his mouth—his eyes were too intense—and was embarrassed by the sudden impulse to kiss it. "I'll call. But please don't talk to anyone else about me."

"You have my word."

She nodded and was moving to her car as he said, "Thank you, Hannah. It means so much to me, finding you."

Exiting Loving Shepherd's driveway, the blood rushed to her cheeks as the words came unbidden to her mind, *Me too, you, Ethan*.

Chapter Fourteen

Hannah spent the remainder of that rainy Sunday morning in front of the fire, fruitlessly trying to concentrate on anything other than the plane crash and its aftermath, and on anyone other than Ethan.

She studied the card he had given her, lingering over the Ph.D. after his name, and the words "Clinical Psychologist" in the lower right-hand corner. She repeated his name aloud—*Ethan Quinn*—relishing the sound of it, then berating herself for acting like a lovestruck teenager.

Three times she read the same page of the Elizabeth George novel before she finally set it aside.

She stared at the phone, wishing there was someone to call. She didn't want to talk to Rose, and she knew Jeli was out of reach, in transit between San Francisco and Los Angeles. The rest of her family were traveling home from Wyoming. There was no one, and she felt a sharp pang of loneliness.

"I guess I *could* call Ethan," she said aloud to Clancy, sleeping soundly beside her on the floor. He stirred, lifted his handsome head and half-opened his eyes to look at her briefly before expelling a deep breath and settling back into sleep. "Don't think much of that idea, do you, pal. You're right, too pushy."

She had no appetite for lunch; instead she sipped a generous two fingers of Jack Daniels, neat, and dozed for a while on the floor by the fire, dreaming that she had stayed home yesterday instead of going to the field with the twin blue silos. The child, Micah, had died, and Grampa was weeping with her when she was awakened by the ringing of the front doorbell.

Clancy barked happily, but a chill ran through Hannah. It couldn't be Rose, who knew Hannah's dislike of unexpected guests and would always call before stopping by. Her mouth dry and her neck aching with tension, she went to the door and peered through the peephole. Standing outside on the doorstep was the last person in the world Hannah wanted to see, today or ever: Vivian.

For years after that July day in 1982 when Papa had ordered her off the property, Vivian had continued to haunt Hannah's nightmares but had been only peripheral in her waking life. Although Vivian had remained in the area, Papa had kept his promise and prevented her from coming near Hannah. Then Vivian's son, Bruce, had been killed in a hunting accident, and Papa's heart had softened toward his stepmother. He had begun speaking with Vivian from time to time, and Hannah had become accustomed on occasion to hearing about what was going on in Vivian's life. Vivian married again in 1989 to an older man, Wilbur Black, who apparently was genial, stone deaf and half blind, and who died shortly after Grampa moved east from Cincinnati in 1992.

Once Grampa was close at hand, year round, Hannah shed all fear of Vivian, now the widow Black—or the "Black widow", as Grampa had dubbed her. He had accurately taken Vivian's measure the first time he met her, on one of her impromptu drop-ins at Papa's house, and had later said that people like Vivian live forever because God doesn't want them. Hannah had laughed with him, but thought that, like most good jokes, there was some truth in it.

It had been clear to Hannah that Vivian wanted to be a part of her stepson's life again, to once again be a grandmother to Hannah and now to young Michael and Matthew. It had also been clear that this would not happen. There was a coldness that clung to Vivian wherever she went; children, especially, were sensitive to it and kept their distance from her. And, because Vivian no longer had any sort of hold over her, Hannah managed to tolerate the old woman.

Then Grampa had died and all of Hannah's Vivian-centered fears and resentments had returned with a thud. Ever since, she had gone to extreme lengths to avoid the Black widow.

And now, today of all days, when Hannah hadn't a spare iota of strength to draw on, here was Vivian, glaring at the peephole as if challenging her to try to pretend she wasn't at home.

Dammit! Hannah thought. If only I'd put my Jeep in the

garage.

She sucked in a breath, took a firm grip of Clancy's collar and opened the door.

"Hello, Johannah," Vivian said, a tight little smile unpuckering her kewpie-doll lips. "May I come in?"

"This isn't a good time for me, Vivian. I'm expecting company."

"I'll only take a few minutes, I assure you."

Hannah opened the door wider and Vivian entered, her step nearly as sure as it had been twenty-one years ago.

Grampa's right, Hannah thought. This woman is going to live forever.

Ironically, nearly all of the physical changes in Vivian over the past two decades appeared to be good ones. She had lost her excess weight, her permed hair was longer and softer, its color a more natural blond, and her skin, which she had religiously protected from the sun, had rewarded her by remaining unmarred and barely wrinkled. Only her mouth, with its deep lines of bitterness on either side, betrayed what Hannah saw as her true character.

This afternoon there was something different in Vivian's eyes that Hannah could not quite identify, but that she associated with illness.

Clancy began a low, rumbling growl, curling his lip back from his upper teeth.

"Behave yourself, boy," Hannah said, secretly glad that Clancy, like Grampa, had quickly taken an accurate measure of Vivian.

"Oh, dear," Vivian said, stepping back nervously. "I'm afraid I'm allergic to dogs."

Without a word, Hannah led Clancy to the back hall, scruffed his ears and shut the kitchen door. When she returned, Vivian was standing in the greatroom.

"Your house is beautiful, Johannah," Vivian said. "I wonder if you realize this is the first time I've been here."

"Yes, I do."

"Yes," Vivian repeated as she pulled out and sat on one of the dining table chairs. "I hope you don't mind if I sit down for a moment."

Hannah said nothing, and remained standing.

Vivian turned her round gray eyes to Hannah as she said, "I won't beat around the bush, Johannah. I know you are the angel of Angler's field."

Hannah felt steamrolled, and silently shot up a quick prayer for composure. "I don't know what you're talking about."

"Of course you do. I've known about you since you were a child. I've been certain since that day you healed my broken arm, the day your poor fawn died."

It was all Hannah could do to restrain herself from smacking this woman in the face. You mean the day you *killed* my poor fawn! she thought. But she neither moved nor spoke.

"When I heard reports of yesterday's plane crash and the healings brought about by a mysterious young woman, I wondered if it had been you. Then I saw the artist's rendering, and I knew for certain."

"That drawing looks like me and a thousand other women."

"But they don't live in Pennsylvania, do they? Where were you yesterday, tell me that."

"I was right here all day," Hannah lied.

"It doesn't matter what you say. I know it was you, and I was content to keep that knowledge to myself." Vivian cleared her throat and pulled a travelpack of tissues from her handbag, removing one and holding it against her forehead. "I have the most awful headache, Johannah. Would you be kind enough to give me a clock of water?"

"A clock of water?"

"What?"

"You asked for a clock of water."

"I did? Well, of course, what I meant is a... a *glass* of water."

Hannah was surprised by a twinge of pity for the old woman, surprised even to think of her as old. She went to the kitchen and returned quickly with the water.

Vivian thanked her and took a few sips before she continued, "As I was saying, I was willing to keep what I knew about you to myself, although I was troubled by the claims being made by the Disciples of the Shepherdess, raising you up in a very inappropriate light. Then this morning I heard about the, uh… that person, that black person, I can't recollect her name, the one who's offering all that money to find you, and I saw the picture of that other son of hers. That's when the Lord spoke to me and told me I was to stop you."

Hannah crossed her arms over her chest as she said, "Stop me from what?"

"It's really quite simple, Johannah. The Lord God Almighty has sent me to tell you that these powers you use, they are not of him. They are of Satan. It was Satan who sent you to that field yesterday, Satan who had you heal that black boy. It is Satan who would lure you with *money*, the root of all evil, to heal that other black boy in… uh, the, uh… that clinic place. You see, it's Satan's will to destroy you, but it's God's will to save you, save you through *me*."

"You're out of your mind."

"You know I speak the truth. I can see it in your face."

"Whatever you think you see in my face is a projection of your own dementia."

"No, Johannah, it's not." Vivian sighed and patted her forehead with another tissue. "The sooner you admit to these things, the sooner we can get on with what needs to be done here."

"And what in the world would that be?" Hannah asked, hating herself for getting hooked into this conversation.

"We need to scourge Satan out of you. There are things you must do to renounce his power."

"I see. You want to *scourge* me. What fun."

"Oh, Johannah, don't make light of this. We must never mock the will of the Lord. If you'll just get on your knees with me now—"

"I don't understand, Vivian. All those lives were saved, so why on earth are you saying that it was Satan's work?"

"I'm not the one saying it, Johannah; the Lord has told me these things. Those lives were saved for Satan's purposes by his work at its most diabolical, masquerading as God's work."

"I see. If the so-called angel had killed people, she would have been doing Satan's work, but since she healed them, she was doing Satan's work in *disguise*. What a bunch of crap!"

"It is not… it's the truth. The Lord has spoken it to me, every word. I can prove it to you, if you'll just bring me a Bible."

"You are too ridiculous, Vivian. After all these years, still trying to force your warped morality down my throat. Don't you have anything better to do?"

"There can be nothing better to do in this world than the Lord's bidding."

"All right, that's enough," Hannah turned to head toward the front door. "I want you to leave now."

Vivian remained where she was. "Please listen to me, Johannah. I'm afraid you will regret it terribly if you don't."

Hannah turned back to her. "I seriously doubt that."

"It's true. You can either accept the Lord's salvation with my help, or take the consequences."

"And what would those consequences be, Vivian?"

Vivian gave a weary sigh. "Believe me, Johannah, I don't want to hurt you. I want to help you. God has ordered me to help you. But if you won't renounce Satan of your own free will, I am to go to Mrs. Lily Severill and tell her who you are."

Hannah was losing it; her hands formed into fists. "What purpose could that possibly serve? Except to get you that big fat reward. Is that what the Lord's will is all about, money for Vivian Black?"

"The money has nothing to do with it. The purpose is that the spotlight would be turned on you and it would become the light of the Lord, and then the truth would be revealed. Satan would be revealed at work in you and his hold over you would be destroyed."

Suddenly, Grampa's voice was in Hannah's mind: *Never mind, honey. This old woman is no more important than flies on a cowpat.*

Hannah took in his words as she struggled to pull herself together. "So. All right. Let me see if I have this straight. You believe that I am the so-called angel who helped yesterday's crash victims. You believe that I am doing Satan's work—in *disguise*, of course. You believe that God has sent you here to free me from Satan. And you believe that if I don't do as you say, you must tell the authorities about me so that I will be stopped, possibly even killed. Is that about it?"

Vivian shook her head. "No, Johannah. You yourself won't be destroyed; that isn't God's will. It's Satan's power *in* you that will be destroyed."

Hannah blew out a breath. "Well, Vivian, thank you so very much for this enlightened message of hope." Hannah moved quickly to the front door and opened it wide. "Now get your ugly ass out of my house."

Vivian was slow to leave the greatroom. As she approached Hannah at the door, she said, "I am sorry to have to do this, Johannah. I don't want to hurt you or your father. But you can't say I haven't warned you."

"No one will believe you, Vivian."

"Of course they will. All they have to do is see you and they'll recognize you. You know I'm right. Why, those crazy Shepherdess people would be on your doorstep so fast, your head will spin."

"Will you get the hell off my property, you old witch!" Hannah gave Vivian a small push between her shoulder blades, reminded suddenly of how often and how hard she had been pushed by this woman.

Hannah closed and locked the front door even as Vivian continued to speak. "You're making a very sad mistake, Johannah. You're not to blame in this unless you turn a blind eye to the Lord God's will."

There was silence for a few beats before Vivian added, "I want to be fair, Johannah, so I will give you one day to see the truth of this. I'll pray for the Lord to open your mind and your eyes, and I'll be in touch with you tomorrow evening for your answer."

When she finally heard Vivian's car head out of the driveway, Hannah leaned her back against the door and then sank to the grayish-brown slate of the foyer. She hugged herself, feeling as if she were about to break into a million pieces.

In her mind she screamed, *Damn you to hell, Vivian! God damn you!*

She heard Clancy pawing at the hall door and hurried to him, holding his warm body and welcoming his slurpy kisses. Within minutes they went out for a run.

Mindless of the chill and the drizzle and mud, mindless of everything but the sensation of her body performing under her control, she ran with Clancy by her side for close to an hour. Two-thirds of the way through, she achieved the high she sought—that timeless euphoria where the world receded and every physical movement became effortless. Once there, it seemed she could continue endlessly, but the rain began again in earnest and washed away the high.

When they were home again, Hannah kept her mind numb by working hard on Clancy, bathing him, drying him and brushing out his coat. By the time she was done, the sweat had dried on her body, so she threw on old warm-ups and went to the greatroom, sitting in the sofa and staring sightlessly out the wall of windows as she finished off the box of chocolate-covered donuts. Then she returned to the kitchen, rummaged for the necessary ingredients, and baked a small batch of Tollhouse cookies, ignoring Clancy's pleading eyes and eating every one of them herself, warm and melty from the oven, washed down with two large glasses of milk. As she licked the last of the chocolate off her fingers, she gagged and fierce pain vised her stomach. She raced to the bathroom and vomited up the whole mess, afterwards remaining on the floor with her head resting on the cold porcelain of the toilet bowl. The tears came then, along with sobs that hurt her throat, tender as it was from the vomiting.

Clancy padded in from the bedroom and began licking her cheek. She put her arms around him and wept into his coat, her heart welcoming his love like the desert welcomes rain. Before long she felt a calm she hadn't experienced all day. She drew back and regarded her golden friend, stroking the sides of his regal head. "How many times is that in the last twenty-four hours, pal? How many times have you put me back together?"

Clancy's eyes began to close under her ministrations.

"I wish you could tell me what to do about all this mess, pal—about that old bitch. I can't stand the thought of her getting money off my back."

As clear as day, Hannah heard Grampa's voice say, "End run, honey. Do an end run around the Black widow."

Hannah was mulling over Grampa's words when the phone

rang. She went to the bedroom and checked the Caller ID screen. It was Rose. She sat on the bed and let the phone ring. When it stopped, she waited a bit and then checked her voice mail, listening to Rose urging her to call immediately; she'd heard the news about Lily Severill's reward. "I know how you're feeling, Jo. Please let me be there for you. Please!"

After she deleted the message, Hannah went to the kitchen and cleaned up the mess she'd made with her cookie binge, then headed to the bathroom for a long shower.

Afterwards, the shower having worked its magic, she knew precisely what she would do, and more or less how she was going to do it. She slipped into black jeans, black loafers, and a black cashmere turtleneck sweater. Pulling her hair back into a green-scrunchied pony tail, she and Clancy left the house.

Chapter Fifteen

A half-hour later, Hannah sat at the desk of her chiropractic office, Clancy lying at her feet as she dialed the toll-free number she'd seen on TV that morning.

"Angel Search," answered a weary female voice.

"I'd like to speak with Mrs. Lily Severill."

"You have information to report?"

"Yes."

"If you will give it to me, with your name and number, I'll pass it along to Mrs. Severill."

"I need to speak to her personally."

"I'm sorry, miss, but we are handling all calls for Mrs. Severill."

Hannah had foreseen this. "All right, then. I'll give you a message for her and call again in five minutes. I believe she'll want to handle my call herself."

"Do you have any idea how many calls we've had today? Mrs. Severill can't possibly—"

"Fine. Will you please just give her my message? Tell her I still have the doll my mother gave me."

"What?"

Slowly and deliberately, Hannah repeated, "Please tell Mrs. Severill that I still have the doll my mother gave me."

"That's the message?"

"Yes."

"And your name is?"

"I'll call back. Five minutes."

"But—"

Hannah replaced the receiver and leaned back in her chair, propping her feet on the desk. She remained there, rocking and idly stroking Clancy for five minutes, trying not to think.

When she again dialed the toll-free number, a man's voice answered, "Angel Search, may I help you?"

"I left a message for Mrs. Severill about a doll."

"Yes, yes, hang on, one minute."

The line went on hold and Hannah wondered if they were trying to trace her call. She assumed it was possible, even though her office number was Caller-ID blocked.

In less than ten seconds, a breathless woman's voice came on the line, saying, "This is Lily Severill. You have a message about a doll?"

"Yes. Its name is the same as yours."

There was a stunned silence before Lily said, "It's you! I hardly dared to hope! Will you help me?"

"Are you tracing this call?"

Lily said, "No," but her hesitation said yes. Hannah hung up.

A few minutes later she called again, and Lily came on the line immediately.

"Please don't hang up!" Lily cried. "I've stopped the tracing, please believe me!"

Hannah did. "All right. Where are you now?"

"Where am I? Why, at my offices in Philadelphia. Where are *you*?"

"I want to speak with you at your home, and I want the same guarantee not to attempt tracing my number."

"At my home. All right. I... let me see... I can be there within an hour."

"Fine. Give me the number there."

Lily recited a phone number, then said, "You *will* call me, won't you?"

"Yes, I'll call. But one more thing. I want you to shut down this toll-free number and let the media know that you're withdrawing the offered reward."

"Gladly. I'll tell them you've called—"

"No! Absolutely not. Tell them nothing until we've talked further except that you're withdrawing the reward."

"All right. Whatever you say. I'll have my staff—"

Hannah firmly replaced the receiver, and looked at Clancy. "Well, pal, the fat's in the fire now. No turning back. So what'll we do for sixty minutes?"

She decided to work on reports some of her patients needed

for their health insurance coverage, and was able to reduce the stack of these by only three when an hour had passed.

Lily answered on the first ring. "Oh, thank God, I didn't miss your call! My driver ran into traffic on the Schuykill and I was—"

"Lily," Hannah said firmly.

"Yes? Oh. Yes, I'm sorry. I'm not usually rattled like this."

"There are some things we need to discuss."

"Of course. Whatever you want, it's yours, if you'll only help me."

"You've put me in a terrible position with this reward of yours. My privacy and my anonymity are what have kept me sane, and you've threatened them both."

"Oh, Lord, I am sorry. Truly I am."

Hannah thought she could hear genuine remorse in Lily's voice.

"You see... won't you please tell me your name?"

Hannah thought of her mother. "You can call me Elizabeth."

"Elizabeth. Thank you. You see, all I could think about was the hope that you'd heal Isaiah as you did Micah. And then when the calls started coming in—all these crazy people preaching about the second coming or claiming they were you or that they knew you and all I had to do was give them the money and they'd lead me right to you—it's been a nightmare, and I saw what a dreadful mistake I'd made. How can I ever make it up to you?"

The news that "crazy people" were calling in did nothing to relieve Hannah's tension. "Have you canceled the reward?"

"Yes. And shut down the toll-free number."

"All right. That's a start. As soon as possible, I'd like you to set up a news conference, explaining your change of heart. I don't care what reasons you give, just take the focus off of me."

"All right. I can do that. I guess... well, I could say that I've withdrawn the reward, quite honestly, because of the insanity it's caused. And I could... well, no, I *will*. I will give the money to my church in thanksgiving for the life of my son Micah. I'll announce that."

"And when they ask if you're still looking for me?"

"I can tell them I've realized I might be causing trouble for you, and that I couldn't continue to do that in good conscience."

174

"That won't be enough. Somehow, you have to make them think you've changed your mind about… who or what I am."

Lily was silent for a moment, and Hannah's throat tightened as she recalled this woman's resolve.

"But I haven't changed my mind, Elizabeth."

"I'm only asking you to convince the media that you have."

"You require this in order to help me?"

"Yes. I do."

"And you *will* help me?"

"I'll do what I can, but you need to know that I have no control over my… abilities."

Hannah could hear Lily silently absorbing this information.

Eventually, Lily said, "I guess that means you're not—"

Hannah interposed her own choice of words: "Supernatural? Not in any sense."

"And you may not be able to heal Isaiah?"

"I'm afraid I've often been unable to help people—even some I've loved dearly."

"Then why were you there yesterday? How did you know my name, and Micah's? Who *are* you?"

Hannah thought for a moment. "In your interview, didn't you say it's not up to you to explain why things happen as they do in the universe?"

"Yes. In *God's* universe."

"Well, it's not up to me either."

Lily was quiet for a time. Finally, in a voice filled with weariness, she said, "I think I understand, Elizabeth. You don't know why you were sent there yesterday, just as you don't know if you can help Isaiah."

"Yes, that's it."

"But you will try?"

"Yes, I will."

"Well, of course, that's all I could ask. I'm sorry that my hopes were so…"

"It's all right. I'm sure the last eighteen months must have been hell for you."

"Oh… they *have*… complete hell… and yesterday… oh…"

Hannah felt the weight of Lily's pain and grief as she listened to her weeping.

Eventually, Lily began to gain control of herself. "So sorry," she said. "Your kindness, it… well, I'm so accustomed to disaster, the opposite breaks right through my defenses."

"I understand."

"You do, don't you. Oh, how I would love to get to know you, Elizabeth! Could we meet somewhere?"

"I don't think so. At least not until this 'angel search' business is dead and buried, and this Disciple group finds a different Shepherdess."

"Lord! I see now what a terrible thing I've done to you. If it helps, I *have* changed my mind about you, and that's what I'll tell the media."

Hannah felt a small measure of relief. "Thank you."

"It's the least I can do. And you *are* willing to come to the Mayo? Because it would be impossible to move Isaiah in his present condition."

The small relief was engulfed in a wave of fatigue. "I was afraid of that."

Lily hurried on, as if she feared "Elizabeth" would back out. "But aside from moving him, literally everything is possible. The Mayo is just as concerned about privacy as you are."

"Their patients' privacy, I'm sure. But the privacy of visitors?"

"I know this sounds ludicrous, coming from me, but if you'll just come to the Mayo, I'll move heaven and earth to protect your identity."

Hannah and Lily spent the rest of their phone conversation discussing precisely what portions of heaven and earth Lily would need to move.

After she hung up with Lily, Hannah used her office computer to research the availability of flights to Minnesota. She learned that there was an airport in Rochester, specifically serving the Mayo Clinic, but her fears of discovery compelled her to book her trip via Chicago and Minneapolis-St. Paul. She arranged for a rental car to drive the seventy-or-so miles south from the Twin Cities to the Clinic, then called Lily and confirmed only that she would be at the Mayo "sometime this week."

Next, she speed-dialed her chiropractic assistant, Kyla

Morgan.

"Hey there!" said Kyla's sunny voice.

"'Hey there'? Why do I think you were expecting a call from someone else?"

"Boss, is that you? Whatcha doin', calling your lowly C. A. on a Sunday?"

"Being magnanimous, as a matter of fact. How'd you like to have tomorrow, Tuesday and Wednesday off with pay?"

"Glory! Who do I have to kill?"

Hannah laughed, and it felt good.

"No homicide required. But I do need you to reschedule my patients."

"What's up?"

"I've decided to take a little time off. A friend from college has persuaded me to spend a few days with her in Chicago."

"A spontaneous holiday? Wait a minute! How do I know you're really Dr. Johannah Kirkland?"

Hannah laughed again. "Ky, you're good for my soul," she said, imagining Kyla's wide, white smile in her exotic, café-au-lait face. "One thing, you could move some of my patients to Friday if that works for them."

"Good Friday? But—"

"I know, you and Rob are heading for the Poconos. That's fine. I really won't need you in the office. So just reschedule anyone you can to Friday, but make it a short day—say, ten till three. Okay?"

"Okay. Why don't I go over to the office right now and get the appointment book. I can call everybody from here tonight… and you want me to refer emergencies to Janet McGaurn's group as usual?"

"Please. And if you would, phone Dr. McGaurn to alert her that my patients may be calling."

"Consider it done."

"Thanks, Ky."

"My pleasure. And have a great time in the Windy City."

Hannah left the office quickly after she hung up with Kyla, and on the drive home dialed Rose on her cell phone.

"Finally, you called! Are you all right?"

"I'm okay, but in a hurry. I've been at the office and I'm going home for Celeste's van before I head to the airport to pick them up."

"Oh, I forgot they were coming in tonight. Want me to go with you?"

Hannah thought, *God, no!* She said, "No, thanks anyway. I just wanted to let you know what's happening."

"You got in touch with her, didn't you—Mrs. Severill."

Fear felt like a golf ball in Hannah's throat. "How did you know?"

"I just watched her press conference—"

"What'd she say?"

"Don't panic. She didn't say much about you, really, which is why I got suspicious. She said she had a complete change of heart because of all the phone calls that came in today—apparently they were mostly from psychos and religious fanatics. She says she now believes it was God and the power of prayer that restored Micah's life, and that you *were* just a helpful passerby. And she's giving the reward money to her church."

"What about Isaiah?"

"That's why I became convinced that you'd contacted her. She said she has faith that God will heal Isaiah 'just the way he healed Micah.' I figured she was being literal, saying God will heal Isaiah through you. Am I right, Jo?"

Hannah couldn't help being impressed with Rose's intuition. "You are, pretty much, except that she does know I may not be able to help Isaiah."

"So I guess things are working out the way you wanted them to."

Hannah didn't miss the disapproving edge to Rose's words. She thought, not the way *you* wanted, eh Rosie? She said, "So far so good," and decided not to tell Rose about Vivian's threat.

"So when are you heading out to the Mayo Clinic?"

"Tomorrow morning, early."

Immediately, there was excitement in Rose's voice. "Oh! Let me go with you! God, how I'd love to be there when you heal that poor little boy!"

"I can't, Rose. I really need you here to maintain the

appearance of normalcy. I've told Kyla and I'll tell Pop and everyone else—except Jeli—that I'm making a spur-of-the-moment visit to Chicago to see a friend from college."

"Who?"

"Remember Robin Langley?"

"Robin? Sure, but what if she calls…"

"Who's she going to call, Rosie? I think this is a pretty safe lie."

Hannah listened for a few moments to the dramatic silence on the other end of the line. Eventually she said, "I know you're disappointed, but I hope you can understand."

"I guess I do. It's just that I know Robin, too, and it would make perfect sense for me to join in this spur-of-the-moment trip. But, oh well. It's obvious you want to do your thing by yourself, as usual, and all you need from me is prayer, as usual. Oh, and of course, you need me to keep the lie solid. Speaking of which, what do I tell them if they want to know why I didn't go too?"

Hannah wanted to scream: *For crissake's, woman, we are not attached at the hip!* Instead, she said, "We don't do everything together, Rosie."

"Well, when we were in college we did. Almost everything."

"But you and Robin were never best buds."

"No, I guess not. But I sure would have liked a break from teaching for a few days."

"Then take one. You don't need me as an excuse."

"So, I probably won't see you or talk to you between now and Thursday?"

"I can call you from Minnesota after I see the boy, if you want," Hannah said, mentally kicking herself for always giving in to Rose in one way or another.

"Oh, good! Please! That would mean so much to me."

Hannah kept her frustration to herself. "Okay. Talk to you tomorrow night or Tuesday, then, depending on when I see him."

"Good luck, Jo! And you know, I will be praying for you the whole time."

"Thanks. I think I'll need it."

Before she left home for the airport, Hannah had time to talk with Jeli in Los Angeles.

"Have you already moved up your return flight for tomorrow?" Hannah asked.

"Yes, I did it first thing this morning. Why?"

Hannah gave Jeli an abbreviated account of the day, omitting only Ethan. There'll be plenty of time to tell her about Ethan, Hannah thought, happy with her sense of the truth in that.

"Look," Jeli said, when Hannah had finished. "I can either come straight home and sort out Vivian, or, if you want me to, I could rearrange my flights so that I can meet you in Minneapolis."

"That's too much, Jeli. I can't ask you to change your tickets again, and I don't know what's going to happen at the Clinic. The press could be waiting to jump on anyone who shows up to see Isaiah."

"You're not asking, dear. I'm offering. If you want me to be with you in Minnesota, then that's what I want, too."

Feeling suddenly like a needy child, Hannah said, "Are you sure? What about the expense?"

"I'm sure."

Relief and gratitude brought tears to Hannah's eyes. "Jeli, how can I ever—"

"Now," Jeli said briskly, "what can we do about Vivian?"

"Well, I'm hoping Lily's withdrawing the reward will take the wind out of Vivian's sails."

"You think she won't go to the media anyway with her story? Maybe try to get some money from this Shepherdess group?"

"Maybe, but I just don't know what else I can do at this point. I won't even be here tomorrow night, if she comes gunning for me again."

"That's true. You're sure you don't want me there to deal with her?"

A small groan escaped from Hannah's throat. "What I really want is for you to be in both places at the same time. Can you please manage that?"

"Funny, I've often wished the same about you," Jeli said, her voice warm with laughter. "One thing, though—I'm wondering if

I have the right clothes with me."

They discussed the identities they would assume for their visit to the Clinic, and agreed to purchase the additional elements of disguise when they were together in Minneapolis.

"This could be wonderfully stealthy," said Jeli.

"If it weren't so deadly serious."

"True. So we're all set, are we? I'll get busy with my flight arrangements. What time do you get into Minneapolis?"

Hannah told her, and gave her the flight number from Chicago, and they arranged to meet at the airline baggage claim area. Jeli would call back and leave Hannah a message regarding what time she expected to be there.

After she hung up with Jeli, Hannah slipped a black denim jacket over her sweater against the evening chill, and drove her Jeep up to Papa's house, where she switched to Celeste's van. On her way to the airport, she retraced her conversations with Lily and Jeli. Things *are* working out the way I want them to, she thought. For once. Now if only God will come through for me with little Isaiah.

And if only God would *really* come through for me and pluck the widow Black off the face of the earth.

Chapter Sixteen

Hannah was approaching the assigned airport gate when, amidst a noisy crowd of strangers heading in her direction, she saw Papa, Celeste, Michael and Matthew, barely twenty feet away. All four wore ski jackets, jeans, and beaming smiles aimed at Hannah, and she felt awash with love at the sight of them.

And here's a treat, she thought. Pop doesn't look at all bleery.

At fifty-two, Papa's golden brown hair had thinned only slightly and he boasted that he could still—almost—fit into the suit he had worn the day he married Celeste. His continuing construction work, along with his snow-skiing and windsurfing vacations, gave his face a year-round tan that handsomely complemented his sea-green eyes.

He wrapped his arm around Hannah and gave her cheek a hearty, breath-minted kiss as he said, "How's my girl?"

"Fine, Pop. Sorry I'm late."

Celeste kissed her other cheek and gave her a half-hug, saying, "You're not, honey. We had a good tail wind, that's all. Thanks for picking us up."

Hannah thought it was so like her stepmother to instantly attempt to alleviate even the smallest of guilts. Celeste at forty-eight was still trim and pretty, her lightly freckled face touched only with faint laugh lines, and her honey-blond hair short and brushed softly back from her face.

Hannah teased her stepmother, "So, you enjoyed the skiing as usual?"

The light in her clear blue eyes dancing, Celeste replied in kind, "It was the best ever. I must have finished ten paperbacks and had three or four bracing walks and five or six luxurious naps every day."

Michael and Matthew stood there grinning and waiting to be acknowledged. Hannah put her hands on the broad shoulders of her youngest brother and smiled up into his eyes. "How'd you like it, Matt?"

"Fantastic! You should've come with us, kiddo," he said, giving her his megawatt grin and bending to kiss her cheek. "You mighta' had some fun for a change."

He's *beautiful*, Hannah thought. God help him.

Hannah worried about Matthew, whose only interests in life seemed to be girls, partying, and sports—preferably in combination. At eighteen, in his freshman year at the University of Pennsylvania, Matthew apparently couldn't have cared less about choosing a major, and claimed he was going to college only for football. And basketball. And baseball. He was on the U. of Penn varsity teams in all three sports, delighting Papa, who made a point of attending every home game for which Matthew suited up.

"So," said Hannah, "I guess that means you creamed only one or two little old ladies in your wild downhills."

"Hey, listen, those little old ladies didn't have what it takes for my hills, anyway."

"The truth is, Jo," drawled Michael, "Matty spent the entire week in the lodge, trying to get the attention of even one female under fifty."

Matthew's grin widened. "Mikey's just jealous." He jabbed Michael's shoulder. "The women were all over me. Had to fight 'em off with a ski pole."

"Okay, Matt," said Celeste. "How about you take some of that energy down to Baggage Claim for us."

Matthew saluted his mother, turned and jogged away as Papa said, "I'll come with you, son."

But Celeste took his arm to stop him. "Walk with me, Paul," she said, and Hannah knew at once that Celeste wanted to give her time alone with Michael.

As Celeste and Papa moved away, Hannah turned to her oldest brother. At twenty, tall, lanky Michael was a studious junior at the U. of Penn, with a major in psychology and a minor in art. Introspective and insightful, he often gave Hannah the feeling that he was reading her as easily as a billboard.

As he did at this very moment when he said, "What's going on, Jo?"

"Oh, Mike," she said, looking up into his sea-green eyes, so like Papa's. "It's a long story." She moved easily into his warm hug.

"Anything I can do to help?" he asked.

Into his strong shoulder, she said, "I promise I'll let you know, okay?"

"You'd better."

As they moved apart, he said, "I wish you'd come with us next time."

"You know I prefer your mom's not-at-all variety of skiing."

"Silly," he said, draping an arm over her shoulders. "Skiing is safe as houses, like Grampa always said."

"Grampa never said that about skiing, and anyway I never did know what it meant."

"Well," Michael said, a smile teasing the corners of his mouth, "it meant that since Pop builds safe houses, that's what skiing is."

Hannah laughed, loving the sweet kid that was never far from the surface in this brother of her heart.

On the way home, with Celeste driving, Hannah sat between her brothers in the back of the van and fed her family the lies about visiting Robin Langley in Chicago. She added that Jeli had decided to join them for a couple days and would be flying home with Hannah on Wednesday evening.

"That mother of mine," Celeste said fondly. "I never could keep up with her."

"When are you leaving?" asked Papa from the front passenger seat.

"First thing tomorrow. I have to be at the airport by seven-thirty. I thought I'd drop Clancy off at your house around six-thirty. That is, if you don't mind taking care of him till Wednesday night."

Celeste said, "Mind taking care of that angel dog? He practically takes care of us."

"You should've let us take the shuttle tonight, baby," said Papa. "So why don't I drive you to the airport in the morning?"

"What are you talking about, Pop? Since when is the chief workaholic in this family not going to be on the job by seven?"

"Since when is the junior workaholic not going to be on the job, period?" Papa laughed. "What happens to your poor, unadjusted patients?"

Celeste said, "I think it's great you're taking off like this, Jo. More power to you."

"Thanks, Cell," Hannah said, noticing that while Matthew seemed to be lost in his own thoughts, Michael had become very quiet. *He suspects something,* she thought. *Please God, don't let him ask me for the truth.*

Steering the van into the top of the driveway, Celeste exclaimed, "What on earth? Is that Vivian on our front porch?"

Hannah's heart jumped into her throat as she heard Grampa's voice in her mind: *Calm, honey. Stay calm. I'm right here with you.*

"What the hell does she want at this hour?" Papa said.

Matthew exclaimed, "I'm out'a here!"

"Matthew," Celeste said firmly. "You'll stay at least until the van is unloaded and you've taken your luggage up to your room."

"Mike'll do it for me, won't ya, Mikey? If I have to hang around that woman, it ain't gonna be pretty. And I promised Justin I'd be over soon as we got back…"

Papa settled it. "Matt, do as your mother says."

Calm, honey.

Celeste pulled the van to a stop at the porch steps.

Calm. I'm holding your hand. Everything will be all right.

Vivian had come to the foot of the steps and was giving them a smile that didn't remotely touch her eyes. "Hello, everyone!" she chirped.

Stepping out of the van, Papa said, "What's going on, Vivian?"

"Are you all right?" added Celeste, climbing out from behind the wheel.

"Oh, yes, I'm fine, just fine. And I'm sorry to bother you at this time of night."

Matthew was already unloading the luggage and ski gear as Michael climbed out of the van's left-side sliding door and waited, apparently expecting Hannah to follow him.

"What's going on?" Papa repeated.

Vivian said, "Rose was kind enough to tell me I might find all of you here. I hope this isn't a problem…"

"Of course not," said Celeste, ever the diplomat. "Would you like to come in? I could get some tea going—"

"Oh, I hate to intrude. I just have something important to discuss with Hannah and I know she's going out of town tomorrow, so I hoped to catch her here." Vivian peered into the van at Hannah, who remained in the middle of the rear seat.

Hannah's thoughts shrieked at her, *How much did Rose tell this old bat!*

Papa and Celeste also peered in at Hannah, and Michael reached in, offering her his hand.

Michael's here for you, too, honey, said Grampa's voice. *You can count on Michael.*

Vivian continued, her voice dripping with honey, "Hannah and I spoke earlier today, and… well, I don't know, do you want to continue our conversation here, Johannah?"

"Are you okay, baby?" asked Papa.

When Hannah finally climbed out of the van, she felt as if she were drowning in quicksand. She couldn't seem to grab hold of anything to rescue herself. Michael put his arm around her, and Grampa's voice continued to urge her to be calm, but all she could do was stare wordlessly at Vivian.

Papa asked again, "Are you okay, Jo?"

"Shall we go inside, then?" said Celeste, putting a gentle hand on Hannah's shoulder.

Celeste's touch seemed to galvanize Hannah. She said, "No," her voice low and steady. "Vivian and I will talk right here. Pop, Cellie, Mike, you three go on inside."

Matthew called from the porch, "Pop, I need your front door key."

All at once—as Papa said, "Coming," and moved to help Matthew, and as Celeste and Michael each moved closer to Hannah, as if to shore her up—Hannah's mind saw three clear truths: Papa subconsciously knew about her but could not let himself face it; Matthew was oblivious, fully absorbed in his own world; and Celeste and Michael knew, and they would stand by her, come what may.

Vivian seemed surprised and suddenly a bit intimidated, facing not only Hannah but Michael and Celeste as well. "I… well, I wasn't expecting that we'd stand out here in the driveway, Johannah. It's rather chilly. Could we go inside? Or perhaps we could talk down at your house."

"I'm not letting you take your garbage… not into my father's house."

Hannah's anger seemed to ignite Vivian's. "Your house will be fine, then. These matters must be settled tonight, Johannah, before you go to… before you leave on your little holiday."

So she suspects where I'm going, Hannah thought. "All right. My house."

When Vivian nodded and moved off toward her Chevy sedan, Celeste and Michael simultaneously said, "I'm coming with you." They looked at each other then in silent acknowledgment, and Celeste reached out and took her son's hand.

Hannah looked from one to the other. "Please don't—"

"I am," said Michael. "You need me."

Celeste said, "Please let me—"

Hannah saw the love and determination in their eyes. "All right," she sighed. "Let's get this over with."

Celeste said, "Mike, tell your dad we're going down to Hannah's for a little while."

Once the three of them were in her Jeep, Hannah said, "You two really don't need to do this. I can handle one old woman by myself."

"Not this one. Not tonight," Michael said from the back seat.

"I agree," Celeste added, in the front passenger seat.

"Why not tonight?" Hannah asked, wanting one of them to get it out in the open.

It was Michael. "You were the one at the plane crash yesterday, weren't you, Jo. And somehow Vivian knows it, and she's threatening you."

Hannah stopped the Jeep and looked at their faces in the dim light from the dashboard. "How long have you known?"

Michael answered first. "Pretty much since fifth grade. Remember Bobby, that friend of mine who was always hanging around the house? Remember what you did when he nearly cut his finger off messing with Pop's tools?"

She nodded. "I was hoping you didn't know what a bad cut it was."

"I may have been young, Jo, but I wasn't stupid. I saw the bone, and when he pulled the bandage off a couple hours later, there wasn't even a mark."

"Why didn't you ever talk to me about it, Mike?"

"Why didn't you ever talk to *me* about it, Jo?"

"You were too young. I didn't want to burden you."

"Right. You protected me just like you've always protected Pop and Mom, and I respected your decision. But now, with what you did yesterday, I can't sit back and pretend not to know anymore. I thought things might get rough, and Vivian being here tonight—now I'm sure of it."

"I am too, Jo," said Celeste. "And I'm glad this came out now. I'm glad for a chance to help you."

"How long have *you* known, Cell?"

"Oh, years and years, I guess. But not really consciously until I saw that drawing of you in the newspaper."

Hannah felt tears on her cheeks, and swiped them away with the backs of her hands. "It's funny... I thought I didn't want anyone to know, but now, with you two here, I feel... stronger, that's it. I feel like I really can face that old dragon."

Celeste added, "Speaking of the dragon, we should probably get down there before she gets any more steamed up."

During the remainder of the drive to her house, Hannah gave Celeste and Michael a quick sketch of her arrangements with Lily Severill and Jeli, and of Vivian's accusations and threats.

Pulling into Hannah's circular driveway, they could see Vivian sitting in her dark sedan while Clancy bounded around it, barking as if he'd treed a cat.

"Why don't we just leave her there?" offered Michael.

Hannah climbed out of the Jeep and moved toward the Chevy, while Clancy changed direction and bounced over to her, nearly knocking her down in his enthusiasm.

"Hey, pal," she said, hugging and scruffing him briefly as she looked through the driver's window at the widow Black.

Vivian sat inside, very still, with her head drooped down and her chin resting on her chest. Suddenly alarmed, Hannah tried the door handle but found it locked.

"Mike, try the passenger door. She's either asleep or... I don't know what."

"This one's locked, too, Jo."

Hannah knocked on the window. "Vivian!" The old woman didn't stir. "Are you all right?"

Celeste had come to Hannah's side, followed by Michael.

"Maybe Clancy scared her to death," Michael said.

"Don't joke about it, Mike," said Celeste. "Something's very wrong."

"What are we supposed to do?" said Michael. "We can't even get to her."

Just then Vivian lifted her head slightly and raised her right hand to the side of her face.

"Vivian!" called Celeste. "Open the door."

Vivian slowly, stiffly turned her head and looked blankly at Celeste, then at Hannah and Michael, her hand still pressed against her cheek.

Hannah said, "Vivian! Can you hear me? Unlock the car door."

Celeste said, "She's not registering."

"She looks like she's asleep with her eyes open," said Michael.

Hannah pounded on the top of the Olds with the palm of her hand. "Vivian! Wake up!"

Finally, Vivian's eyes focused. She moved her right hand from her cheek until it covered her mouth, as if she were embarrassed by something she'd said.

Hannah said, "Vivian, can you hear me? Can you understand what I'm saying?"

Vivian slowly lowered and raised her head.

"All right, then unlock the car doors so we can help you."

"There she goes," Michael said, as Vivian slowly reached for the door lock button.

As soon as she heard the locks release, Hannah opened the driver's door. "Are you all right?" she asked Vivian, aware of an unexpected, unwanted feeling of compassion for this old nemesis of hers. "Can you hear me?"

"I… I… think… I think… I'm…"

"What's wrong?" Hannah asked.

Suddenly, Vivian pulled herself up straight.

"Don't be ridiculous. Nothing is wrong with me. I… believe… I must have simply dozed off for a moment."

Hannah, Celeste, and Michael moved back as Vivian stepped out of the Chevy and closed its door behind her. She appeared to have entirely regained her fighting stance. "If you will kindly remove that *dog* somewhere out of my way, Johannah, we might get on with this."

Shortly, Clancy was closed in the back hall and Hannah, Celeste, and Michael stood in the greatroom facing Vivian.

"This is ridiculous," Hannah said. "Why don't we all sit down."

They did, Hannah and Celeste on the sofa and Michael and Vivian in matching overstuffed chairs angled at either end of the coffee table.

"What is it you want to say, Vivian, that you didn't already cover this afternoon?"

"Well, dear, you've managed to change things a good deal since this afternoon, haven't you, forcing that Severill woman to withdraw her reward, and now…" Vivian looked pointedly, first at Celeste, then at Michael. "Now you've brought these two into the matter."

"It was our decision to be here," said Celeste.

"Because you know that Johannah is the person they're calling the 'Angel of Angler's Field,' isn't that right?"

Celeste responded: "What we know, Vivian, is that you're making wild accusations and threats against someone we love very dearly."

Vivian blinked her eyes and shook her head, seeming momentarily confused. Then she said, "The Lord God Almighty has opened my ears and my eyes to the truth, and I'm sorry for you and your son, if you're too blind to see."

"Whatever the truth is, Vivian," said Celeste, "you seem to be trying to batter Hannah with it."

"I am doing only what the Lord has told me to do," Vivian declared. "And although Hannah is resisting, she can't help that.

There is a mighty battle being waged for her soul. You see, it's Satan's work she's doing, not the Lord's, and she must make the decision to cast out Satan."

"Jesus!" Michael said, lurching to his feet.

"The Lord spoke to me—"

"Sit down, Michael," said his mother. "What exactly do you want, Vivian?"

Michael moved around the room, keeping his eyes locked on Vivian.

Hannah felt washed by a wave of love for her brother and stepmother. I should have confided in them years ago, she thought.

"What I want is for Johannah to acknowledge that she is the one who was at the plane crash yesterday, and for her to renounce Satan's power so that she can be saved."

"Enough!" Michael said, striding to Vivian's chair and looming over her.

"Michael! Sit down!" cried Celeste. "Now! You're not helping at all."

Michael didn't budge.

Apparently unperturbed, Vivian spoke to Michael while looking at Celeste. "Michael, you must do as your mother says. I assure you, your size and strength do not… do not… your…"

The old woman's chin dropped to her chest again, as it had been in the car, and her body sank in on itself as if her bones had been abruptly removed.

Now Michael did step back, while both Hannah and Celeste moved quickly to Vivian's side.

"What's wrong with her?" Michael asked.

"She may be having small strokes," said Celeste, and Hannah nodded in agreement. "We need to make her comfortable. Mike, give me a hand—and Hannah, call 911."

With ease, Michael lifted Vivian and put her on the sofa.

Hannah called for an ambulance, then retrieved a bedroom quilt and tucked it around Vivian.

"Is this my fault, Mom?" Michael asked. "Did I—"

"Don't think that for a minute, honey. She was already having a problem out in the car."

"And from what I saw, Mike, she wasn't afraid of you," Hannah added, affectionately stroking his broad back and feeling him relax a bit. "You're really just a big cream puff, you know. Couldn't scare a mouse."

Celeste stood after examining Vivian. "Her pulse is pretty rapid, but not off the charts. And her pupils look all right. How long for the ambulance?"

"Probably another ten minutes, at least," Hannah said. "Is there something else we should do?"

"Do you have a small pillow to support her neck?"

Hannah found one and put it in place. Then they all sat on the coffee table and were quiet for a few moments.

"Strange, isn't it," Hannah said.

"What?" asked Michael, as Celeste said: "Very."

"Did I miss something?" Michael said.

"No, honey," said Celeste, patting his knee.

"I guess your mom and I are both thinking what a strange thing it would be if this was the end of Vivian's threats."

Michael nodded solemnly.

"The thought of her dying is bizarre to me," Hannah said. "Totally disorienting, as if the world would be an unfamiliar place without her. Most of my life I've had the feeling that she's been watching me."

Vivian stirred then and opened her eyes, blinking a few times.

Celeste knelt beside her. "Vivian? Can you hear me?"

"What... I... what's..." She seemed to be struggling to sit up, apparently confused by her surroundings.

"It's all right," Celeste said, applying light pressure to her shoulder. "You should rest. An ambulance is coming to take—"

"Ambulance?" Vivian asked, sounding more puzzled than alarmed. She lay back into the sofa and stopped struggling. "What's wrong with me?"

"How do you feel?" asked Celeste.

"Oh... I... I... tired... tired. My head..."

"Well, you rest now," Celeste said, stroking Vivian's forehead. "You'll be all right."

Hannah wondered if that were true. And—for the first time ever in the presence of a person's physical distress—she was grateful that her hands were stone cold.

In Vivian's sedan, Celeste and Michael would follow the ambulance to Chester County Hospital's Emergency Room. They would take care of Vivian's car and return it to her when she was released from the hospital.

Celeste was behind the wheel of the Chevy, with Michael in the passenger seat, waiting for the ambulance to pull out of the drive. She was insisting that Hannah stay home and get to bed. "My mind boggles at the thought of your going to the Mayo Clinic to help that child after the weekend you've had."

Hannah leaned against the side of the car by Michael's open window. "Well, at least call me and let me know what's wrong with her. I won't be able to sleep anyway."

"I'm not going to call you, Jo," Celeste insisted. "They'll admit her for observation, and after that she's out of our hands—at least for tonight."

"Well, then, leave me a note, will you, so I can find out when I drop Clancy off in the morning."

"I'll be up. I'll see you then."

"So will I," said Michael.

"That'll be the day," Hannah smiled. "You on vacation, out of bed before noon."

"I'll be up, Jo. I want to see you before you go."

Hannah saw the concern in his eyes and leaned further into the car, giving him an awkward hug. "You two are the best."

"Love you, honey," Celeste said, as they pulled away.

Me too, you, Hannah thought, waving goodbye in the dark.

After they'd gone, Hannah fed Clancy, washed and dried a load of laundry, and checked her voice mail, noting Jeli's arrival time in Minneapolis. Then she paid a couple of bills by computer, packed her carry-on suitcase, and was in bed by eleven-thirty—wide awake, her mind spinning with all that had happened in the past thirty-six hours.

She thought how bizarre it was, Celeste's and Michael's unequivocal support, and then Vivian suddenly—if temporarily—taken out of the picture. Bizarre, and also miraculous. But, with effort, she stopped herself short of considering that God might have come through for her in this moment of need. To her way of thinking, if God existed, it could not be as an omnipotence that willy-nilly caused or relieved suffering; such a God would be too capricious to deserve contemplation.

She considered trying to reach Celeste for news about Vivian, but decided not to risk waking anyone. Anyway, Vivian's going to live forever, she reminded herself. I won't be done with her so easily.

She allowed her thoughts to linger awhile with Ethan. She thought about his eyes, his voice, his mouth, his skin. She wanted—*longed*—to touch his skin, to feel its heat. If it weren't so late, she would have phoned him, intuitively knowing she could tell him anything and everything. She wished he could go with her to Minnesota.

Is he the one, Grampa? Is he? She imagined the light in Grampa's eyes dancing as he said, "Honey, that's something you're going to have to discover for yourself."

After a while, she gave up on sleep, got out of bed and went with Clancy to her computer room, a stiff drink in one hand and some Milk Bonz in the other. She played Free Cell, and then, sometime later, awoke with her cheek resting on the computer keyboard. Shutting everything down and rinsing out her glass in the kitchen, she dragged herself to bed and achieved the sleep of the innocent—or the dead—until the alarm woke her at five-thirty.

Chapter Seventeen

Hannah had been a white-knuckle flyer until she tried valerian. Now, as long as she swallowed one or two of those magical capsules within a half-hour of boarding, she could relax and let the pilots be responsible for keeping the plane in the air.

Unfortunately, that Monday morning she was running way behind schedule. She wasn't at all sure she could park her Jeep, get her boarding pass and make it to the gate with anything like a few minutes—much less valerian's thirty—to spare. The traffic on Route 322 between Chadds Ford and I-95 was hellious, frustrating her so that she was silently hurling curses at the drivers of every other car on the road, then at everyone who had ever worked for the Pennsylvania highway department, and eventually at nearly everyone and everything that came to mind.

In truth, she was furious at herself. Weighed down by her vivid memories of Saturday's plane crash and her certainty that she'd be unable to help Isaiah, she had dawdled and procrastinated this morning. She had spent too long in the shower, too long getting dressed—in the plainest clothes she owned, working her hair back into a tight, matronly bun low on the nape of her neck, bundling up in a calf-length camel-hair coat against the cold Minnesota winds—too long securing her house, too long talking with Celeste and Michael, too long saying goodbye to Clancy.

If she missed the flight this morning, there was no one to blame but herself. And, oh, how she wanted to miss the flight!

I wish I could just turn this Jeep around and go home, she thought. I could phone Kyla and ask her to put my schedule back together. Then I could go to work and spend this day doing what I do best.

She thought about her patients, her wonderful, beautiful patients; she loved them all—skinny or fat, familiar or new, young or old, cranky or sweet. She loved greeting them, seeing their faces. She loved checking their condition, hearing how they were doing, even hearing their complaints and worries, knowing that they trusted her. She loved the feel of their backs and their necks under her hands as she adjusted their subluxations, the near-trance into which her intellect could settle while her hands diagnosed and repaired under a knowledge and skill all their own. She loved that an intelligence seemingly separate from hers would occasionally find an underlying problem or disease and set her hands on fire for its healing, and that the healed patient never knew he or she had been given a miracle. She loved the way—

Suddenly she noticed the sign: *Philadelphia International Airport, 1 1/2 Miles*. She glanced at the digital clock on the dashboard. Only seven thirty-five. Oh, well, she thought... Isaiah, for better or worse, here I come.

Because she'd booked her ticket only the evening before, Hannah felt lucky with her seat for the three hour flight from Philadelphia to Chicago. Although near the back of the plane, she was on the aisle, with no one between herself and a teenaged boy who appeared to be entirely absorbed by the window view and whatever music he was listening to on his CD player.

Relaxed by the valerian, she said "no" to the proffered headset and "yes" to the waffles-and-sausage breakfast, minus the sausage. She drank the grapefruit juice but skipped the coffee, and then dozed for the remainder of the flight, her mind lightly touching hundreds of thoughts but dwelling on none.

In Chicago, she had more than enough time to reach the gate for her connecting flight, and spent part of it in a Starbucks, drinking a decaf cappuccino, eating an apricot scone, and glancing through a local newspaper someone had abandoned at her table. She was pleased to find only a brief article on the second page of the first section concerning the ongoing interest in the whereabouts of the mysterious blond "angel" of Saturday's plane crash. She's right here, she silently announced, just an ordinary mortal scarfing down at Starbucks.

On the plane to the Twin Cities, she found herself between two bulky men, one of whom had a heavy-duty body odor problem. Still, she was thankful not to be on a DC-10 in the middle of one of those torturous rows of six seats, and managed to settle back and let her thoughts drift again for the eighty-minute flight.

At the sight of Jeli, dressed much like Hannah, entering the United Airlines Baggage Claim area in the Twin Cities' airport, Hannah's first thought was of Gabriel, the little brown wren she'd loved in that cataclysmic summer of 1982 and ever since. Gabriel, who had perched on her head as a lookout the afternoon she crawled through the tall, wet grass toward the back of the witches' house, toward her first encounter with Jeli. Gabriel and Jeli had become connected in Hannah's mind that summer, and although she hadn't seen him again after she finally persuaded him to fly south that September, the sight of Jeli often brought loving thoughts to her heart on the wren's tender wings.

At sixty-eight, Anjelica Whitney Thayer was everything that Hannah hoped to become some day: serene, graceful with her years, in love with life, and illuminated from within. Unlike Vivian, Jeli had enjoyed nearly every outdoor activity that exposed her skin to fresh air and the warmth of the sun; as a result, the elements had punished her complexion. In combination with her solar-white hair, which she wore in a pixie cut for easy maintenance, and her glasses with their silver-toned metal frames, her skin made her look older than her years, a fact she seemed to relish. "I earned all these wrinkles," she would say, with a laugh. "And I wouldn't part with a single one of them if you paid me." She had a story to go with every line, and would arbitrarily point to one on her forehead, deepening it with a frown, and saying something like, "See this one? That's the night Celeste was born after eighteen hours of labor. If you're really bearing down, giving birth your all, God rewards you with a wrinkle just like this one."

"There you are, Jo!" Jeli said, the love in her wide smile reflected in her clear blue eyes.

They dropped their various bags and moved into each other's arms and a warm hug.

Hannah delighted in Jeli's soft, clean-scented hair, and the gentle strength of her arms. "I am so glad you're here," she said.

"So am I, sweetie," said Jeli. "I couldn't stand for you to be doing this on your own, after all that's happened the last few days."

Hannah picked up her shoulder bag and carry-on, and said, "Let me carry this," as she relieved Jeli of a suitcase. "Did you hear about Vivian?"

"Indeed I did," she said, picking up her purse and a small carry-on bag. "I spoke to Cellie before I left the hotel this morning. She said to tell you they'll be doing a few more tests and Vivian will probably be released this afternoon. Too bad they won't keep her longer—"

"Permanently would be nice."

". . . but her EEG is normal."

"How that woman manages to have a normal EEG is beyond me," Hannah said.

Jeli nodded and smiled. "But isn't it miraculous how those spells of hers—whatever their cause—happened just in time to get her out of your hair?"

"For now, anyway. I can't help thinking she'll be lying in wait for me when I get home."

"But I'll be with you then, and Celeste." Jeli chuckled. "And Michael's talking about taking time off from classes to, as he puts it, 'settle that old bag's hash.' So why don't we just put Vivian Black out of our minds while we're here."

"I'll give it a shot. And speaking of bags, do we need to collect the rest of yours?"

"I put everything but these two in a locker," Jeli said. "We can pick it all up on Wednesday before the flight home."

"Good, so we might as well get—" Hannah broke off, mid-sentence, suddenly disoriented by the press of people and noise around her.

"Are you all right, dear? You look awfully pale."

"Maybe… just sit for a minute."

They found two empty seats near the Alamo Car Rental desk, and sat in them, putting their bags on the floor at their feet.

Jeli put an arm around Hannah and took her hand, squeezing it gently. "Everything will be all right, honey."

"Mm. You sound like Grampa."

"Good."

"But what if everything is *not* all right, Jeli? The media, or even the Shepherdess people—they could be waiting at the Mayo, and I could fail completely with Isaiah. Vivian could go to the Local News with her story tomorrow, while I'm still out here, and they could believe her."

"I'd be anxious too." Jeli stroked Hannah's hair. "You don't have to do this, you know. Nobody would blame you for turning around and going home."

"I'd blame me."

"Then why don't we just sit here awhile and relax together. You've had precious little time to relax lately."

The loving acceptance in Jeli's voice soothed Hannah, and they did sit quietly, side-by-side, for a few minutes.

Eventually, the rental car sign registered on Hannah. "Alamo," she said. "That's where I've reserved a car for us."

"Are you ready then?"

Hannah stood and held her hand out to Jeli. "I am."

"Sure? You don't have to go any further with this."

"I know. But I want to, and I'm ready. Let's go get our car and find a store where we can buy the rest of our camouflage."

At a department store in Minneapolis, they found everything they needed to complete their disguises: a plain white cotton blouse for each of them, a dark blue blazer for Jeli, and black low-heeled shoes for Hannah. Even all these years after her husband's death, Jeli still wore her plain gold wedding band, and Hannah had brought the one that belonged to her mother. In a dressing room, they added the simple wooden crosses on black cords that Sophie Muller had given Hannah and Grampa several years ago. Then they scrutinized each other, and once Hannah reworked the bun holding her wild hair in place, they pronounced themselves ready.

Several miles south of the Cities, on Route 52 to Rochester, with Hannah behind the wheel of their rented Honda Accord, Jeli clicked off the radio and sat back in her seat after searching in vain for a classical music station. "This your first time in Minnesota, Jo?"

"First time. But it seems familiar. All this pristine farmland, I keep expecting to see an Amish horse and buggy with that hideous orange triangle on the back."

Jeli smiled. "It is a bit like Pennsylvania. A lot colder, though."

Hannah appreciated the sense of familiarity she was experiencing, as if Minnesota were welcoming her. Before long, she found herself telling Jeli about Saturday, from waking up knowing where she had to go that day and what she had to do, through her doubts and her nervousness, her careful preparations, and the certainty that had settled on her by the time she neared Gettysburg.

Describing the accident itself and the living nightmare of the wreckage, Hannah felt lightheaded. "Sorry," she said, slowing down and steering the Accord onto the highway's shoulder. "Would you mind driving for a while?"

Once they were back on the road, with Jeli behind the wheel, Hannah began to talk about Ethan Quinn, from her first visceral response to him in the plane wreck, through her sense of his significance in her life during their brief conversation outside of church yesterday morning. "I can't stop thinking about him, and I feel like a silly adolescent with her first crush."

"But this is wonderful, Jo! I think it's exactly what you need in your life right now."

"What about Craig?"

"Oh, my dear, I'm sure even Craig knows your relationship has run its course."

"Really? I didn't know anyone thought that except me."

"Well, in fact, even your grampa knew Craig was short-term. He doesn't have a clue about your gifts, does he?"

"No."

"Well, there you are. You've been dating him... what... two years, is it? And he still doesn't really know you. That says it all, as far as I'm concerned. And now, look what's happened. You've met a simpatico man in the midst of using the very gifts you've kept hidden from Craig. A little much to be simple coincidence, wouldn't you agree?"

Hannah murmured assent, pleased by Jeli's sight-unseen approval of Ethan.

"Speaking of a little much for coincidence, I find it so odd that you were sent to the plane crash specifically for little Micah, and you end up out here two days later for his younger brother."

"I know. It's bizarre. Rose says that it's proof God wants me to stop hiding away in my comfortable little life."

"Ah, Rosie. If only we could all be so sure about what God wants."

Shortly after six o'clock, they came upon Rochester's skyline against the backdrop of a sailors-delight sunset.

"Shall we find the Transplant Center before we look for a motel?" Hannah suggested. "Sort of spy out the lay of the land for tomorrow morning?"

"Sure. Are you planning to see Isaiah tonight?"

"I don't think I can. Not tonight."

"Understood. So let's take a peek at the Center and then scout up some food and a motel room."

It was ten-fifteen and Jeli and Hannah were each lying in their own double bed, in a non-smoking room of the Holiday Inn Express, not fifteen minutes from the Transplant Center.

Jeli was reading a book, and Hannah was holding one, unable to concentrate. She wished she had her computer, or even an actual deck of cards, so she could play solitaire. Even more, she wished she had a bottle of Jack Daniels.

Apropos of nothing she said, "Have I told you how glad I am that you're here?"

Jeli chuckled softly. "Frequently."

"Well I am."

A bit later Hannah asked, "Do you really believe that everything will go well tomorrow?"

"I do, sweetie. Really. I think Lily Severill has laid the groundwork, and I think the Mayo Clinic goes to great lengths to protect the privacy of its patients."

"But what about Isaiah? Do you think I'll be able to help him?"

"If there's any justice, you will."

But *is* there any justice? Hannah wondered.

Later, considering the worst of her fears, the words slipped out. "What if he dies?"

"If Isaiah dies?"

"Uh-huh. I mean, what if that is the only sort of healing he can have, an end to his suffering. And what if it happens when I touch him?"

Jeli put down her book, got out of her bed and moved to sit beside Hannah. With her fingertips, she brushed the hair back from Hannah's cheek. "Darling Jo, I wish I could make everything all right."

"I'm sorry, being whiny like this. I'm just so scared."

"Of course you are, honey," Jeli said, smoothing Hannah's brow. "Anybody would be. But you've done the right thing coming out here to help this little boy—risking so much you hold dear—and I believe that whatever happens, things are going to turn out for the best."

"Thanks, Jeli. I wish God saw things the way you do."

There was an infectious twinkle in Jeli's eyes as she said, "Maybe she does, honey."

Chapter Eighteen

Hannah was relieved to see no evidence of the media when she and Jeli arrived at the Transplant Center just after nine o'clock the next morning.

"Remember, Jeli. Don't look at the security cameras."

"Right."

The Center's foyer was large and decorated, somewhat like Hannah's own chiropractic offices, in mauves, grays, and smoky blues, with indirect lighting, industrial strength carpeting, and occasional potted plants.

"Nice," Jeli pronounced. "Utilitarian, but attractive."

Still just a hospital, Hannah thought. I hate hospitals.

There were three women busy at the reception counter. The one who greeted them was middle-aged, with a pleasant smile and sporting a nametag that read, "S. Russell." "May I help you?" she asked.

"Yes, please," said Hannah. "My name is Sister Marie Joseph, and this is Sister Ruth Thomas. We're here to see Isaiah Severill."

"One moment, Sister," said Ms. Russell, tapping some words into her computer keyboard and watching the screen hidden beneath the simulated marble countertop. After a few moments, she looked up, her smile mingled now with a curiosity that put Hannah's nerves on alert. "Yes, Mrs. Severill told us that we might expect you, Sister Marie. However, she didn't mention your companion."

Hannah thought fast. "I'm sorry, this is my error. I must not have mentioned to Mrs. Severill that our Order does not permit us to travel alone. Sister Ruth has accompanied me for that reason, and will also be offering prayers for the little boy."

"I see. But I'm afraid I'll have to check with Mrs. Severill regarding Sister Ruth's presence before I can issue a pass for her."

Dammit, Hannah thought. Now Lily will know I'm here. She said, "If you would allow me, I could call Mrs. Severill myself and save you the trouble."

"It's no trouble at all. Mrs. Severill happens to be here, with her son, at this very moment. I'll ring the nurses' station. Perhaps you and Sister Ruth would care to take a seat," Ms. Russell said, gesturing to chairs grouped around the foyer.

Hannah gritted her teeth as they moved to sturdy chairs near one of the tall, narrow windows. She sat with her back to the reception counter, and Jeli settled into a chair at right angles to hers.

Hannah spoke softly, "Lily's *here*. This is terrible."

"Did you ask her to stay away?"

"It never occurred to me she'd turn right around and come out here. How am I going to explain you? What if she recognizes you from one of your books?"

"Explain me as your friend, honey, here to support you. And don't worry about her recognizing me. People don't pay much attention to dust-jacket photos."

"She might have seen you on TV, one of those interviews."

"So what if she has? Couldn't an author be a friend of yours who is willing to support you here?" Jeli reached across and patted Hannah's hands, clenching and unclenching in her lap. "Honey, try to relax. You look like you're about to be guillotined."

"I should've had some valerian."

"I'm glad you didn't. I think you'll need all your faculties today." Jeli rested her hand on Hannah's arm. "It's going to be all right, Jo."

More than Jeli's words, Hannah felt the warm reassurance in the hand resting on her arm. For the next few minutes they were silent together, Hannah meditating on the healing power she believed to be intrinsic in every human being who loved. For most, she thought, it was a profound, unrecognized and untapped resource. For others, like herself, it was the blessing and bane of living.

S. Russell appeared beside them, proffering two I.D. tags with metal clips. "Here you are, Sisters. Mrs. Severill is waiting for you with Isaiah."

Hannah and Jeli stood and attached their I.D. tags to their

jackets as Ms. Russell gave them directions to the Pediatric ICU area.

In the elevator, on the way up to the third floor, Hannah held Jeli's hand and did her best to breathe normally.

They checked in again at the nurses' station on Isaiah's floor, and Hannah felt some relief over the Clinic's security measures. Surely we'll be safe from the media here, she told herself.

A Pediatric ICU nurse introduced herself as Elise Merritt. She was tall and slender in her nurse's uniform, with black curly hair over pale skin, and intelligent brown eyes. She presented Hannah and Jeli with gowns, transparent masks, surgical gloves, and booties that fit over their shoes, and waited while they donned the protective gear. Then she guided them personally to Isaiah's room.

Hannah's heart sank when she caught a clear view of Lily through the nearly floor-to-ceiling windows separating the room from the hallway. We might as well be in a fishbowl, she thought. How on earth will I get any time alone with the child?

As if sensing Hannah's doubts, Jeli laid a gentle hand between her shoulder blades, and they entered the room.

The air in Isaiah's room seemed dry and overly hot, with a pervasive odor that instantly took Hannah back to Grampa's sickbed. She had been assaulted by that odor on Grampa's breath during his last weeks of life; it's the stench of death, she'd decided then. And here it was again, now, cloaking the air in this child's room. The smell, combined with the rapid blipping of Isaiah's heart monitor and the sight of various tubes snaking into his body, nearly propelled Hannah back out the door.

Lily approached them, smiling, her smooth dark skin beautifully offset by the creamy white knit dress she wore. Her hair was cropped short, revealing the fine shape of her head, and she wore large, creamy white button earrings and an ornate gold cross on long, gold rope necklace. She had her eyes glued to Hannah as she spoke. "It is you, isn't it, even though your hair— well, it's lovely, and that's its real color, I'm sure, since I did think you were wearing a wig on Saturday. But I do recognize you, even with that mask... I so loathe the dreadful precautions we have to take here—except for me, of course, since I'm with him so often. But your eyes, what an extraordinary color! Are they contact lenses? Oh, forgive me, I'm being so silly, never mind... I just... you're here, you really are here, and I don't know how I can ever thank you." Lily opened her arms wide to embrace Hannah.

Hannah felt the tense withholding of her own body, even as she allowed herself to be hugged. A memory flitted through her mind of someone years and years ago—was it Vivian?—saying they couldn't bear being hugged by strangers, and Hannah was ashamed for feeling the same way in that moment.

Evidently sensing Hannah's restraint, Lily quickly pulled back. "I'm sorry. I'm simply so... overwhelmed that you're truly here, you've come all this way for my poor Isaiah, and I can't tell you how much it means to me."

"Lily, this is my friend, Sister Ruth," Hannah said, moving to the side of Isaiah's crib.

"How do you do?" Lily nodded and smiled at Jeli. "It's so good of you to come with, um, Sister Marie."

"It's my pleasure," Jeli responded.

Lily and Jeli stepped to either side of Hannah, who was gazing down at the small, sleeping form in the crib.

"Here's my precious lamb," Lily said, tightly gripping the crib rail as if she couldn't trust herself to touch her son. "Poor little darling, they keep him tranquilized so that he sleeps most of the time now, and the steroids have puffed him up dreadfully. Sometimes, when he does open his eyes, it's almost... well, it frightens me because I think he can't see me or he doesn't recognize me, and if he's going blind along with everything else, I don't know if I can bear it. They say God never gives you more than you can bear, but I'm not sure anymore. I'm coming apart at the seams these days, and what with the plane crash and my sweet Micah dead right there on my lap until you came along, Elizabeth... Sister Marie... Sister Marie? Are you all right?"

With her first sight of Isaiah, Hannah was enshrouded by a sense of other-worldliness, as if something inhuman were present in the room. This, she knew, was the source of the stench. She looked at the child and suddenly it seemed she was peering into the wrong end of a telescope, with Isaiah at an unbridgeable distance. Worse, his small form was resting in thick, liquid darkness, like tar, that was entering his pores, sucking at him and pulling him down, down and away. Hannah reached out to touch him, and saw her gloved hands—her left on the top of his head and her right on his diapered hip—through the same wrong end of the telescope, as if they were miles away and not remotely connected to her. And her hands were cold, as was Isaiah's body. Despite the heat of the room, everything was cold, especially the sucking darkness that began to encompass her fingers. She tried to pull her hands away, but they resisted like damp flesh stuck to a metal ice cube tray.

Someone lightly touched Hannah's back and at once the malevolent images vanished. "Oh!" she gasped, turning her head, seeing Jeli's face, heavy with worry. "Oh, Jeli—"

"Are you all right, honey?"

"I... yes, uh... no," Hannah said, dazed. "Where's—"

"Lily seems so tightly strung, I thought you might want her out of here for a few moments. So I asked her if she could arrange for you to hold the boy."

"Oh. Good," Hannah said, her gaze falling back to Isaiah, who now appeared to be only a small, critically ill child.

"What happened? Can you tell me?"

"I saw death, Jeli. It's all around him, pulling at him."

"Oh God."

"Can't you smell it in the air?"

Jeli shook her head.

"Then when I touched him, it started on me." Hannah gripped Jeli's arm. "We don't have any time. He could die any minute."

"Can you be sure? Maybe death has been here, waiting for weeks."

"Maybe. But I don't think it's just waiting. I think it's taking him. Lord, Jeli, what am I supposed to do?"

Jeli put a steadying hand on Hannah's shoulder. "Don't lose heart, love. Death may be simply trying to scare you away."

Listen to her, honey, said Grampa's voice in Hannah's mind. *Put old Death in the closet and bar the door.*

Lily returned just then, her upbeat energy feeling like a slap to Hannah's face. How can this woman be so oblivious to what's happening? Hannah wondered, at once feeling guilty for her intolerant thoughts. She's a nervous wreck, Hannah silently reminded herself. And who wouldn't be? On some level, Lily probably does know precisely what's happening. And, God help me, she believes I can stop it.

Lily was gushing, "The nurses will be here in a moment, and they'll set up that nice rocker over there for you, on this side of the crib. They've done this before for me, it's really quite simple. All they have to do is lower the crib's railing and lift Isaiah onto your lap. They'll remove the boards from his arms—he doesn't really need them now, anyway, because he's always sleeping—and of course, they're very careful about keeping the tubes untangled and making sure nothing gets dislodged." She looked at Hannah like a child expecting praise for a job well done.

"I wonder," Hannah said. "Could Sister Ruth and I have privacy in here with Isaiah? Can these hall windows be covered?"

Lily's dark brown eyes widened for a moment in apparent surprise; then she seemed to remember her promise to Hannah. "Of course. Whatever you want. But, well, we have no way to easily cover the windows onto the hall, but we could pull the privacy curtain around the bed. Would that be enough?"

Hannah felt ridiculous for not having noticed the privacy curtain. She nodded. "That'll be fine."

Several minutes later, Hannah settled into the rocking chair and watched Nurse Elise Merritt prepare to lower a blanket-wrapped Isaiah into her arms. As with S. Russell at the reception desk, Hannah recognized curiosity in the nurse's expression, and managed to drive the sudden alarm from her thoughts by unnecessarily adjusting the angle of the chair set beside her for Jeli... for Sister Ruth.

Isaiah's weight felt surprisingly substantial in Hannah's arms, and she automatically began rocking the chair while the nurse pulled the privacy curtain and Lily came to stand at her side.

Jeli sat in the other chair, moving it slightly closer to Hannah's rocker.

"Will this be all right?" Lily asked, her voice sounding strained.

Hannah looked up at her, seeing that the earlier ebullience had vanished, replaced by trembling lips and teary eyes. "This will be just fine," Hannah reassured her. Cradling Isaiah in her left arm, she reached out and took Lily's hand. "Are *you* all right?"

"Oh. Well." A big tear slid down Lily's cheek. "Me. Well, I'm… I just wish there was something I could do. What shall I do? Isn't there some way I can help? I would so like to be here and watch you heal him."

"Lily, please," Hannah said, tears suddenly burning behind her own eyes. "You have to remember that I may not be able to help him at all. If you think my simply being here is a guarantee of his healing, the pressure is too much for me. Do you understand?"

"Oh!" Lily pressed her fingers against her lips for a moment, as if she were shushing herself. "Of course. So stupid of me. I didn't… I mean, I'm not… I do know that, I really do. I know he may be beyond help. Even yours, even after what you did for Micah. The thing is, I simply have no idea what I'm supposed to do now."

Feeling her tension level rising intolerably, Hannah looked to Jeli for help.

Jeli took the cue. "Why don't you take a break, Lily?" she said. "Is there somewhere you could go for some refreshment or a rest? Perhaps there's a Borders where you could read and relax with a nice cup of coffee."

"Tea. I prefer tea, and there's a Borders not far from my hotel. I could do that. But… well, I was hoping I could stay here with you and—"

"I'm sorry, Lily," said Jeli. "But I'm not even sure that I'll be staying. It depends on what Sister Marie needs."

"What Sister Marie needs…" Lily repeated. "I see. Of course. Well, there's a chapel here at the Center. I could wait there."

"That sounds just right," Jeli offered.

Lily crouched beside Hannah, who was rocking Isaiah and lightly stroking his cheek with her gloved fingertips. "But *could* I stay? It would mean so much."

Hannah looked into Lily's pleading eyes and felt sympathy. "I wish I could say yes, but I really need to be free of all distractions."

"But what about all those distractions on Saturday? They didn't stop you then."

"But that was completely different, Lily. The healing was already at work when I stepped into the wreckage. Now it's not."

Lily rubbed her forehead. "And what if it doesn't come at all this time? What happens then? I'm going to lose him, aren't I. He'll die, won't he. What if he dies right here with you, while I'm off somewhere drinking my nice little cup of tea?"

Lily's words squeezed Hannah's heart. My own worst fear, she thought.

Jeli stood and helped Lily to her feet. "Why don't you show me where the chapel is, Lily? We could pray there together awhile."

"All right, all right, I can do that," she said wearily, leaning on Jeli as the older woman helped the younger out of the room.

When Hannah heard the door close softly behind them, her thoughts shifted to the child whose life at the moment quite literally rested in her hands. She lowered him onto her lap and continued to gently rock the chair. With a great effort of will, she forced all thoughts of the sucking black death and its stench out of her consciousness. Then, taking care not to disturb any of the tubes that were supporting his life, she pulled back the blanket and let her eyes rest on Isaiah's body.

She decided it was a beautiful body. True, it was bloated, its brown skin slightly ashen and unnaturally stretched tight, but nonetheless it was a baby's body and therefore beautiful. "You are a perfect child of God, sweet Isaiah," she murmured, lightly stroking his hair, thick and close-cropped like his mother's. "Did you know that, little love?" She traced her fingertips over his brow and across his delicate eyelids and his thick black lashes that brushed the tops of his puffy cheeks, longing to remove the gloves she'd been forced to wear. Longing to truly touch his warm skin, to feel his mouth—a generous cherub's bow—and his ears, so perfectly placed on each side of his heart-shaped face. She raised his right hand—the arm not hindered by tubes—and watched it curl reflexively around her fingers. She pressed his hand to her cheek above the mask, then to her lips through it, her thoughts brushed by the memory of Gabriel's fragile little wings. She ran her fingers over his legs—legs that had probably never held his toddler's weight—and lifted each of his soft, disproportionately long feet to her lips, kissing them through the mask, imagining the sweet scent of his skin, and thinking that with such feet, he'd be a tall man some day. If he lived.

Finally, Hannah placed her gloved palm lightly on his chest, absorbing his warmth and giving back her own, feeling his irregular heartbeat and his shallow breaths. Loving on him, as Grampa would say.

Please, God, she prayed silently. Please, God, help this child. Heal this child.

Hannah rocked him and she loved on him and she silently repeated her version of the Jesus prayer for him, all the while aware of warring voices in her head, undermining her concentration. It was as if there were several Hannahs present in Isaiah's room: the one who lovingly rocked the child, and the others crowding around her in angry contentiousness.

Lord Jesus Christ, have mercy on this child.

This isn't going to work, and you know it. You might as well give it up now, Johannah.

Blessed Lord Jesus, grant this child your peace.

It never works when you most want it to.

Lord Jesus Christ, have mercy on this child.

Look what happened with Grampa. This is exactly the same.

Blessed Lord Jesus, grant this child your peace.

No, this is worse than with Grampa. This poor baby will probably die while you're here alone with him.

Lord Jesus Christ, have mercy on this child.

Nobody blamed you for Grampa, but everybody'll blame you for Isaiah.

Blessed Lord Jesus, grant this child your peace.

Give it up, fool. Put him on the bed and get the hell out of here.

Lord Jesus Christ, have mercy on this child.

The sooner the better. There's probably a lobby full of reporters waiting downstairs.

After a time, Hannah knew her efforts were fruitless. The gloves and mask were minor irritants; the self-criticism was a land mine.

I'll do what I do best, she decided.

She took a pillow from the foot of the crib and placed it on her lap, under Isaiah. Then she turned him gently onto his right side, facing her, and reached around the various tubes with her right hand, carefully feeling the bones of his neck and back. Sweet Jesus, all these subluxations! she thought. I'd need to adjust him every day for weeks. I wonder if they have a chiropractor on staff here.

Silently, she moved her hand along his back and his neck, finding and applying pressure, oh-so-gently, to each disordered vertebra, feeling no real change at all. Her intellect couldn't seem to distance itself from this particular patient in order to allow her hands to work on their own.

It's these blasted gloves for one thing, she thought, grateful that she didn't have to wear them normally in her practice. And it's also that I'm trying too hard. I can't make myself let go of control here.

Poor Isaiah, she thought eventually, her eyes welling up. I can't help you, sweet child.

Gently, she lowered him onto his back and pulled the lightweight cotton blanket around his body. Then she rested one hand on his brow and the other on his chest, and leaned her head against the high back of the rocker. Closing her eyes, she rocked and softly hummed the tune to "Jesus Loves Me."

Sometime later, she was startled by the sound of the door opening.

Jeli slipped around the privacy curtain and sat in the chair next to Hannah, studying her eyes. "It's not going well?"

"It's not going at all."

"Honey, I'm so sorry."

"Where's Lily?"

"She went to her hotel to try to get some rest. Poor woman hasn't slept since Friday night."

Hannah looked at Isaiah and felt the tears threatening again. "I had no idea how much I'd care, how much I wanted to be able to help this little guy."

"This is too much, Jo. Why don't you let me hold him awhile, and you go take a break. It's almost noon. You could get some lunch."

"It's that late? I must have dozed off. Lord, what if I'd dropped him?"

"That settles it. You need a break. The nurses probably have things they need to do for Isaiah, anyway, so why don't we both go out for lunch."

On the way down in the elevator, Hannah asked, "Do you think the nurses suspect who I am?"

"Even if they do, it doesn't matter. They're the soul of discretion."

They went to a diner down the block from the Transplant Center. Hannah wanted only a bagel and a cup of coffee, and Jeli managed to eat only half of her chef's salad.

"We're a jolly pair, aren't we," Jeli said.

"Not a lot to be jolly about just now."

"Oh, I don't know. How about the fact that there's been no sign of Disciples or reporters?"

"Mm. Yes, that's good."

"And that no one has challenged us with questions about our 'Order.'"

"True," Hannah said, beginning to smile. "And I *didn't* drop Isaiah while I was sleeping."

"Oh, yes, indeedy. That's worth a lot of jolly."

"And how about your persuading Lily to get some rest."

"Definitely rates on the jolly-meter."

They both ordered dessert, a cake the menu listed as "Death by Chocolate."

"Nothing like a dose of chocolate in the bloodstream to lift the spirits," Jeli said, smiling brightly, as she finished the last of her slice.

Hannah laughed out loud. "Unless its the sight of one famous author's chocolate-coated teeth."

They shared random light thoughts over mugs of coffee, and by the time they returned to the Center, Hannah felt refreshed and ready to face whatever the afternoon held in store.

As it turned out, what the afternoon held in store was nearly a repeat of the morning, except for Lily's absence and Jeli's presence in Isaiah's room.

Hannah and Jeli took turns holding and rocking Isaiah, and Hannah found herself better able to pray; with Jeli at her side, the contentious Hannahs were kept at bay.

When the nursing shift changed, Hannah and Jeli both went to the Center's chapel for a while. It was small and non-denominational, and Hannah was comforted by her sense of the countless prayers that had been offered there over the years. *You can feel the prayers hanging from the walls*, Grampa would have said.

Lily returned to the Center shortly after five-thirty, having changed out of her knit dress into designer jeans and a soft, yellow cotton sweater, looking rested and years younger than she had that morning.

Hesitantly, feeling weighed down with shame, Hannah told Lily of her lack of success with Isaiah.

Lily revealed that far more than her outfit had changed. "I know you've done your best," she said calmly, taking her son into her arms and settling into the rocker vacated by Hannah. "And I count it a blessing that he has survived one more day. Who knows? We could get the news any minute that there's a donor heart for him."

Hannah knelt beside Lily. "You're remarkable," she said.

Lily gave a sad little smile. "Just a mother who loves her sons."

Hannah stroked Isaiah's forehead for a few moments, then stood. "We'll be back after we get a bite to eat."

"Good. Thanks. By the way, I apologize for making such a fuss this morning. I wasn't myself. But I'll be all right now."

"You know," Hannah said, "I feel sure you will."

Jeli and Hannah each ate a light meal in the Center's cafeteria, and then returned and stayed with Isaiah and his mother until visiting hours ended at nine-thirty.

After they removed their protective gear, put on their blazers and gathered their coats, they met Lily at the elevators.

"I'm so sorry," Hannah said. "It breaks my heart that I couldn't… that it didn't—"

"Please don't apologize, Elizabeth. There, I've called you by your real name. The whole charade about your being a nun seems almost silly now."

"It does, but I thank you for all you did to stop the media blitz."

"By the way, I have something here for you." From a back pocket of her jeans, she removed a folded white envelope addressed to "Sister Marie Joseph." "Please don't open it until you're on the plane tomorrow, all right?"

"All right. But whatever it is, thank you."

They looked at each other steadily for a long moment. "I'm sad that I may never see you again, Elizabeth."

"Me too, Lily. But maybe someday… you never know."

"True. And, Sister Ruth—whatever your real name is, it's been wonderful to meet you. You've looked so familiar to me all day, once I saw you without your mask. I feel as if we've known each other for years."

Hannah glanced at Jeli's face, glad that it revealed nothing. "I know what you mean, Lily. It's as… Elizabeth here used to say, 'Maybe we knew each other in heaven.'"

A bit later, on the way down in the elevator, Hannah said, "I feel like crying for a month. He's so sweet, and she's so brave."

"Do you want to come back and see him briefly in the morning before we go to the airport?"

"Maybe. If we're up early enough. Let's see how we feel."

They were quiet the rest of the way back to their motel, Hannah dreading the phone calls that she'd be making to Rose, and Celeste and Michael. Dreading telling them she had failed.

Chapter Nineteen

Hannah and Ethan went hand-in-hand to her kitchen, Gabriel flitting around them, and Clancy dancing in front of them, nearly tripping them. Gabriel landed on Hannah's shoulder as she picked up the last tray of hors d'oeuvres, while Ethan brought another bottle of champagne out of the refrigerator. They kissed lightly, then they kissed again, and then they nearly put everything down so they could get into the kissing more earnestly, but Gabriel flew to Ethan's head and began to do his nesting routine, so they returned to the greatroom where everyone—Grampa, Papa, Celeste, Jeli, Michael, Matthew, and Rose—was waiting with big smiles and raised glasses. Papa said, "A toast to the happy—," and was stopped by Vivian's shriek from above. Hannah looked up and saw the Black widow, being lowered on wires from the cathedral ceiling. She held a flaming torch in one hand and with the other pressed a small bundle of something against her chest. Hannah almost laughed, thinking Vivian had arrived at the party dressed as the Statue of Liberty, but suddenly she took in what the old bat was shrieking: "GOD WILL NOT ALLOW YOU TO HAVE A NORMAL LIFE, JOHANNAH! GOD WILL NOT BE MOCKED! YOU'VE MURDERED THIS CHILD!" and she held the torch under the bundle, setting it on fire, and hurled it at Hannah, who caught it and saw that it was Isaiah, and his eyes were open and filled with fear and with fire, and his voice tried to scream through his burning mouth but instead it breathed flame into Hannah's face and she too began to burn...

Hannah was nearly dressed when she heard Jeli stir in her bed.

"Jo? Are you all right?"

"I have to go to the hospital. I'm burning up."

"You've got a fever? Let me—"

"It's my hands. I have to get to Isaiah."

"Oh, Lord," Jeli said. "Give me a minute, I'll come—"

"Don't have a minute." Hannah slipped into her coat and picked up her shoulder bag.

"Let me drive you then," Jeli said, putting on her coat over her pajamas. "You shouldn't drive when you're like this."

They were soon in the Accord, Jeli behind the wheel. "It's four in the morning, Jo. How on earth will you get in? What if the building's locked?"

"I don't know, but I will. I have to."

"I'll come with you."

"No, you can't help me this time."

"Well, then I'll go back to the motel and get dressed and pack our things, then I'll come to the Center and wait for you. Or I'll come up, if they'll let me."

Hannah didn't fully register what Jeli was saying, so focused was she on getting to Isaiah.

The Center's main doors were not locked, and the lobby was dimly lit and empty, except for a balding man in a security police uniform behind the reception desk. His face went quickly from boredom to alarm as Hannah burst through the doors and ran straight at him.

"I have to see Isaiah Severill right away," she said.

"That's impossible. Visiting hours don't begin—"

Hannah was already on her way to the elevators, and by the time the man came out from behind the reception desk, hollering for her to stop, she had pressed the button for Isaiah's floor and the doors were closing.

Moments later, she rushed past a burring telephone at the nurses' station. That'll be the lobby guard, Hannah thought. But he's too late.

She raced into Isaiah's room, peeling off her coat and dropping it on the floor as she went to the side of the hospital crib, reaching in for Isaiah with her bare, burning hands.

She was dimly aware of people rushing into the room, grabbing her arms, pulling at her. But she was already holding Isaiah, cradled in her left arm while she pressed her burning right hand against his chest and her lips to his forehead.

An urgent female voice said, "Wait, she'll drop him, be careful!" And that was the last thing Hannah heard before she lost consciousness.

Hannah's awareness returned gradually, beginning with the sense of hard wall at her back and hard floor beneath her. Then voices filtered in, and she opened her eyes to find herself still in Isaiah's room, in the corner by the windows onto the hall. Color had returned to her vision, and her hands were cool and slightly damp.

It was over, she knew that, but had she done any good?

A somber-faced security guard in his mid-thirties stood by the door, and three other people in nurse's whites—two women and a man—clustered around Isaiah's crib, talking in subdued voices.

"I don't understand it," said the taller of the two female nurses, shaking her pretty blond head. "This is crazy."

"Totally nuts," the male nurse agreed. He was of medium height with broad shoulders, his dark brown hair pulled back into a discreet ponytail.

"What's keeping Jensen?" asked the shorter nurse, her plump frame stretching the fabric of her uniform.

Just then, another woman hurried into the room, her presence immediately asserting authority. She was very tall, with bobbed, salt-and-pepper hair, and wore a white lab coat over a dark gray wool dress.

The three around Isaiah's crib stepped aside, making room for her.

"You're not going to believe this, Doc," said the male nurse, as the doctor leaned over the crib with her stethoscope.

Moments later, the doctor said, "What is this? He's got a perfect sinus rhythm. What's going on here?"

"That woman over there," said Mac, gesturing at Hannah. "She came tearing in here and picked him up, and by the time we got her off him… well, you can see for yourself."

Dr. Jensen looked at Hannah. "Who are you?" she asked, her voice imperious.

"A friend of Mrs. Severill's," Hannah replied, feeling very small.

"Isaiah's mother sent you here?"

"She… I was here with her—"

The doctor cut her off, asking Mac, "Did you call Mrs.

Severill?"

"No, not yet," said the man. "I thought you'd want to examine him before—"

"Right, I do."

Dr. Jensen ordered the two female nurses back to their stations, and said to Mac, "Isaiah's your patient tonight?"

"Yes," Mac answered. Hannah watched his hands clutch each other behind his back.

"Then you stay. Who's on at eight?"

"Elise Merritt, like yesterday."

"All right. Call her, ask her to come in early, as soon as she can. Then get back here. I want a thorough workup on Isaiah, *stat*."

"What's your name," she asked the security guard.

"Martin VanHoltz."

"VanHoltz. All right. I want you to take this woman to the station office. Get somebody up from Admin to deal with her."

"You want me to call the cops, Doctor?"

"No. She doesn't look like she'll run. Admin can handle the police."

Martin VanHoltz stood outside the nurses' station office while Hannah sat inside on a hard plastic chair, her heels up on the seat and her arms wrapped around her legs. She had put on her camel-hair coat and still could not get warm, although she guessed the temperature was around seventy-five degrees in that cramped little room. Her pulse beat hard behind her eyes and she felt the beginnings of a monster headache.

Hannah knew the security guard was waiting for someone from Administration, and she despairingly wished Lily might arrive first. She wondered if she would be arrested, and whether Isaiah had been healed. Would Jeli be allowed to come up when she got here, and would they make their flight to Chicago? She wished she had some aspirin for the pounding behind her eyes, and a bottle of Jack Daniels for her nerves. And some food, some chocolate-chip cookies, or a couple of donuts. Maybe not even the bourbon; something warm instead. Cocoa, cocoa with marshmallows, or a s'more with a Hershey bar and graham crackers and melty marshmallows, and a hot toddy. Thinking about booze and food was infinitely better than thinking about jail.

The nurse named Mac had appeared in the office, his face exhibiting both curiosity and resentment. He stood over her—keeping the upper hand, she thought—and began asking questions, noting her responses on a clipboard. When he expressed disbelief that she was a nun, she held her tongue to keep from admitting that she didn't blame him. Dressing at the motel, she'd simply grabbed what was handy. Now, her wild auburn hair loose around her face and shoulders, and wearing her black turtleneck sweater, black jeans and Reeboks, she guessed she looked about as much like a nun as he did. He also didn't believe that she had come to the hospital merely to hold Isaiah Severill, and she held her tongue again, because that was the truth. Mostly. He asked for the name and address of her convent and where she was staying in Rochester, and she refused to reply, saying she would wait until Mrs. Severill arrived before answering any more questions. Finally, when he left, he looked angrier than when he had arrived, and Hannah suspected he'd be catching more hell from the formidable Dr. Jensen.

Hannah had been in the little office for forty-five minutes or so, and was warm at last. In fact, she had begun to sweat over the prospect of legal charges being brought against her by the Mayo Clinic, when she heard a woman's voice in the hall. Someone was talking to the security guard, evidently telling him he could leave. Hannah watched the door, expecting to see Dr. Jensen or the dreaded "someone from Admin," and was surprised when Elise Merritt rushed into the room, her pale, pretty face flushed pink.

She took hold of Hannah's hand and said, "We've got to get you out of here right away."

"What—"

"Come on, follow me." Elise went to the door and looked out, then pulled Hannah behind her, heading down the hall in the opposite direction from the elevators. "We'll take the stairs," she whispered, opening the door into the stairwell.

"Thank God, Security sent Martin up to guard you," Elise was saying as they started down the first flight of switchback stairs. "He's been asking me out for months, so it was easy for me to persuade him that he was supposed to get back down to the first floor office."

Hannah said, "But what's—"

"See, I recognized you right away this morning, and I knew why you were here and I kept hoping all day that you'd be able to help that sweet baby. By the time I went to bed, I figured it just hadn't happened, but then Mac called... you know, the nurse on duty for Isaiah tonight?... and he told me to come in, that this crazy woman had done something to Isaiah, and I've never moved as fast as I did getting here, and thank God I did, 'cause the vultures are starting to gather out front of the hospital."

"Vultures?"

"The press. And some of those Shepherdess people. We're lucky, there's a local ordinance keeping them a distance from the Center itself."

"But how did they find out?"

"My guess is Jack at reception. He loves the spotlight."

"This is awful. What about... my friend? She was coming back for me."

"You mean the other *nun*?" Elise gave a little laugh. "She was just ahead of me in the lobby, thank God again. I sent her back out to the parking lot. She's waiting there for you."

They had reached the first floor, but Elise continued down another flight.

"I'll get you out through the restaurant's service entrance. There shouldn't be anyone around at this hour."

"What about you? Will you lose your job?"

"I don't think so. But even if I do, it's been worth it, meeting you—and now, what you've done for Isaiah, I wouldn't've missed this for anything."

Elise had been wrong: a few of the kitchen staff were already at work. Still, she and Hannah appeared to stir no interest, and quickly made it to the kitchen's panic door. Hannah pushed on the bar, but then stopped and turned to face Elise. "Thank you for helping me."

They hugged briefly, and Elise whispered, "Godspeed, and

thank *you*, angel."

Making her way toward the visitors' parking lot, panic rose in Hannah's throat like vomit when she saw the crowd of men and women that had stationed itself about twenty-five feet from the front of the Center. There were TV-channel trucks, cameras, and klieg lights waiting to be switched on when the mystery woman was escorted from the building.

God! Hannah thought. Thank you for Elise Merritt.

When she reached the street, she turned left, away from the parking lot, and hurried two blocks in the wrong direction before doubling back and looking for Jeli. She found her standing beside the Accord, facing away from Hannah toward the front of the hospital.

She coughed softly, wanting to alert Jeli to her presence without startling her. Jeli turned, saw Hannah and gave an exaggerated sigh as she pressed a hand to her heart. Then she climbed in behind the wheel of the car while Hannah opened the back door on the driver's side, got in and hunched down on the floor as best she could. "Okay, go," she whispered, and Jeli started the engine, steering the Accord around to the parking lot's rear entrance. They exited without having to pay a fee—free parking between 10 P.M. and 6 A.M.—and before long were on the highway out of Rochester, heading toward the Twin Cities.

Jeli broke the tense silence. "How's Isaiah?"

"I think he'll make it, Jeli. I heard the doctor say he had a perfect sinus rhythm."

Jeli reached back through the gap between the front seats, found Hannah's hand and squeezed it gently. "Ah, love—this is wonderful!"

"But now they know exactly what I look like, and Vivian has her goddam proof." And so does everyone else who's interested, Hannah thought.

She heard Grampa's voice in her mind. *I'm proud of you, honey. You did what was right.*

Sorry, Grampa, Hannah silently answered him. But I need a lot more than your pride in me right now.

"I wonder, Jeli," she said aloud, "what wise person said, 'No good deed goes unpunished'?"

Chapter Twenty

It was a little after seven that evening when Hannah brought her Jeep to a stop beside her father's house. She turned off the engine and stepped out, bending and stretching briefly, unkinking a bit from the long day of travel in cars and airplanes. Then she made her way around the side of the house toward the back, toward the addition that Papa and Carl Kingsley had built in early 1984, soon after their business began to take off. It was a sprawling, airy space, with arched windows and skylights, combining a luxurious kitchen and dining area with a large, comfortably furnished family room.

Michael was coming out the back door before she reached it. "Hey!" he said, swooping her up in a bear hug.

"Hey, yourself," she laughed. "How'd you know—"

"Gran called after you dropped her off at home."

Celeste stood in the doorway. "There you are," she said, hugging Hannah close. "Welcome home."

When Hannah stepped through the door, Clancy bounded into her, and she knelt to hug him and receive his enthusiastic welcome. Yes, she thought. I'm home. Thank God.

Clancy's weight maneuvered her into sitting, and she slipped out of her coat as he draped himself across her legs. "I guess we know who's in charge here, don't we, pal," Hannah said, stroking the silky length of his back. "I hope he hasn't been too much of a dictator around here the last couple of days," she said to Celeste, who was stirring something on the kitchen's island cooktop.

"That little cupcake? Putty in my hands."

"Speaking of putty," Michael said, settling his long frame onto the Spanish-tile floor beside Hannah. "Mom decided you'd need some of her cure-all hot chocolate with marshmallows."

"She's right. In fact, Cell, where were you at five-thirty this morning?"

"Why? What was going on at five-thirty this morning?"

"I was sitting in a tiny little office, fantasizing about cocoa and headache remedies and jail." Hannah chuckled, but stopped abruptly when she saw the look on Michael's face, and on Celeste's, who had turned toward her.

Michael put a hand on the back of Hannah's neck and squeezed lightly. "Don't be joking about jail. Things were pretty tense around here till you called from Minneapolis."

Hannah patted his arm. "I'm sorry, Mikey. You too, Celeste. We should have stopped to call between Rochester and the airport."

"You don't have to apologize," Celeste said, bringing Hannah a mug of hot chocolate topped with melting marshmallows. "You must have been terrified they'd catch up with you." She sat on a barstool by the island. "Before I forget, Rose called about a half an hour ago and seems pretty tense herself. Do you want to call her from here, let her know you're home?"

"I guess I should," Hannah said, dreading yet another episode of defending herself with Rose.

Michael seemed to hear her thoughts. "I'll do it," he said, getting to his feet. "I'll tell her you're with us and that she should relax."

"I owe you one, Mikey. And if she wants to come over, tell her—"

"I'll tell her no. I don't have a problem saying no to Rose."

"What d'you think, Jo?" said Celeste. "Would Clancy let us move over where it's more comfortable?"

As she stood, Hannah asked, "Where are Pop and Matt?"

Celeste settled into a soft, caramel-colored leather chair while Hannah sat in the middle of the matching sofa, and Clancy scootched a good portion of his upper body onto her lap.

"Matt had to be back at Penn on Monday for baseball," Celeste said. "And your dad is supervising one of his crews, putting some finishing touches on that restaurant that's supposed to open on May first. I don't expect him home much before eleven."

"I see. I was just wondering if either of them knows about... what I've been doing."

"Matt doesn't, I'm sure. As for your father, I'd guess he

consciously knows nothing except what you told him about your trip to Chicago. Unconsciously… well, who can say?"

"Does it bother you that Pop's in denial like this?" Michael asked, coming to sit beside Hannah on the sofa.

"I'm glad, really. Any other way, he'd feel responsible for me and that'd drive him nuts. Drive us all nuts. Now tell me, master negotiator, did you succeed with Rose?"

"Of course. She even said to remind you that if you can't call her tonight, she's your last patient tomorrow afternoon and she'll see you then."

"I'm impressed. How'd you do it?"

"Piece of cake. I only had to promise her your first-born child."

As they laughed, Hannah felt such a rush of love for him and for Celeste, such a sense of complete safety, that everything within her relaxed. She settled back into the sofa and began to tell them the story of the past five days, beginning with Saturday's plane crash.

"Jeli changed out of her nun clothes at the Twin Cities airport and we went looking for our gate, and once we found it and sat down, I zoned out, and I think she did too," Hannah said. "After that, we probably didn't say more than twenty words for the rest of the trip home. Sheer exhaustion."

Hannah had been avoiding Celeste's and Michael's eyes for the past few minutes, unnerved by the emotion she saw there. "I don't know how your mother does it, Cellie. I hope I have half the energy at her age."

No one spoke, and Hannah struggled to keep her focus on Clancy, to keep herself from pleading with them to remember who she was: still Johannah, still the same person they'd known all these years, not some magical being who'd floated into their midst from over the rainbow.

As if they had read Hannah's mind, Celeste moved to sit on the sofa and Michael slid closer to her, Celeste wrapping her left arm, Michael his right, around her back. They stayed there beside her for a while, quietly loving on her.

Hannah absorbed their love and their silent support, feeling like a five-year-old who's just discovered Christmas. She began to weep, then to sob, covering her face with her hands and leaning into Clancy's warm body, feeling Michael's and Celeste's arms and hands on her back and neck and shoulders, and taking in without comprehending their murmured words of comfort. After awhile, when the tears began to slow, Hannah felt herself start to pull away; she was congenitally able to receive only a certain amount of love at any one time, and she'd reached her limit. Embarrassment began to set in, and she lifted her head, saying, "Thanks, guys. Thank you." Swiping at her cheeks with her hands, she asked for some tissues, and Michael sprang up to get them from the powder room.

Celeste kissed Hannah's cheek and stood, picking up Hannah's cocoa mug, staring into it as if she'd never seen it before. "This has gone cold," she said. "I think I'll just zap it for a minute."

Watching her carry the cocoa mug to the microwave oven, and seeing Michael come back into the room, proffering a flowered box of tissues, Hannah realized with a sense of relief that they, too, were embarrassed. They, too, had difficulty with displays of emotion.

What was needed, she saw, was a complete change of subject. "Somebody tell me the news from the Mayo Clinic."

"Mom didn't have you listening to KYW on the drive home?"

"She didn't even mention it. I think we were both still trying to put distance between ourselves and all that."

Celeste handed Hannah her nuked cocoa and sat again in one of the leather chairs. "Well, let's see… the best news is, Isaiah's heart is beating as steadily now as any healthy eighteen-month-old's, and—"

"It is?"

"You didn't know?"

"Not for sure. I hoped, but—"

"It's true," said Michael, popping a beer for himself and settling beside Hannah on the sofa. "Mission accomplished."

"Thank heaven. Any more good news?"

"Lots, I think," Celeste said. "The Clinic doesn't plan to take any legal action against you—if they could even find you—

because Isaiah's doing so well. Also because of pressure from Lily Severill, would be my guess. And the only employee getting the boot is the guard who was at the reception desk this morning. He's the one who called the media."

"Mm. Elise thought he might be."

"Elise?"

"Isaiah's day nurse."

"Oh, right. There've been interviews with her and the night nurse, and also the doctor who first came on the scene after you… did what you did."

"Do they know Elise helped me get out of there?"

"If they do, they're not saying."

"But they have a perfect description of me now, don't they."

Michael said, "Not *perfect* by a long shot. That nurse and Isaiah's mom, both of them are doing a great job muddying the waters about what you look like, swearing up and down that you were wearing a wig and contact lenses at the hospital."

"But what about the male nurse, Mac? He's no friend of mine. Neither is that doctor who showed up."

"I don't think you have to worry about them, Jo," said Celeste. "The doctor apparently wasn't paying much attention to what you looked like, and the male nurse agrees with Lily and Elise Merritt, says no one's eyes could be your color naturally."

"What about the security camera film?"

"Were you avoiding them on purpose, Jo?" asked Michael. "They don't seem to have any good shots of you."

"We were doing our best."

Michael smiled. "Where'd you and Gran get your CIA training?"

"So, are you telling me we've had unbelievably good luck across the board with this thing?… No, I can see it on your faces. Okay, what's the bad news?"

Michael nodded at his mother, as if asking her to be the messenger.

"It's the feeding frenzy over finding you," said Celeste, moving again to the sofa to sit beside Hannah. "I've never seen anything like it. Not just the news media, but the Disciples of the Shepherdess. Naturally, they're more convinced than ever that you're... who they say you are. I'm just afraid they won't give up until... well—"

"Mom and I think you need some kind of plan," Michael said, putting a hand on Hannah's shoulder. "You need to decide how you want to deal with it if they do catch up with you."

Hannah felt as if she were in a falling elevator. She lifted Clancy's head from her knee and looked into his contented, half-closed eyes. "I'll have to go away, won't I," she said. "I'll have to leave my life... all of you, everybody. My patients. My home. Everything."

"You're not going anywhere without me," said Michael.

"Can you do that, Jo?" Celeste asked, very gently. "Is that the choice you would prefer? Because if it is—whatever choice you make in this—you know we'll all support you one hundred percent."

"What other choice is there for me, Cellie?"

Michael answered her. "You could stand and face it, Jo, with me and Matt and Pop protecting you."

She shook her head. "They'll destroy me," she said. "Some will claim I'm the antichrist like Vivian says. Others will get into this Shepherdess thing. Either way, they'll tear me apart."

Michael said, "They won't, Jo. We won't let them. We can get you the best security people. Carl Kingsley's sons, you know, they're in that business. We'll get protection around the clock..." He trailed off, apparently aware of the sort of picture he was painting. He shook his head. "Sorry. Got carried away."

Celeste gently squeezed Hannah's knee. "You know, sweetie, there are other genuine healers around these days who seem to be able to live fairly normal lives."

"If you're wondering why I believe that way isn't open to me, I can't explain it. It's just something I'm sure about, and I wish I weren't."

Seeing the concern on Celeste's and Michael's face somehow strengthened Hannah. She took hold of their hands. "I need to think about this, and I need to ask Grampa what I should do. And Jeli, I need to talk some specifics with her. Meanwhile, we won't get discouraged, right? We're the fightin' Kirklands of Chester County and we ain't givin' in." She squeezed their hands and stood up abruptly, sending Clancy scampering backwards. "Now, this particular fightin' Kirkland is going home with her loyal mutt."

Celeste and Michael went with her to the door.

"By the way," she said with a smile, "Vivian's not waiting down at my house with a horde of reporters, is she?" She felt her smile fall away when she saw the look on Celeste's face.

"I'm sorry to have to tell you this, Jo. Vivian has a brain tumor. It's malignant and it's inoperable."

Hannah felt as if she'd been punched in the stomach; her knees buckled and she sat down hard on the floor.

"Whoa!" Michael said, crouching beside her. "You all right?"

"She's... I... why didn't you tell me?"

Celeste knelt beside her. "We didn't want you to have anything else on your mind."

"But... wasn't her EEG normal, you said?"

"She had an MRI late Monday morning."

Hannah suddenly became aware of a throbbing headache. She put her hands to her head, pressing, as if she needed to keep it from breaking open. "My head..."

"Mike, get her some aspirin. Come on back to the sofa, Jo."

"Just... just let me lie here for a minute," she said, stretching out where she was.

Michael brought the aspirin and a small throw pillow for her head. He draped her camelhair coat over her and lay down beside her, resting a hand on her shoulder. Clancy stood by her, whimpering.

"There, there, Clancy," Celeste said, stroking his back. "I promise she'll be okay, big fella."

"What is it, Jo?" Michael asked, his voice nearly a whisper.

"Don't know. Should be dancing, shouldn't I. Not knocked out like this."

"It's probably the shock on top of everything else," said Celeste. "No matter how you feel about her, she's been in your life—"

"Forever," said Hannah, covering her eyes with the back of her arm. "So what's her prognosis? How long does she have?"

"It's spreading quickly," answered Celeste. "She'll be losing consciousness more and more often as time goes on. They're giving her meds, and they've started her on radiation, but they think nothing's going to help much."

Michael said, "They're saying two to six months, tops."

"They're keeping her in the hospital?"

"For a while," said Celeste. "Then she'll go to a nursing home. And there's one other thing, Jo; she's begging for you to come see her."

"God, no."

"It's okay. Nobody's going to force you. I just thought you should know. To me, she seems utterly changed since Sunday."

Hannah shook her head. "A changed Vivian. Impossible to imagine." She took her arm away from her eyes and looked at Celeste. "I need to go home."

"Mike, help Hannah to her Jeep and drive her down."

Hannah watched Michael jump up, idly wondering if her body would have energy like that ever again.

"I'll stay with her and drive her to work in the morning," Michael said, helping Hannah to her feet.

"No, honey. I want you to help her get settled and then come on home."

"Sorry, Mikey, but your mom's right. I need to... I don't know... maybe I need to just *be* for a while."

By ten o'clock Hannah was in bed, slipping down quickly, gratefully, into oblivion.

Chapter Twenty-One

The next morning, Hannah awoke before six and lay in bed for a few minutes while fear slithered into her mind, threatening to imbed itself like a leach. She sat up and shook herself mentally. *I had a great sleep,* she thought. *I'm well rested and that will have to be good enough.*

Minutes later, she slipped a UB40 CD into her Discman and went out for a run with Clancy. Inhaling the chilly, dew-freshened greening of early spring, she turned off the Discman and listened instead to the morning birdsong. Soon she was in that timeless, mystical place where earthly problems had no meaning, where she wished she could stay forever. When she finally headed home, she felt—for the moment—as light and carefree as a kitten.

After she showered and dried her hair, she dressed for work in her usual soft khakis—black, today—and silk shirt—today she chose a long-sleeved, bright, rebellious red. She slipped into her Mephistos and went to the kitchen, where she fed Clancy and let him out. Then she sat down to a breakfast of orange juice, a nearly overripe banana, and a bowl of Grape-Nuts with the last of a quart of milk.

I'll pick up some coffee at Wawa on the way to the office, she thought. *Please, God, don't let Sally be on the job today.*

She had just started on her cereal when she remembered the envelope that Lily had handed her at the hospital elevator on Tuesday night. "Please don't open it until you're on the plane tomorrow," Lily had said. Immediately curious, Hannah went to her shoulder bag and retrieved the envelope, brought it back to the table and opened it. Inside were several handwritten sheets of Lily's business stationery and an oblong piece of paper that fluttered out onto the floor, face down. She picked it up and turned it over, and her mouth dropped open; it was a cashier's check for fifty thousand dollars. "Jesus!" she said aloud, slapping it onto the table, face down again. She stared at the back of it for a few moments, shaking her head. What are you doing, Lily? she thought. There's no way in hell I can keep that.

She turned her attention to the letter. It was dated Monday, April 14—before Lily could have known for certain that Hannah would show up at the Clinic.

She read:

"Dear Elizabeth,

I know that's probably not your real name, but it's a name I love and it suits you.

Compared to what you've done for me and for my family, this money means nothing. Please don't hesitate about accepting it. You gave my son Micah's life back to me and that alone is a gift beyond measure. And if you're reading this, that means you've come to the Mayo at great risk to your anonymity to try and help my poor Isaiah. As I said, this money means nothing by comparison.

The real gift that I hope to give you is of a very different sort. After we spoke yesterday (once I understood what your privacy means to you), I began to think about what I could do to repair the damage that I've done in my thoughtless, public search for you. I've concluded that there is nothing <u>concrete</u> within my power that will lessen the furor over finding you. Instead, I've decided to approach that furor head-on in the hope of directing its power onto myself (and my extensive personal and business resources), rather than on you.

My plan is that when I return from the Mayo Clinic later this week, I will hold a news conference and announce that I have met with you in person and have become thoroughly convinced that it is my role to guard your privacy. I will tell the world what you have told me— that your healing powers are <u>not under your control</u>, and that sometimes they have not been available even for your near-and-dear ones. I expect that there will be much skepticism about this—people do long for miracles—but I will do the very best I can to convince everyone (as I am convinced) of its truth.

Otherwise, I intend to embroider the truth wherever I can to mislead the public, but I will not answer any questions about your real identity or even what you look like. (This is because I'm fairly certain that the blond shag was a wig, and I'm fearful that any misdirection about your appearance might go horribly wrong and turn out to be an accurate description!)

Of course, human beings have an almost universal need for healing, so I fear that many will continue their pursuit undaunted (especially this Shepherdess group that says they've prophesied you). There is no question in my mind that the world needs you, just as I have and do. But my hope is that this effort of mine will take a little of the pressure off of you for now.

And please know, dearest Elizabeth, if there is ever any way that I can help you further, you have but to ask!

With Easter coming up in just six days, it seems very fitting to me that God has chosen this time of year to present the world with an angel. I've long known that the definition of angel is 'messenger', and that fits, for you are a messenger of God's love for the world. Now if we can just insure your protection so that you may continue with your life of healing in privacy, with only the eye of the Lord as your witness, we will have much to celebrate this Easter.

With my love and gratitude forever,

Lily Severill

P.S. If, by some terrible circumstance, your identity is revealed against your will, I will still come forward and claim that they have the wrong angel and that I, alone, know the identity of the right one. After all, who should know better than I?"

Hannah's Grape-Nuts had turned to gray-brown goo by the time she finished reading Lily's letter, but it didn't matter. She had lost her appetite and her mind was racing. It was as if everything Lily had said had put reality back in front of Hannah's face. The good sleep she'd had, the good run, the chance to get back to work—no matter how Hannah wished things could be as they were six days ago, the truth was that everything had changed irrevocably.

She looked at Clancy where he sat next to her, watching her expectantly. He wagged his tail back and forth in broad sweeps on the kitchen floor. "What do you think, pal?" she asked him. "Do we have to run away now, or turn and take a stand?" Clancy lifted his ears and opened his eyes wider, as if he were giving their options serious thought. "Or could I just go to work and try to hope that everything will gradually return to normal?"

Worst case scenario, she thought, Lily's efforts will at least buy me some time.

Thinking about time, she realized it was getting late. She wrote a quick note to Lily—"Thank you, but I can't accept this. And thank you for your plan; that I do accept with gratitude."—and put it along with the cashier's check in a stamped envelope addressed to Lily at her offices in Philadelphia, planning to drop it in the mailbox near the Wawa. Then she threw her dishes into the sink, brushed her teeth, put on her Burberry, loved on Clancy for a few moments, and was headed out of the driveway by seven-fifty.

Hannah mailed the check, then got her coffee, the *Philadelphia Inquirer*, and a Daily Local News at the Wawa, grateful for the absence of nosy Sally. When she was about to climb back into her Jeep in the parking lot, she stopped and thought for a moment. Then she turned, retraced her steps, and stuffed the newspapers into the trash can by the store's right-side door. Temporary insanity, she thought, buying those papers. The last thing I want this morning is to read about people scrambling to find me.

She parked in the lot behind her office building on North Church Street shortly after eight-ten, and moments later entered her reception room to find Kyla Morgan already behind the counter.

"Hey, Ky!" she said. "Aren't you the early bird."

Kyla came out from behind the counter, her long African-print cotton dress flowing softly around her slim figure. "Just trying to make a good impression on the boss," she said with a grin.

They gave each other a substantial hug, then Kyla stepped back and made a show of studying Hannah, head to foot. "What's up with you, Doc?" she asked, shaking her head, making her huge, gold hoop earrings swing. "You're supposed to be all rested up from a few days off, but you look like you could use a few days off."

Hannah laughed and rubbed her knuckles on the top of Kyla's soft, curly black hair. Kyla batted at her hand and put on an aggrieved look.

"Not all of us lead such carefree lives as you, Mrs. Morgan," Hannah said. "If I recall correctly, you were griping last spring after a two-week honeymoon in Hawaii that you needed time off for re-entry."

"Listen, girlfriend," Kyla said, "If you had to come back to work from two weeks of love in paradise, you'd be griping too. My guess is the mid-west wasn't all that relaxing for you."

Hannah caught the knowing look behind Kyla's dark, smiling eyes, and realized that here might be one more person who had correctly identified the "Angler's angel".

Briskly, she turned to business. "Have you been collecting the voice mail?"

Picking up her cue, Kyla handed Hannah a small pile of pink, phone-message slips. "Ma'am, yes ma'am, couple times a day. I rescheduled everyone, and filled up your schedule for tomorrow like we said, ten till three. I also scheduled two new patients with the usual hour each, next week and the week after I'll tell you, lady, you've got one full appointment book for the next month."

"Good. Any patients have problems that couldn't wait till I got back?"

"A couple, but Dr. McGaurn took care of them."

"Bless her. Anything else I need to know?"

"I've put the mail, the personal stuff, on your desk, and I saved some voice mails for you to hear. A couple of them are from a Reverend Yarnell—says he's your grandmother's pastor, and would you please come to see her at the hospital. I don't know what that's all about, since I didn't even know you had any living grandmothers, but I guess mine is not to reason why."

"She's my step-grandmother, not a blood relative, and she's been the bane of my life for... well, for most of my life. Now she's in the hospital with inoperable brain cancer."

"Oh, Hannah, I'm sorry. That's really tough. Do you want me to call the Reverend back and put him off somehow?"

Hannah considered for a moment. "What would you say to him? 'I'm very sorry but Doctor Kirkland is unwilling to have anything to do with that sick old crone'? No, just call Matlack Florists and get them to send a nice big arrangement of something springy to Mrs. Vivian Black at Chester County Hospital, with a get-well card signed from Johannah. That'll hold her awhile, I hope."

"How much do you want to spend?"

"At least a hundred. I'm feeling extravagant today."

Kyla grinned. "I see," she said, turning *see* into two syllables. "Is it time, then, to discuss my raise?"

"Sure. You've got it. Fifty cents more a week. How's that."

"Wow. Now I can buy that gumball I've had my eye on."

"You really should save it up for that rainy day, y'know," Hannah laughed. Then she turned her attention to the pink slips in her hand. "So, two of the voice mails were from the pastor. And these others?"

"Two from a Lynn Thomkins. Called herself your cousin, she and her sister Marcia. The first one was Tuesday night, from California, letting you know that they were flying in yesterday to see their grandmother in the hospital—I guess that's your Vivian Black, yes? Then the second one, last night from the Holiday Inn, urging you to call them a.s.a.p. Something about seeing you on TV?"

Lord, Hannah was thinking. Lynnie and Marcie. Twenty-one years since I've seen them, and they recognize me on TV? What next? "Okay, I'll give her a call. Anything else?"

"One last one, kind of peculiar. I got the feeling this guy had been calling a lot, getting frustrated with the voice mail, and finally decided to leave a message. Says his name is—"

Bill Tyler popped into Hannah's mind, as Kyla said, "William Tyler."

Not a wild card anymore, Hannah thought. "What did he

want?"

"He started out by saying he wanted to talk to you, and that he thinks you know why. Then he seemed to change his mind and he took a new tack, asked you to call him back so he could make an appointment for an adjustment. Said he was in an accident on Saturday. Then he changed direction again and said he'd just stop in to see you on Friday, if he hadn't heard from you. By the end, he sounded so miserable that I had to laugh. Made me think of all the times I've left a babbling phone message and wished I could call back and erase the whole thing."

Something in Hannah's expression wiped the mirth from Kyla's. "Are you all right, Doc?" she asked. "Do you want me to get rid of this character for you?"

Hannah gave a wry laugh. "Planning to hire a hit man, are you? No, it's okay. I'll have to face him eventually." She sighed. "I'm pretty sure he doesn't really want an adjustment, so just call him and ask him if he'd like to meet me here tomorrow afternoon, say around three-thirty."

"Will do. So, Doc, I can't help wondering... is there something going on that you want to tell me about?"

Hannah returned Kyla's steady gaze as she said, "Probably. But not just yet. I have to sort out some things first. Okay?"

"Of course. I just hope you know I'm here for you."

"I do, Ky, and I'm grateful. So, that's it, then?"

"That's it. Oh, except, what's your music mood today?"

"Soothing and unintrusive, I think. Let's do all Bach."

"You got it. Becca Robinson's your first patient, at nine."

"Good. I can't wait to get back to work. Feel like I've been off for months."

"Sure sign of a lady who loves what she does for a living."

"Speaking of love," Hannah said as she headed toward the back rooms. "Remind me to tell you about the man I met this weekend."

"Hey! That's no fair. I have to hear now!"

"Patience is a virtue," Hannah said with a laugh, pulling the door to her private office closed behind her.

She sat at her desk and wondered why in the world she'd given Kyla a hint about Ethan. After all, what was there really between herself and this man she'd seen twice in her life? I'm being completely ridiculous about him, she thought.

Deliberately, she pushed Ethan out of her mind and phoned Celeste, telling her about Lily's intentions. "Just in case she has that press conference today, I wanted you to know."

"This is good, Jo, don't you agree?"

"At least it might give me some breathing room."

"Right. I'll tell Mike when he gets up. And do you want me to call Mom?"

"Would you, please? I've got some more calls to make and my first patient's due in at nine."

"Consider it done."

She listened then to the saved voice mail, ill at ease with Lynn's message and oddly soothed by Bill Tyler's patent nervousness.

Next she dialed the number for the Holiday Inn, and moments later heard a breezy female voice say, "Hey."

"Lynn, is that you? It's Hannah."

"Hann! How ya doin'?"

"All right. How about you and Marcia?"

"I'm fine, but Marce, she's... so when can we see you?"

"I'm with patients till after five today. But tell me what's the matter with Marcia?"

"How about we get together tonight? We'll fill you in on everything then. Come over here and we'll figure out something to do for dinner."

Hannah considered inviting them to her house, but dismissed the idea. After all, they were practically strangers. "Okay. I could make it sometime after six-thirty."

"Great. We're in room one-three-three."

"Fine, I'll be there."

"Hannah, just a sec. I... we need to know, and I can't wait till tonight. That gal on TV at the Mayo Clinic? Marce and I both think she looks like the picture of you we got with your Christmas card a couple years back. So we're wondering... well, *was* it you?"

Hannah forced a small laugh. "You can't imagine how many people have asked me that. I guess I've got a *doppelgänger*."

There was a silence down the line that made Hannah nervous. "Is something wrong, Lynn?"

"Well, see, what's the matter with Marcie is leukemia and I guess we were hoping maybe you could... you know, fix her up."

Hannah's heart sank. "Oh, Lynn. I'm so sorry."

"Thanks, Hann. I'm sorry too. I shouldn't have put you on the spot like that. Actually, Marce is doing pretty good. She's been in remission for a while. But then when we saw that woman on the TV news, we couldn't help getting kind of excited. Thought maybe we'd struck gold, coming out here to see a grandmother we hardly remember, and finding a cure for this damn disease in the bargain. I guess the truth is we got pretty stupid, like hoping we had the winning lottery ticket or something."

"Never stupid to hope," Hannah said, finding herself hoping that her hands would burn tonight for Marcia.

When she hung up with Lynn, she drummed her fingers lightly on the glass-topped desk for a few moments, then took her wallet from her shoulder bag, found the gray-blue calling card and dialed the office number it listed.

"Ethan Quinn," answered his warm baritone.

"Hi," she said, her voice little more than a squeak. She felt herself blush as she cleared her throat and tried again. "Hi. It's Hannah."

"Hannah!" he said. "Are you all right?"

"I'm okay," she said, feeling shaky all of a sudden.

"Are you sure? I know you've been... busy."

"No, I'm okay. I think so, anyway. I would like to, uh... could we talk sometime, you and I?"

"Please. Every time the phone has rung since Sunday morning, I've hoped it would be you. When can we meet?"

She knew her cheeks were still red and was glad he couldn't see her. "Could we start with a long phone conversation?" she asked, blushing deeper with the sudden memory of how such a phone call ended in a romantic comedy from the '90's called *The Truth About Cats and Dogs.*

"I understand. You don't know anything about me. When could we talk?"

"Tonight? Shall I call you at your home number?"

"Fine. What time?"

"Say, around nine-thirty, ten?"

"Right, nine-thirty. And, Hannah—"

"Yes?"

"You *will* call me, won't you?"

Hannah was quiet for a moment, remembering his face and the deep blue of his eyes. "I will. I promise. But I have to meet some people for dinner and... well, if things get complicated, how late could I call?"

"Call me anytime, it doesn't matter."

"You're sure."

"I can't even begin to tell you how sure I am."

Hannah had to restrain herself from echoing the deeper meaning she heard in his words. "Okay, but I'll try to call by nine-thirty."

"Hannah, thank you. I hate to be trite, but I feel as if I've known you all my life."

From when we were still in heaven, Hannah thought.

Chapter Twenty-Two

Hannah was grateful for her thoughts of Ethan that flowed beneath the bridge of the day like a peaceful stream, enabling her to remain calm and focused.

Despite the fact that she saw speculation and, occasionally, outright recognition in the eyes of a few of her patients, her hands took over, using their chiropractic skill and training, giving her intellect time off. As a result, she was relaxed with each of her patients, able to tune in to their needs and, best of all, help them feel better physically and emotionally. Days like this reaffirmed her conviction that hers was the world's best profession.

A few minutes' conversation with Jeli, mid-morning, only strengthened Hannah's sense of calm. "Celeste told me what Lily intends to do, and I'll be keeping my fingers crossed for her success on a grand scale," Jeli had said. Then she'd added, "I hope you don't need reminding—I'm quite literally here for you if you need me."

Michael had come by the office around noon, and they had walked a few blocks to a café for lunch together. Over gourmet sandwiches named for streets in town, he had told her he didn't think much of Lily's plan. "In reality, Jo, what can she do to protect you?" And he was worried; he needed to get back to school to work on a paper—he couldn't concentrate at home—but he didn't want to leave Hannah unguarded.

"Remind me," she had said, deadpan. "How long does it take you to get from Penn to my house?" She watched his slow grin.

"Okay, I get the point. But call me, will you, if anything happens?"

"You'll be home Sunday?"

"Sure, maybe sooner. Matt's coming home late Saturday night."

"Good. I have a feeling it'll be a nice Easter," she said, imagining Ethan returning to the house with her after church. "Maybe even a terrific Easter."

Hannah had remained relaxed even though Rose arrived at four-fifteen, half an hour early for her adjustment. She was accustomed to Rose's early arrivals, and was usually annoyed by them, but today she'd been able to stay focused on the patient under her hands. Today she felt accepting of Rose with all her irritating idiosyncrasies. A Rose is a Rose is a Rose, she'd reminded herself.

When it was Rose on the high-low table, Hannah said, "I'm sorry I haven't called you. It seems like there's been one thing after another, and my head has been spinning half the time."

"That's okay, Jo," Rose said, her voice muffled slightly by the table's face rest. "You can fill me in over dinner."

"Dinner? I can't, not tonight."

"Didn't Michael tell you I wanted to have dinner with you after my adjustment?"

"I'm sorry, but I've promised to meet with Lynn Thomkins and her sister Marcia. Do you remember my telling you about them, Vivian's granddaughters?"

"No."

"Well, I'm sure I did, a long time ago. And now they've come out to see her. I'm guessing she had her pastor send them an S.O.S. like she did with me." Hannah touched Rose's shoulder and said, "You can turn on your side now."

Rose turned on her left side and Hannah went to work with the drop-head piece. "What's going on with Vivian?" Rose asked.

"Vivian… I can hardly believe it, but she's been diagnosed with a malignant brain tumor, inoperable."

Kyla knocked and poked her head in the door just then to say goodnight. Hannah gave her a solid hug and wished her a nice weekend.

"You too, boss," Kyla said. There was a somber note in her voice as she added, "Behave yourself, okay."

"Always. Please don't worry about me."

She returned to the table, and Rose said, "That's awful about Vivian. Does it means she's dying?"

"I guess so, although it's hard to take in."

"And she wants you to come to see her?"

"Yes," Hannah said, indicating that Rose should turn onto her right side.

"Will you go?"

"I don't know. Eventually, I probably will."

"What if she wants you to heal her, Jo?"

Hannah hadn't told Rose about Vivian's accusations on Sunday. "Why do you say that?"

"Because I think she's always known about you."

"You can sit up now," Hannah said. "When she called you looking for me on Sunday night, did she tell you she thought I'm the Angler's angel?"

"Well, in fact, she did. She was really quite friendly, and I—"

"You didn't *confirm* it for her!"

"No, of course I didn't."

"But when she's friendly like that, Rose, I've told you a million times, watch out for what's really going on."

"I know, I know. I'm not an idiot. It's just that since she did guess the truth, I figured now she's likely to ask you to heal her."

"It seems to me, if she wants my help, she has an awful lot of bridges to unburn first."

"Speaking of burning, if you go see her and your hands start to heat up, *would* you heal her?"

"Aw, Rosie, I don't know. I can't... I don't want to even think about it right now."

"Sure, but it could happen, you know. God certainly wants you to forgive her, and what better way than to heal her?"

The anger rose in Hannah like a flash flood. She walked to the window and looked out on the weathered stockade fence that separated her offices from the residence next door. "Why do you always have to do this, Rose?"

"Do what?"

"Push me. You're always pushing me to deal with things that may not even happen, when what's already happening is hard enough."

"I'm just asking you a simple question. I didn't mean to get you all upset."

Hannah turned around to face her. "And it's not only pushing me, you're always telling me what God expects of me. Other than Vivian, you're the only person I know who does that."

"That's a low blow. The only thing I have in common with Vivian Black is my faith in God."

"There's also your unceasing efforts to control the faith of others."

"Hannah! What's come over you? You never talk to me this way."

"Maybe it's time I did."

"How can you say that? You've been my best friend all these years. You saved my life!"

"And you seem totally bent on *fixing* mine. Can't you just let me be?"

"What do you mean, let you be? I'm always letting you *be*! I don't camp out on your doorstep and spy on you and tell you what to do."

"Sometimes, that's exactly how it feels! Like I have to answer to you in every aspect of my life. And I'm never, ever going to get it right."

"What in the world are you talking about? No one loves you more than I do."

"The truth is, no one tries to *control* me more than you do, and I can't stand it anymore."

"What are you saying?" Rose asked, her voice suddenly gone small.

Hannah looked at her there, sitting sideways on the table, looking more like a child than ever, with her feet dangling several inches off the floor. She saw the fear in her eyes, the tightness around her mouth, the waif look of her once-crippled body, now nearly buried in clothes that were too big. And something within Hannah wanted to relent. As usual.

But there was something else in Hannah in that moment, something more powerful than forgiveness. "Look, Rose, we have to talk. Let's sit over here."

They moved to upholstered armchairs on either side of the window. Rose's nearly swallowed her small frame.

"What's the matter, Jo? I feel like you're about to tell me you never want to see me again."

"I meant it when I said I can't stand it anymore. I can't go on with things the way they've been." Hannah tried to breathe evenly, to rise above the rage. "You have to stop telling me what to do. No, what I mean is, you have to stop telling me what God wants me to do."

"But I've told you over and over again, Jo, I *can't* stop. God is using me to communicate with you and I must obey him."

"I don't believe that. In fact, I think it's ludicrous to imagine that any sort of deity would order you to do one of the things that most *turns me against* him."

"I can't help what you don't believe, Jo! I—"

"Exactly! Listen to what you just said. You can't help what I don't believe. Don't you see? That's precisely what I'm talking about."

"Don't play semantics with me. I'm saying I must obey God's word as I hear it."

Hannah sat back in her chair and blew out a breath. "Then I think we've reached an impasse."

"How do you mean that?"

"Simply that I can't or won't change, and neither will you." Hannah was looking at Rose but not really seeing her. She was thinking about how it had all started, nearly twenty-one years before. How this complex, convoluted relationship had begun with her own simple desire to turn Maybelle into something other than she was, and how it seemed to be ending with Maybelle-Rose's similar desire toward Hannah.

"So what are we supposed to do, Jo?"

"I'd like to take a break."

"From what?"

"From us."

"What do you mean?"

"I'd like to not see you for a while, or talk to you. And then, maybe in a week or two, get together and find out where we are with our impasse."

Rose pushed herself off the chair onto her feet. "Then you *are* saying you don't want to see me anymore!"

"Only for a little while."

"Only for a little while? What about Easter? We're always together on Easter! And what about my adjustments every week? Am I supposed to go to someone new? What if the media finds you? You don't need my support anymore?"

The more shrill Rose became, the more calm Hannah felt. "I always need your support, Rose. But only if it's support for me just as I am, not as you want me to be."

Rose stared at Hannah for a few moments, then dropped back into the chair and put her head in her hands. "I can't live without you, Jo."

Hannah went to her immediately, knelt beside her chair and put a hand on her shoulder. "Of course you can. You have your job and your church and your faith. All these years, haven't you been telling me the Lord's right there with me, every step of the way, and doesn't that apply to you too?"

Rose shook her head, keeping her face covered. "You don't understand."

"What don't I understand?"

"My life, it's…" She raised her head and looked at Hannah. Tears were pouring down her cheeks. "My life *is* you. I think about you all day long and I dream about you at night. Whatever happens to you, happens to me too. Your family is my family. The men you've dated, well, I just block that part out of my mind, like they don't exist. In a way, they don't. They're not real. *You* are all that's real, and without you, there's nothing. … Nothing."

Stunned, Hannah sat back on her heels.

"You saved my life, Jo, so it belongs to you. If you don't want to see me anymore, my life is over."

Surprised by the calm in her voice, Hannah heard herself say, "Rosie, we need help. These feelings of yours, we can't deal with them on our own."

Rose nearly screamed the words, "I will not go to a psychiatrist!"

Hannah leaned forward and wrapped her arms around Rose; it felt like holding a terrified child. "It's okay, Rosie. Nobody's going to make you do anything you don't want to do. How about if we see somebody together, you and I? A psychologist, not a psychiatrist. Somebody who's had a lot of experience with relationships."

"You know somebody like that?"

Hannah had been thinking of Ethan. "Well, I do know a man who's a psychologist, but I think we should see a woman, don't you? Maybe he'd give us the name of a woman who could help."

"I need some Kleenex," Rose said.

Hannah handed her a box of tissues from the table under the window, and Rose used several tissues to wipe her eyes and face and blow her nose. Eventually, she raised a timid gaze to Hannah and, in a near whisper, said, "You'd go with me?"

"Yes."

"It's not just me, then? You don't think I'm crazy?"

"Aw, Rosie, I think everybody's kind of crazy, don't you? But I also think that what's wrong with our relationship is something we can fix if we want to, with a little professional help."

"It's worth it to you, our friendship?"

"Of course it is."

"Oh, Hannah…" Rose began to weep again, softly. "Thank you. I'm sorry I acted like that, said all those things."

"I'm *glad* you did," Hannah said, realizing it was true. "For the first time in a long time, I feel hopeful about us." She stood up and held out her hand to Rose. "C'mon. I need to get going."

"You'll find someone for us to talk to?" Rose asked as she stood.

"Yes, as soon as I can."

"And you'll keep on talking to me in the meantime, till we find somebody?"

"Sure. Just not so intense, all right? And you'll lay off the sermons?"

"I'll try, I really will. … So could we get together soon, maybe tomorrow night or Saturday?"

Hannah felt a twinge of claustrophobia setting back in. "Let's wait and see what's going on. What with Vivian and Marcia and Lynn, and now Bill Tyler coming to see me tomorrow—"

"Oh, no."

"Oh yes." She tapped in the office alarm system numbers and they headed out the door. "But for some reason, he seems like small potatoes at this point."

"I'm not surprised. Every time I hear the latest news about—"

"Wait, stop! Whatever's happening, I don't want to hear about it. I just can't deal with anything else right now."

Rose made a gesture of locking her mouth and throwing away the key. "But just remember, Jo, the Lord is right there beside you every—"

"Rose! If you finish that sentence after what we've just been through, I'll wring your neck."

Chapter Twenty-Three

Hannah stopped at home before going to the Treadway. She fed Clancy and rough-housed with him a while, fatigue heavy on her shoulders. She wished she could relax at home tonight with her golden pal, have a nice long conversation with Ethan, and follow it with a few ounces of Jack Daniels and a luxurious soak in the bathtub. Instead she took a quick shower and changed into gray slacks and a pink shirt, combed her hair with her fingers, and left the house just after six-thirty.

On the drive to the Holiday Inn, she considered what she knew about Marcia and Lynn Thomkins, twenty-one years after the day she last saw them. Through their Christmas cards, she'd learned that both had become paralegals and worked with the same law firm in Monterey, where they'd moved when their mother remarried in the late 1980s. Beyond that, and the fact that they shared the same street address, she knew nothing at all, except that they seemed to have remained very protective of each other. That didn't surprise her; she would never forget the loathing she'd felt for Bruce Thomkins as an uncle, and could barely imagine what it must have taken to survive him as a father.

When she arrived at room one-three-three, she found the door ajar and tapped on it lightly. "Marcia, Lynn? It's Hannah. Sorry to be late."

They both came to greet her and Hannah felt as if she'd seen them just yesterday. She would have recognized them anywhere, they each so resembled her memory of their petite, blue-eyed mother.

Lynn, at twenty-nine, was maybe an inch taller than her sister and looked like she'd just come back from the beach or was headed there. She wore slim, white jeans, a little yellow shirt, and white sandals. Her naturally blond hair was short and tousled, and she appeared to need no makeup for her sunny complexion.

By contrast, Marcia at thirty-one looked like a fifteen-year-old

249

Alice in Wonderland. Her blond hair was straight, cut in bangs and reaching below her shoulder blades. She wore a short-sleeved, high-waisted Laura Ashley dress that seemed at least one size too large and reminded Hannah of Rose's wardrobe. Marcia, too, appeared to be without makeup, and Hannah thought she'd never seen skin so bloodlessly pale.

There were hugs and smiles all around, everyone agreeing how good it was to see each other.

"So what shall we do, guys?" Lynn asked. "Shall we stay here? We could order in room service. Or we can go out on the town."

"How about you, Marcia? What would you prefer?" Hannah asked.

"Don't ask *her*. She's not allowed to drink because of her meds, and she's got the appetite of a fruit fly."

"You'll have to forgive my sister, Hannah. She still thinks I can't speak for myself."

"Is it true you don't have an appetite?"

Marcia nodded. "I'm afraid it is, but it really doesn't bother me to be with people who do. So I vote that we go somewhere."

Because the sisters didn't seem like strangers to her after all, Hannah made a quick decision. "Why don't we go to my house? We can pick up a pizza or whatever, and I've got a big furry friend I want you to meet."

"This is heaven," Marcia said, settling more deeply into the greatroom sofa.

"You got that right," said Lynn from the floor on the other side of the coffee table. She had stretched out facing the wall of windows, and Clancy had snuggled up beside her. She had her head propped in one hand, and with the other stroked the length of Clancy's back. Hannah thought she could hear him purring.

"If I had a house like this, I think I'd never go anywhere," Marcia said.

On the sofa beside her, Hannah drank the last of a Yuengling Lager and set the bottle in the empty, open pizza box on the coffee table. She said nothing, as comfortable with these two women as if they'd been her lifelong friends.

"You already don't go anywhere, Marce."

"Of course I do. I go to work five days a week."

"But when was the last time you went somewhere just for fun? When was the last time you went outside *except* for work?"

"You know, I really get around a lot more than you do."

"*Virtual* getting around doesn't count."

"Well, it should. Which one of us has been to Japan and Alaska and South Africa? Which one of us spends almost every night and weekend with people from all over the world?"

"The real question is, which one of us spends every night and weekend with a machine?"

"What kind of computer do you have, Marce?" Hannah asked.

Lynn answered, "She's in this obsessive relationship with iMac, ever since she met him in '98."

"Me too," laughed Hannah. "Although I've never gotten into the swing of the internet. I'm still kind of intimidated by it."

"Oh, you shouldn't be!" Marcia exclaimed, sitting up and looking at Hannah. "It's wonderful. It's opened up the whole world for me. I can't begin to tell you all the terrific people I've met. There's even an interactive website for people with leukemia." She sat back again. "If I had a party and invited all my internet friends, there'd be a hundred people crammed in our townhouse."

Lynn drawled, "You might invite a hundred people, but how many would show up? My guess is zero. You're all too scared of being face-to-face with another living, breathing person."

"That's not true, Lynz. I wish you wouldn't be so hard on people you don't even know."

"Well hell, Marce, you don't know them either."

"Anyway, Hannah," said Marcia. "You really should check out the internet sometime. I bet you'd love it."

"Hannah's got a real life, Marce. She doesn't need a virtual one."

Hannah saw Marcia flinch, and wished she could rescue her from Lynn's barbed teasing. She tried for a change of subject. "So how did the visit go with Vivian today?"

"It was strange," Marcia said. "I kind of liked it. I kind of liked *her*."

"Really?"

"So did I," said Lynn. "Weird."

"Unbelievable," Hannah murmured. "What did she want?"

"Just to see us, I guess," Lynn said. "And she asked us to beg you to come see her, too. So consider yourself begged."

Marcia added, "She said she wanted to apologize for anything she ever did that hurt us."

"Yeah, that's what was so weird. We hardly ever saw her when we lived in Virginia and here she is apologizing all over the place."

"I think she needs to clear her conscience before she dies," Lynn said.

The mention of death silenced them all for a time. Hannah looked at her hands, wondering at their coldness; wondering, too, if there would be any point in telling the sisters the truth about herself when apparently she was going to be unable to help Marcia.

"Do you remember the fawn we found that day, Hannah?" asked Marcia.

"Joey. Sure I do."

"He was so soft and sweet. I always wondered what happened to him."

Hannah was surprised by the tears that rushed to her eyes and the sudden longing she felt to hug Clancy. She couldn't tell them what their grandmother had done to soft and sweet Joey. "I didn't have him very long."

"He needed to be set free, didn't he," Lynn said. "The way Marcie is with animals, if Joey'd been hers, he'd be caged up in our house today."

"You've got pets, Marce?"

"Only one, now. A Cairn terrier called McDuff. But Lynn's right, I do have a thing about animals. Growing up, I had hamsters and gerbils and white mice, guinea pigs. I'd have had cats, except I'm allergic to them. Duffy's my second Cairn terrier, and I love him to pieces. He looks like Toto in the *Wizard of Oz*. Remember Toto?"

"Sure. Adorable."

"So's Duffy."

"You're forgetting about Gabriel," said Lynn.

Hannah was surprised. "Gabriel?"

"We named him after that little bird of yours," Lynn said. "He's a canary Mom let us get soon after we moved to Monterey."

"Well, that was the first Gabriel," Marcia added. "This one's the second. I hope you don't mind us using that name."

Hannah grinned. "Not at all. It's a compliment." Thoughts of Gabriel led her to thoughts of Jeli, and then to Papa and the rest of her family. "How long are you staying in town?"

"Till Sunday afternoon," answered Lynn. "We've both gotta get back to work on Monday."

"I didn't want to fly on Easter," said Marcia. "But the airfare is ridiculous if you don't stay through a Saturday night."

"Does my dad know you're here?"

Lynn answered, "We haven't been in touch with him. Why?"

"Because I think he'd like to see you, and I'd like you to meet the rest of my family. It just occurred to me that the place we found the deer—that old house Pop was working on?—that's Jeli's house, my stepmother's mom. I know you'd like her and vice versa. Celeste, too, and my brothers. It's hard to believe that the last time we saw each other, Michael and Matthew didn't even exist." Except in heaven, she silently added.

The sisters agreed that they wanted to see Hannah's dad and meet the rest of her family. "We really know next to nothing about you," said Marcia.

"By the way," added Lynn, sitting up and leaning on the coffee table, facing Hannah. "I'm sorry we put pressure on you about that Mayo Clinic thing."

"It's okay," Hannah murmured, her throat tightening.

"Did you see what's-her-name on TV this afternoon?"

"Who?"

"The mother of those two little boys, Lily something?"

"No. No, I didn't."

"She gave a press conference, said she's putting everything she's got—mega bucks, I guess—she's putting it all behind protecting the identity of this miracle-worker. She said the angel wants to keep her privacy, and she's determined to help her do that. She also said the angel can't control the healing, it just happens whenever it happens."

Hannah was having trouble breathing normally. "Huh."

"But I don't buy that. I mean, if this angel does the healing out of the blue, are we supposed to believe she just *happened* to be in that field on Saturday?"

Hannah was aware of Marcia, silent beside her, and of a weight to the older sister's stillness, as if she were probing Hannah's psyche.

"It's a little much to just be coincidental, don't you think?" Lynn added.

"Mm." As if drawn by a magnet, Hannah turned her head and locked on Marcia's eyes. "What's your take on all this, Marce?" she said, thinking: If she asks again whether it was me she saw at the Mayo, I'll tell her the truth.

But Marcia slid her gaze away. "Oh, I don't know. I guess it bothers me that this one woman has both of her sons healed because she's got all this money, and now she's using her money again to keep the rest of us from getting what we need."

Hannah was stunned. "You think this healer helped Lily for money?"

"Don't you?" asked Lynn. "To me it's obvious. Like one of the commentators said, those people in the front of the plane who died anyway? None of them had big bucks like this Severill woman."

Hannah closed her eyes and leaned back into the sofa cushions. A new nightmare, she thought. An awful twist she'd never considered. They not only think I'm in control of the healing, they also think I do it for money.

As he did so often, Clancy seemed to sense Hannah's mood and came over to her, nuzzling her elbow and whining softly.

"You want to go out, big guy?" said Lynn, jumping up and moving to the French doors.

Clancy stayed where he was and Hannah sat up and put her arms around him.

"He's comforting you, isn't he, Hannah," said Marcia. "Duffy's like that with me when I'm down. I think he reads my mind."

"You're not feeling so good, Hann? Maybe we should take off."

"It's not that, is it Hannah," Marcia said levelly.

Hannah looked at her and read the question in her eyes. "No," she sighed. "It's not that."

"I think I missed a step here," Lynn said. "What're you two talking about?"

"I lied to you, Lynn. It *was* me you saw on TV."

Lynn said, "Holy shit!" while Marcia breathed, "Thank God."

Sometime later, at the end of her abbreviated version of all that had happened since last Saturday, Hannah said, "If you two don't stop looking at me that way, I'll scream."

Marcia brought her hands to her cheeks. "I'm really sorry, but I just can't help it. It's... well, it feels like a miracle."

Lynn shook her head. "We really did have the winning lottery ticket after all."

"Except that I can't control it. I need you to believe that."

"You're saying you won't be able to help me?" asked Marcia.

"I'm saying I don't *know* if I will. I can't cause the healing; it happens or it doesn't."

"You mean, just all of a sudden, like Lily Severill said?" Lynn asked. "Then you really were at that field on Saturday by chance?"

"Oh. No, not that. I woke up knowing I had to go there, first to Gettysburg, then north, looking for those two blue silos. It's sort of like following your nose."

"You sure must have one powerful sense of smell," Lynn laughed.

Marcia said, "Like your intuition tells you something and you really listen."

"Right, except it's not so much words as images, pictures in my mind."

Lynn asked, "So did you *see* the plane crash before it happened?"

"Not the crash itself, but the aftermath, very much as it looked in reality."

"What about the people?" said Marcia. "Did you see them before you actually saw them, if you know what I mean?"

"Only the little boy, Micah, and his mother. I've wondered about that ever since, especially once I knew about Isaiah."

"Weird," Lynn declared.

"There must be some reason why Micah was supposed to live,"

Marcia said.

"Or Isaiah, like maybe one of them will grow up to be another Einstein," added Lynn.

"Maybe," Hannah said. "But I've been wondering if it's simply the way this extra sense of mine works. It's limited, like my other senses, so it doesn't see the whole picture, just enough to get me there."

"You don't think there's a divine plan at work in the things you do?" Marcia asked.

Hannah wanted to say she had trouble with the concept of divine plans, but stopped herself. She saw where the conversation might go if she answered that question, and knew she didn't have the energy for venturing into what she considered Rose's rocky terrain. She shook her head. "I'm sorry, but I guess I'm not up for theological discussions tonight."

"I understand completely," said Marcia. "After the week you've had, I'm just happy you'd get together with us." She hesitated a moment before she added, "And listen, please don't feel bad about maybe not being able to help me. Really, I'm so much luckier than a lot of people with leukemia. Mine's chronic, not acute, and I've got something like a ninety percent chance of staying in remission."

"Right," added Lynn. "And if she did need a bone marrow transplant, we're a perfect match. But they're doing mostly the stem cell transplants these days, and for those you're your own donor."

Hannah looked back and forth between the sisters. "You two are amazing, sitting here working at making me feel better about Marcia's disease."

Marcia smiled, and Lynn said, "I feel bad, though, for saying what I did about her—about you—healing for the money."

"So do I," said Marcia.

"I guess a lot of people must believe that now." Hannah thought of Lily's fifty-thousand-dollar cashier's check. "Maybe even Lily. She did try to pay me."

"That's natural, I think—I mean, about Lily," Marcia said. "People have a hard time receiving gifts, period, and with your sort of gifts, they must feel very indebted."

"I guess," Hannah said, suddenly feeling claustrophobic. Deliberately, she stood up and announced, "I need to get some air.

Why don't you two come for a walk with Clancy and me. We can head up toward Pop's."

"In the dark?" Marcia asked.

"I've got flashlights."

"Shouldn't we, well, call your father first? I wouldn't want to intrude on his evening."

"I was thinking we'd just walk up that way, but we can stop by if you want to."

"Oh, no. No, not tonight. I thought you meant... unless *you* want to. I mean I really do want to see him and meet Celeste and everybody, but I don't know, tonight I'm just—"

Lynn interrupted. "There's nothing to be afraid of, Marce. Hannah's not asking you to dance naked in Times Square."

Marcia looked so embarrassed that Hannah rushed to her rescue. "My youngest brother teases me like that, and all I can do is try to let it roll off my back."

"I wish I could. The thing is, she knows all my buttons and pushes them deliberately."

"Matthew's the same way with me," Hannah said, as she and Marcia both looked at Lynn's impish grin. "But, remember, it's because of our vast wisdom and maturity that you and I choose not to sink to their childish level of button-pushing."

"Wait a minute," Lynn said. "Vast wisdom?"

"And maturity," said Marcia, linking an arm with Hannah's. "So quit messing with me, pipsqueak."

They went for a walk with Clancy, but the night had turned chilly and they didn't stay out long. When they returned to the house, Hannah suggested something warm to drink, and they ended up at the kitchen table, drinking mugs of hot chocolate and talking quietly.

Before they left, it was decided that Marcia and Lynn would move into Hannah's house for the next two nights, staying in Grampa's old room where she'd put her double bed last November, when she bought a new queen-sized one for herself.

As the sisters drove away in their rental car, Hannah stood in the driveway, waving to them, reminding herself of when she'd done the same thing on a July Friday, nearly twenty-one years before.

Chapter Twenty-Four

It was nearly ten forty-five by the time Hannah finally stretched out in bed and dialed Ethan's home number.

He answered on the second ring. "Hello?"

"Hi, it's me. I'm sorry it's so late."

"It's all right. I'm just glad you called. How are you?"

"Mm. Good question. You're probably pretty experienced in asking that, as a therapist, am I right?"

"Sure, but in a session the question has nothing to do with me."

"Now it does?"

"Of course."

"In what way?"

"I hope I don't have to explain that to you. And it occurs to me here that you've successfully deflected the question itself."

Hannah imagined the dancing light in his eyes. "So what was the question?"

He laughed. "I forget. But how the heck are you, anyway?"

"I think I'm okay. Down maybe, but not out yet."

"Down doesn't surprise me, but I'm glad to hear the 'not out'. Do you... I've wanted to ask you a question... truthfully, I've wanted to ask you a lot of questions, but this particular one, I'm not sure how to phrase it without prying into your personal life. I don't mean to pry, but I'm hoping you've got plenty of support, plenty of family and friends who are there for you."

"Is that the question?"

Ethan laughed again. "Matter of fact, yes it is."

"I do have family and friends around—surprisingly more than I knew last Saturday."

"People are coming out of the woodwork?"

"Not really. I guess the surprise is how easily I've opened up with these people, after so many years of keeping myself a secret."

"Congratulations," he said.

"You think so, Ethan? You think it's a good thing?"

"Letting people be there for you? A very good thing."

Hannah heard something in his voice that told her he wanted to be there for her, too. "So what about you, Ethan? Do you have family and friends around here?" Are you married or engaged? she wanted to ask, and wondered if he was fishing for the same information about her.

"I do. My parents live in Haverford, and I've got three brothers, all in the Chicago area. Jenny—my niece on the plane— I was bringing her out for a week with my folks, over her Easter vacation."

"Is she all right?"

"Sure is, right as rain."

"Right as rain! I can't believe you said that. Nobody says that anymore." Nobody since Grampa.

Ethan chuckled. "Busted. It was one of my grandfather's favorite expressions."

"Mine too. So Jenny really is okay?"

"She's fine. She can't stop talking about it—and about you— with her typical eleven-year-old enthusiasm. You might think she'd been to her first prom. But her parents and my parents, no one's willing to let her fly home on Sunday afternoon. My brother, Michael, and his wife are driving out to get her."

"I'm not surprised they don't want her to fly. Do they know about me? I mean that you and I are… in touch?"

"No. I'm keeping that for myself."

"Thank you."

"No need to thank me. Some of my motives are completely selfish."

Hannah felt herself blush, and quickly searched for safe ground. "Is one of your other brothers by any chance named Matthew?"

"No. John and Luke. Why do you ask?"

"Because I have a brother named Michael."

"And one named Matthew?"

"Yup. And here's another coincidence for you. My grandfather's name was Ethan."

"Hannah, you're not going to believe this, but so was mine,

my mother's father, the one who said 'right as rain'. I was named for him."

"Now this is getting a little spooky. His last name wasn't Bailey, was it?"

"As a matter of fact…"

She loved the laughter in his voice. "Seriously, Ethan. What *was*—"

"Kirchner, so I think we're safe."

"Whew!"

"Right. But it's amazing, isn't it, these coincidences. I bet we'll stumble on others as we go along."

"I don't stumble," Hannah said.

"Oh, pardon me, of course you don't. You glide over the most treacherous of terrains."

"Yes, sylph-like."

"In your diaphanous gown of silken moonbeams."

"This is getting sickening," she laughed.

"I thought we were just getting good. But if you'd like to shift gears, tell me about your family."

She did, beginning with her mother and father, and then Celeste, Michael and Matthew, and ending with the fact that her father and her youngest brother were the only two in the family who still didn't know about her.

"You really do have support. I'm glad."

"Me too."

"Have you lived around here all your life?" he asked.

"Yup, most of it in a big house right up the hill from where I live now. How about you?"

"Haverford was my home base until I went into practice out here."

"Is it a successful practice?" she asked, blushing again when she realized that it was a rude question. Might as well ask him about his gross annual income, she thought.

He seemed to read her thoughts, and chuckled. "Yes, it is. How about you? What do you do for a living?"

For the first time in the conversation, Hannah hesitated. Exactly how much solid information about herself was she ready to share with him? If she told him her profession, he could find her easily in the phone book. "I'm sorry. I guess I need to hold off on that a little longer. I hope you understand."

"Of course I do. I meant it about not wanting to pry. Anything I ask you, tell me if you don't want to answer, all right?"

"Okay. Thanks."

Now she sensed him hesitating. "Huh. I'm sorry again, that wasn't fair of me. I need to be honest with you. I'm pretty sure I already know what you do for a living."

He sounded so sheepish, Hannah smiled in spite of what he was saying. "I saw a client yesterday afternoon who swears that the angel of Angler's field is none other than her chiropractor, Jo-*hannah* Kirkland."

That's that, she thought... and felt just fine about it. "Oh, well. Ditto on the 'busted'."

"I'm sorry. I promise I won't presume—"

"I know you won't, and it's okay. Really it is."

"So I can come in for an adjustment tomorrow?"

His dry humor brought a bubble of laughter out of her.

"Okay, okay. Forget the adjustment," he said. "Tell me how you're coping with the media circus?"

"I've got the perfect way to deal with that. I don't read the newspapers or watch TV or listen to KYW."

"Masterful coping skills."

She thought for a moment before she asked, "Why? Is there anything in particular that you thought might be upsetting me?"

"You don't really want me to report what you've been avoiding."

"Mm. I guess not. I know things are bad, I'm just wondering if they're getting worse. I've thought about my cell phone, the one I used to call nine-one-one from the crash site. Even though the number's unlisted, I'm wondering if that call could be traced."

"I haven't heard anything along those lines, but I suppose anything's possible with electronics these days."

"Do you think there's any chance the story might just die out?"

"Truthfully? Maybe the media would find a hotter story, but I'm afraid I don't see this Shepherdess cult giving up."

Hearing his concern, remembering her appointment with Bill

Tyler the next afternoon, Hannah felt a sinking of hope. "My brother and stepmother want me to have a plan of action, they're that sure I'll be found."

"Is there anything I can do to help?" he asked.

"I don't think so, but thanks for the offer."

"It's sincere. I'd... I would like to be one of the people who are there for you."

"I think that's already a given," she said, suddenly needing to change the subject. "I'm feeling a little like Richard Kimball. Can we talk about something else?"

She heard his smile as he said, "You bet. So, um, how about church? How long have you been at Loving Shepherd?"

"Grampa and I worshipped there for years. But I slacked off a lot after his funeral there last April."

"Unhappy associations with the place?"

"No. More like with religion in general. God let me down in a big way with Grampa."

"Your grandfather was very significant in your life." It wasn't a question.

"You can't imagine."

They were both silent for a time, Hannah lost in thoughts of Grampa and of how he would have liked this other Ethan.

". . . Hannah?"

"Mm?"

"There's a world of conversation I want to have with you. I want to know about your grandfather, and your childhood, and a million other things, and the phone just isn't going to cut it. So can I see you sometime soon? Will you have dinner with me?"

Without a conscious thought, Hannah said, "Are you married or engaged?"

Ethan laughed again, and the warm richness of the sound went into Hannah's ear, directly to her heart. "No to both. Although I was engaged for a while a couple of years ago."

"What happened?"

"It's a long and boring story."

"You don't want to tell me?"

"I think I'm a little embarrassed. This might prove me to be something less than perfect."

"Yikes."

"Think you can handle it, Dr. Kirkland?"

"I don't know, Dr. Quinn, but you can't back out now."

"Okay. Here goes." His voice took on a more somber tone. "Four years ago, when I was twenty-six, I finally admitted I was in big trouble with alcohol. My two older brothers had traveled this route ahead of me, and so had my father, so it was the most natural thing for me to go straight to AA, Alcoholics Anonymous. … Are you with me so far?"

"I'm glad you're telling me about this, Ethan."

"Not disillusioned by my imperfections?"

"Pobody's nerfect," she said with a smile.

"Thank God. … So, I started going to AA meetings and I was lucky, able to get sober right away. I kept running into this woman named Linda at the meetings, and after a few months I asked her out. To make a long story short, a year later we were engaged, and six months after that it was over."

"Your decision or hers?"

"Mutual, really. She wasn't sold on AA, like I was. Like I am. She started drinking again and stopped going to meetings, and I had to choose between recovery and marrying her, so there really wasn't any choice at all."

"Did it take you a long time to get over her?"

"No, which says a lot about the relationship, doesn't it."

"Mm, I guess it does."

"Now do I get to ask you if you're married or engaged?"

Hannah felt a twinge of guilt with the thought of Craig. "Neither one."

"So will you go out to dinner with me? Tomorrow night or Saturday, or both?"

"I can't either night. My cousins are staying with me till Sunday."

"How about Sunday night then? Or Monday, or both?"

"We could start with Sunday," she said with a laugh, immediately counting on Monday night too. *Ouch!*—another thought of Craig.

"Great! I'll take you to your favorite restaurant."

"Where's that?"

"That's your part of the deal. You have to tell me."

"I like the Dilworthtown Inn."

"Terrific, so do I. Where can I pick you up?"

"Oh. Let me think... I guess I'd better meet you there, this time."

"'This time.' I like that. But it just occurred to me, they might not be open on Easter night. I'll find out and call you... at your office?"

How much do I trust him? she asked herself. And heard her answer as she gave him the numbers for her home and cell phones.

"It's a date then, Hannah?"

Oo! Craig again. "It's a date."

After they hung up, Hannah lay in bed for a while, replaying their conversation in her mind. She'd enjoyed it; he was wonderful to talk with, as if they'd known each other for years. But that business about his commitment to AA—that was sticking in Hannah's craw.

He gave up the woman he loved for sobriety, she thought. Doesn't bode too well for my future with him, unless I quit the booze. And it sounds like his whole family is on the wagon. Must make for boring parties, everybody sitting around stone cold sober, a room full of American Gothic characters.

She heard Clancy's tags jingling as he padded over to her. "Reading my mind are you, pal?" She stroked his head and looked into his eyes. "We've got a little predicament with this new Ethan, you know. What d'you think, should I swear off the booze myself?" Clancy didn't voice an opinion; instead his eyes were drooping with contentment. "Looks like you don't really care a whole heck of a lot about this problem, Clance. Leaving it up to me, aren't you."

She lay in bed awhile longer, petting Clancy and considering her relationship with alcohol. It's not as if I'm an alcoholic, she thought. I hardly ever drink, and always alone, except for beer or wine. Nobody has ever seen me drunk. Really, I don't *get* drunk. I just like the taste of the stuff, and it relaxes me, lets me get a good sleep when nothing else works. If things continue to go well with Ethan, I could give up the booze in a heartbeat. He'd never have to know.

That's what I'll do, she decided. Sunday night, if I have a good time with him, I'll toss out all the liquor in the house as soon as I get home. No problem. And I can do it without AA. He won't have to know I was ever a drinker.

Satisfied with her plan, she kissed Clancy on the top of his head and turned off the bedside lamp.

A few minutes later she turned the lamp back on and went to the kitchen for a drink... one or two fingers of Jack Daniels as a sort of farewell.

Five or six fingers of Jack Daniels later, she returned to bed and quickly fell asleep.

Chapter Twenty-Five

Hannah awoke Friday morning in a rotten mood, with a pounding headache that forced her to cut short her run with Clancy. Some aspirin and a long, hot shower eased the pain, but the mood worsened when she found herself without fresh fruit or orange juice or milk, and wound up breakfasting on a container of yogurt whose taste was well past its expiration date.

After she ate, she stayed at the kitchen table, gloomily pondering her day and wishing that she could spend the next couple of evenings at home alone with Clancy rather than entertaining Marcia and Lynn.

Jeli called then, apparently picking up on Hannah's distress signals, and Hannah wound up pouring out all her gripes, including the fact that the house needed cleaning, the kitchen needed food, and Bill Tyler was coming to her office that afternoon.

Jeli took on the persona of a Mother Betty Crocker Teresa, insisting that she and Celeste would host everyone for dinner tonight and tomorrow, and that Marcia and Lynn would be far more comfortable in her big house, rather than on Hannah's old double bed. Finally, she announced that she would bring a cleaning crew down to the house while Hannah was at work.

Hannah felt as if Jeli were offering to lift a *Sumo* wrestler off her back. "I can't let you do all this," she protested.

"Don't be silly. You need help and I'm offering it, so just say, 'Thank you, Jeli, I would appreciate it.'"

"Would I ever. You're an angel, Angelica."

"Of course I am. Now, I'll call Celeste about tonight, and when you talk to your cousins, tell them that I insist they stay with me."

When she hung up with Jeli, Hannah realized she felt better, less ready to pick a fight with just anybody. She also realized she hadn't told Jeli about her conversation with Ethan and her date with him on Sunday night. She asked herself why, and was hit again with the jangling unease about his commitment to AA.

Dammit, Ethan, she said to herself. I guess you're not going to be a peaceful stream for me today, are you? Why can't there just once be a man who fits perfectly with me and vice versa? Why do there always have to be these compromises and trade-offs?

Having gotten herself back to irritated, Hannah phoned Marcia and Lynn at the Holiday Inn. Lynn answered and Hannah relayed Jeli's offer.

"That's really nice of her, Hann, but she doesn't even know us. We'll be fine on your double bed. Unless you'd rather we stayed with her?"

"Not at all," Hannah lied.

"Okay then, we'll stay with you. When could we come over?"

Hannah thought of her patients and her appointment with Bill Tyler, and suggested they meet at her house around four-thirty.

"We'll be there," Lynn agreed. "And hang on a sec, will you? Marce wants to talk to you."

Hannah waited, wondering why she felt so annoyed with these women today, when last night they had seemed like newly-rediscovered best friends.

Marcia came on the line saying, "I just wanted to thank you again, Hannah. I had the best sleep last night I've had in ages."

"Good... but, well, I hope you're not counting on my being able to—"

"No, it's not that. It's just knowing you. Whether you see a divine power behind what you do, it doesn't really matter, because I see it. You've given my shaky faith such a shot in the arm."

Hannah felt ashamed of her own mean-spiritedness. "I'm glad for you, Marcia."

"I feel so fortunate to be seeing God at work through you, Hannah. I want to tell the world—"

"Please, Marcia," Hannah interrupted. "You're making me awfully nervous here."

"Oh, I'm sorry. It's just hard to—"

"It's okay, but I've gotta run now. See you later," she said, breaking the connection quickly.

She rested her head on the kitchen table then, wishing she could bag everything and take off for the day. For the weekend, would be better. Or, better yet, ten days at Jeli's house in Avalon, New Jersey. Empty beaches, sunrise runs along the sand, bracing, salty sea breezes. Best of all, few people this time of year.

I'm feeling crowded, that's what it is, she thought. Like people are pressing in on my life, hoards of people, and if I don't stop them, it won't be *my* life at all anymore. *I wish you could tell me what to do, Grampa*, she said to him in her mind. There was no response.

Blowing out a breath, she pushed up from the table and got busy, starting a load of laundry, and making up the double bed in Grampa's room with pale blue percale sheets and a white, heirloom-style bedspread. Then she dressed in tan khakis and a cream-colored silk shirt, gathered clothes to take to the cleaners, and headed down the driveway by nine-twenty. She was about to turn onto Brandywine Road when she reconsidered, turned the Jeep around and drove back to the house. Clancy came bounding to her, barking joyously as if he hadn't seen her for hours, and she opened the passenger side door for him. He gave her a look that seemed to say, *What, me? You want me, really?*

She said, "Yes, you, pal. I want you with me today."

He leaped onto the passenger seat, trembling with excitement, and began to lick her face enthusiastically.

"Okay, okay. Cut it out or I'll have to take another shower."

In spite of Clancy, Hannah's mood blackened further when she encountered Sally on duty behind the cash register at the Wawa. Sally didn't say a word when Hannah paid for her donuts and coffee; in fact, she didn't once look her in the eye, and kept her thin lips pressed together tightly as if she were trying to keep herself from speaking. Seeing Sally this way gave Hannah a terrible feeling, worse than having the woman accuse her outright.

She knows about me and she has big plans to turn me in, Hannah thought. Maybe she's done it already.

Back in the Jeep, on the way to her office, Hannah felt like the car itself was closing in on her, compressing the air she needed to breathe.

Over the course of the day with her patients, Hannah was repeatedly grateful for Clancy's presence. Not only did he distract her thoughts, but he also distracted her patients. Kept them, she hoped, from noticing her utter lack of chiropractic skill that day.

She dropped off her cleaning at lunchtime and brought back to the office a generous chef's salad from Arianna's Café. She consumed every bit of it, and spent the next two hours wishing only for a nice long nap.

Now, with nothing but a few minutes separating her from Bill Tyler, she was again thinking about taking off and heading for the beach.

When she heard the soft tone that signaled the opening of the front office door, she glanced at the clock; he was ten minutes early. She decided he'd just have to wait. Not wanting to make any noise to alert him, she stayed at her desk, silencing Clancy with her thoughts—unnecessarily, because he was sound asleep at her feet. Finally, an excruciatingly-long ten minutes later, she stood up and went to the door of her private office, opening it and immediately jerking back in surprise at the sight of Bill Tyler, just outside in the hallway, looking at her.

"What!" she yelped.

"Hey!" he said, apparently as surprised as she was.

They both spoke at once, Hannah saying, "I was coming out to see you," while Bill Tyler said, "I didn't know if anybody was—"

Clancy barked and rushed at Bill, who quickly held out the back of his hand for Clancy to sniff.

He's good with dogs, Hannah thought, softening slightly. "Clancy, meet Bill Tyler."

"He's a beauty," Bill said, stooping to scruff Clancy's brisket.

"You have dogs?"

"Always have, since junior high. Right now it's Murphy, a black lab." Bill straightened and looked sheepishly at Hannah. "I'm sorry I startled you like that. I was coming back to see if you were here."

"It's all right," Hannah said, steering him away from her private office. "Why don't we go out front and talk."

Bill sat on the waiting room sofa and Hannah pulled one of

the chairs around and sat a few feet away from him.

Unwilling to make the situation easier for him, she studied him in silence. He was about her height and appeared to be in good physical shape, and had blow-dried dark brown hair, a wide mouth, brown eyes and heavy eyebrows. Today he wore a dark suit and a subdued tie with a white shirt, and Hannah wondered if he'd dressed this way to impress her somehow. She felt very unimpressed as she watched him nervously fiddle with the knot of his tie and look around the room as if he hoped to find what he wanted to say painted on the walls.

His face reddened when he finally met her gaze. "I'm sorry. I'm... I... hardly know where to begin."

Clancy put his head on Bill's knee and Bill began petting him; Hannah felt herself softening a little more.

"I wanted to see you, Johannah... well, now that I am seeing you, I'm sure... I'm sorry, I can't seem to think straight here." He blew out a breath and started again. "I wanted to see you because... I guess I might as well get right to it. I thought that... was that you at the plane crash on Saturday?"

The expression in his eyes was so earnest and hopeful, Hannah instantly relented. "Yes. It was me."

"Oh my God," he said, apparently surprised by her simple admission. "It really *was* you."

Hannah caught the glint of tears in his eyes and knew something more was going on here than she'd anticipated. "What is it you want, Bill?"

Apparently embarrassed, he swiped at his tears. "I know you must think I'm out to harm you, but I'm not. I swear that's the last thing in the world I'd want. I'll do whatever you want me to do, anything really, if you'll just help me."

"How do you need my help?"

"It's my daughter. She's... her name is Tessa and she's just two years old, and the thing is, she's in a coma and it's..."

He lowered his head, and Hannah strained to hear his words.

"It's my fault... happened a few weeks ago... I dropped her... like I *threw* her, really, when she let go . . . hit the TV so *hard*... her head, her beautiful head... coma ever since... my wife, never forgive me... never forgive myself..."

Hannah's heart flooded with compassion for this man, his daughter and his wife. She put a hand on his trembling shoulder as she silently repeated the Jesus prayer for him and his family.

After a time, she went behind the reception desk and brought out a box of tissues, offering them to Bill.

He took a handful and held them to his eyes. "Sorry, so sorry," he said, shaking his head. "Things must be hell for you these days... never meant to break down like this."

She sat again across from him. "You've been going through hell yourself lately."

"Yeah. And, I have to tell you, Saturday when the plane was going down, I told myself it made sense. For crissake, can you believe that? I figured I was finally being punished for what I'd done, dropping Tessa like that. My wife, Suzi, she always told me not to spin Tess in the air that way." He grimaced. "I called it 'playing airplane'." He wiped at his eyes again. "So I figured, the plane going down Saturday was justice for me, but what was I *thinking*. God, it wasn't justice for everybody else on the flight! I was going to be found guilty of killing all those others as well as myself. I thought I'd already died and this was hell."

"Surely the plane crash wasn't your fault."

"No, but I thought it was then. I didn't know what I'd done, but I was sure it was my fault. I'd made some horrible mistake, I thought, so I could punish myself. All of that insanity was going through my head from when the trouble started with the plane, and then when we were down and I was still alive, I figured that was the real punishment. I'd made a mistake and killed all these people, and I was going to have to live with that forever. I'll tell you, if I could've shot myself then and there, I would have. And with that little kid, that Severill boy, I tried so hard to get him to breathe. Thought if I could just save one person, maybe... that's when you came along and I recognized you right away. Not your name, but I knew that I knew you. I figured you were on the flight and helping out, and I'd catch up with you later. 'Cause I saw what you did with that boy. I saw you bring him back to life, and all of a sudden I knew I'd found my salvation. I knew God had forgiven me by sending someone who could heal Tessa. Later, when I found out you were missing, you hadn't been on the flight at all, I went crazy. I'd seen my redemption and I'd let it slip away. That's when it popped into my head who you were, your name, clear as day, like a theater marquee: *Johannah Kirkland*." He finally looked into her eyes. "I knew you were my savior, Johannah."

"Bill, *please*. I'm not anybody's savior. I was there at the crash because I woke up knowing I had to be there, and I knew I had to help little Micah. But beyond that, please believe me, I have no say whatever about who I can help or when."

"But what about with the other Severill kid, in Minnesota? His mother asked you, and you went out there and made his heart like new. "

"I went out there because she wanted my help, but I had no idea whether or not I'd be able to do anything for Isaiah. I'm not in charge of this gift, Bill. In fact, most of the time it's as if I don't have any gift at all. I'm as normal as everybody else, until all of a sudden the heat comes up in my hands and I can do these *ab*-normal things."

"But would you at least *try* with Tessa? I'd give you everything I own if you'd just see her and try to heal her."

"Where is she?"

"Twenty minutes away, at Paoli Memorial."

"I'll see her, yes. I'd like to do that. But I can't promise it'll do any good."

"Will you come with me now?" He started to rise.

Hannah felt unnerved by the excitement in his eyes. "I need… could we just talk a little more? I'd like to have a better sense of exactly what's going on." A better sense of exactly how high your expectations are, she wanted to add.

He sat again. "Okay. Whatever you need, that's fine with me."

"Let me make a phone call, then we could go somewhere for a cup of coffee."

"God, I can't thank you enough, Johannah."

"Just 'Hannah' will do."

"Sure. Hannah. Got it. I'll wait here for you."

Clancy remained with Bill while Hannah went to her private office, closed the door behind her and dialed Celeste's number.

Jeli's voice said, "Hello?"

"Jeli? Did I dial the wrong number?"

"No, sweetie. I'm here at Cellie's. Did Bill Tyler show up?"

"He's here now. That's why I'm calling. I'm afraid I need another favor." She told Jeli about Bill Tyler's daughter and her intention to go see the child in Paoli.

"Oh, honey. Are you up to this?"

"I don't know. I hadn't given it a thought. But, really, what choice do I have?"

"How about 'no.' Or how about, 'I'm very sorry, but I'm only human and I'm worn out.'"

"My mouth doesn't know how to form those words at the moment. You want to come over and say them for me?"

"I will if you want me to."

"No, it's okay. Bill Tyler's little girl—I do want to see her."

"Well then, what *can* I do?"

"The favor is, Lynn and Marcia will be waiting for me at my house around four-thirty and I was wondering if you could let them know—"

"I'll go down and intercept them and bring them straight up here."

"That'd be perfect. You really are my Good Friday angel, you know."

"I'm delighted to have the chance to help you a little."

"Jeli, I think you've been helping me since we were in heaven."

Bill Tyler and Hannah sat in a booth over coffee at the Burger King on south High Street. Through the window, Hannah could see Clancy in the Jeep, staring at her, reminding her she'd be in big trouble if she came back to the car without a couple of bacon cheeseburgers for him.

Bill had been telling Hannah about the FAA and NTSB investigations into the cause of the plane crash. He didn't look at her as he spoke, keeping his gaze trained on his coffee cup. "There are dozens of state-of-the-art safety features to guarantee it wouldn't happen that way, but I suppose they can say that about most accidents."

"Sounds like it could have been even worse if you hadn't

found that field when you did."

"Right. No question, we were lucky. Well, everybody who made it, that is."

"I guess there's a lot of blame and guilt floating around now."

"Yeah. More than enough."

"On top of what you've already got because of your daughter."

He glanced at her. "Right."

"Did the airline know about your daughter?" As soon as the question was out of her mouth, she regretted it; she could see that she'd hit a nerve.

"I should've told them, but I didn't. I couldn't. They would've grounded me. It's company policy, anybody who's dealing with grief and the like. I knew I couldn't handle that. Flying's what keeps me sane." He gave a brief laugh that sounded more like a groan. "*Sane.* Right."

"So you've been adding that guilt to all the other?"

"That's what I mean. More than enough guilt to last the rest of my life."

In that moment, Hannah realized she cared very much about this man. She felt the familiar, terrible pressure of wanting to help someone and knowing it might not happen.

"So what's next, Bill, with you and the captain, the rest of the flight crew? Do they send you up again soon, like putting you right back on the horse?"

"Just the opposite. Minimum of a month out of the cockpit, mandatory, for processing the accident—like debriefing—plus a lot of hours in the flight sims—simulators—and some R and R."

"I'm sure you could use the R and R."

"Maybe. But I damn well don't deserve it. Anyhow, there's nothing I want to do. I'm not going anywhere until Tessa's... while she's in the hospital. They'll be transferring her to a rehab soon, probably the DuPont."

"That's a good sign, isn't it?"

"I don't know. Makes me think the hospital's giving up."

"But at least she's not on life support."

"Yeah, you're right. Still, the whole concept of R and R's a joke. I can't even sleep."

"Is your wife—"

"She moved out, back with her folks in Downingtown. Won't have anything to do with me, her whole family."

"Have you thought what you'd tell her about me?"

"Suzi?"

"If we should bump into her over at the hospital."

He looked blank, as if she were talking gibberish.

"You know I've been doing everything I can to elude the media."

He nodded.

"Well, I don't want to stir up any interest when I go to see your daughter. I need some sort of cover story, for your wife and for the nurses and doctors, anybody we might run into there. And for myself, if I visit Tessa alone."

"You mean, like being a nun when you went to the Mayo Clinic?"

"But I wouldn't try to disguise my identity, since I've lived here all my life. I just mean a reason why I've taken an interest in your daughter's situation. Do I know your wife from school? Was she at Downingtown?"

"No, Unionville."

"By any chance, do you get chiropractic adjustments?"

"No. Never have."

"Well, would your wife question your saying that you've begun to see a chiropractor?"

"I don't think so. We never talked about it. But why would you come to see Tessa if you're my chiropractor?"

"I adjust children all the time. In fact, some of my patients are newborn babies."

"Really? That's it then. You've been doing such a great job with my... my spine?"

"Just say your back or your neck. Sounds more natural."

"Okay. You've been doing such a great job with my neck— God knows, it's aching all the time these days—so I asked you to come up and see if you could help Tessa. How's that?"

"Good. I just wish I *had* given you an adjustment so that you'd have a better sense of what we're talking about."

"Couldn't we stop back at your office and do that?"

Half an hour later, as Hannah retrieved Clancy from the yard behind her office and prepared to head for the Paoli Memorial Hospital, Bill Tyler was enthusiastically proclaiming himself to be a true believer in the wonders of chiropractic.

Other than saying she was glad the adjustment had helped, Hannah stayed silent. She couldn't tell him what had happened. She couldn't tell him that the color had washed from her vision and the heat had come into her hands almost as soon as she touched his back while he lay there on the high-low table; that what he was experiencing now was only in small part due to having his bones and muscles properly repositioned; that God had seen fit to heal the father rather than the daughter. She couldn't tell him that there was now little point in her going to see Tessa.

Now, as Bill Tyler exuded positive energy and optimism, Hannah fastened a leash to Clancy's collar, thinking murderous thoughts about God.

Chapter Twenty-Six

There was no opposition to Hannah's seeing Bill's daughter at Paoli Memorial Hospital that evening. Tessa's mother had left and wasn't expected back until the next morning. In addition, the nurse on duty, Martha Frenz, was enthusiastic about a chiropractic adjustment for her comatose, two-year-old patient. She herself had been getting adjustments on a regular basis for years. "It's helped me with everything from allergies and headaches to sore feet," she told Bill and Hannah.

As Bill led the way to the room his daughter shared with another pediatric patient, Hannah felt as if invisible hands were holding her back. I'm about to see the sucking, black death again, she thought, and to smell its stink. Then, entering the room, she was surprised to encounter nothing of the sort. Instead, the toys and alphabet blocks on the wallpaper, and the matching curtains at the windows seemed to welcome her. The only smell she noticed was of something equally welcoming, clean and soft like baby lotion.

There was a pajama-clad little girl of about five sitting on the bed nearest the door, watching Nickelodeon on the wall-mounted TV. She looked at Hannah and gave her a gap-toothed smile. "Hi," she said. "My name's Angie. I got pendixitis."

"My name's Hannah, Angie. Are you all better now?"

"All better. The doctor took it away. Did you bring me a present?"

"Oh, I'm sorry. I didn't. I'm here to see your roommate."

"She's really sick, lots more than pendixitis. Did you bring her a present?"

Hannah thought, I *wish* I had a gift for her. "No, I didn't bring any presents at all tonight."

"That's okay," Angie announced solemnly. "She never wakes up anyhow."

"Hey, little Angie," said Martha Frenz, breezing into the

room. "Why don't you come with me up to the desk while these nice people visit Tessa? I have something really interesting to show you."

"Okay," Angie said brightly. "Look what I can do, lady." She held up the TV's control. "See, I can turn it off from all the way over here."

Hannah said, "Good for you, Angie," and waved goodbye as the little girl took hold of Martha's hand and skipped out of the room in her footed pajamas.

Bill was waiting on the far side of the room's other bed—a hospital crib like the one Isaiah had been in—over near the wall, giving Hannah easier access to his daughter.

As she approached the crib and looked down at the child, she felt pain gathering around her heart. Unlike Isaiah, Tessa had clearly enjoyed a robust, active childhood until the terrible accident a few weeks ago. Curly brown hair softly framed her sweet face, long dark eyelashes lay tenderly on her baby's cheeks, and her perfect mouth seemed to be asking for a little kiss. If it weren't for her pallor and the IV and oxygen tube, she might appear to be simply taking a good long nap after a typical toddler's day.

"She's beautiful, Bill," Hannah said, looking up to find him leaning back against the wall with his eyes closed. "Are you all right?"

"Kind of light-headed."

"Go get some air. I'll stay with Tessa awhile."

"I don't want to leave. I'm okay."

Hannah turned her attention back to the child, and suddenly she was telescoped away, as if she had fallen up to the ceiling and was watching herself with Tessa from above.

God, what is this? she wondered. What's happening?

It's all right, honey, she heard Grampa's voice say in her mind. *Relax and let it carry you.*

What is it, Grampa? she silently asked him.

Shhh, honey. Look.

Hannah blinked and refocused her eyes from her ceiling vantagepoint, seeing at once that the scene below her had changed. Daylight now flooded the room, and Bill Tyler stood beside his daughter's crib, gazing across it at Hannah… no, at some other woman standing where Hannah had been, a woman with short dark hair who was looking across the crib at Bill. He held out his hand to the woman and she grasped it, and then a small, two-year-old hand appeared between him and the woman, and a child's merry giggle danced around them and resolved itself into words: "Patty-cake, Mommy! Patty-cake, Daddy!"

And just as suddenly as she had left her body, Hannah returned to it. She looked again into the crib and found Tessa exactly as she had been moments ago, pale and still and quiet.

"Bill," Hannah said softly.

"Hm?"

"Did you notice I haven't touched her?"

"What?"

"I want you to notice that I haven't touched Tessa yet, okay?"

"I guess so. I mean… well, my eyes were closed. What's—"

"Then just take my word for it. I haven't touched her."

"Okay, I believe you. But why—"

"Because I want you to know that she's going to be all right, and it has nothing whatever to do with me."

"She's… she'll be all right? She'll come out of this and be her old self?"

"I'm absolutely certain, yes."

He leaned into the crib, patting Tessa as if to reassure himself that she was still there, that he wasn't dreaming this. "She looks the same. What happened?"

"I saw her and I heard her, laughing and talking with you and your wife."

"You saw her?"

"And heard her. I'm sure you'll be able to take her home in a few days."

"But what about her EEGs? How can the docs be so wrong?"

"I don't know. Maybe they made a mistake. Or maybe you've been given a miracle, you and your wife and your daughter. These things do happen, completely separate from people like me."

"You mean it, don't you. It's true."

"It's true."

"Oh, my God, Hannah," he exclaimed, looking at her with

279

awe, and reaching out to touch her.

"No," she said, stepping back. "That's what I was trying to tell you. This has nothing to do with *me*."

He shook his head. "I'm sorry. I don't believe that. I was over here feeling a kind of peace I've never felt before… Christ, I was feeling *forgiven*. And then you tell me she's going to be fine. I think it has everything to do with you."

Hannah remembered the healing Bill had been given at her office, and couldn't press her point. She felt dizzy with exhaustion, and leaned back against the safety rail of Angie's bed, rubbing her face with her hands. When she looked up again she asked, "Have you told anyone about me, Bill?"

"Just one person, my mother."

"Your mother," Hannah said softly, remembering what Jeli had told her about Ramona Tyler. "Would you be willing to not tell anyone else?"

"That's really important to you, isn't it, keeping yourself hidden."

"You have no idea."

"But what are you afraid of, Hannah? These gifts you have, don't you think they're meant to be shared with the world?"

"I guess I'm afraid of what the world does to people like me."

Bill appeared to take that in. Thoughtfully, he said, "I can't argue with you." He shook his head. "Really, after what you've done for me, I'll do anything you want. Anything."

"Then you'll keep this between us and your mother?"

"If that's what you want, absolutely."

"Thank you," Hannah said, the words coming out with a sigh of relief.

"You sure you wouldn't rather I shout the good news about you to the world, see you get the accolades and the rewards you deserve, and then I could take you to Philly for a five-star meal at *Le Bec Fin*?"

She studied his expression, relieved to find gentle humor. "Maybe in the next millennium."

They smiled at each other, and for the first time that day Hannah felt safe. "Would you like me to give Tessa an adjustment anyway?"

"Please. I'm a believer, remember?"

Hannah was glad he'd said yes; she'd been aching to touch the child. She switched sides with Bill and lowered the crib's railing. Then she reached in and gently rested her right hand on Tessa's chest and with her left began stroking the child's forehead. "She is so beautiful, Bill. You're very fortunate."

"I know," he whispered.

Careful not to dislodge the IV or nose tube, Hannah turned Tessa onto her left side. "Put your hands there," she told Bill, gesturing to his daughter's chest and thighs. "Keep her from rolling over any further."

Hannah bent over and carefully, slowly examined Tessa's neck and spine with her hands. "Not too bad," she said quietly. "Nothing that can't be put right with a period of regular adjustments."

"Thank God."

Hannah had begun to apply very gentle pressure to areas of Tessa's spine when Angie burst into the room, with Martha right on her heels telling her to slow down.

"Look, lady!" Angie said, rushing over to Hannah.

Hannah continued to adjust Tessa but looked at the piece of computer paper Angie proudly held out to her.

"See, it's my name all in *exes*! I did it all myself on the 'puter, but Martha kinda helped me a little bit."

"It's very nice," Hannah said.

Angie's eyes grew wide. "Whatcha doin' to Tessa? Does it hurt?"

Martha intervened. "It does just the opposite of hurt, Angie. See how softly the doctor is touching Tessa's back?"

"Tessa likes it?"

Martha nodded. "I'm sure she does."

"Ooo. So will you do that to me too, lady?"

Bill said, "Here's another believer come into your fold, Hannah."

She glanced up at him, grateful to see the peaceful light in his eyes.

On the road toward home from Paoli, Hannah's thoughts drifted back through the day. She realized her frame of mind had done a hundred-and-eighty-degree turn since morning, and couldn't remember what had made her start off the day so cranky. "What the heck was my problem?" she asked aloud, startling Clancy out of his snooze on the passenger seat.

She reached over and stroked his back. "What was my problem, eh, Clance?"

As if her golden friend had answered her loudly, Hannah heard the word "booze" reverberate in her ears.

Instantly, Ethan was standing there in her mind's eye. Ethan. Probably everything she wanted in a man, maybe even a partner for life, the father of her children. She imagined him wearing jeans and a soft blue shirt, untucked. He was barefoot, and his jeans were rolled up a bit, as if he were about to wade in water. His hair was ruffled by an easy breeze, and his eyes were alight with joy. She realized he was standing on the beach—it must have been early morning, she could see the sun over his shoulder—and he was asking her something and beckoning to her, wanting her to go with him. For a walk? For a run? She didn't know where, but it didn't matter; she wanted to go. She heard herself say, "Wait a minute," and was surprised when the words came out in a child's voice. Ethan stood still, looking at her, and she saw the light seem to slip out of his eyes. He came toward her then, and she knew she must be sitting on the sand because he was looking down at her. He knelt in front of her, on one knee, and she could suddenly see not only Ethan but parts of herself, her hands and her arms. They *were* a child's hands and arms; she was a little girl about the age of Angie back at the hospital, and she was sitting there on the sand, playing with something instead of getting up and going with Ethan. What was it she played with? She couldn't quite see it, but she felt a terrible, childish hatred of it. She wanted to set it aside and go with Ethan, wherever he went. She ached with longing to get up and go. So why was she dawdling there? "C'mon, Hannah!" she said to herself. "Stop that, whatever you're doing! Stop it now! I said stop!"

STOP! The word reverberated in her ears as "booze" had earlier, and Hannah jammed her foot on the brake pedal… just in time to avoid being hit by cross traffic at the Five Points Road stoplight. "Jesus!" she said aloud, staring at the red light and feeling her heart lurching back toward a normal rhythm.

Minutes later, she pulled her Jeep into the parking lot of the Wawa on Route 3 and turned off the engine. "I'm afraid it's not safe for me to be on the road tonight, Clance. You want to drive?"

She stayed in the Jeep awhile, stroking Clancy and thinking about her daydream. She knew full well what she'd been playing with there on the sand while Ethan waited. And she wondered if, in reality, he *would* wait. Wait for me to grow up, she thought. A longing swept through her—to talk to him, to be with him, to be held by him.

Sunday night, Hannah, she told herself silently. Sunday night he'll hold me.

Craig Stafford pushed his way into her thoughts just then. "What the hell do you think you're doing, Hannah?" he asked. "For crissakes, grow up!"

You're right, Craig, she thought. I'm a mess.

She looked over at Clancy. "Hey, pal," she said quietly. He opened his eyes and cocked his head. "Thanks for not caring that I'm a mess, and thanks for coming with me today. You want anything from the Wawa before we head to Pop's?"

She thought she heard him say, *You're welcome, and I wouldn't mind some Entenmann's chocolate chip cookies.*

Chapter Twenty-Seven

From the brick path leading to the back of her father's house, Hannah peered into the greatroom through a side window, and found not only Celeste, Jeli, Marcia and Lynn, but also Michael and Rose.

They've turned it into a bloomin' party, she thought, feeling as if lead weights were dragging from both feet as she made her way to the back door.

Clancy flew into the house ahead of her as Hannah said, "Hi," and then realized that everyone was staring at the sixty-inch TV screen. "What's happening?"

Six pairs of eyes turned to her with slightly glazed expressions.

Hannah's tension level rose several degrees, pushing her to joke, "I think I've walked in on the *Night of the Zombies*."

Everybody seemed to jump into action. Michael got up from the floor as he clicked off the TV and tossed the remote control to Rose, who blushed as she slipped it under a *Newsweek* on the coffee table. Meanwhile, Jeli and Celeste, their faces filled with concern, came over to greet Hannah, and Marcia and Lynn both stood and said "hi," looking embarrassed, like kids caught with their hands in the cookie jar.

"Good God," said Hannah. "What's going on here?"

Everyone answered her, talking over each other, reassuring her that nothing was going on, it was just something on TV and they were all aware that she didn't want to hear the news.

"Well, I might as well hear it since you guys have already scared me silly with that nothing's-going-on routine."

Michael smiled. "You didn't think we were smooth?"

"Smooth as track cleats. So what's happening out there in the big cold world that I've been avoiding?"

Jeli took her arm and steered her over to the sofa, sitting and pulling Hannah down beside her. "It's really nothing you should worry about, honey."

"That's true, Jo," said Celeste.

Hannah was studying their faces. "Then why are you all looking at me like that?"

"It's disorienting, that's all," Lynn said.

"Right, that's it," Michael added. "Watching TV and then seeing the source of it all walk in through the back door."

"Please don't worry, honey," Jeli said, patting Hannah's arm. "You know we'd tell you if we thought it would help."

Hannah decided to let it drop; she didn't have enough energy for anything else. "Okay, everybody. You win."

Just then, Clancy barked and bounded to the door as it opened to let in Papa, along with a gust of chilly night air.

"Hey, gang," he said. "You having a party without me?"

Everyone returned his greeting, as Celeste and Hannah crossed the room to him. Shrugging off his jacket, he kissed Celeste and gave Hannah a hug. "Hey, baby. How's my girl?"

"Fine, Pop. But don't you know you're not supposed to work so late on a Friday night?"

"Tell those fool restaurant owners that for me, will you? Now who have we here?" he asked, with an exaggerated look of surprise at Marcia and Lynn. "Wait. Don't tell me. Can it possibly be little Marcie and little Lynnie Thomkins?"

They laughed and stood to give him a hug as Celeste said, "He's so full of it, girls. I called him this morning and told him you'd be here for supper."

"What is it, about twenty years since I took the two of you to Richmond?" Papa said, shaking his head. "I must be a hell of a lot older than I thought."

"You don't look a bit older," said Lynn.

"Now here's a woman of commendable insight," said Papa with a grin.

"Knock it off, Lynn," Michael said. "He's already got a swelled head."

"Good to see you too, Mikey. You get your paper finished? And here's Rose. This *is* a party."

"Hi. I didn't mean to horn in like this. I was looking for Jo and I stopped by to tell her—"

"You want to get your shower, Paul?" Celeste interrupted.

"We're all hungry, and dinner can be ready in fifteen minutes."

"I'll do that," he said, waving to Jeli. "Hey, Ma. Good to see you."

"You too, dear."

As he left the room, Celeste said, "Would some of you come give me a hand or twelve?"

Marcia and Lynn simultaneously went to help, and Rose followed along behind them, as Michael pulled Hannah back to the sofa next to Jeli.

"Michael," called Celeste. "Get a fire going for us, would you?"

Hannah leaned back into the sofa and reached for Jeli's hand.

"You must be exhausted, honey," Jeli said quietly.

"Yes," Hannah breathed. "But I need to talk to you."

"I'm here."

Hannah turned to face her, and spoke softly. "Michael and Celeste told me on Wednesday night that they think I need a plan, in case the media catches up with me. Really, it was more like they said *when* the media catches up with me."

"Ah, love," Jeli said, cocooning Hannah's hand in both of hers.

"You think so too, don't you?" Hannah searched Jeli's eyes.

Jeli nodded slowly, and Hannah's heart skipped a beat or two.

"What in the world am I supposed to do, Jeli?"

"It'll have to be your decision, Jo. But you know we'll all support you."

Hannah sighed and shook her head. "I can't even think what my choices are, except to stay and tough it out or run away. But where would I go?"

"I've been giving this some thought, honey. You know my house at the shore is yours whenever you need it, but if you want more distance, how about San Francisco or Hawaii?"

Hannah smiled, then took in the expression on Jeli's face. "You're serious?"

"I have friends with vacation homes in both places—good friends who wouldn't ask questions if I said my granddaughter and I needed a place to stay for a few months."

"You'd go with me?"

"Of course I would, honey. In a heartbeat."

Hannah closed her eyes, remembering. "I've always loved San Francisco."

"So have I," Jeli said.

Hannah looked at her again. "You know… I… there aren't any words to thank you."

Jeli gave her a gentle smile. "Remember, honey, they may not find you at all. I'm simply agreeing with Celeste and Michael that you need to be prepared."

Hannah turned and sat back into the sofa, blowing out a breath. "Prepared," she said. "Yes, prepared is good."

"Hannah?" Marcia said, from where she was setting the dining table.

"Hm?"

"I've been commissioned to beg you to pay Vivian a visit tomorrow."

"So have I, *again*," called Lynn.

"How's she doing?"

"The same," Marcia said. "But she's driving everybody crazy, asking for you."

"What's the big deal?"

"Whatever it is, she insists on talking to you about it."

Hannah rolled her eyes. "All right, all right. I'll go."

"We're off the hook?" said Lynn.

"You're off the hook," Hannah said, and quietly added to Jeli, "And I'm on it. What if the old bat is planning to sic reporters or these Disciple people on me as soon as I show up there?"

"I hear she's a changed person, honey."

"She'd better be. I've had my fill of hospitals this week."

"How did it go with Bill Tyler's little girl?"

"It was good. Really, it was amazing." Hannah told Jeli about the healing Bill had been given in her office, and the healing little Tessa was receiving quite without Hannah's help.

"Thank heaven," Jeli said. "Maybe that will be the last of the briar patches for a while."

Just then the front doorbell sounded.

"Who in the world?" said Celeste.

"I'll get it, Mom," Michael called, heading to the front of the house.

Hannah felt a terrible certainty tighten her throat. "My God. It's Craig."

"Craig?" Jeli asked. "I thought he was in Japan until next week."

"He was. But now he's here," Hannah said softly, her eyes fixed on the doorway.

Michael returned, looking at Hannah as if he knew he was delivering bad news. "Look who I found."

He was followed into the room by a tall man with light brown hair and pale blue eyes, wearing a sportcoat over a dark gray shirt and slacks.

"Craig," Hannah said, finding that her legs didn't want to bring her out of the sofa. Jeli squeezed her hand, somehow giving her the boost she needed, and she stood and went to him. She hoped her face didn't show what she was feeling.

I'm not ready for this, she thought, as he wrapped his arms around her. She felt trapped in his embrace, repelled by the invasive smell of his cologne.

"Jo," he murmured in her ear. "At last."

Hannah pulled back as soon as she could and looked up at him. "I thought I was picking you up at the airport on Tuesday night."

"If you ever checked your home voice mail, you'd know I finished up in Japan a few days early."

"Oh, no. I'm sorry. Were you expecting me to meet you today?"

"It's okay. I caught the shuttle," he said, and chucked her under the chin.

Hannah was thinking how much she loathed being chucked under the chin as she introduced Craig to Marcia and Lynn, and Craig said hello to Jeli and Celeste and Rose.

"You're just in time for dinner," said Celeste. "Hannah, set another place for Craig."

"Please don't bother," Craig said, patting his flat stomach. "First class treated me too well."

"But you'll sit with us, won't you? Paul should be down in a few minutes."

"I will, thanks."

Hannah caught the admiration in Lynn's eyes and Marcia's, and wished she could tell them that Craig was fair game. Go for it! she wanted to say. He's available, even though he doesn't know it yet. Instead she said, "Craig's a consultant for humongous computer systems, Marcia. I think you two must talk the same language." She felt mild relief then as conversation began between Craig and the sisters.

After supper, as Hannah helped clear the table, Lynn quietly told her they had decided to accept Jeli's offer of beds for the next two nights.

"You don't need to," Hannah said. "Craig won't be staying with me." Saying this, she realized that Craig was going to be surprised by this news.

As Lynn appeared to be. "After three weeks in Japan? What a hunk he is. Reminds me of a younger Michael Douglas, like he was in *Wall Street*."

Hannah realized Lynn was right, and remembered how she'd loathed the actor in that role.

Lynn was saying, "There's no way we're going to stay with you."

"Honestly, Lynn, it's not a problem."

Lynn looked disbelieving, and shrugged her shoulders. "Whatever, but we'll stay with Jeli anyway. She's terrific, and we want to see the inside of that big old house of hers."

Hannah wished she too could spend the night at Jeli's. Ever since Craig had walked into the room, she'd felt self-conscious and tense, as if he were finding fault with everything about her. At the same time, she'd watched him match drink for drink with her father, becoming more tightly controlled while Papa became more loose and sloppy.

By the time they said goodnight to everyone and Craig climbed into his sleek black Mercedes to follow Hannah in her Jeep down to her house, she was wondering how she had managed to date this man for nearly two years. She knew she had to break up with him tonight, but didn't know if she could summon the energy. On the other hand, if she delayed, he would expect to make love to her and to spend the night, and that was inconceivable.

She reached over and brushed her fingertips along one of Clancy's silky ears. "Looks like we've found ourselves another briar patch after all, doesn't it, pal."

Chapter Twenty-Eight

At Hannah's house, Craig took over as if nothing had changed. He hung his sportcoat over the back of one of the dining table chairs, got himself a scotch on-the-rocks and a beer for Hannah, turned the stereo on to a twenty-four-hour jazz station, and settled himself into the greatroom sofa, slipping out of his shoes and propping his feet on the coffee table.

"It's great to be home," he said.

Hannah hoped he meant home in the United States, not home on her sofa. Seeing him there, acting as if he owned the place, she struggled with an impulse to kick him, hard, in one of his immaculately clad shins. She was considering the possible effect of such action when Craig patted the space beside him. "Come here," he said.

She shook her head and sat on the overstuffed chair at right angles to his end of the sofa. "I want to be able to see you."

Apparently misunderstanding, he said, "I love seeing you, too, doll. Where have you been all week? I couldn't even reach you at the office."

"I know. It's been... things have been very weird."

"Why? What's been happening?"

"Nothing," she said "Well, things have happened, yes, but it's, I don't know, I guess it's been..." She let her sentence trail off, because she had no clear idea of how to tell him what she needed to say.

"Is something wrong, doll?" Craig asked, studying her over the rim of the glass as he took a sip of his drink.

She shook her head, loathing herself for not getting on with it. "Nothing's wrong. Just tired I guess. So tell me about Japan, how'd it go?"

He folded his hands behind his head and settled back into the sofa, launching into a description of his work with one of Japan's most famous electronics companies.

Craig relished talking about his work, while Hannah's computer literacy extended only so far as operating the fun and friendly Macintosh system. So while he talked, Hannah went into a familiar mode of feigning interest as her mind journeyed among other matters. She told herself it was time to stop being a wuss, that she needed to "hitch up her britches," as Grampa would say, and confront Craig with the truth about her feelings. She imagined how she could begin, that she would tell him she'd been giving their relationship a lot of thought while he was away, and that...

She realized that Craig had stopped speaking and was looking at her as if he expected her to respond to what he'd just said. She hadn't a clue what response would be appropriate, so she took a shot with, "Tell me what's next on your agenda."

Suddenly there was a look in his eyes that got her complete attention.

He sat forward eagerly, as if he were about to make a sales pitch. "In fact, I have something I want to tell you. I've been doing a lot of thinking these past few weeks, about us, and I've decided we should get married. You could quit your job—really, you'd never have to work again, just let me treat you like a queen, like you deserve. We could settle down somewhere else, maybe California. I've been thinking about relocating my headquarters there, anyway. We can have kids, you can do that whole stay-at-home mom routine, except we'd get an *au pair* for when you wanted to travel with me."

As Hannah listened to Craig, she wondered if he knew her at all.

"So how's that sound, doll?" he asked, giving her a confident grin.

All she could think was that his lips were too thin and pinched, that his mouth was selfish, not generous like Ethan's. The idea of ever kissing those thin lips again made her feel queasy.

She blinked a few times, trying to clear her thoughts. "Was that a proposal?"

He laughed and reached for her hand. "Of course it was. Want me to get down on my knees?"

"No. Don't." She stood and went to the stereo, turning it off. "I don't like jazz much. I never know where it's going next," she said, returning to the chair.

"What are you talking about? I ask you to marry me and you tell me you don't like jazz."

"I need to talk to you, Craig."

"Sure. But sit over here, will you? Let me hold you while you talk."

"I can't think when you're touching me."

He narrowed his eyes and grinned at her. "So who says you need to think, doll. You know thinking was never your forte." He ran his hand up the back of her leg.

She quickly moved out of his reach. "Damn it, Craig! I hate it when you treat me like that."

He held up his hands in mock surrender. "Okay, okay. Don't bite my head off. I thought you agreed you're an emoter, not a thinker."

"You make me sound like an idiot."

"Well, if the shoe fits…" he said, laughing.

"That's not funny."

"Oh, lighten up, doll. You know I'm just kidding. And we're getting off the subject here, aren't we? As I recall, I had just asked you to marry me. So now's when you're supposed to give me a resounding 'YES!'"

"No. My answer is no."

He sat back, a bemused smile on his lips. "You're kidding."

"No. I don't want to marry you. In fact, I *can* think and I've been doing a lot of it myself these past few weeks. And I've decided we're not right for each other."

"That's ridiculous. We're completely right for each other. We've been right for each other for more than two years now."

"Maybe that's how you see it, Craig."

"That's not just how I see it, Johannah, that's how it is. So cut this crap. What's really going on here?"

"This is what's really going on, Craig. I hope… well, I'd like it if we could be friends, but I'm simply not…" She lost the courage to say it.

Clancy scratched at the French doors and Hannah moved

quickly to let him in, grateful for the interruption.

Clancy went straight to Craig, who ignored him. "I want you to be my wife and you want to be my friend, is that what you're saying?"

She sat on the coffee table across from him, keeping her eyes averted from his. "I'm sorry. I don't mean to hurt you."

"Christ!" he said, shooting to his feet, nearly knocking her over. "You don't mean to hurt me? What a crock!" Clancy clambered away as Craig strode to the windows. "I can't believe this. I'm planning our future while you're planning to end us." He turned around and glared at her. "What the hell happened to you in the past three weeks?"

Hannah shook her head. "You wouldn't believe it if I told you."

"What do you mean? Tell me. I deserve to know."

Hannah shook her head again. She couldn't tell him there was another man; Ethan was only a small part of this breakup, and Craig would blame him for all of it. And she still didn't trust him enough to tell him the truth about herself.

"Tell me, Hannah, goddamit. You owe it to me to tell me what's been going on here."

She felt as if her mind had ground to a halt, like an engine that's run out of fuel. "I can barely think, Craig. I'm so tired."

"Oh, woe is me, Craig, I'm so tired," he said, in a singsong imitation of her voice. "Poor Hannah. She's just too tired to tell me why this knife with her fingerprints on it is sticking out of my back." He took hold of her shoulders and pulled her to her feet. "Talk to me, Jo! Look at me and tell me what's happened."

She kept her eyes trained on the middle of his chest, reminded suddenly of how she'd always avoided Vivian's eyes. "I really am sorry, Craig. I know I'm making a mess of this and my timing stinks, but our relationship hasn't been working for me for a long while."

"What's that supposed to mean, not 'working for you'?"

"I'm not myself with you. I'm not honest."

"Well then, for crissakes, *get* honest."

"It's not that simple."

"Of course it's that simple. Just say the first honest thing that comes into your head."

She finally looked into his eyes. "I don't love you."

He pushed her away, and she sat hard on the coffee table. Clancy growled at him.

"Get that goddamned dog away from me before I boot his hairy ass across the room!"

"C'mon, boy," Hannah said, quickly taking hold of Clancy's collar and dragging him to the French doors. She opened them and pushed him out, then turned again to face Craig.

He looked at her steadily. "So that's it? All of a sudden in the last three weeks you stopped being in love with me, and now I'm supposed to graciously bow out of your life? I don't think so. Come and sit down with me, will you? Oh, don't look at me like that. Sit at the other end of the sofa if you want to, but let's have an adult conversation about this."

He sat on the sofa and she returned to the overstuffed chair.

"When did you make up your mind about all this?" he asked.

"It's been coming for a while, Craig. I even wondered... I hoped maybe you'd feel the same way I do about our relationship."

"And how is that?"

"That it had reached its logical conclusion."

"You're being completely ridiculous. Anybody with half a brain would see that the 'logical conclusion' of our relationship is marriage."

"I'm sorry. I guess I can't say anything right."

He stared at her, then shook his head. "You say you're tired and you can't say anything right and you're making a mess of this. Seems to me you're proving my point about you and thought processes. So why don't we drop it for tonight, get a good sleep and talk again tomorrow."

"We can talk tomorrow, but my mind isn't going to change."

Clancy was scratching on the door, and Hannah went to let him in again.

"Wait. Don't!" In one movement, Craig stood and came at her, and Hannah automatically flinched and put up her hands to stop him.

"What the hell, Johannah? You think I'm going to hit you?

That's how little you know me. I just want to hold you." He softened his voice. "Please let me hold you, Jo. For old times."

"Please don't, Craig. It's over."

"It's not over for me." He put his arms around her and pulled her close, pressing her back against the windows, murmuring, "Come on, Jo. Let me make love to you. You know how good we are together in bed." He tried to kiss her lips, but she turned her head away. "Come on, doll. Don't be like that."

Hannah forced herself to go limp, to offer no resistance, and gradually she felt his ardor dissipate. Finally, he stepped back and glared at her.

"You're acting like a mindless bitch, you know. And you're going to regret it. Whatever the hell's been going on with you, when you come to your senses, you'll regret having done this to me."

"I'm sorry, Craig. I really am. I'll always be grateful to you. You helped me through rough times when Grampa—"

"Screw the gratitude."

She looked at him, stayed silent.

He held her gaze for a long while. Then he cursed her viciously and turned away.

In that moment, knowing their relationship was over, Hannah felt a glimmer of compassion for this man who had been a bridge over the time following Grampa's death. "I hope you can forgive me," she said.

He turned back to her, and the look she saw on his face held such malevolence that, for the first time, she was genuinely afraid of him.

"Don't hold your breath on that one." He slipped into his shoes. "On second thought, bitch, feel free to hold your breath for the rest of your miserable life." He slung his jacket over his shoulder and slammed his way out of the house.

Hannah realized she was trembling and her heart was racing. I should have made him give me his key, she thought. What if he comes back?

She ran to the front door and put on the safety chain, then returned to the greatroom and let Clancy in, tightly securing the French doors. She stood there in the greatroom for a few moments, feeling utterly naked and vulnerable. Then she raced around checking locks, turning off lights, and finally hurrying to the privacy of her bedroom. There, she dropped fully clothed onto the bed and folded the quilt back over herself, hoping for instantaneous sleep—or at least an end to the trembling. Instead, she found herself lying there, looking up into the dark, wondering if she'd ever again feel safe in her own home.

Clancy jumped halfway onto the bed and slurped Hannah's nose.

"Hey!" she said, shoving him away. Immediately she felt sorry, and reached over, turning on the bedside lamp. Clancy sat beside the bed like a golden statue, gazing at her with his soulful eyes. "I'm sorry, pal," she said, scootching over a bit and patting the bed. He jumped up fully this time and settled beside her. "You're trying to cheer me up, aren't you. You think I'm just tired, and that things will look better in the morning." She leaned close to his face and stroked his ears. "And you're saying that if Craig should try to get back in here and hurt me, you'd scare the bejesus out of him, right?"

Clancy licked her nose again.

"You are cheering me up, pal. Once again."

Knowing sleep was far away, Hannah climbed out of bed, took off the khakis and silk shirt she'd been wearing all day, and slipped into warmup pants and a T-shirt. After she washed her face, brushed and flossed her teeth, she sat on the edge of her bed and reached for the phone. She pressed the button for her home voice mail, quickly deleting three messages from Craig and two from Rose, and then listening intently to every nuance in Ethan's voice as he said, "I wanted to let you know we're in luck, the Dilworthtown Inn is open Easter night, and I've made a reservation for eight o'clock, the earliest I could get. And I have to confess I also wanted simply to hear your voice. Please call me anytime, Hannah. Anytime at all." She listened to the message repeatedly before finally saving it, "for thirty days," as the electronic female voice informed her.

She climbed under her covers, turned off the light and cocooned her head just so in her down pillows, then closed her eyes and tried to relax.

Five minutes later, she turned on the light and got out of bed, putting on socks and a sweatshirt, and going to the kitchen for a bottle of Jack Daniels, a glass, and some dog biscuits for Clancy. For the next couple of hours she played computer games and sipped bourbon, until the brightly flashing images behind her eyelids persuaded her to try for sleep again.

Once she was back in her bed, with the light off, she heard Vivie's voice in her head, telling her she didn't deserve to sleep. *Through and through, you know you are very bad, Johannah*, said the Vivie of twenty-one years ago.

I can't believe this, Hannah thought. You're dying in the hospital and I'm six years old again, listening to you tell me how horrible I am.

Nobody likes a smart aleck, Johannah. Remember, bad things only happen to bad people.

"Except for hurting Craig," Hannah whispered, "what have I done that's so bad?"

Vivian replied immediately, *This isn't about Craig. It's about your running away from what God wants for you. It's about putting your own will before God's.*

It was always so easy for you, Vivian, she thought. You always knew exactly what God willed for you and for everybody else.

Suddenly, there was Grampa's voice. *And think of all the people she hurt with her self-righteousness, honey.*

Oh, Grampa, Hannah cried in her mind. Where are you? I need you. I can't do this anymore.

The tears started then, and Hannah turned over, burying her face in her pillows, letting the pain and the fear have their way.

After a while she fell into a restless, exhausted sleep.

Chapter Twenty-Nine

It was nearly nine when Hannah woke up the next morning; even so, she felt sick with exhaustion. It took all her willpower to haul herself out of bed, change clothes, do a few minimal stretches, and start off on a run with Clancy.

The air was warm and heavy with the fragrance of new grass and forsythia, smells Hannah found stifling. She and Clancy had covered less than a half-mile when a spasm of pain hit her stomach and she moved off the road, vomiting up the bourbon she'd consumed the night before. Clancy came to her, whining, and she rubbed behind his ears. "I'm okay, pal. Just paying the price for my indulgences."

She started to run again, but broke out in a sweat so profuse that she wondered if she'd come down with something since yesterday. I never get sick, she thought. Then again, I never have weeks like this one.

Soon she was gasping for breath, as if she'd hit the wall in a marathon, and she slowed to a walk, turning and heading for home.

Clancy loped in front of her, apparently trying to herd her back in the other direction. "Sorry, pal. I can't do it, not today. I know, I know—not yesterday either. I owe you one. Two, right, I owe you two."

She felt marginally better after her shower and some aspirin, and by ten-fifteen was headed to Giant with Clancy, a lengthy grocery list tucked into the pocket of her jeans.

It was close to eleven-thirty when she was home again with the groceries put away, eating a bowl of Grape Nuts with fresh strawberries and milk, and considering how she wanted to spend her day. She was pouring boiling water over her Morning Thunder herbal teabag when she reached for her cordless phone to call Jeli, listening instead to a new voice mail message.

It was Lynn. "Good morning, sleepyheads. It's ten-thirty and we figured you two might want the day to yourselves, so we're off to Philadelphia with Rose and Celeste to see the Chagall exhibit at the Art Museum. Jeli says to tell you to be here by six for dinner tonight—and bring that handsome hunk with you, of course—and that your brother Matthew's coming out too. Also, Marce and I want to wish you good luck with Vivian. Really, Hann, I think you're going to be surprised by her. We'll see you later."

Hannah speed-dialed Jeli's number and left a message on her voice mail, thanking her for the house-cleaners, and saying she'd be there this evening by six o'clock. Just before cutting the connection, she added, "Oh, by the way, I broke up with Craig last night, so there'll be one less for dinner."

She speed-dialed her father's house then, hoping to find Michael at home and willing to accompany her on the visit with Vivian. The phone rang six times before the voice mail kicked in, and she hung up without leaving a message.

"Well. That's that, I guess," she said aloud, causing Clancy to sit up and press himself against her legs. "Right, pal," she added, crouching down in front of him, stroking his sides. "Looks like it's going to be just you and me today. Funny how much I wanted that *yesterday*, but yesterday I didn't have to face the dragon. And even if she is an old, mortally ill dragon, I sure do wish you could face her with me. Maybe give her a few of your most fearsome snarls." She gently tugged his lips back on either side of his face and studied his resulting loopy smile. "Some snarl. But come with me anyway, will you, Clance? You'll give me moral support even while you're snoozing in the Jeep."

It was after twelve-thirty and patients' lunch trays were being removed to a large cart in the hallway when Hannah arrived at the door of Vivian's room at the Chester County Hospital.

She held her hands up in front of her and silently ordered them: *Don't you even think about healing this old bat. If you start to burn, I'm out of here and you're going with me.* Then she took a deep breath and pushed open the door.

There was a single hospital bed in the room, the head raised about forty degrees, and the woman who lay on it looked so unlike the Vivian of six days ago that Hannah almost turned back to recheck the room number.

But the woman said, "Johannah. You've come." So Hannah stayed.

"Yes, Vivie," she said, unconsciously reverting to the name she'd last used twenty-one years before. "It's me."

"Pull that chair around, won't you, and sit down. I need to see you."

Hannah did as directed, wondering at the astonishing physical change in this woman. Her hair was lank, gray-brown and thinning, and her mouth, without lipstick, had lost much of its former kewpie-doll pucker. She wore thick-lensed glasses in pale frames that made her round gray eyes look small and set impossibly deep within the rest of her face. Her face itself had gone from rosily made-up to sickly ashen.

"I know I look horrible," Vivian said. "But there doesn't seem to be any point in wearing my wig and makeup and contact lenses in here… especially now."

Hannah was at a loss for words, surprised to find herself oddly moved by this vulnerable old woman. "I'm sure it's much more comfortable this way," she murmured.

"Yes."

Unable to look at Vivian's eyes, distorted as they were through her glasses, Hannah stood and pulled off her jacket. "Hot in here."

"Why don't you hang that on the back of the door."

Hannah did, and reluctantly returned to the chair.

"What a lovely shirt you're wearing. That peachy color looks so nice with your hair, and you favor silk, don't you."

Hannah bit her lip to keep from saying, *None of your business.*

"By the way, Johannah, thank you for the beautiful flowers. Did you see them? The nurse had to take them out to the station because the arrangement is so large. But look at this." Vivian pointed to a small vase on the adjustable table; it held a few limp daffodils, some feathery ferns and two droopy red tulips. "She pulled these out for me so I could enjoy them in here. I'm afraid they're on their last legs now, but they were simply lovely."

"I'm sorry the arrangement was too big."

"Oh, no. I didn't mean to… I'm not complaining. Really, it

was beautiful and I loved it. So good of you." Vivian's hands were nervously smoothing the top of the sheet, folding it down over the blanket. "I know it was hard for you to come here, Johannah, and that makes it even more special to me. There's so much I need to say to you, but now that you're here, I find myself tongue-tied."

Hannah remembered being young and tongue-tied with her father, wanting to say just the right thing because she loved him so much. Unexpectedly, here in yet another stuffy, overheated hospital room, she felt a weakening of her defenses. She thought if she didn't do something immediately, if she didn't take charge, the fortress she had built painstakingly over much of her lifetime to protect herself from this woman would soon be washed away like yesterday's sand castle. "I can't stay long, Vivian."

"Of course, I understand, you're so… you have such a full life and so little time. Forgive me, I…" She pulled some tissues from the box on the bedside cabinet and dabbed at her face with them.

Hannah was horrified to see the tears streaming out of Vivian's tiny, faraway eyes. "Why did you want to see me, Vivie?"

"Oh, I need to get to the point, don't I. You see… how can I explain?… Did you know how much I admired your mother?"

Hannah couldn't imagine any question that would have surprised her more. "You did?"

"Yes. Beyond all reason." Vivian removed her glasses and rested her head back against the pillow, closing her eyes. "She was beautiful and gracious and so feminine, so gentle. Sometimes when I saw her, I'd feel a real pulling inside my heart, as if it hurt to look at someone so lovely. She was perfect, really. She was everything I always wanted to be."

Hannah was stunned into silence.

"And then you were born, and something happened inside of me. You had everything, a perfect mother, a wonderful father, and all the love any baby could ever need. Looking at you in your mother's arms, the way she would cradle you and gaze at you with all that love in her beautiful eyes, and when she was nursing you—I've never felt such pain. It was as if a fire started inside me. I had never envied anyone like I envied you."

Vivian's left hand lay at her side, on top of the blanket;

Hannah resisted the impulse to reach out and hold it.

"When your mother went back to work, it seemed natural that I should take over caring for you during the day. After all, your father and she had never even hinted that they wanted me to move out and find my own place. So that's what I did, I took care of you as if you were my own daughter, all during the workweek. I'd feed you and bathe you and change your diapers, and I used to drive you into town and take you for walks around Marshall Square Park or Everhart in your carriage, and later in your stroller. And… well, I'm embarrassed to admit, but if somebody was admiring you and I didn't know them, I'd tell them you were my baby sister. You see? That made your mother *my* mother too." Vivian blew her nose on more tissues and again rested her left hand at her side.

"Of course, nobody believed me. I was too old. But it didn't matter, because I let myself believe it. And then, at night when your mother would come home from work at the hospital, she'd take over with you and she hardly paid any attention to me at all. Me, her first-born daughter. Oh, I know how crazy that sounds. I knew even then that it was just make-believe, but I couldn't stop how I felt. And your father, he was so in love with your mother and with you, he'd barely say a word to me for days on end. I'd never been so lonely as I was then, living there with you and your mother and father."

Vivian turned her head and tried to focus her myopic eyes on Hannah. "You've never been lonely, have you, Johannah. You've always been adored. You've always been needed."

Hannah had a dozen retorts on the tip of her tongue in response to Vivian's ridiculous assumptions, but she managed to remain silent.

"Well, I'll tell you, there is no more painful feeling in the world than loneliness and knowing that no one wants you around." Vivian let out a long breath and closed her eyes again. "But there was nowhere else for me to go. I had no job, no training for a job, no friends outside of a few acquaintances at church. I had no life other than caring for your mother and father and taking care of you. So nothing changed, everything went on the same way, year after year, me living in the house with all that love and not one drop of it for myself." She shook her head and pressed her hands to her face. "And then the unimaginable happened. Evil came and punished us all by taking your precious mother away." Her tears started anew and she reached for more tissues.

After awhile, she continued, "I remember how I envied you at the funeral, because you were allowed to cry like that. You were still so young, and losing your mother that way, everybody expected you to be devastated. But *I* wasn't allowed to show the pain I felt. I was supposed to be strong for you and your father. Well, I wasn't strong. Inside, I was a child like you, wailing for her lost mother. It was as if I died with her, and I wished I could have. I wished they could have buried me right beside her that very day."

Vivian peered again at Hannah. "Can you possibly understand any of this?"

Hannah was experiencing waves of pain. She was glad Vivian couldn't see her face clearly. "Go on," she said softly.

"Well, you can probably guess the rest. Now you know why I was so hard on you. I couldn't stop envying you because you'd had your mother's deepest love and I'd had nothing. Your father, too—if he barely noticed me before, well, afterwards, it seemed like he was avoiding me on purpose. The only person who ever showed me any kind of genuine affection was my poor Bruce."

Hannah expected to see a fresh tide of tears, but there were none. Instead, Vivian's face seemed oddly emotionless as she spoke of her dead son.

"Of course, I loved him like any mother loves her child, but he was so much like his father that a lot of the time I hated him, too, and I'm afraid he must have known that. Anyway, it didn't matter. His love for me wasn't what I craved; the love I craved was gone forever with your mother. So I envied you and... well, I'm ashamed to say it, I hated you too, you were so bright and so pretty and you had your mother's eyes. It was as if I didn't have any choice but to be hard on you. I told myself I did it to make you strong. I told myself I did it to make you into someone like your mother."

Vivian put her glasses on and reached a hand out to Hannah.

Out of long habit, Hannah flinched away from her touch.

"Poor Johannah, you were only a child. You had no way of knowing, did you."

Hannah shook her head and strained to hold back her tears.

"No, of course you didn't. And I think when your mother died, I think that's when Satan stepped in. But he stepped into *me*, not into you."

Vivian closed her eyes again. "After she died, I lost control of myself. I could no more have stopped myself from doing the things I did, from treating you and your father that way, than I could have flown to the moon. Even though nothing, not one single thing, ever turned out the way I wanted it to.

"And then I..." Vivian pulled her glasses off and brought her hands up over her face. "I can't... I don't want you to see me now. Don't look at me."

Hannah turned her gaze toward the blank TV screen.

"Are you looking at me?" Vivian asked, her voice sounding like a whiny three-year-old's.

"No."

"You promise you're not?"

"I promise."

". . . The thing is, I *did* kill your poor little fawn. I'm so sorry. Can you ever forgive me? Please say you can forgive me."

This is too much, Hannah thought, lowering her head and closing her eyes. "It was a long time ago, Vivian."

"Don't look at me!"

"I'm not."

". . . You see, when I did that, when I killed that little fawn, I felt like somebody else was doing it, some cruel old woman I didn't even know, and I was powerless to stop her." Vivian sobbed, but kept on talking. "And then, do you remember, you healed my broken arm! Sweet Jesus, I killed your fawn and you turned right around and healed me! Can you imagine how that tortured me? It's haunted me all these years." Her sobs took over now, and she leaned forward into her hands.

Hannah stood up and stiffly put her right arm around the old woman's bony shoulders. "Vivian, it was twenty-one years ago."

"It doesn't matter, I can never forgive myself," Vivian wailed.

"Never! Not in a million lifetimes! And now I have only a little left of this one."

Hannah's mind searched wildly for a way out of the room. She couldn't think clearly and she could barely get her breath. "I have to go."

"No, please!" Vivian cried. "I'm sorry. I'll stop. Please don't leave me now. I need—"

"I have to."

"I promise, I'll stop. Please—" Vivian grabbed Hannah's hand.

Hannah pulled her hand out of Vivian's grasp, but sat again, shaking her head. "I'm sorry, but it's impossible for me to take this in. A few days ago you accused me of being a servant of Satan, and now you're asking me to forgive you."

"I know. It's pitiful, and I really don't expect you to forgive me at all. I'm just so thankful that you've let me tell you these things. I had to tell you these things. I had to. Like a confessional." She lay back into her pillows, looking deeply exhausted. "I think this tumor... I think it's God's grace, saving me at last. Those episodes I was having, with every one it seemed that my thinking would change a little more, and after they did the MRI and told me... what they told me, well, it was as if something just lifted off my back that's been there all these years." She put a tentative hand on Hannah's arm. "Those things I said to you on Sunday? Now it seems like somebody else entirely who said them."

Somewhere Hannah had heard the expression, "dying grace". She wondered if that's what she saw at work in Vivian.

"I don't know anything about psychology, Johannah, but I've been thinking I must have been under Satan's power all those years, starting with the craziness when your mother died, or maybe even before that. And then, when I got sick and they found the tumor, well, maybe then the Lord God Almighty could finally get through to me."

Hannah was having a hard time remaining open-minded, hearing words like "Satan" and "lordgodamighty" coming from Vivian's mouth. She felt suddenly light-headed. "I really do have to go, Vivie," she said as she stood again.

Tears started once more in Vivian's eyes. "Please..."

"I'll come back. Maybe tomorrow. But for now, I'm too... I'm overwhelmed."

"I'm so sorry. You've been so patient and I forgot about all you've been through in the past week, with the plane crash and that little boy in Minnesota, and the press and those Shepherdess people hounding you."

Hannah was retrieving her jacket, but Vivian's words brought her quickly back to the bed.

"Oh, my dear," Vivian said. "Please don't look at me like that." She motioned for Hannah to lean down and then spoke softly into her ear. "I won't tell anyone about who you are."

Hannah pulled back and looked hard into Vivian's eyes. "You won't?"

"I promise. Your mother was a healer too, you know. I think that's one of the reasons I've been so… envious of you all these years."

"Vivian, if you'll keep this between the two of us, it will mean a lot to me."

"I will, Johannah. I swear on my love of the Lord."

Hannah felt the truth of Vivian's words. She hesitated a moment, then leaned over and kissed the old woman lightly on her downy cheek. "I believe you."

Vivian's nurse came into the room just then. "Everything all right in here? Vivian, anything I can do for you?"

"Not unless you're a priest," Vivian said, her hand on her cheek over Hannah's kiss.

"Do you want me to call your minister?"

"No, no. I'm all right." Vivian patted Hannah's arm. "Meg Gowan, meet my granddaughter. Her name is Dr. Johannah Kirkland and she is the best chiropractor in all of Pennsylvania, probably in all the world."

Hannah couldn't help smiling at Vivian's excess. "We met at the nurse's station when I arrived, Vivie."

The pretty, dark-haired nurse gave Hannah a warm smile that lit her expressive brown eyes. "We did indeed, Mrs. B., and your granddaughter is just as lovely as you've been telling us. Now, let me check your pulse and your blood pressure, so I can let you two get on with your visit."

"Johannah's just leaving," Vivian said. "And anyway, I don't know why you even bother. What earthly difference can it make how my pulse is doing, with that hideous lump I've got growing in my head? It seems to me that the better my pulse is, the happier my lump will be."

Hannah was startled to realize that Vivian was making light of her situation.

"Now behave yourself, Mrs. B. You know we have to make sure the radiation and the meds aren't causing any additional problems."

"All right, all right, just get on with it," Vivian grumbled, winking at Hannah.

My God, Hannah thought. The Black widow just winked at me and I feel like winking back.

Chapter Thirty

Hannah sat in her Jeep in the hospital parking lot, with Clancy asleep on the passenger seat beside her. She stared out through the windshield, blind to the sunny spring afternoon, as she idly stroked Clancy's golden coat.

She was disoriented. The monster of her twenty-seven years had been transformed into a fragile little old lady, shifting the familiar structure of Hannah's life. She felt lost in the new terrain.

"What am I supposed to do without a monster, Clancy?" she said aloud.

He lifted his head and looked at her, his eyelids at half-mast.

Am I supposed to trust this new Vivian? she wondered. Then again, what difference does it make? She hasn't played an important part in my life for years, so why should she start now?

Hannah was satisfied with her logic, but bothered by some deeper thought she couldn't quite reach. Something about everything being different now, and about trust.

Her cell phone rang just then. She withdrew it from her jacket pocket and pressed the *On* button. "Hello?" she said.

"Hannah!" said Ethan's voice.

She heard the alarm in his voice. "What's wrong?"

"They've found you, the media. I just heard it on KYW, and I tried you at home—"

"Found me?"

"The media's staked out now, some at your office and a bigger crowd at the foot of your driveway. Where *are* you?"

"Oh my God…"

"I know. I'm so sorry, Hannah. What can I do? Let me help you."

"I need to think." In her mind she heard Craig laughing at her, reminding her that thinking wasn't her forte.

"Where are you?" Ethan repeated.

"In a parking lot," she said, for the first time noticing her surroundings. "With lots of other cars. I think it's okay. Do they know my license number?"

"Probably."

"You said they're parked at the *foot* of my driveway? They're not on the property itself?"

"I think they can't be on the property legally unless they're invited."

"Do you have the TV on?"

"Now I do."

"What are they showing as my driveway?"

"There's a tall lamp post and two mail boxes and some flowering trees back from the road."

"That's what I thought, it's my father's. There's a different driveway to my house. I wonder if I could get home without being seen."

"Do you need to go to your house?"

"I don't know, I don't know."

"Can I go there for you?"

"Let me think…" Craig laughed again.

"Where's your family?"

"Everybody's in Philadelphia except my father—he's probably working—and Michael, my brother, he might be playing racquetball, I don't know. My father… God, I never wanted him to find out about me this way."

"Hannah, I know I can help you if you'll let me."

Her mind raced through her options, and she realized that everyone she trusted was out of reach… except Ethan.

"Yes, please," she said.

"Good. Just tell me what to do."

"Would you come get me now?"

"Absolutely. Where are you exactly?"

She told him, and he said, "I'll be there in ten minutes."

When they broke the connection, Hannah speed-dialed her father's house, again hearing six rings before the voice mail clicked in. This time she left a message.

"Pop, if you're the one hearing this, please forgive me. Please understand that I didn't tell you about myself because I didn't want you to worry. And don't worry now. I'll be all right. And

Mike, if you're hearing this before Pop, please reassure him that I'm not a child anymore and it's not his job to protect me—or yours either, for that matter. I'm not sure right now what I'm going to do, but I'll call you as soon as I know."

She called Jeli then and left another message. "I'm assuming you know what's happened, and I wanted to tell you that Ethan Quinn is helping me—remember, I met him on the plane? I'll try to call you later when I know where I'll be, but meantime, would you contact your friends about the possibilities we discussed? Oh, and I've got Clancy. I'm so sorry all of you have to go through this with me. I wish... oh, well, just know that I love you, and I'll be in touch as soon as I can."

Hannah took the next several minutes to think in as straight a line as she could, despite the barbs from Craig, while keeping an eye out for Ethan—or for anyone who might be too interested in the license plate of her army-tan Jeep.

As soon as Ethan pulled up behind her in a Honda CRV, she climbed out her door and went to him, her legs turning wobbly when she saw the expression in his eyes.

She suddenly felt shy, and said the first inane thing that came to mind. "I guess we're both partial to army-tan four-by-fours."

"Great minds," he replied, his gaze steady on hers.

"Could we drive around in your car awhile?" she asked, glad that her voice, at least, felt normal.

"You bet."

"Is it okay that I have a dog? Clancy's a golden retriever."

"My favorite breed."

Hannah let Clancy out of the Jeep and locked it, pocketing the keys.

"No car alarm?" Ethan asked, as she let Clancy in the back and climbed into the front seat of the CRV.

"I don't want it going off accidentally and drawing attention."

"Good thinking." He looked back at Clancy, who was tail-wagging and drooling happily. "Great dog."

"My loyal pal," she said, fastening her seat belt.

"So where to?"

"Any place out of the way. I'd like to run some ideas by you, see what you think."

"How about my house?"

She considered for a moment and realized she felt perfectly safe now. "That's fine, unless it happens to be next to my office."

He smiled at her. "It's down near Everhart Park, the opposite end of town if I'm right about where your office is."

"Perfect," she said, as he drove toward the parking lot exit. "Funny, but that's the second time today Everhart Park has come up."

"Must be fate."

"Fate… yes. Feels like a lot of fate lately."

Ethan's house reminded Hannah of both Papa's and Jeli's. It was an older house of gray stone with a wide, covered porch along the front, separated from neighboring homes by a few acres of mature trees, trim lawns, and privet hedge.

"This is nice," Hannah commented, as Ethan steered the CRV to a stop under the portico.

"Thanks. It belonged to my grandparents."

"You must enjoy mowing."

"It's Astro-Turf," he said, so earnestly that Hannah almost believed him for a moment.

Inside, Ethan led Hannah through a large living room centered around a baby grand piano.

"You play?" she asked.

"Marginally. It was my grandmother's, and no one else wanted it."

She followed him then, out into a brightly-sunlit space that combined a country kitchen with a family room. "This is nice," she said again. She noticed the abundant array of succulents along the south-facing windows. "And you have a green thumb."

"My mother's thumb, I'm afraid. She insists on maintaining a cactus garden for me out here. Claims she doesn't get enough light at home, but I think it's really her way of keeping tabs on me."

"How does she keep your jades so healthy?"

"I'm not sure, but it could be all the intimate conversations she has with them. … Now, a couple of these chairs, you don't want to sit in them unless you've got time for a nice long nap.

Upholstered sleeping pills."

"Best kind."

He handed her a slim black device. "Here's the remote and there's the TV, help yourself."

"Thanks."

"Could I get you something to eat or drink?"

"You have any Pepsi?"

"Wild Cherry, I think."

"My favorite."

"Fate again," Ethan said, going to the refrigerator.

"Which chairs are the sleeping pills?" Hannah asked.

"Guess."

She settled at one end of the sofa.

"Ah," he said, pouring the Pepsi over ice in two glasses. "So you're going to play it safe."

"All these chairs are lethal. I can tell by the way Clancy's begging for permission to nest in them."

Clancy settled at her feet as she clicked on the TV that stood against the opposite wall.

The first image on the screen was of the back of Michael's car as it headed up Papa's driveway. A female reporter was saying that, so far, Michael Kirkland had been the only person seen entering or leaving the Kirkland property that afternoon. "And as you just saw, Jim, he was unwilling to speak with the press. So at this point in time, the whereabouts—"

"Poor Michael," said Hannah, muting the TV sound. "What a shock that must have been for him."

Ethan handed her one of the glasses of Pepsi, then sat at the other end of the sofa.

"Do you want to call him?"

"I do, but I'm feeling kind of paranoid about how they can listen in on phone calls these days." She took a sip of her drink. "Anyway, I left a message on my father's machine while you were coming to get me, and I'm hoping Michael has heard it by now." She skimmed quickly through the TV channels, including CNN, and found only normal broadcasting. "Nothing else," she said, her eyes still fixed on the blank screen after she clicked off the TV.

"How could there be when the story's sitting right here on my sofa?" He held up his drink to her. "A toast to calmer days?" he asked.

"To calmer days," she agreed.

They clinked glasses, looking at each other.

"Your eyes are extraordinary," he said.

She felt her cheeks burn and looked away from him, taking another sip of her Pepsi.

"I'm sorry," he added. "I didn't mean to embarrass you."

"It's not that," she said. "It's… well, I was thinking the same thing about your eyes."

He set his drink down on the coffee table. "There's fate again. Maybe it's you and I that are fated."

"Whatever it is, it's scaring the wits out of me."

"If it's any comfort, me too."

She couldn't help smiling. "So this isn't *pro forma* for you either?"

He returned her smile. "Hardly. In fact, it's so far outside my comfort zone that I'm not sure of my moves."

The look in his eyes was so compelling that she scrambled for safer ground. "Can we talk about the problem at hand?"

"Sure. Why don't you tell me what you're planning."

"Nothing brilliant, really. Long term, there are a couple of possibilities if I decide to relocate. And, short term, I thought I'd go down to the shore, at least for tonight and maybe tomorrow—you know, get away and try to decide where I go from here."

"That's good."

"Then you don't think I'm being a coward, running away?"

"Not at all. You're getting yourself some breathing room and giving yourself time to think calmly. Even if you should decide to relocate, I wouldn't call it running away."

"I'm afraid I would."

"But it's not, Hannah. You know you'd leave the area only if you could see no other way to continue using your gifts."

"But it would also be to save my own hide."

"Even the grandest act of altruism contains a bit of self-interest."

She studied his face for a moment. "You're determined to

make me feel better, aren't you."

There was a warm smile in his eyes as he said, "If helping you see yourself as you really are makes you feel better, then yes, I am determined."

"I think you're in the right profession, Dr. Quinn."

"That's good to know."

"So, how about telling me what I should do?"

"I can't, Hannah."

"Just your opinion, then."

"My opinion? All right. I think you should do exactly what your heart tells you to do."

"That's cheating," she said, loving his wonderful smile. "I need guidance and you tell me to follow my heart."

"Best guidance there is."

"Phooey."

"Phooey? The eminent Dr. Kirkland says 'phooey'?"

"You remind me of Grampa."

"Well, that's good, isn't it?"

"I guess, but he could drive me crazy, always telling me I already knew the answer to whatever question I was asking him."

"He was right, wasn't he."

She gave a small sigh. "Probably."

"Good. So you'll go to the shore and you'll sort out your next move. And I guess it's out of the question for me to go with you."

"If you're not going to tell me what to do, I'm probably better off alone. Except for Clancy," she added, reaching down to stroke his back. "He's a terrific sounding board."

"Where will you go?"

"Avalon."

"Is anything open? Any motels where you can have Clancy?"

"My stepmother's mother has a house right on the beach."

"You can get in?"

"I know where the keys are."

"Perfect. And I think you should use my Honda."

"Oh, I can't take your car."

"Unless you've got a spare license plate for your Jeep, I think the CRV's the answer."

"But what about you? It's not a good idea for you, either, to be driving around in front of my license plate."

"I was thinking I'd rent a car while you're using mine."

Hannah shook her head. "I'm accumulating too many debts."

"How do you mean?"

"Too many people are doing too much for me. I don't even know how to sufficiently thank them—you, for example—much less repay the favors."

"Maybe you're getting back a small measure of what you've given all your life."

She felt her cheeks redden again. "That's a kind thing to say. Thank you."

"You're not the only one who has trouble accepting help."

Hannah nodded. "Much easier to give. No strings attached."

"Right. There's a whole bunch of disorders most of us suffer from labeled 'fear of strings.'"

"Intimacy."

He gave her a gentle smile. "The 'i' word."

"What I'm so nervous about with you," she admitted.

"Ditto back at you."

They both sipped their Pepsis, and then Ethan said, "Is there anything I can do to help with your family?"

Hannah imagined her family and Rose and Kyla on a ship in a storm, bouncing off each other in their efforts to stay on course, while the navigator hung out in Avalon, studying maps. Add Ethan to the mix, and instantly the sea became calm. "Would you be willing to sort of present yourself at my father's house later today?"

"I'd be happy to."

"Not the ideal way to introduce you, I guess—"

"I disagree. I'm thinking they'll be feeling lost at sea while their captain has taken a leave of absence, and there I am, responding to their S.O.S."

"I can't believe you said that. It's exactly the image I had, except I thought of myself as the navigator."

"Fate again?"

"Great minds again."

"So what would you like me to tell your family?"

"Oh," she said, raking her hands through her hair. "My

family. I'd give anything to have them out of this mess."

"Understandably. But I'm guessing they want to rally around you, that they wouldn't have it any other way."

Hannah shook her head. "You're right, of course. So just tell them I'm okay. They'll know where I've gone. And do you think you could get them to not *talk* about where I've gone, not even call me on my cell phone? I think the media can listen in on anything these days. Am I being ridiculously paranoid?"

"Not at all. Smart and cautious."

She looked directly into his eyes as she said, "You *are* making me feel better, Ethan. I really can't thank you enough."

He reached for her hand and she gave it to him easily, then immediately thought of Craig.

"There's something I have to confess, Ethan."

"Whatever it is, you're absolved."

"You better hear it first." She looked down at her hand in his, momentarily distracted by the warm strength of him. "The other night, when I said I wasn't engaged or married... well, that was true, I'm not, but I have been involved with someone for a long time. Nearly two years, in fact, and I wasn't going to tell you about him when we met for dinner tomorrow night." Although he continued to hold her hand, she sensed that he withdrew a little.

After a few moments he said, "I'm glad you told me, Hannah. Secrets can be toxic."

She looked up at him again. "Funny thing is, I might have kept it secret, except that he came home early from three weeks in Japan, and I broke up with him last night."

"Last night? You broke up with him? You're saying it's over?"

She nodded. "It's over."

He moved close to her then and brought her hand to his lips, kissing the back of it, turning it over, kissing the palm, tracing the lines and stroking the length of her fingers. She thought how small her hand looked in his, and how appropriate, as if it had found its safe haven. She wondered if she might have found her own safe haven.

She rested her head on his shoulder, warmed by the current that flowed from his body into hers. Loving the clean, woodsy smell of him.

He put his hand on her cheek and turned her face, tilting it up and looking into her eyes for a long moment before he gently, very gently, kissed her lips. Then he kissed her again and she felt a rising of desire within her that took her breath away.

"I should go," she whispered.

"Yes."

"I don't want to go."

"No," he said.

"But I have to."

"Yes."

"Someday, Ethan…"

"Soon, please God."

"Yes, very soon," she said. "But if I decide I have to move—"

"Where?" he asked.

"Somewhere. If I can't stay here and tough it out…"

"I've always wanted to live *somewhere*."

"What about your practice?" she asked.

"What about yours? If you can start again, so can I."

They were quiet awhile, holding each other, Hannah resting her head on his chest, lulled by the strong, steady sound of his heart.

He kissed her then, longer and deeper. When he pulled back, he said, "You sure you don't want me in Avalon with you? I could be there and quietly hold your hand while you listened to that wise heart of yours."

She wanted to say yes. "Trouble is, if you did, maybe my heart wouldn't be focusing in the right direction."

"Mm. I see your point."

She stroked his cheek lightly with the back of her hand. "Thank you for this oasis, Ethan. I don't know what I would have done without it. But now I guess I'd better get on the road."

He nodded but stayed seated, keeping hold of her hand as she stood and clucked at Clancy. "Okay, pal. Say goodbye to Ethan."

Clancy stood and shook himself, as Ethan finally got to his feet. "Hang on a second," he said, and left the room.

While he was gone, she retrieved her jacket and looked around, memorizing the light and peace and comfort of his home, in case she didn't see it again for a while.

When he returned, he handed her another of his blue-gray calling cards. "I've added my cell phone number. I'll keep it with me, so you can use that number to call me."

"I guess I *could* make calls with my cell phone. They can't find out where I am when I'm using it, can they?"

"Your guess is as good as mine, but I hope the infamous *they* aren't nearly as all-powerful as the movies make them out to be."

She smiled and tucked his card into her pocket. "Your mouth to God's ear," she said, and then gave him directions to her father's house. "Are there any quirky things I should know about the CRV?" she asked.

"Only that it's already crazy about you."

". . . You're making this awfully tough, you know."

"I'm sorry," he said, moving close and slipping his arms around her.

"You're lying. You're not sorry at all."

"You're right." He kissed her again, and Hannah was thinking maybe he should accompany her to the shore after all, when Clancy jumped up and planted his forelegs, one on Ethan's hip, one on hers, smiling and panting at them.

"Doggone it, Clancy," said Ethan. "What kind of pal are you?"

"Maybe the one with the clearest head," Hannah laughed. "Now, should I take you to the car rental office?"

"No need. Enterprise will deliver a rental to my front door."

When Hannah was in the CRV, about to turn on the ignition, she stopped and looked at Ethan through the open window. "Thank you for all of this. Just when my worst fears were coming true, there you were to turn everything around for me."

"Believe me, Hannah, it's my pleasure."

"Good luck with my family."

"I'm looking forward to it. In fact, I was hoping I might see you in church tomorrow and you might invite me to meet them afterwards. This way, I meet them a day sooner."

She turned on the ignition. "I would have liked to spend Easter with you."

He leaned down and kissed her lingeringly. "Maybe fate will give us a lot of Easters together."

As she steered the CRV out of the driveway, she saw him in the rearview mirror, standing there, watching her. "Please God," she whispered, "a lifetime of Easters together."

Chapter Thirty-One

Hannah was a good distance past the New Jersey side of the Delaware Memorial Bridge when she was startled by the sound of her cell phone. When she checked the caller ID screen and saw the name, she felt an immediate chill. *Craig.* How could she have forgotten that Craig, like everyone else, would now know the truth about her. She clicked the phone on and put it to her ear.

"Where are you, Jo?"

His aggressive tone stirred her defenses. "Why?"

"Because I want to see you. We have to talk."

"What about?"

"Don't be ridiculous. You *know* what we have to talk about. Why you lied to me. Why you've lied to me all this time. The real reason you ended us last night."

She didn't have the energy to keep on hedging. "This is only part of the reason, Craig."

"Nonsense. You didn't want me to know about you because you were trying to protect me. Well, now I know and I intend to protect *you*."

"But I don't want your protection. I don't need it."

"Of course you do. Now tell me where you are."

She said nothing.

"Look, Jo, I'm coming to you, whether you like it or not. We're in this together. In spite of everything, I still want to marry you."

Don't do me any favors, she thought. And remained silent.

"All right. If you won't tell me where you're going, I'll find you on my own. … In fact, I bet you're headed for Avalon, aren't you."

Hannah's heart jumped into her throat. "No!"

"I knew it! I'll be right behind you. You don't have to be alone anymore, doll."

"Craig, please! I want to be alone now. I really do. I *need* to be alone to sort out what happens next."

"Bull! That's the last thing you need, being alone with your convoluted emotions. You need my help with these Shepherdess loons. They intend to own you, Jo, and you're going to have to face them. You know you've never been good at dealing with more than one person at a time, while that's one of my strong points."

"Craig, please listen to me."

"I'm listening. I'm driving to Avalon and I'm listening."

Suddenly, she didn't know what to say. Short of brutal honesty, how could she persuade him to leave her alone?

"I'm list-en-ing, Jo-han-nah," he sing-songed at her.

His ridicule was just the push she needed. "I don't want you with me, Craig. I meant it when I said I don't love you."

"Sorry, but I'm not buying it. I know what we've had together, and you can't just change your mind about something as good as that."

"I haven't changed my mind. I think I've finally *spoken* my mind."

"You're trying to tell me you've been faking it for two years?"

Ouch! "I wasn't faking. I just didn't know what I really wanted."

"And now you do?"

Yes, she wanted to say. Now I know Ethan. "I guess I'm a slow learner."

"What's that supposed to mean?"

"That it's taken me two years to see the significance of not wanting to tell you about myself."

He was silent for a few moments, and Hannah wondered if she might be getting through to him at last.

But then he said, "Maybe I didn't know their magnitude, but I've always known you had these gifts."

Liar, she thought. "But I haven't told you, have I? I haven't trusted you enough to tell you, to believe you would understand and accept me just as I am."

"What difference does that make? I know now and I accept you fully. Why do you think I still want to marry you?"

She felt like screaming. "If you really accepted me, you'd let me handle this my own way."

"Not when I see you're handling it with your emotions, instead of with your mind. Look at yourself, Jo. You're so ruled by your fears that you're turning tail and running off to Avalon. What the hell good is that going to do you? You need to stand and face these people down, not let them drive you off."

He made it sound so easy. "You may be right about what I should do, but can you understand that I have to decide for myself?"

He was silent for a few beats before he said, "Look, I have an idea. Don't go to Avalon; they may already know about Jeli's house there. Come with me instead. We can go down to the Smokies or even the Outer Banks for a couple weeks. I can protect you while you take all the time you need to decide for yourself, and I can keep you from letting your emotions do your thinking."

God, could he be right? she thought. What if reporters were already keeping an eye on Jeli's house in Avalon? Even so, the idea of spending two weeks anywhere with Craig at this point was intolerable.

Time for the brutal honesty. "Craig, I've met someone else." When the words were out of her mouth, she sensed that his thoughts had come to a dead stop. She decided to push her advantage, to make Ethan more real to Craig, so she said, "It was in the plane crash, he was one of the passengers toward the front, and it turned out he's a member at Loving Shepherd. I saw him at—"

"Wait!" he interrupted. "Wait a minute. You're saying you met this guy last Saturday?"

"Yes."

"And *he's* the reason you're dumping me? Two years down the drain after one goddam week?"

"Well, no, not really. I mean, it had been coming for a long time. That's what I was trying to—"

He hurled an abusive curse at her and broke the connection.

She stared at her cell phone for a moment, feeling a mixture of surprise and relief. "Is that all it takes?" she said.

As if in response to her rhetorical question, the phone

sounded again. This time, she decided not to answer. If Craig was determined to follow her to Avalon, she'd have to deal with him there. And maybe she wouldn't stay at Jeli's after all. She'd leave her options open on that, maybe spend the night in Ethan's car, somewhere along the beach in Cape May. For now, she set the cell phone to vibrate, tucked it into her pocket, and returned her full attention to the road.

At least she tried to return her full attention to the road, but her mind was still in the conversation with Craig. Here he was again, accusing her of being incapable of rational, linear thinking, and of allowing her emotions to dictate her decisions. How many times was that in the past twenty-four hours, either in her mind or in reality? Many months ago, she'd decided that she preferred her way of thinking over Craig's, meandering through all the nuances of the alphabet rather than rocketing directly from *A* to *Z* as he did. But this time his accusation bothered her. She wondered if he was right. Would she be unable to sort out her options and set the best course for herself, *by* herself? As her cell phone finally went silent, Hannah realized that at least one thing was certain: if she needed someone's help, it would never be Craig's.

She shifted her mind to where it had been since she'd left Ethan's house and before she'd spoken with Craig, again allowing her thoughts to sort through the events of the past week. She wanted to find her path for the future in the signposts of the past seven days, but those signposts seemed to indicate a direction so fearful that they stole her breath away and set her heart racing. Of fight or flight, only the latter seemed possible for now.

Thinking about flight, she reached out a hand and petted Clancy's warm, sleeping head, wondering if there were a place on earth where the two of them could make a home as fine as the one they'd be leaving behind. She wondered if he'd like San Francisco, and whether he'd have to be in quarantine for a while if they moved to Hawaii. Her thoughts went from Hawaii to the pretty, rented house on the coast of Maine, near the town of Camden, where she and Grampa and Sophie Muller had spent several happy summers. From Maine, her imagination took her to Alexandria, Virginia—a place she loved, a place much like her hometown. Yes, she thought, I could be happy in Camden or in Alexandria.

Before long, Hannah was touring the world in her mind, choosing the places where she definitely would, or definitely would not, consider spending the rest of her days.

She was still on her world tour as she neared the exit for Avalon from the Garden State Parkway. Suddenly feeling ravenous, she drove on in search of drive-through fast food in Cape May Court House. An hour later, replete with Burger King's finest—which she had shared liberally with her golden pal—she pulled the car to a stop along a deserted stretch between Stone Harbor and Avalon, and took Clancy for a walk across the dunes to the beach.

Daylight was fading, and the air was heavy with the smells of sand and beach grasses and ocean life that never failed to lift Hannah's spirits. Clancy pranced toward the surf, happily scattering seagulls, then backpedaling in a hurry when the foamy edge of the cold water touched his feet. The calm sea reflected the slate-gray sky, dense with clouds, and Hannah saw that she and Clancy were in for some serious rain. She decided they'd have to chance it at Jeli's; exhaustion was pressing on her neck and shoulders, and spending a rainy night in Ethan's car—even if it was by the sea in Cape May—no longer seemed an option.

First, she thought, what about checking on the home front? Snoopers can't trace me to a *beach*, can they? I'll make it short.

She pulled her jacket close around her and sat on the hard-packed sand, then retrieved her cell phone and speed-dialed her father's home phone number.

Michael answered after the third ring. His "hello" sounded apprehensive.

"Are they giving you a hard time, Mikey?"

"Jo! Where are you? I mean, no, I mean, *how* are you? Are you okay?... Wait! Everybody's running to extensions. Hang on! Man, I'm glad you called! Are you okay?"

She heard Matthew trying to argue the phone away from Michael.

Papa's voice came on the line with, "Baby! Are you all right?"

Then she could hear Jeli and Celeste on other extensions,

asking variations of the same question. In the background, Lynn was hollering, "We're rootin' for you, Hannah!"

Hannah laughed. "This is exactly what I needed, hearing all of you. I'm okay. Honestly. I just wanted to make a quick call and find out if you guys are managing all right."

"We're doing great," said Michael, as Jeli was saying, "Don't be worrying about us, sweetie."

"Why didn't you tell me?" Papa asked, sounding wounded. "Didn't you know you could trust me?"

"Now, Paul," said Celeste, "you promised you wouldn't get going on—"

"We're okay, baby," Papa amended. "Just damn glad you called. What are you going to do?"

"I'm not sure yet, Pop. But as soon as I am, I'll let you know. Has anybody heard from Craig?"

"Craig?" said Michael, as Papa was saying, "Jeli told us you broke up with Craig last night."

"It's just that he called me earlier and he's figured out where I am. I was hoping he—"

"Is he threatening to come there?" Jeli asked.

"He was, but I may have changed his mind."

"You want us to find him and stop him, baby?"

"No, Pop. Don't worry. If he shows up, I'll—"

"Let me come down there, Jo," Michael said.

"No, Mike, I don't want you to."

"I'm coming, too, Jo," said Matthew, evidently having grabbed the phone away from Michael. "Mike and I can handle Craig for you."

"Thanks, guys, but I hope I can handle him myself. I just wish I knew what he's up to."

"How can we help you, honey?" Jeli asked.

"I don't think you can, not with Craig. But don't worry. I'm sure he wouldn't do anything to hurt me."

"Mike and I are coming down," Matthew insisted.

"No, Matt, please don't. I can deal with Craig, and I really do need tonight alone."

"But we could—"

"Matthew, enough!" Papa interrupted. "But if you change

your mind, Jo, you know we can be there within a couple of hours."

"Thanks, Pop, I do know that. And I really do feel very safe here." She smiled to herself as she watched Clancy scattering sandcrabs. "I guess I shouldn't stay on much longer, but I need to know, are things okay there? The media people aren't coming up to the house, are they?"

"No, not on the property, baby. Don't worry."

Matthew added, "Pop went down after Ethan got here, and told the press you'd gone out of town for a while. A lot of 'em booked after that."

Hannah took in only that Ethan was with her family. The image of all of them together surprised her with the warmth and comfort it carried.

"Hannah?" said Celeste, "You still there?"

"Mm, yes. Just thinking. So what about the Shepherdess groupies?"

Jeli answered, "Apparently they're planning to hold an all-night prayer vigil by candlelight."

"Oh, no."

"But they're very peaceful, sweetie. Not a bit aggressive."

"And they're not coming around the house, either?"

"Against the law, Jo," said Michael, who apparently had repossessed the extension from his brother. "Not without being invited."

"Good. Then there's really nothing going on up there for me to worry about?"

Almost simultaneously, their voices reassured her that everything was all right.

"Just take the time you need," said Jeli. "We'll be fine."

Hannah felt a stab of disappointment that they were coping so well without her. But she said, "Great!" and tried to mean it. Then, with reluctance, she added, "So I guess I might as well get going."

"We're here if you need us," Celeste offered.

"I'd have to throw in the towel if you weren't."

"Jo…" Papa's voice broke.

"Hey, Pop, please don't… I'm okay. Honest I am."

"Just want you to know, I'm so proud of you."

Hannah felt her own tears threatening. "I love you, every one of you," she said. "I'll call you in the morning." She broke the connection, immediately feeling very lonely.

Apparently observing that Hannah was no longer talking to that little silver thing, Clancy bounded over to her expectantly.

She stroked his silky ears as she said, "Time to reconnoiter Jeli's house, pal. You ready?"

Clancy drooled happily.

Chapter Thirty-Two

Hannah was surprised to feel uneasy when she first saw Jeli's beach house that evening. A light rain began to fall as she circled around the neighborhood twice more, finding no sign of Craig's Lexus.

Clancy had been sitting upright, watching with obvious pleasure as she had approached Jeli's house the first time. Just like his predecessors, this Clancy loved summer weekends in Avalon, and he knew the territory well. Now, as Hannah drove past Jeli's for the third time, Clancy stared at her as if he were waiting for some explanation.

Hannah caught the look on his face. "I know, pal. But it just doesn't feel right to me. Does it to you?" The house seemed almost ominous, not at all the pretty, welcoming summer home she'd loved ever since she first saw it as a child. She felt as if it were warning her away. "And where *is* Craig if he's not here and not at Pop's?" It's not like him to give up this easily, she thought.

Clancy shifted closer and propped his head on her shoulder. She stroked his right ear as she said, "Or am I just being ridiculous and paranoid? I told everybody I could handle him, and I can. ... Can't I?"

Clancy gave her cheek a hearty slurp, making her laugh out loud. "You're right, pal. With you along, Craig's a piece of cake."

So, on her fourth approach, she finally pulled Ethan's CRV off the street and into one of the stone-covered parking spaces beside Jeli's house.

She shut off the engine and stepped out of the CRV, letting Clancy go for a run. She knew he wouldn't go far in the rain. By the time she had retrieved the house key from its hiding place on the beach porch, Clancy was at her side. She unlocked the door and Clancy rushed into the house ahead of her, happily exploring the bedrooms on the lower floor while she disarmed the security system and turned on some lights.

She headed upstairs then, aware of the slightly musty smell the house took on when no one had been there for some time. Still, with lights on, and with the scent of the ocean air overlying everything, and the sound of the waves and the rain, Hannah felt the tension begin to flow out of her body.

She pulled the drapes back from the sliding glass doors. Looking across the upstairs deck to the beach and the water and the dark clouds that were raking the sea with rain, she wondered how on earth this wonderful house could have spooked her only a few minutes ago.

She put some water in a bowl for Clancy, and popped open a can of Diet Coke from the refrigerator for herself. Then she lit the gas fire in the fireplace and settled into the cream-colored sofa that faced the sliding glass doors. With the rain and the encroaching darkness, there wasn't much of a view, but it didn't matter. Hannah thought that here, finally, in the familiar comfort of Jeli's beach house, she would be able to make the right decision. She kicked off her shoes and thought about looking for a pair of socks.

Having thoroughly checked out every corner of the house, Clancy had settled contentedly in front of the fire. Suddenly, he lifted his head with his ears perked up, and a moment later the doorbell chimed. With a half-bark, Clancy jumped to his feet, bounded to the stairs and raced down to the front door.

Hannah stayed on the sofa, feeling paralyzed. In her mind, she heard the voice of the Vivie she used to know. *For heaven's sake, Johannah, don't be such a baby! You can't really pretend to be shocked that Craig is here. You can't possibly think the lordgodamighty would let you throw this man out like yesterday's garbage. Now stand up and go let him in!*

The doorbell chimed insistently, now in combination with some clamorous barking from Clancy. Hannah wondered if her golden pal was angry because he knew who was on the other side of the door. *I'd watch your jugular if I were you,* she said to Craig in her mind.

She pushed herself up from the sofa, feeling like an old woman, and made her way slowly downstairs to the door. As soon as she touched Clancy, he stopped barking and sat down abruptly.

"It's alright, Clance. Everything's alright," she said, kneeling beside him and looking into his eyes. "It's important to me that you mind your manners now, okay?"

The doorbell chimed again. Hannah stood and called, "Who is it?" and immediately felt silly.

"Don't be ridiculous, Hannah," came Craig's voice from the other side of the door. "You know exactly who it is."

She unlocked the door, and Craig pushed his way into the house. "About time," he said.

She smelled liquor on his breath. "Where's your car?" she asked, feeling stupid again.

"Where d'you think it is? Parked out front."

"But I didn't—"

"See it when you searched the neighborhood?" he cut her off, turning and heading up the stairs. "No, of course you didn't. I've been coming by every thirty minutes or so." At the top of the steps, he turned around and looked down at her. "And this last time, imagine my surprise at finding some stranger's CRV parked beside your grandmother's house. So where'd you get the car, Hannah?"

Hannah looked up at him, not liking their relative positions on the steps. She moved on past him with Clancy close at her heels. "None of your business," she said, thinking she sounded like an adolescent.

"None of my business? Christ, Hannah, what the hell has happened to you? You're being a complete bitch."

Deciding he was right, Hannah was stung by his words. She turned her back to him and went to the sliding glass doors, looking out but seeing nothing except darkness. The lights in the room reflected her grim-faced image back at her.

"I know whose car it is," Craig went on. "It's the bastard you met a week ago, isn't it."

"What bastard?" Hannah said, wondering if she'd be able to say anything to him tonight that didn't instantly make her feel stupid.

"This new love of your life. You've been having sex with him all week, haven't you."

She swiveled around, exclaiming, "I have not!" Then she

cursed herself when she saw the satisfied expression on his face. "Dammit, Craig! Why did you have to come down here?"

"I'm here because you need me, baby." He came to her and put his hands on her upper arms. "You know you do."

She shrugged his hands off. "I don't! You're the last person I need right now."

"You don't mean that, baby. This is just a very stressful situation for you, and the truth is, you're lost." He cupped her cheek with his hand. "I can help you. Let me help you."

She removed his hand from her cheek and looked straight into his eyes. The liquor was strong on his breath, and the look in his eyes triggered a small alarm in her mind. "You can't help me, Craig. You and I are finished, and I think you'd better leave now."

"Well, I'm not leaving. You can count on that." He turned away and went to the kitchen. "There are some things we have to talk about."

"I don't think there's anything more to say."

"Maybe not for you," he said, as he took a large juice glass from the cupboard and filled it halfway with scotch, no ice. "But I've got plenty to say. And I think you owe it to me to listen."

Hannah felt like screaming and tearing her hair and throwing furniture. Then she noticed Clancy sitting beside her, leaning his weight against her leg. She dropped to the floor and put her arm around him, feeling a little calm settle on her. "Go ahead and talk, then. Get it all off your chest. But after that, you're leaving."

When Craig came and stood over them, Clancy lowered his head and gave a growl so menacing that Hannah herself was startled. She stroked his side and said, "It's okay, pal. It's okay."

"Like hell, it's okay! Put that damn dog downstairs before I kick him."

Hannah came to her feet and took Clancy by the collar. "Let's go, pal," she said, silently adding, *But thanks for trying to protect me.*

Downstairs in her bedroom, Hannah knelt beside Clancy and loved on him awhile. "You just take a nice snooze down here, Clancy, okay? I'll get this over with and be back for you in no time flat." She realized Clancy was shaking. "It's alright, boy, really it is. Everything will be okay. I promise I won't let Craig hurt you. Not in a million years." For some reason, Hannah thought of the wren and fawn of twenty-one summers before. Well, she told herself, at least I protected Gabriel.

She kissed Clancy's head, stood and left the room, closing the door behind her. Then she waited there for a moment, irrationally wishing that Clancy would break through the door, rush upstairs and force Craig to leave. She heard her pal lie down against his side of the door, and she whispered to him, "See you in a few minutes, Clance." Why don't I believe that? she wondered. What am I so afraid of? It's only Craig. She walked away and resolutely climbed the stairs.

Craig sat on the sofa, at the end where Hannah had been sitting when the doorbell chimed. In his right hand he held a different glass; this one contained ice and an amber liquid that Hannah assumed was more scotch.

"Alright," she said. "I'm here, so say what you need to say." She switched off the gas fire and sat at the far end of the sofa from him.

He took a swallow of his drink and put his glass on the floor. Then he slid over next to her and tried to put his arms around her.

"No!" she yelped, jumping up and moving over by the glass doors.

"What, I can't even touch you while we talk? At least come sit here," he said, patting the seat of a wicker chair angled near his end of the sofa. "I won't bite, you know. Not like that dog of yours."

"Clancy's never bitten anyone," she muttered, sitting in the wicker chair. But I wouldn't have minded if he'd started with you tonight, she thought.

He leaned forward and reached over, trying to take her hand in his. When she pulled away, he said, "Jo, come on. At least let me hold your hand. What's the big deal?"

"The big deal is I don't want you here, and I don't want you touching me. Not even my hand."

He sat back in the sofa and gave her a sly look. "Well, well, well. I think our little Jo is actually mad at me. She sure is cute when she gets pissed off, isn't she."

Jesus, she thought. What did I ever find appealing in this man?

"Please, Craig. Just say what you have to say and get out of here."

He grabbed his glass and swallowed the last of his drink. Then he stood and went to the kitchen, tossing the ice in the sink and opening the bottle of scotch.

"No more, Craig," she said, going to him and taking the bottle away. "You've had more than enough."

"Give me that!" he roared, grabbing the scotch back from her. "Don't you ever try to tell me what to do!" The bottle slipped out of his hand and smashed on the tile floor. Liquor and bits of glass flew everywhere.

"That's it," she said, moving to the stairs, wincing as a glass shard pierced her bare right foot. "You're drunk," she said, turning to look at him. "Get out." Hannah saw anger spark in his eyes, and she reflexively took a few steps backwards.

He came at her fast then and vised her in his arms, crushing his lips to her mouth. She turned her face away, getting her hands between them and pushing at his chest. Still, he held her tight and kissed her ears and neck, murmuring, "C'mon, Jo. Don't be like that. C'mon, let me kiss you. Let me make love to you."

"No, Craig, let me go! Please!" She summoned her strength and gave his chest a fierce push that sent him sprawling.

Immediately, he lunged at her legs and brought her to the floor, throwing his weight on top of her. The hardwood floor was cold under her back as he pressed her down and sat on her thighs.

Hannah felt a panic rising in her like nothing she'd ever known before. It wasn't lust she saw in Craig's eyes; it was rage. As she struggled to free herself, she frantically tried to remember everything—anything—she'd ever learned about how to stop a man who was intent on raping her.

But her ability to think deserted her; all that reverberated in her mind were the words *No!* and *Stop!* and *Wait, please wait!* And all she could do was fight. She squirmed and flailed under his weight, desperate to free an arm or a leg. She wanted to scratch him, but her hands were trapped. Repeatedly she tried to bite his face or neck, but he managed to keep himself out of reach. She needed to scream, but his pressure on her chest drove the air from her lungs. Still, as she kept on fighting him, she began to sense a tiny hope that she could wear him out, make him give up.

But then he somehow had his forearm across her neck and lights started flashing in her eyes. Flashing lights, paralyzing fear... then nothing.

When she opened her eyes, she was sitting in a far corner of the room, near the fireplace, watching herself lie there motionless under an ugly, grunting man she recognized as Craig. She no longer felt any panic; she was merely curious about whether she might be dead. She watched as Craig rutted at her apparently lifeless body. Then she watched him finish and roll off of her, turning his back to her as he began pulling his clothes together.

She saw then that her prone self was not dead; it moved a little and made a sound like a small groan. She wished her prone self would get her clothes in order too, like Craig; she was ashamed of that Hannah for lying there, half-naked, disheveled and defeated.

It creeped into her awareness that Craig was talking; or, more accurately, that he was forming syllables with his voice. She supposed he was saying something that might be intelligible in some foreign country, maybe Japan, and was mildly curious about how he had learned to speak Japanese so quickly. She thought, on the other hand, that it didn't really sound like Japanese, and she let her mind take a little tour of other countries he might have visited lately.

Then, abruptly, Craig spoke six words in clear English that brought Hannah instantly back to her body.

"It's not over between us, Hannah," he declared, standing over her now.

Hannah looked at the empty corner where she'd been a moment ago. Suddenly mortified, she tugged her clothes into place and turned on her side, curling up on herself.

Craig was still talking. "I know you see the truth of that now. We'll always have this strong bond. We'll always be part of each other's lives."

In Hannah's mind, his words trailed off again into that alien language. She gazed out at blackness through the sliding glass doors, numb except for a mild stinging in the sole of her right foot.

A while later, the sound of Craig's voice stopped, and she heard Clancy's cries from the bedroom downstairs. *Good dog,*

Clancy, Hannah said to him in her mind. *You're such a good dog. Good dog.*

Her mind played with the word *dog*, how it was the reverse of the word *god*. God dog, that's what Clancy is, she thought. Maybe that's why they called them dogs in the first place, because they're like gods. Better even, because they're so loyal and loving. And they're always there for you, to protect you. Yes, she thought, you can really trust a dog. Listen to him down there, going crazy because he can't be up here making me feel better.

Still, she lay curled on the cold floor, amusing herself by reversing words in her mind. Some time passed that way until it occurred to her that Craig had left the house. It seemed like an *a-ha!* moment, it was so significant. She realized she could now go downstairs to lock the front door, and could let Clancy out of his bedroom prison. As she got to her feet, she was surprised by how stiff and achy she felt. Then she noticed the broken glass widely scattered in amber liquid, and set about cleaning up the mess. Can't have my pal cutting his feet, she thought, wincing again at the pain in her own foot.

With paper towels and a sponge mop, Hannah cleared away the remains of the broken bottle of scotch, managing to keep her weight off the pad of her right foot. Now and then she called to Clancy, reassuring him that she'd be there soon, silencing his whimpering for the moment.

When the floor was clean and drying, she limped downstairs, locked the front door, turned on the security system, perimeter only, and hurried to the bedroom door. As soon as it was open, Clancy bounded into her with a yelp, and she let herself settle on the floor while he ministered to her. "Not there, pal," she told him when he tried to lick the wound on her foot.

Normally the slightest contact with Clancy's warm, golden body would be a comfort for Hannah, but tonight his nearness and slurpy kisses seemed to have no effect at all. "It's okay, Clance," she reassured him, over and over. "I'm okay. Everything will be alright." She wondered if she was trying to persuade Clancy or herself.

Eventually she stood and hunted for tweezers, finding them in the first aid kit in the larger downstairs bathroom. She sat on the edge of the bathtub and removed the splinter of glass from her foot, wiping the cut with hydrogen peroxide. That done, she noticed Clancy sitting very still in front of her. She thought he looked worried. "It's nothing, pal. Just a little cut." It occurred to her that he was worried about more than her foot, and she felt the first small flicker of something like warmth in her heart. "Thanks, my friend," she murmured, stroking his ears and kissing the top of his head.

Resolve settled on her shoulders, and she drew in a deep breath, stood and went to her bedroom, Clancy close behind her. She dug through drawers and then headed back to the bathroom armed with clean underwear, jeans, and a soft flannel shirt. Peeling off her clothes, she felt a pang of sadness that she would have to throw them away—or, better yet, burn them. She had always loved the peach silk shirt she'd worn that day. But even touching these clothes now made her feel like vomiting.

Clancy lay on the bathroom floor while Hannah showered and washed her hair. She turned off the water and was about to step out of the shower stall, then changed her mind and began the whole process again, this time scrubbing herself all over with a back-brush and antibacterial soap. She stopped only when she saw that the stiff-bristled brush was close to drawing blood. She dried herself and dressed as quickly as she could, wondering if she would ever again feel comfortable without a lot of clothes covering her body. "I'll have to get over this if I want to swim this summer, won't I, pal." Clancy wagged his tail in apparent agreement.

At that moment, the reality of her situation hit Hannah; it felt like someone had swung a baseball bat into her stomach. She dropped onto the damp bathroom floor and hugged Clancy close to her. Where do I expect I'll ever swim again? she wondered. Where will I even be this summer? Now that Craig... now that *this* has happened, is it even an option anymore for me to go home? How can I face people? How can I ever face Ethan again?... But then, no one has to know it even happened, do they. Craig isn't going to talk about it. ... But what if he *does*? God, what if he thinks I liked it? What if he wasn't speaking a foreign language at all, but he was saying something I didn't want to hear about *making love* with me? Could his perception of it all be that skewed?

Some diabolical spike of fear brought the worst question into her mind: *What if I'm pregnant?* She stood and began filling the bathtub with hot water.

Chapter Thirty-Three

Over the next several hours, after a bath so hot that it left her skin red and itchy, Hannah felt like she was living in a nightmare. She couldn't relax; she couldn't even settle down anywhere in the house. And to go outside—even to Ethan's CRV so that she and Clancy could leave Avalon entirely—was not an option as long as it was dark. Resting on a bed downstairs was out of the question; she felt far too vulnerable on the first floor. Upstairs, everything reminded her of Craig. She couldn't rest on the sofa because he had sat there too recently. She couldn't stretch out on the floor; in fact, she was fairly certain she'd never even sit on that floor again. Faced with the problem of Clancy needing to go outside, the best she could do was telling him—feeling compelled to whisper— that he had to hurry, then opening the downstairs door just far enough and long enough for him to get out and then back in. Her heart raced and her skin prickled in these brief moments downstairs, and she would have laughed at herself for her paranoia if her sense of humor hadn't deserted her.

So for hours she prowled the upstairs of Jeli's house, reminding herself of a wild animal in a tiny cage. She scanned the kitchen cupboards for food, finding canned peaches and canned pears but realizing she couldn't have eaten even if someone held a gun to her head. She thought about getting good and drunk on the Jack Daniels, but the smell of Craig's scotch lingered in her mind and brought bile to her throat. She considered taking another bath or a shower, but the fear of being downstairs, vulnerable to all those street-level windows, stopped her.

The pressure of making the decision about her next move increased as the night wore on. Finally desperate to at least stop pacing, she pulled the wicker chair over to the sliding glass doors and sat down. She peered through the glass, trying to catch sight of the ocean, but all she could see was her own reflection. She decided she had never looked uglier, so she turned her gaze away, toward the innocuous kitchen. Before long her neck started to ache, so she stood and turned the chair with its back to the window, then sat again—only to find herself looking at the stairs where it had all started.

"God!" she groaned, closing her eyes and resting her head against the hard chair back.

Clancy had been moving with her, staying close. Now he put his head on her thigh. She began to stroke him, but kept her eyes closed. She remembered hearing somewhere that when I'm alone with my thoughts, I'm in bad company. She fleetingly considered talking to Grampa, but was stunned silent by the coldness in her heart toward him now.

"Oh, Clancy, if only you could talk."

Clancy responded with a sigh so loud that Hannah couldn't help opening her eyes to look at him. The sight of his big golden head squarely planted on her thigh, with his mournful, pleading eyes angled up at her, brought her a flicker of warmth, a tiny push toward a smile. She sat up and hugged him close, relishing his warmth. "It doesn't matter that you can't talk, pal. I hear you anyway."

She decided to try a few timeworn decision-making methods. She got a quarter from her wallet and tossed it, heads I go away, tails I go home. It came up heads, so she decided to try for the best out of three. Still not satisfied, she then went for best out of five, seven, nine, eleven, and finally gave up and threw the coin across the room in disgust.

She went to the cabinet in the dining area and hunted through board games and decks of cards until she found a lined tablet. Then she retrieved a pencil from the kitchen and sat cross-legged in the wicker chair. She made a line down the center of a tablet, and wrote "Go" at the top left of the line, and "Stay" at the top right. On the "Go" side she wrote, "Save my skin," then thought a moment before adding, "I hope." On the same side she wrote, "Live in a different city/state." Seconds later she had added the same sentence to the other side, thinking again how much she loved the home Papa had built for her and Grampa. She stared at the tablet for a while, considering some of the other additions she should make to the "Stay" side, such as her family and her patients. Eventually she tossed both tablet and pencil in the same direction as the loathsome quarter.

"Must be Easter morning by now," she said to Clancy, who lay on the floor beside her. Hardly the Easter I'd hoped for, she thought. Hardly the Easter anyone would hope for. No feeling of celebrating anything, Just waiting here at Jeli's. Waiting for the rain to stop. Waiting for the fear to stop. Waiting for an epiphany. Waiting for *something* to illuminate the path I'm supposed to follow.

Ethan's right, she thought. The decision has to come from my heart. But my heart isn't functioning just now.

Something prompted her to look out through the sliding glass doors, and she saw immediately that the rain had stopped. "Thank you, God!" she cried, startling Clancy away as she jumped to her feet.

Within minutes she had uncovered one of the deck's wrought-iron lounge chairs and settled on it with a couple of clean, well-worn beach blankets she retrieved in a hurried trip to the downstairs linen closet. Clancy was on a blanket she'd put on the deck beside her, sitting up straight and alert, apparently on guard for Hannah's next move.

She lay back in the chair, taking in the clearing sky and the chilly air redolent of rain and sea. Hannah watched the stars gradually appear, as if a curtain were being withdrawn to reveal a glorious stage set, and eventually saw the moon painting a rhythmic silver trail on the water.

Very quietly, with barely even a whisper in her mind, she felt safe.

She decided she'd stay out here on the deck until daybreak or until she reached a decision, whichever came first.

Clancy must have sensed that she had settled in; he began kneading his blanket and circling until everything was just right, then curled up with a grateful sigh.

Even with the feast for her senses, even with the feeling of safety there on Jeli's deck, Hannah's thoughts remained a muddy jumble. She pulled the blanket up under her chin and watched the winking stars until her vision blurred and she drifted into sleep.

She sensed Grampa next to her on the deck, in his wheelchair on the other side of Clancy. From the corner of her eye, she saw that he was bundled against the chill and the damp in a plaid stadium blanket and a matching, soft flannel shirt. He was silent and she was glad of that; she didn't want to hear anything he might have to say.

Against her will, she smelled the clean, evergreen fragrance of him, and felt his warmth. She wanted to get up from the chaise and go into the house, but couldn't seem to move any part of her body.

After awhile the silence became unbearable, and she willed him to speak. Say something! she yelled at him in her mind. Say something so I can scream at you and tell you to leave me alone.

He reached for her right hand with his left. Once more against her will, she let him hold her hand. She noticed how strong and young his hand felt, not at all the parchment-skinned bones she'd held when he was dying.

"I'm so sorry, honey," he said, his voice soft and sad. "I'm so terribly sorry."

Instead of screaming at him, Hannah began to weep. The pain radiated out from her center, just like the healing fire, and touched every cell of her body. She thought her heart was going to burst out from her throat. She knelt beside Grampa's wheelchair, not knowing if he'd pulled her there or she'd made it on her own, and she buried her face in his soft shirt and strong chest. She was faintly aware of Grampa stroking her hair and her back and murmuring words of comfort, and of Clancy sitting next to her, leaning heavily against her side. But all she really knew was that she had tapped into a bottomless well of tears and would be forced to cry for the rest of her life.

Later, through the moaning within her, she began to hear the sounds of the ocean—the waves breaking on the sand and skittering out again. Sometime after that, it seemed that she could breathe normally once more, that her throat was no longer in danger of breaking open. And her eyes, though burning and tired, were no longer pouring tears. Before long, she found herself resting comfortably with her cheek on Grampa's chest, and listening with interest to the soothing, steady thump of his heart.

She opened her eyes then, surprised to see that it was still night.

"I'm sorry, Grampa," she whispered.

"Oh, honey, there is nothing in heaven or earth you need to apologize for."

"No, I think I really messed up. Flirting with Ethan like that, enraging Craig, making him…"

Grampa laid a gentle hand on her mouth. "Shhh, honey. You are not to blame for any of what has happened."

Hannah moved her mouth away from his hand, "But now I could be pregnant, Grampa, and I don't have a clue how to handle my own life, much less a baby's."

"You will do exactly as you've always done, sweetie. You will make the best decisions you can with whatever life sends you."

Hannah pulled away and sat cross-legged on the deck between chaise and wheelchair. "Right. Me and decisions. Have you noticed what a great job I'm doing with the current one?"

With a contented sigh, Clancy curled up on the deck in front of her, and Hannah began idly scratching his furry head.

"I've been thinking about this current decision, honey, and I'm wondering if you're up to telling me a couple of stories."

"Stories?"

"Sure, honey. Like we used to do when you were little, only this time not make believe. This time, I'd like to hear a story about what happens if you move away, and a story about what happens if you stay."

Hannah looked at him, feeling a faint glimmer of interest. "You should tell them, Grampa. Your ability to see the future was always better than mine, and now that you're dead, well, there's really no comparison."

He smiled at her. "But you know the future isn't written in stone, honey. To a large extent, you're the one who creates it, so you're the one who has to tell the story."

She sighed and climbed up onto the chaise. Clancy climbed up and lay beside her. "You want me to tell it like when I was a child?"

"Precisely."

"This seems silly, Grampa."

"Would you indulge your old, dead grandfather, honey?"

"Jeez. I guess I can't say no to that. So okay, here goes." Hannah looked up at the sky for inspiration, and felt a lifting of spirit at the sight of the dancing stars. "Once upon a time, Hannah decided to take off for San Francisco. Jeli and Celeste helped Ethan sell her Jeep and get her a different four-by-four, and they packed up the clothes and things she'd need, and Hannah and Ethan swapped cars somewhere. In Gettysburg, that's a nice touch."

"Mm. So far so good," offered Grampa.

"You don't think I'm being too presumptuous about Ethan doing all that?"

"Not at all, honey. Although he may have a lot more helpers than just Jeli and Celeste."

"True. Kyla will want to help."

"And your father and brothers, don't forget. And Rose."

"Right. But Kyla... I'm really leaving her in the lurch, aren't I. I don't know if I can do that."

"It's something to consider, honey. But go ahead with your story."

"Okay. So Hannah drives off into the sunset—with Clancy, of course—and after five or six days, winds up in San Francisco at Jeli's friend's house."

"Is it a nice house, honey?"

"Well, I don't know, do I? I mean, I don't even know who the friend is. I guess I was hoping it might be on the water somewhere, rambling, California-style, with lots of windows and plants."

"Sounds lovely. So there is Hannah, in this very nice house on the water, and what happens next?"

"Well, Jeli comes to San Francisco and... well, I guess Hannah makes a plan for setting up an office where she can be a chiropractor again."

"Does she have to change her name?"

"That's an awful prospect, Grampa."

"But a realistic one, wouldn't you agree? It's not as if San Francisco were another country."

"No, you're right. Hannah has to get a new identity somehow... Maybe she *should* move to another country."

"Do you suppose it's easier to get a new identity in another country?"

"They do it all the time in the movies, Grampa."

"True. I guess one can hope it's possible in real life."

"I think you just have to find the birth certificate of someone who was born the same year you were but who died, and then you take her name and social security number. Something like that."

"Sounds awfully complicated, honey, but I suppose Hannah could manage it."

"Right. So I get... I mean, so Hannah gets a new identity and sets up her practice in San Francisco or in another city, and—"

"I don't mean to interrupt, but what about Jeli?"

"What about her?"

"Does she stay with Hannah whatever-her-name-is-now, or does she come back home?"

"Well, of course she doesn't stay with me indefinitely."

"Are you lonely, then, without her?"

"Well, I'm hoping Ethan will move to... wherever with me, and I'm sure I'll have new friends."

"And a new family?"

"Eventually, sure, but... why am I getting the feeling you don't particularly like this story, Grampa?"

"Honey, as you so correctly pointed out, I'm dead now. It follows that my enjoyment of stories now is dependent entirely on yours."

"You're saying *I* don't like this story?"

"Do you?"

Hannah stayed silent, feeling rebellious.

"Well then, are you about done with story number one?"

"I guess."

"So let's hear story number two and see how much you enjoy that one."

"Okay." Hannah sat up straight in the chaise and looked out at the moonlit sea. "Story number two. Hannah hitches up her britches—"

"Oh, I like that."

"I knew you would. So she hitches up her britches and... and what? I don't know where to even begin."

"Try baby steps, honey. What's the first baby step you might take?"

"First? After I cleaned things up here at Jeli's? Well, I guess I'd call Pop and tell him I'm coming home."

"Yes. And what would he say?"

"Oh, that's easy, he'd be ecstatic. No question, they all want me to stay."

"And would he want to help you somehow?"

"Of course he would. They all would."

"What sort of help could they offer, do you suppose?"

"Hm. I guess Pop could help me with my house, so I could get some kind of privacy in the greatroom."

"I'm sure he could."

"Because I do love that house, Grampa. I don't want to have to move."

"It's a wonderful house."

"And Jeli, she'd probably move in with me for a while till things settle down. I'd like that. It's always a comfort, too, having Celeste nearby. I know I can always count on her. And of course Michael, at least, would expect to live with me. He's so protective. But I couldn't let him do that. He has to finish the semester. And I guess Rose would be hanging around a lot, not that that'd really be a help, although I do appreciate her prayers. I wonder if Lynn and Marcia would move back here from San Diego? You never met them, Grampa, but you'd like them a lot. Kyla'd be terrific with all this, she's so capable, so professional. And Mike reminded me about Carl's sons in the security business; maybe I'd contact them to see what's possible. Oh, and I can't forget about Lily Severill; she'd put herself front and center, I think, wanting to oversee everything."

Hannah was silent for a few moments before she added, "And then there's Ethan."

"Ah, yes. Your Ethan."

"*My* Ethan, Grampa? You think so?"

"It seems quite clear to me, honey."

"Good. My Ethan. He'd be wonderful." Thinking about Ethan brought Craig to Hannah's mind, and with Craig came a horde of strangers with anguished faces. She sank back against the unforgiving chaise. "All of a sudden, I feel like I can't breathe."

"Scoot over closer to me, honey."

Because she knew she was dreaming, Hannah thought the wrought iron chaise next to Grampa's wheelchair, and it was so.

Grampa caressed her cold hand between his warm ones. "Okay, now. I'm right here with you, holding your hand."

"I always used to feel like I could do anything if you were with me, Grampa. Now I'm not so sure."

They were silent for a time. Then he said softly, "So tell me what happens when Hannah goes home."

"I... she... I don't know. I can't think. Or I'm thinking too much."

"Could you tell me some of the thoughts?"

"It's people, people crowding around me, pushing me, trapping me. I can't move, I can't catch my breath. And they all want something from me. And some of them, they hate me so much they want to kill me. Or at least I feel like they do."

"The crush of people."

"Yes."

"All wanting something."

"Exactly."

"And can you tell me your very worst fear about all of this?"

"My very worst? Well... that they'll kill me, I guess. Or... no, I think it's that I'll get handicapped somehow, you know? Paralyzed, literally. Unable to take care of myself anymore. Dependent on other people for the rest of my life." She felt that fear in every cell of her being. "How can I possibly go back to that, Grampa? How could anyone choose to face all that?" She looked at him and saw through his wire-rimmed glasses that his eyes were unusually solemn. "Even you can't encourage me now, can you."

"This time, honey, I think the encouragement will have to come from within yourself."

She looked away from him and withdrew her hand, raking it through her hair. "Like that's really going to happen."

"Well, tell me, how do you think a person gets the courage to deal with such difficulties, Hannah? Because, you know, people do it every day of their lives. What is it that makes them able to go forward?"

Hannah felt unaccountably irritated with him. "I'm not stupid, Grampa. I know what you want me to say."

"What's that?"

"Oh, for God's sake. You want me to say they have faith that something will see them through."

"Is that such a bad thing, honey?"

"Of course it's not bad. But you know as well as I do what I think about trusting God."

"Yes, I do know that. But apart from God, is there nothing good in your life that will see you through?"

Hannah didn't want to answer him. She didn't even want to think about what he was asking. So she said, "I think if a person doesn't trust, nothing will change that."

"So everything seems hopeless, honey?"

"Yes. Hopeless."

They sat there for a time with only the steady sounds of the sea breaking the night silence.

Then Grampa said, "We're at the heart of it now, aren't we, honey. Your inability to trust in anything beyond what you can know with your five senses."

She silently agreed with him, feeling very small.

Gently he stroked her cheek with a forefinger. "What if I tell you not to be afraid, that God exists and loves you and will help you?"

"I guess I wouldn't believe you."

"Because I'm dead and you're just dreaming this?"

"I guess so."

"And nothing anyone says is going to make a difference?"

"I guess not."

"Then your only option is flight?"

Hannah took in a deep breath. "I don't know, Grampa. I really don't know. That whole scenario sounded ridiculous when I was telling it to you, getting a new identity and all that. But if the other option means facing crowds of needy people, where am I supposed to get the guts for that?"

Grampa gave a small sigh and settled back in his chair. "With all the terrible accidents that can and do happen every day, I used to be amazed that people had the guts even to get out of bed."

Hannah felt a rush of angry energy. She sat up and glared at him. "I don't believe this! You're giving up? You're not going to do something to convince me that, quote, *everything will be all right, honey*?"

"What can I do? You said nothing would make a difference."

"But I didn't want you to agree with me, Grampa! You're the only one who *can* make a difference for me."

"What can I say? You're determined to not believe me."

"You can tell me… I don't know. Tell me something like… well, tell me what happens after death, for example. Tell me where you really are, and tell me about my mother."

"Tell you these things, you who've read everything ever written about near-death experiences?"

"Yes, but those people didn't really die, Grampa. Not like you. So tell me what happened to you."

"The problem is, there's no common language between this dimension and the next one. There are no words to describe—"

Hannah sat back in the chaise and crossed her arms over her chest. "I knew you'd say that. It's such a typical excuse for why there's no tangible, rational proof about what happens."

"Ah, so we want not only proof, but tangible, rational proof."

"Well, any real proof would be rational, it'd make sense."

"Like a legal argument, honey? Guilty until proven innocent beyond a shadow of a doubt?"

She had to smile. "Something like that, yes."

Grampa was silent for a while before he said, "This is a very tall order, you know, proving what can be proved only in the experience of it."

She scooted off the end of the chaise and stood, turning to look at him hopefully. "Not too tall for you, though, is it, Grampa?"

He looked up at her. "Let me see if I've got this straight, honey. You want incontrovertible proof that there is nothing to be afraid of, so that you can turn and face whatever threatens you, real or imagined, trusting that God exists and will support you unfailingly."

"Yes. Right."

"And you want me to prove this in some way that you can't negate with the facts that, one, I'm dead, and, two, you're dreaming."

"Yes. That's it exactly."

Hannah watched him as he closed his eyes, apparently in prayer. Then she had a sense of a vacuum building around them, as if the air were being sucked away from the space they inhabited in anticipation of some explosive event. She felt real fear, her thoughts racing in panic over what she was asking of him.

Then, all of a sudden, as if propelled by a rocket, Grampa leaped out of his wheelchair. In a blaze of light, the stadium blanket became a kilt and Grampa became an Irish dancer, his arms straight at his sides while his body lifted in impossible jumps and his feet made intricate moves at the speed of sound, his winter-white hair flying in rhythm with his leaps, his lips clamped together in solemn contrast to the joy of his dancing, and only the light in his eyes revealing the merriment of his soul. He leaped and bounded, stepped and twirled, uncannily like the male lead in "Riverdance" except that he was still Grampa, still the dearest friend of Hannah's heart as he jumped and spun around Jeli's deck.

And Hannah felt a surprise of laughter so big and so profound that it seemed to have issued from the center of the earth. She laughed as she had never laughed before, with uncensored joy and release, with a celebration of life that filled her soul and lifted her heart straight to heaven.

Still laughing, Hannah awoke as the faintest suggestion of light had begun to draw a thin line between the dark water and the dark sky.

She lay on the chaise and thought about her dream. *That was my proof, Grampa?*

She watched then as the stars dimmed and the luminous aura deepened on the horizon. Before long she heard the first birdsong of the morning. Not a gull, as she might have predicted, but... *is it a wren? I think it is.*

"Hey, Clancy," she whispered. "How'd you like to have a little bird friend? Maybe we can find a wren this spring who isn't afraid of us. We'll name him Gabriel the Second. Or the Third, if we count Lynn's. He can teach you how to sing, and you can teach him how to chase squirrels."

She closed her eyes and imagined herself flying. Clancy was with her, floating as if he were on a magic carpet, looking mesmerized by the sea and the ground rushing past hundreds of feet below him. And Gabriel was there, Gabriel the First, singing his joyous melodies so loudly that she thought he could awaken the world.

When she opened her eyes, she felt a certainty spread from her center like the heat of the healing, until it permeated every cell of her body.

Yes, she thought, Grampa's dance was my proof.

As the sky turned from gray to pale yellow and the sun itself began to peek over the far edge of the sea, she stood and stretched.

"Let's go home, Clancy," she said.

And in the first ray of the Easter sun that touched her face, Hannah felt the warmth of Grampa's beautiful, crookedy-toothed smile.

Printed in the United States
26001LVS00001BD/43-255

9 781931 456395